PRAISE FOR *THE CREAK ON THE STAIRS*

'Fans of Nordic Noir will love this moving debut from Icelander Eva Björg Ægisdóttir. It's subtle, nuanced, with a sympathetic central character and the possibility of great stories to come' Ann Cleeves

'Beautifully written, spine-tingling and disturbing, this is a simply stunning debut, heralding a thrilling new voice in Icelandic crime fiction and the start of an electrifying new series' Yrsa Sigurðardóttir

'An exciting and harrowing tale from one of Iceland's rising stars' Ragnar Jonasson

'Rich in atmosphere, bursting with suspense and with beautiful, quiet and sophisticated writing reminiscent of Ruth Rendell, this debut author has succeeded in creating an intricate and wholly realistic portrait of a small town and its secrets' Goldsboro Books

'*The Creak on the Stairs* is full of suspense and intrigue. Not only did the mystery surrounding the body of the woman at the lighthouse have me gripped, I also really enjoyed getting to know Elma and her new colleagues … Chilling, absorbing and I absolutely loved it!' Novel Deelights

'*The Creak on the Stairs* is clever and intricate, but the story flows so effortlessly that you don't even realise just how clever and intricate it is, until you've turned that final page and start thinking back' From Belgium with Booklove

'The plot of the book is not over-elaborate, nevertheless, it keeps the reader glued to his seat due to the author's exhilarating writing style that creates a terrific, claustrophobic atmosphere in the small, secluded Icelandic town. *The Creak on the Stairs* is one of the best debut crime thrillers originating from the Nordic countries in the last few years and it leaves the reader hungry for more' Tap the Line

'A chilling and troubling debut ... reminiscent of Jorn Lier Horst's Norwegian procedurals. Much of the narrative is restrained and minimal, practical, honest, matter-of-fact, pretty grey, even. This means that the key emotional aspects of the story, and its moments of action, seem to stand out even more. It's a book that makes an impact, but gives itself time to sink in' Crime Fiction Lover

'A compelling story that will break you piece by piece while revealing horrible secrets ... The book develops slowly, creating tension gradually, letting us into the painful darkness. You'll be under a spell, word after word, not believing how heart-breaking the truth is' Bookaholic Me

'A truly unforgettable read ... We have characters here that I can, and do, root for, and writing that is both emotionally manipulative and brilliant at creating a sense of place and time, and that holds the atmospheric and almost hauntingly melancholic tone of the story from the first page to the last. Sterling stuff. Highly recommended' Jen Meds Book Reviews

THE CREAK
ON THE STAIRS

ABOUT THE AUTHOR

Born in Akranes in 1988, Eva Björg Ægisdóttir studied for an MSc in Globalisation in Norway before returning to Iceland and deciding to write a novel – something she had wanted to do since she won a short-story competition at the age of fifteen. After nine months combining her writing with work as a stewardess and caring for her children, Eva finished *The Creak on the Stairs*. It was published in 2018, and became a bestseller in Iceland. It also went on to win the Blackbird Award, a prize set up by Yrsa Sigurðardóttir and Ragnar Jónasson to encourage new Icelandic crime writers.

Eva lives in Reykjavík with her husband and three children and is currently working on her next novel. The second book in the Forbidden Iceland series, *Girls Who Lie*, will be published by Orenda Books in 2021. Follow Eva on Instagram @evabjorg88 and Twitter @evaaegisdottir.

ABOUT THE TRANSLATOR

Victoria Cribb lived and worked in Reykjavík for a number of years and has translated more than twenty-five books by Icelandic authors, including Arnaldur Indriðason and Yrsa Sigurðardóttir. Her translation of *CoDex 1962* by Sjón was long-listed for the Best Translated Book Award and the PEN America Translation Prize in 2019. In 2017 she received the Orðstír honorary translation award for services to Icelandic literature.

THE CREAK
ON THE STAIRS

Orenda Books
16 Carson Road
West Dulwich
London SE21 8HU
www.orendabooks.co.uk

First published in the United Kingdom by Orenda Books, 2020
First published in Iceland with the title *Marrið í stiganum* by Veröld Publishing,
2018
Copyright © Eva Björg Ægisdóttir, 2018
English translation copyright © Victoria Cribb, 2020

A catalogue record for this book is available from the British Library.

Paperback ISBN 978-1-913193-04-1
Hardback ISBN 978-1-913193-23-2
eISBN 978-1-913193-05-8

The publication of this translation has been made
possible through the financial support of

ICELANDIC LITERATURE CENTER

Typeset in Minion by typesetter.org.uk

Printed and bound by CPI Group (UK) Ltd, Croydon CR0 4YY

*For sales and distribution, please contact info@orendabooks.co.uk or visit
www.orendabooks.co.uk.*

No. 570
One of 750 numbered copies
of the first edition of

THE CREAK ON THE STAIRS

Eva Björg Ægisdóttir

Translated by Victoria Cribb

Signed by the author

**ORENDA
BOOKS**

in association with Goldsboro Books

ICELAND

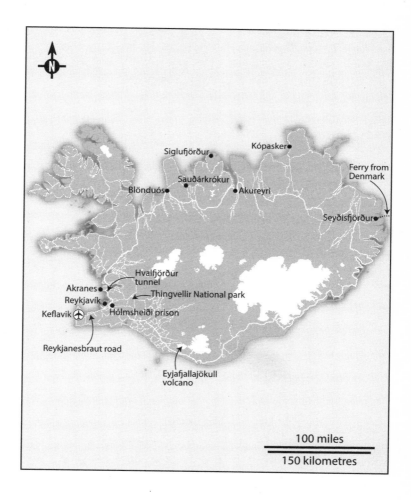

PRONUNCIATION GUIDE

Icelandic has a couple of letters that don't exist in other European languages and which are not always easy to replicate. The letter ð is generally replaced with a *d* in English, but we have decided to use the Icelandic letter to remain closer to the original names. Its sound is closest to the voiced *th* in English, as found in *th*en and ba*th*e.

The Icelandic letter þ is reproduced as *th*, as in *Th*orgeir, and is equivalent to an unvoiced *th* in English, as in *th*ing or *th*ump.

The letter *r* is generally rolled hard with the tongue against the roof of the mouth.

In pronouncing Icelandic personal and place names, the emphasis is always placed on the first syllable.

Names like Elma, Begga and Hendrik, which are pronounced more or less as they would be in English, are not included on the list.

Aðalheiður – AATH-al-HAYTH-oor
Akranes – AA-kra-ness
Aldís – AAL-deess
Andrés – AND-ryess
Arnar Arnarsson – ARD-naar ARD-naarsson
Arnar Helgi Árnason – ARD-naar HEL-kee OWRD-nasson
Ása – OW-ssa
Ásdís Sigurðardóttir (Dísa) – OWS-deess SIK-oorthar-DOEH-
    teer (DEE-ssa)
Bergþóra – BERG-thoera
Bjarni – BJAARD-nee
Björg – BYURRG
Dagný – DAAK-nee
Davíð – DAA-veeth
Eiríkur – AY-reek-oor

Elísabet Hölludóttir – ELL-eessa-bet HURT-loo-DOEH-teer
Ernir – ERD-neer
Fjalar – FYAAL-aar
Gígja – GYEE-ya
Gréta – GRYET-a
Grétar – GRYET-aar
Guðlaug – GVOOTH-loig
Guðrún – GVOOTH-roon
Halla Snæbjörnsdóttir – HAT-la SNYE-byurs-DOEH-teer
Hrafn (Krummi) – HRAPN (KROOM-mi)
Hvalfjörður – KVAAL-fyurth-oor
Hörður – HURTH-thoor
Ingibjörn Grétarsson – ING-ibjurdn GRYET-arsson
Jón – YOEN
Jökull – YUR-kootl
Kári – COW-rree
Magnea Arngrímsdóttir – MAG-naya ARD-greems-DOEH-teer
Nói – NOE-ee
Rúnar – ROO-naar
Sara – SAA-ra
Silja – SILL-ya
Skagi – SKAA-yee
Sólveig – SOEL-vayg
Sævar – SYE-vaar
Tómas – TOE-maas
Viðar – VITH-aar
Þórný – THOERD-nee

THE CREAK
ON THE STAIRS

She hears him long before she sees him. Hears the creaking as he climbs the stairs, one cautious step at a time. He tries to tread softly as he doesn't want to wake anyone – not yet. If it was her climbing the stairs late at night she would make it all the way up to the top without anyone hearing a thing. But he can't do it. He doesn't know them like she does, doesn't know where best to tread.

She shuts her eyes, clenching them so tight that the muscles around them ache. And she takes deep, slow breaths, hoping he won't be able to hear how fast her heart is beating. Because a heart only beats that fast when you're awake – awake and terribly afraid. She remembers the time her father had her listen to his heart. He must have run up and down the stairs a thousand times before he'd stopped and called her over. 'Listen!' he'd said. 'Listen to how fast my heart's beating. That's because our bodies need more oxygen when we move, and it's our heart's job to provide it.' But now, although she's lying perfectly still, her heart is pounding much faster than her father's was then.

He's getting closer.

She recognises the creaking of the last stair, just as she recognises the rattling the roof makes when there's a gale blowing outside, or the squeaking of the door downstairs when her mother comes home. Tiny stars appear and float across her eyelids. They're not like the stars in the sky: those hardly ever move, and you can only catch them at it if you watch them for a long time and you're very lucky. She's not lucky, though. She's never been lucky.

She can sense him standing over her now, wheezing like an old man. The stink of cigarettes fills her nose. If she looked up she would see those dark-grey eyes staring down at her. Instinctively, she pulls the duvet a fraction higher over her face. But she can't hide. The tiny movement will have given her away: he'll know she's only pretending to be asleep. Not that it will make any difference.

It's never made any difference.

Elma wasn't afraid, though the feeling was similar to fear: sweaty palms, rapid heartbeat. She wasn't nervous either. She got nervous when she had to stand up and speak in front of people. Then the blood would rise into her skin; not only on her face, where she could disguise the flush with a thick layer of make-up, but on her neck and chest as well, where it formed unsightly red-and-white blotches.

She'd been nervous that time she had gone out on a date with Steinar in year ten. A fifteen-year-old girl with a blotchy chest and far too much mascara, who had tiptoed out of the house, praying that her parents wouldn't hear the front door closing behind her. She had waited for him to pick her up on the corner. He'd been sitting in the back of the car – he wasn't old enough to drive yet, but he had a friend who was. They'd not driven far, and had barely exchanged a word, when he leant over and stuck his tongue down her throat. She'd never kissed anyone before but, although his tongue felt very large and invasive, she hadn't drawn away. His friend had driven calmly around while they were kissing, though from time to time she'd caught him watching them in the rear-view mirror. She'd let Steinar touch her through her clothes too and pretended to enjoy it. They had been driving down the same road she was on now. Back then they had Lifehouse on the speakers, bass pounding from the boot. She shuddered at the memory.

There were cracks in the pavement outside her parents' house. She parked the car and sat staring at them for a minute or two. Pictured them widening and deepening until her old Volvo was swallowed up. The cracks had been there ever since she was a little girl. They'd been less obvious then, but not much. Silja used to live in the blue house opposite, and they'd often played games on this pavement. They used to pretend that the biggest crack was a huge volcanic fissure, full of red-hot lava, and that the tongues of flame were licking up towards them.

The blue house – which wasn't blue anymore but white – was home these days to a family with two young boys, both blond, with identical *Prince Valiant* pageboy haircuts. She didn't know where Silja lived now. It must be four years since she'd last talked to her. Longer, perhaps.

She got out of the car and walked up to her parents' house. Before opening the door, she glanced back down at the cracks in the pavement. Now, more than twenty years later, the thought of being swallowed up by them didn't seem so bad.

Several Weeks Later –
Saturday, 18 November 2017

Elma was woken by the wind. She lay there for a long time, listening to it keening outside her window as she stared up at the white ceiling of her flat. When she finally got out of bed it was too late to do anything but mindlessly pull on some clothes and grab a blackened banana on her way out of the door. The bitter wind cut into her cheeks the moment she stepped outside. She zipped her coat to the neck, pulled up her hood and set off through the darkness at a brisk pace. The glow of the streetlights lit up the pavement, striking a sparkle from the grey tarmac. The frost creaked under her shoes, echoing in the silence – there were few people about on a Saturday morning in mid-November.

A few minutes after leaving the warmth of her flat, she was standing in front of the plain, pale-green building that housed Akranes Police Station. Elma tried to breathe calmly as she took hold of the icy door handle. Inside, she found herself in front of a reception desk where an older woman with curly blonde hair and a tanned, leathery face was talking on the phone. She held up a finger with a red-varnished nail as a sign for Elma to wait.

'All right, Jói, I'll tell him. I know it's unacceptable, but it's hardly a police matter – they're feral cats, so I recommend you get in touch with the pest controller … Anyway, Jói…' The woman held the telephone receiver a fraction away from her ear and smiled apologetically at Elma. 'Listen, Jói, there's not much I can do about that now. Just remember to close the window next time you go to the shops … Yes, I know those Moroccan rugs cost a fortune. Listen, Jói, we'll have to discuss it later. I've got to go now. Bye.'

She put down the receiver with a sigh. 'The feral-cat problem in Neðri-Skagi is beyond a joke. The poor man only left his window open while he popped out to the shop, and one of the little beasts got in there and peed and crapped on the antique rug in his sitting room. Poor old boy,' the woman said, shaking her head. 'Anyway, enough about that, what can I do for you, dear?'

'Er, hello.' Elma cleared her throat, remembering as she did so that she hadn't brushed her teeth: she could still taste the banana she'd eaten on her walk. 'My name's Elma. I've got an appointment with Hörður.'

'Oh, yes, I know who you are,' the woman said, standing up and holding out her hand. 'I'm Guðlaug, but please call me Gulla. Come on in. I'd advise you to keep your coat on. It's freezing in reception. I've been on at them for weeks to repair that radiator, but apparently it's not a priority for a cash-strapped police force.' She sounded fed up about this, but then went straight on in a brighter voice: 'How are your parents, by the way? They must be so pleased to have you home again, but then that's how it is with Akranes: you just can't beat it, and most people come back once they realise the grass isn't greener down south in Reykjavík.' She produced all this in a rush, barely pausing for breath. Elma waited patiently for her to finish.

'They're fine,' she said as soon as she could get a word in, all the while racking her brains to remember if Gulla was someone she ought to know. Ever since she'd moved back to Akranes five weeks earlier, people she didn't recognise had been stopping her in the street for a chat. Usually it was enough to nod and smile.

'Sorry,' Gulla added. 'I tend to let my tongue run away with me. You'll get used to it. You won't remember me, but I used to live in the same terrace as you when you were a little thing, only six years old. I still remember how sweet you looked weighed down by that great big backpack on your first day at school.' She laughed at the memory.

'Oh, yes … that sounds vaguely familiar – the backpack, I mean,' Elma said. She dimly recalled a big yellow burden being loaded onto her shoulders. It can't have weighed less than a quarter of her bodyweight at the time.

'And now you're back,' Gulla went on, beaming.

'Yes, it looks like it,' Elma said awkwardly. She hadn't been prepared for such a warm welcome.

'Right, well, I suppose I'd better take you straight through to see Hörður; he told me he was expecting you.' Gulla beckoned her to follow, and they walked down a linoleum-floored corridor and came to a halt outside a door where 'Hörður Höskuldsson' was engraved on a discreet metal nameplate.

'If I know Hörður, he'll be listening to the radio with his headphones on and won't be able to hear us. The man can't work without those things in his ears. I've never understood how he can concentrate.' Gulla gave a loud sigh, rapped smartly on the door, and opened it without waiting for a response.

Inside, a man was sitting behind a desk, staring intently at his computer screen. The headphones were in place, as Gulla had predicted. Noticing movement, he looked up and quickly took them off.

'Hello, Elma. Welcome,' he said with a friendly smile. Rising to his feet, he extended a hand across his desk, then gestured to her to take a seat. He looked to be well over fifty, with greying hair hanging in untidy locks on either side of his long face. In contrast, his fingers were elegant, with neatly manicured nails. Elma pictured him sitting in front of the TV in the evenings, wielding a nail file, and instinctively hid her own hands in her lap so he wouldn't see her bitten-down cuticles.

'So, you've decided to move back to Akranes and give us the benefit of your expertise,' he said, leaning back with his fingers clasped across his chest as he studied her. He had a deep voice and unusually pale blue eyes.

'Well, I suppose you could put it like that,' Elma said, straightening her shoulders. She felt like a little girl who had done something naughty and been summoned to the headmaster's office. Feeling her cheeks growing hot, she hoped he wouldn't notice their betraying flush. There was every chance he would though, as she hadn't had time to slap on any foundation before coming out.

'I'm aware you've been working for Reykjavík CID. As luck would have it, one of our boys has decided to try his chances in the big city, so you'll be taking over his desk.' Hörður leant forwards, propping his cheek on one hand. 'I have to admit I was quite surprised when I got the call from your father. What made you decide to come back here after so many years in the city, if you don't mind my asking?'

'I suppose I was missing Akranes,' Elma replied, trying to make it sound convincing. 'I'd been thinking about moving home for ages,' she elaborated. 'My whole family's here. Then a flat I liked the look of came on the market, and I jumped at the chance.' She smiled, hoping this answer would do.

'I see,' Hörður said, nodding slowly. 'Of course, we can't offer you quite the same facilities or fast pace as you're used to in town,' he continued, 'but I can promise you that, although Akranes seems quiet, we've actually got more than enough on our plate. There's plenty going on under the surface, so you won't be sitting around twiddling your thumbs. Sound good to you?'

Elma nodded, unsure if he was being serious. In her opinion Akranes was every bit as quiet as it appeared to be.

'As you probably know,' Hörður said, 'I'm head of CID here, so you'll be working under me. We operate a shift system, with four officers on duty at any given time, and a duty officer in charge of every shift. Here at Akranes CID we're responsible for the entire Western Region. We operate the usual day-shift rota that you'll be used to from Reykjavík. Shall I give you a quick tour of the station?' He got up, went over to the door and, opening it, beckoned Elma to follow him.

Apart from being considerably smaller, Akranes Police Station was much like her old workplace in the city. It had the same institutional air as other public-sector offices: beige linoleum on the floor, white roller blinds in the windows, light-coloured curtains, blond birchwood furniture.

Hörður pointed out the four holding cells at the other end of the station. 'One of them's occupied at the moment. Yesterday seems to have been a bit lively for some people, but hopefully the guy will wake up soon, and we can send him home.' He smiled absently, stroking the thick, neatly trimmed stubble on his jaw. Then he opened the door to reveal an empty cell, which looked pretty much like the cells in Reykjavík: a small, rectangular room containing a narrow bed.

'The standard set-up, nothing that exciting,' he said.

Elma nodded again. She'd lost count of the times she'd seen the same kind of cells in the city: grey walls and hard beds that few people would want to spend more than one night on. She followed Hörður back down the corridor, which now gave way to offices. He stopped by a door, opened it and ushered her inside. She glanced around. Although the desk was small, it had plenty of room for a computer and anything else she might need, and had lockable drawers too. Someone had put a pot plant on it. Fortunately it appeared to be some kind of cactus that would require little care. Then again, she'd managed to kill even cactuses before now.

'This is where you'll be kicking your heels,' Hörður said with a hint of humour. 'Gulla cleaned it out a few days ago. Pétur, your predecessor, left behind a mountain of files and other junk, but I think it should be ready for you to start work on Monday.'

'Looks good,' Elma said, smiling at him.

She went over to the window and stared out. A chill came off the glass and she could feel the goose bumps prickling her arms. The view was depressing: a row of dreary modern blocks of flats. When she was small she used to play in the basements of those buildings. The corridors had been wide and empty, and smelled of stale air and the rubber of the car tyres stored in the bike sheds. A perfect playground for kids.

'Right, well, that's pretty much everything,' Hörður said, rubbing his hands. 'Shall we check if the coffee's ready? You must have a cup with us before you go.'

They went into the kitchen, where a man, who introduced himself as Kári, one of the regular uniformed officers, was sitting at a small table. He explained that the other members of his shift were on a callout – a party at one of the residential blocks had gone on until morning, to the dismay of the neighbours.

'Welcome to the peace and quiet of the countryside,' Kári said. When he grinned, his dark eyes creased up until all that could be glimpsed of them were his glittering black pupils. 'Not that you can really call it the countryside anymore, after all the development we've seen around here. Houses are flying off the market. Apparently everyone wants to live in Akranes these days.' He gave a loud bark of laughter.

'It'll make a change, anyway,' Elma replied, and couldn't help grinning back. The man looked like a cartoon character when he laughed.

'It'll be good to have you on the team,' Hörður said. 'To be honest, we were a bit worried about losing Pétur, as he was one of the old hands. But he wanted a change of scene after more than twenty years here. He's got a wife in Reykjavík now, and both his children have flown the nest.' Hörður filled two cups with coffee and handed one to her. 'Do you take milk or sugar?' he asked, holding out a purple carton.

Akranes 1989

Her daddy hadn't come home for days and days. She had given up asking where he was. Her mummy got so sad when she did. Anyway, she knew he wasn't coming back. For days she had watched people coming and going, heard them talking to each other, but no one told her anything. They looked at her and patted her on the head, but avoided meeting her eye. She could guess what had happened, though, from the little she had overheard. She knew her daddy had gone out on the boat the day he left. She had heard people talking about the shipwreck and the storm; the storm that had taken her daddy away.

The night he vanished she had been woken by the wind tearing at the corrugated-iron sheets on the roof as if it wanted to rip them off. Her daddy had been in her dream, as large as life, with a big smile on his face and beads of sweat on his forehead. Just like in the summer, when he'd invited her to come out on the boat with him. She had been thinking about him before she went to sleep. Once, her daddy had told her that if you think nice thoughts before you go to bed, you'll have nice dreams. That's why she'd been thinking about him: he was the nicest thing she could imagine.

Days passed and people stopped coming round. In the end it was just the two of them, just her and her mummy. Her mummy still wouldn't tell her anything, no matter how often she asked. She would answer at random, waving her away and telling her to go out and play. Sometimes her mummy sat for a long time, just staring out of the window at the sea, while she smoked an awful lot of cigarettes. Lots more than she used to. She wanted to say something nice to her mummy, say that perhaps Daddy was only lost and would find his way home. But she didn't dare. She was afraid her mummy would get cross. So she stayed quiet and did as she was told, like a good little girl. Went out to play, spoke as little as possible and tried to be invisible at home so her mummy wouldn't be annoyed.

And all the while her mummy's tummy kept growing bigger and bigger.

The sky was growing perceptibly paler by the time Elma re-emerged from the police station, though the streetlights were still on. There were more cars on the roads now and the wind had dropped. Since returning to her old hometown on the Skagi Peninsula, she had been struck by how flat and exposed it seemed in comparison to Reykjavík. Walking through its quiet streets, she felt as if there was nowhere to hide from prying eyes. Unlike the capital, where trees and gardens had grown up over the years to soften the urban landscape and shelter the inhabitants from Iceland's fierce winds, Akranes had little in the way of vegetation, and the impression of bleakness was made worse by the fact that many of the houses and streets were in poor repair. No doubt the recent closure of one of the local fish factories had contributed to the air of decline. But the surrounding scenery still took Elma's breath away: the sea on three sides; Mount Akranes, with its distinctive dip in the middle, dominating the fourth. Ranks of mountains marching away up the coast to the north; the glow of Reykjavík's lights visible across Faxaflói Bay to the south.

Akranes had changed since she was a little girl. It had spread and its population had grown, yet in spite of that she felt it was fundamentally the same. It was still a small town of only seven thousand or so inhabitants, and you encountered the same faces day in, day out. Once she had found the idea stifling, like being trapped in a tiny bubble when there was so much more out there to discover. But now the prospect had the opposite effect: she had nothing against the idea of retreating into a bubble and forgetting the outside world.

She walked slowly, thinking of all the jobs that awaited her at home. She was still getting settled in, having only picked up the keys to her flat the previous weekend. It was in a small block with seven other apartments on two floors. When Elma was a girl, there hadn't been any buildings there, just a large field that sometimes contained horses, which she used to feed with stale bread. But since then a whole new neighbourhood had sprung up, consisting of houses and apartment blocks and even a nursery school. Her flat was on the ground floor and had a large deck out front. There were two staircases in the building, with four flats sharing the small communal area on each. Elma hadn't met her neighbours properly, though she did know that there was a young man living opposite her, who she hadn't yet seen. Upstairs was an older man called Bárður, chairman of the residents' association, and a childless, middle-aged couple who gave her friendly nods whenever they met.

She had spent the week decorating the flat, and now most of the furniture was in place. The contents were a bit of a mixed bag. She'd picked up all kinds of stuff from a charity shop, including an old chest with a carved floral pattern, a gold-plated floor lamp, and four kitchen chairs that she had arranged around her parents' old dining table. She'd thought the flat was looking quite cosy, but when her mother came round, her expression had indicated that she didn't agree. 'Oh, Elma, it's a bit ... colourful,' she had said in an accusatory tone. 'What happened to all the furniture from your old flat? It was so lovely and tasteful.'

Elma had shrugged and pretended not to see her mother's face when she announced casually that she'd sold it when she moved. 'Well, I hope you at least got a decent price for it,' her mother had said. Elma had merely smiled, as this couldn't have been further from the truth. Besides, she liked being surrounded by these old, mismatched pieces; some were familiar from her childhood, others felt as if they probably came with a story attached.

Before moving here, she had lived with Davíð, her boyfriend of many years, in the desirable west end of Reykjavík. Their flat, which was small but cosy, had been in the Melar area, on the middle floor of a three-storey building. She missed the tall rowan tree outside the window. It had been like a painting that changed colour with the seasons, bright green in summer, reddish-orange in autumn and either brown or white in winter. She missed the flat too, but most of all she missed Davíð.

She stopped outside the door of her flat, took out her phone and wrote a text message. Deleted it, then wrote the same message again. Stood there without moving for a moment, then selected Davíð's number. She knew it wouldn't do any good but she sent the message anyway, then went inside.

It was Saturday evening and Akranes's most popular restaurant was packed out, but then there wasn't much competition. Despite the unpromising exterior, it was contemporary and chic inside, with black furniture, grey walls and flattering lighting. Magnea sat up a little straighter as she surveyed the other diners. She knew she was looking her best this evening in a figure-hugging black jumpsuit and was conscious of all the eyes straying inadvertently to her cleavage. Bjarni was sitting opposite her, and whenever their gazes met she read the promise in his eyes about what would happen once they got home. She would have given anything to be dining alone with him instead of having his parents seated either side of her.

They were celebrating the fact that Bjarni was finally taking over the family firm. He had been employed there ever since he finished school, but despite being the boss's son, he had been forced to work hard for the title of managing director. He'd put in a huge number of hours, often working evenings and weekends, and had, in practice, been running the firm alongside his father for several years. But now, at last, it was official: he was formally taking over as managing director. This meant double the salary and double the responsibility, but this evening, at least, he was determined to relax.

The waiter brought a bottle of red wine and poured a splash into Bjarni's glass. After he had tasted it and signalled his approval, the waiter filled their glasses, then retreated, leaving the bottle behind on the table.

'*Skál!*' Bjarni's father, Hendrik, raised his glass. 'To Bjarni and his unstoppable energy. Now he can add the title of managing director to his list of achievements. As his parents, we're hugely proud of him, as we always have been.'

They clinked glasses and tasted the expensive wine. Magnea was careful to take only a tiny sip, allowing no more than a few drops to pass between her red-painted lips.

'I wouldn't have got where I am today without this gorgeous girl beside me,' Bjarni said, his voice slurring a little. He'd had a whisky while they were waiting for his parents and, as always when he drank spirits, the alcohol had gone straight to his head. 'I've lost count of the times I've come home late from the office and never, not once, has my darling wife complained, although she has more than enough to do at work herself.' He gazed adoringly at Magnea and she blew him a kiss over the table.

Hendrik turned an indulgent look on Ása but, instead of returning his smile, she averted her eyes, her mouth tight with disapproval. Magnea sighed under her breath. She had given up trying to win her mother-in-law round. These days she didn't really care anymore. When she and Bjarni had first moved in together she had made a real effort to impress Ása, making sure the house was immaculate whenever his parents were coming over, baking specially for them and generally bending over backwards to earn her mother-in-law's approval. But it had been a lost cause. Her efforts were invariably rewarded with the same critical look; the look that said the cake was too dry, the bathroom wasn't sufficiently sparkling clean and the floors could have done with another going over. The message was clear: however hard she tried, Magnea would never be good enough for Bjarni.

'How's the teaching going, Magnea?' Hendrik asked. 'Are those brats behaving themselves?' Unlike his wife he had always had a soft spot for his daughter-in-law. Perhaps that was one reason for Ása's hostility. Hendrik never missed a chance to touch Magnea, put an arm round her shoulders or waist, or kiss her on the cheek. He was a big man, in contrast to his dainty wife, and had a reputation in Akranes as a bit of a shark when it came to business. He had a charming smile that Bjarni had inherited, and a powerful, slightly husky, voice. Regular drinking had turned his features coarse and red, yet Magnea liked him better than Ása, so she put up with the wandering hands and the flirtation, which all seemed harmless enough to her.

'They usually behave themselves for me,' Magnea replied, smiling at him. At that moment the waiter came back to take their order.

The evening went pretty smoothly: Bjarni and Hendrik chatted about work and football; Ása sat in silence, apparently sunk in her own thoughts, and Magnea smiled at the two men from time to time, contributing the odd word, but otherwise sat quietly like Ása. It was a relief when the meal was over and they could leave. The cold night air sneaked inside her thin coat once they were outside and she took Bjarni's arm, pressing close to him.

They had the rest of the evening to themselves.

It wasn't until Bjarni had fallen asleep beside her in bed that she remembered the face. She saw again the pair of dark eyes that had met hers when she glanced across the restaurant. For much of the night she lay wide awake, trying to ward off the memories that flashed into her mind with a stark clarity every time she closed her eyes.

Monday, 20 November 2017

Elma sat at her new desk in her new office, on her first day, trying to keep her eyes open. Conscious that she was slouching, she straightened up and forced herself to focus on the computer screen. She had spent the previous evening wandering restlessly around her flat before deciding on an impulse to paint the sitting room. The tins of emulsion had been sitting there untouched ever since she moved in. As a result, she hadn't crashed out until the early hours, too exhausted to scrub the paint spots off her arms.

Remembering the text message she had sent Davíð, she pictured him opening it and the faintest smile touching his lips before he sent a reply. But that was wishful thinking; she knew he wouldn't answer. She briefly closed her eyes, feeling her breath coming fast and shallow, and experiencing again that suffocating sensation as if the walls were closing in on her. She concentrated on taking deep, slow breaths.

'Ahem.'

She opened her eyes. A man was standing in front of her, holding out his hand. 'Sævar,' he said.

Elma hastily pulled herself together and shook his large, hairy hand, which turned out to be unexpectedly soft.

'I see they've found a home for you.' Sævar smiled at her. He was wearing dark-blue jeans and a short-sleeved shirt that revealed the thick fur on his arms. The overall impression – dark hair, dense stubble, heavy eyebrows and coarse features – was that of a caveman, but this was belied by a pleasant hint of aftershave.

'Yes, it's not bad. Pretty good, actually,' Elma said, brushing her hair back from her face.

'How are you enjoying life out here in the sticks?' Sævar asked, still smiling. He must be the other detective Hörður had mentioned. Elma knew he'd been working for the Akranes force since he was twenty but didn't recall seeing his face before, though he couldn't have been more than a few years older than her. The town only had two schools and one community college, and the smallness of the place meant that you generally encountered all your contemporaries sooner or later – or so Elma had thought.

'Very much,' she replied, trying to sound upbeat but afraid she was coming across as a bit of an idiot. She hoped the black circles under her eyes weren't too obvious but knew the unforgiving fluorescent lights would only exaggerate any signs of weariness.

'I hear you were in Reykjavík CID,' Sævar continued. 'What made you decide to have a change of scene and come here?'

'Well, I grew up here,' Elma said, 'so … I suppose I was missing my family.'

'Yes, that's the most important thing in life,' Sævar said. 'You realise when you start to get old that family's what it's all about.'

'Old?' Elma looked at him in surprise. 'You can't be that old.'

'No, maybe not.' Sævar grinned. 'Thirty-five. Best years still to come.'

'I certainly hope so,' Elma said. As a rule, she tried not to dwell on her age. She knew she was still young, and yet she was uncomfortably aware of how fast the years were winging by. If anyone asked how old she was, she almost always had to stop and think, so she tended just to give the year of her birth – her vintage. As if she were a car or a wine.

'That makes two of us,' Sævar said. 'Anyway, the reason I'm here is that we got a callout at the weekend after some people heard a woman screaming in the flat upstairs, and a lot of shouting and banging. When we got there, it was a mess. The man had beaten his girlfriend so badly his knuckles were bleeding. The woman insisted she didn't want to take it any further, but I expect charges will be brought anyway. Still, it helps if the victim's prepared to testify, even when we have a medical report and other evidence to back up our case. She's home from hospital now, and I was thinking of having a chat with her, but I reckon it would be better to have a female officer present. And it wouldn't hurt if she'd studied psychology as well,' he added, with a twinkle in his eye.

'It was only for two years,' Elma muttered, wondering how he knew about the psychology degree she had been taking before she dropped out of university and enrolled at the Police College instead. She didn't remember the subject coming up in conversation, so presumably he must have read her CV. 'Sure, I'll go with you but I can't promise my knowledge of psychology will be any use.'

'Oh, come on – I have complete faith in you.'

They were met by a strong smell of cooking when they knocked on the door of the house. After a bit of a wait they heard signs of life inside. Sævar had told Elma on the way there that the woman they wanted to see was currently staying with her elderly grandmother.

A few moments later the door opened with a feeble creak, and a small, wizened woman with a deeply lined face appeared in the gap. Her skin was covered in brown liver spots but the pale-grey, shoulder-length hair, drawn back in a clip, was unusually thick and handsome for her age. She raised her eyebrows inquiringly.

'We're looking for Ásdís Sigurðardóttir. Is she in?' Sævar asked. The old woman turned round without a word, beckoning them to follow her.

Elma guessed the house hadn't changed much since it was built, probably in the seventies. There was a carpet on the floor – a rare sight in Iceland where they were considered old-fashioned and unhygienic – and the walls were clad in dark wood panelling. The smell of meat stew was even more overpowering inside.

'That arsehole,' the old woman burst out, startling Elma. 'That pathetic bastard can rot in hell for all I care. But Dísa won't listen to me. Won't even discuss it. So I told her she could pack her bags. If she won't listen, she can get out of my house.' The old woman turned without warning and took hold of Elma's arm. 'But I can't talk – I've always been a soft touch myself, so she probably got it from me. I can't throw her out, not after what's happened. But maybe you can get through to her. She's in there, in her old room.' She pointed down the hallway with a knobbly, brown-splotched hand, then shuffled off and left them to it, muttering under her breath.

Elma and Sævar stood there for a moment, trying to work out which door she had meant. There were four rooms opening off the hallway and Elma wondered how the old woman could afford such a large house when, as far as they knew, she usually lived there alone. After a moment, Sævar tapped tentatively on one of the doors. When there was no response, he opened it warily.

The girl sitting on the bed was considerably younger than Elma had been expecting. She was hunched over the computer in her lap but raised her head as they entered. She couldn't have been more than twenty-five, and her dark-blue hoodie and white pyjamas with a pink pattern contributed to the impression of youth. Her eyebrows were pencilled black and looked much darker than her brown hair, which was scraped back in a lank pony-tail. But it was hard to take in anything apart from her battered face. Her lips had split and the swelling round her eyes was mottled blue, green and brown.

'May I?' Elma asked, gesturing to the office chair at the end of the bed. She and Sævar had agreed beforehand that she would do most of the talking. The girl was bound to find it easier to speak to a woman after what that man had done to her. When the girl nodded, Elma sat down.

'Do you know who I am?' she asked.

'No, how should I know that?'

'I'm from the police. We're assisting the prosecutor with the case against your boyfriend.'

'I'm not pressing charges. I told them that at the hospital.' Her voice was firm and uncompromising. As she spoke, she sat up a little straighter.

'I'm afraid it's out of your hands,' Elma said, trying to sound friendly, and explained: 'When the police are involved, they have the power to investigate the incident and prosecute if they deem it necessary.'

'But you don't understand … I don't want to prosecute,' the girl said angrily. 'Tommi's just … he's been having a hard time. He didn't mean to do it.'

'I see, but that's still no excuse for what he did to you. Lots of us have problems but we don't all react like that.' Elma leant forward in her chair, holding Ásdís's gaze with her own. 'Has he done it before?'

'No,' the girl answered quickly, before qualifying in a low voice: 'He's never hit me before.'

'The doctor found old bruises on you. Bruises from about a month ago.'

'I don't know what can have caused them, but then I'm always falling over,' Ásdís retorted.

Elma studied her searchingly, reluctant to put too much pressure on her. She looked so small and vulnerable as she sat there in bed, in clothes that seemed far too big for her.

'He's almost forty years older than you, isn't he?'

'No, he's sixty. I'm nearly twenty-nine,' the girl corrected her.

'It would really help if you'd come down to the station with us so we could take a formal statement from you,' Elma said. 'Then you'd get a chance to put your side of the story.'

Ásdís shook her head, stroking the initials embroidered on the duvet cover. They looked to Elma like *Á.H.S.*

'You know, there's all kinds of help available to women in your situation,' Elma continued. 'We've got a counsellor you could talk to and there's a women's refuge in Reykjavík that's helped lots of…' Elma trailed off when she caught the look on Ásdís's face.

'What does the H stand for?' she asked instead, after a brief pause.

'Harpa. Ásdís Harpa. But I've always hated the name. My mother was called Harpa.'

Elma didn't pursue the subject. There must be some reason why Ásdís couldn't stand being named after her mother, even though the woman was dead. And why, at nearly thirty, she was still living sometimes with her grandmother, sometimes with a much older man who treated her like a punch bag. But sadly Elma had seen many worse cases and could tell straight away that there was little to be done until Ásdís was prepared to take action herself. Elma just hoped she wouldn't leave it too late. Ásdís had turned her attention back to her laptop as if there was no one else in the room. Elma raised her eyebrows at Sævar with a defeated look and got to her feet. There was no more to be said.

Nevertheless, as they were leaving she paused in the doorway and turned: 'Are you going back to him?'

'Yes,' Ásdís replied, without looking up from the screen.

'Well, good luck. Don't hesitate to call if … if you need us,' Elma said, putting out a hand to close the door.

'You lot don't understand anything,' Ásdís muttered angrily. Elma stopped and looked round again. Ásdís hesitated, then added in a low voice: 'I can't press charges; I'm pregnant.'

'All the more reason to stay out of his way, then,' Elma said, meeting her eye. She spoke slowly and deliberately, stressing every syllable in the hope that her words would sink in. But she didn't really believe they would.

It was past four and already getting dark outside when Elma wandered into the kitchen. The coffee in the thermos turned out to be lukewarm and tasted as if it had been sitting there since that morning. She tipped the contents of her mug down the sink and started opening the cupboards in search of tea.

'The tea's in the drawer,' said a voice behind her, making her jump. It was the young female officer Elma had been introduced to earlier that day. Elma struggled for her name: Begga, that was it. She looked quite a bit younger than Elma herself; well under thirty, anyway. She was tall and big-boned, with shoulder-length, mousy hair and a nose that wouldn't have looked out of place on a Roman emperor. Elma noticed that she had dimples even when she wasn't smiling.

'Sorry, I didn't mean to startle you,' Begga said. She pulled open a drawer and showed Elma a box of tea bags.

'Thanks,' Elma said. 'Would you like some too?'

'Yes, please. I may as well join you.' Begga sat down at the little table. Elma waited for the kettle to boil, then filled two mugs with hot water. She fetched a carton of milk from the fridge and put it on the table along with a bowl of sugar-lumps.

'I know you from somewhere.' Begga studied Elma thoughtfully as she stirred her tea. 'Were you at Grundi School?'

Elma nodded. She'd attended the school, which was on the southern side of town.

'I think I remember you. You must have been a couple of years above me. Were you born in 1985?'

'Yes, I was,' Elma said, sipping from her steaming mug. Begga was much older than she'd guessed; almost as old as her.

'I do remember you,' Begga said, her dimples becoming more pronounced as she smiled. 'I was so pleased to hear there was another woman joining us. As you may have noticed, we're in a serious minority here. It's a bit of a man's world.'

'It certainly is. But I like working with these guys so far,' Elma said. 'They seem really easy to get along with.'

'Yes, most of them. I'm happy here anyway,' Begga said. She was one of those people who appear to be perpetually smiling, even when they aren't. She had that sort of face.

'Have you always lived here?' Elma asked.

'Yes, always,' Begga replied. 'I love it here. The locals are great, there's no traffic and everything's within reach. I've no reason to go anywhere else. And I'm absolutely sure my friends who've moved away will come back eventually. Most people who leave come back sooner or later,' she added confidently. 'Like you, for example.'

'Like me, for example,' Elma repeated, dropping her gaze to her mug.

'Why did you decide to move back?' Begga prompted.

Elma wondered how often she would have to answer this question. She was about to trot out the usual story when she paused. Begga had the sort of comfortable manner that invited confidences. 'I was missing my family, and it's good to get away from the traffic, of course, but...' She hesitated. 'Actually, I've just come out of a relationship.'

'I see.' Begga pushed over a basket of biscuits, taking one herself as she did so. 'Had you been together long?'

'I suppose so – nine years.'

'Wow, I've never managed more than six months,' Begga exclaimed with an infectious giggle. 'Though I am closely involved with a gorgeous guy at the moment. He's very fluffy and loves cuddling up to me in the evenings.'

'A dog?' Elma guessed.

'Nearly.' Begga grinned. 'A cat.'

Elma smiled back. She had taken an instant liking to Begga, who didn't seem to care what other people thought of her. She was different, without making any conscious effort to be.

'So, what happened?' Begga asked.

'When?'

'With you and the nine-year guy.'

Elma sighed. She didn't want to have to think about Davíð now. 'He changed,' she said. 'Or maybe I did. I don't know.'

'Did he cheat on you? The guy I was seeing for six months cheated on me. Well, he didn't actually shag someone else, but I found out he was using dating sites and had a Tinder profile. I came across it by chance.'

Elma caught her eye. 'So you were on there yourself?'

'Yeah, but only for research purposes. It was purely academic interest,' Begga said with mock seriousness. 'You should try it. It's brilliant. I've already been on two Tinder dates.'

'How did they go?'

'It worked the second time – if you know what I mean.' Begga winked at her and Elma laughed in spite of herself. 'But I'm not actually looking for anyone,' Begga went on. 'I enjoy the single life. For the moment, anyway. And my heart belongs to my liddle baby.'

'Your baby?'

'Yeah, my boy cat,' Begga explained and burst out laughing.

Elma rolled her eyes and smiled. Begga was one of a kind all right.

Akranes 1989

The baby came in May. The day it was born was beautiful and sunny, with barely a cloud in the sky. When she went outside the air was damp from the night's rain and the spicy scent of fresh greenery hung over the garden, tickling her nose. The sea stirred idly and far beyond the bay she could see the white dome of the Snæfellsjökull glacier rising on the horizon. Closer at hand, the reefs peeped up from the waves every now and then. She was wearing a pair of snow-washed jeans and a yellow T-shirt with a rainbow on the front. Her hair was tied back in a loose pony-tail but her curls kept escaping from the elastic band, so she was constantly having to brush strands of hair from her face.

It was a Saturday and they had woken early, then eaten toast and jam for breakfast while listening to the radio. The weather was so good that they decided they would go for a walk on the beach to look for shells. They found an empty ice-cream tub to take with them and she sat on the swing while waiting for her mummy to finish her chores. As her mummy hung out the washing, she swung back and forth, reaching her toes up to the sky. They were chatting and her mummy was just smiling at her and stretching her arms to hang up a white sheet when suddenly she clutched at her stomach and doubled over. She stopped her swinging and watched her mummy anxiously.

'It's all right. Just a bit of a twinge,' her mummy said, trying to smile. But when she stood up, the pain started again and she had to sit down on the wet grass.

'Mummy?' she said anxiously, going over to her.

'Run next door to Solla's and ask her to come over.' Her mother took a deep breath and made a face. Drops of sweat trickled down her forehead. 'Hurry.'

Without waiting to be told again, she ran as fast as she could across the road to Solla's house. She knocked on the door, then opened it without waiting for an answer.

'Hello! Solla!' she shouted. She could hear voices coming from the radio, then a figure appeared in the kitchen doorway.

'What's up?' Solla asked, regarding her in surprise.

'The baby...' she panted. 'It's coming.'

Several days later her mummy came home with a small bundle wrapped in a blue blanket. He was the most beautiful thing she had ever seen, with his dark hair and plump, unbelievably soft cheeks. Cautiously, she stroked the tiny fingers and marvelled that anything could be that small. But best of all was the smell. He smelled of milk and something sweet that she couldn't put a name to. Even the little white pimples on his cheeks were so tiny and delicate that it was a sheer pleasure to run your finger over them. He was to be called Arnar, just like her daddy.

But her beautiful little brother only lived for two weeks in their house by the sea. One day he wouldn't wake up, however hard her mummy tried to rouse him.

Saturday, 25 November 2017

The only sounds in the house were the ticking of the sitting-room clock and the regular clicking of her knitting needles as they turned out the smooth, pale loops. The little jumper was almost finished. Once Ása had cast off and woven in the loose ends, she laid the jumper on the sofa and smoothed it out. The yarn, a mix of alpaca and silk, was as soft and light as thistle-down. She tried out several different kinds of buttons against the jumper before opting for some white mother-of-pearl ones that went well with the light-coloured wool. She would sew them on later, once she had washed it. After putting the little garment in the washing machine, she switched on the kettle, scooped up some tea leaves in the strainer, poured the boiling water over them and added sugar and a dash of milk. Then she sat down at the kitchen table. The weekend paper lay there unopened, but instead of leafing through it, she cradled the hot cup in both hands and stared unseeingly out of the window.

Her hands always got so cold when she was knitting. She wound the yarn so tightly round her index finger that it was bloodless and numb by the time she put down her needles. But knitting was her hobby, and numb fingers were a small price to pay for the pleasure she derived from seeing the yarn transformed into a succession of pretty garments. Pretty garments to add to the pile in the wardrobe. Hendrik was always grumbling about her extravagance. The yarn didn't come cheap, especially the finest-quality soft wool, spun with silk. But she carried on regardless, ignoring Hendrik's nagging. It wasn't as if they couldn't afford it. All her life she had been thrifty and watched every penny. It was how she had been brought up. But these days they had plenty of money; so much more than they needed, in fact, that she didn't know what to do with it all. So she bought wool. She wondered at times if she should sell the clothes or give them away so others could make use of them, but something always held her back.

She gazed out at the garden, where the blackbirds were hopping among the shrubs, attracted by the apples she had hung out for them. Time seemed to stand still. Ever since she had given up work, the days had become so long and drawn out that it was as if they would never end.

Ása heard the front door open and close, then Hendrik walked into the kitchen without a word of greeting. He was still going into the office every day, and Ása doubted he would ever give up work entirely, though he was intending to cut down now that Bjarni was taking over. When not at work, he spent most of his time on the golf course, but golf had always bored her rigid.

'What's the matter with you?' Hendrik sat down at the table and picked up the paper, not looking at her as he spoke.

Ása didn't answer but went on staring out of the window. The blackbirds were noisy now, singing shrill warning notes from the bushes. Ever louder and more insistent.

Hendrik shook his head and snorted, as if to say that it didn't matter how she was feeling or what she was thinking.

Without a word, she slammed down her cup so violently that the tea splashed onto the table. Then she stood up and walked quickly into the bedroom, pretending not to notice Hendrik's astonished expression. Sitting down on the bed, she concentrated on getting her breathing under control. She wasn't accustomed to losing her temper like that. She had always been so docile, so self-effacing, first as a little girl growing up in the countryside out east and later as a woman working in the fish factory in Akranes. She had moved young to Reykjavík and, like so many country girls, attended the Home Economics School. While boarding there she had soon discovered that life in the city offered all kinds of attractions that the countryside didn't, like new people, work and a variety of entertainment. Shops, schools and streets that hardly ever emptied. Lights that lit up the night and a harbour full of ships. It was meeting Hendrik that had brought her to Akranes. He had been working on a fishing boat that put into Reykjavík harbour one August night. The crew had gone out on the town where Ása was partying with her friends from the Home Economics School. She had met him as he walked in through the door of the nightclub.

Ása had known from the first instant that she had found her husband, the man she wanted to spend the rest of her life with – *Him* with a capital H. He was tall and dark, and the other girls had gazed at him enviously. This was hardly surprising as she had never been considered much to look at herself, with her ginger hair and her complexion that burst out in freckles at the first hint of summer.

Thinking about it later, she was convinced it was her vulnerability that had attracted him. He had seen that she was a girl who wouldn't stand up for herself. Instead, she smiled shyly and folded her arms meekly across her stomach; she always laid the table and never walked ahead of him when they were out; she ironed his shirts without having to be asked or ever being thanked. When she and Hendrik had first got to know each other, he had said that her timidity was one of the things that had captivated him. He couldn't stand strident women, referring to them as 'pushy cows', but she was a girl after his own heart, who knew when to keep quiet and let others do the talking. Who was nice and submissive. Who would make a good mother.

She wiped away the tears as they spilled over. What on earth was the matter with her? Why was she suddenly so easily upset? After all, she had coped with so much over the years. And she had Bjarni. He hadn't been a bad son to her – quite the opposite. Although he took after his father in appearance, his expression was gentler, lacking all hardness. Despite being nearly forty, he had held on to his boyish looks. When he smiled, her world seemed brighter, but when Ása saw him with the boys he coached at football, something seemed to break inside her.

She knew he wanted children. Not that he'd mentioned it, of course, but she knew. She was his mother, after all, and knew him better than anyone else. The only thing standing in the way was *her*. *She* was too self-centred to have children. And because of *her*, the family line would die out with Bjarni. Ása didn't know if she could bear it, but what choice did she have?

She drew the curtains, changed into her nightie and got into bed, pulling the duvet over herself, though it wasn't yet evening. It wasn't Bjarni's childlessness that had caused her to react so violently just now, but the visit she had received that morning. What had happened then had distressed her so much that she needed to lie down. She was too old to start reopening old wounds. She'd been through enough suffering. Now all she wanted was to go to sleep. To sleep and never to wake up again.

The wardrobe was crammed to bursting with clothes. Old dresses and coats were tightly packed on the hangers and there was a heap of shoes and bags on the floor. Elma couldn't picture herself ever wearing anything in there again.

'For some reason I've never got round to going through it all.' Her mother, Aðalheiður, stood there in her loose shirt, hands on her hips, glasses perched on the tip of her nose. She was a small, slightly plump woman, with short, blonde hair. To Elma, she never seemed to change.

They were standing in Elma's old room, contemplating the over-stuffed wardrobe that had been used for storage in recent years. The task seemed hopeless.

'Still, it's a good thing you hung on to it all. I mean, I could wear this at Christmas,' Elma said, holding up a shiny red dress with frilly sleeves. 'And this would look great with it,' she added, pulling out a beige velvet jacket.

'Oh, you looked so smart in that jacket,' Aðalheiður said wistfully, taking it from her. 'Try it on for me. Go on. Please.'

'*Mum*, I wore that to my confirmation,' Elma said, laughing. 'I doubt I'd be able to squeeze into it now.'

'You've lost so much weight over the last few weeks,' Aðalheiður said accusingly.

Elma rolled her eyes but didn't reply. She knew it was true from the way her clothes hung off her, though she hadn't dared to get on the scales.

'Oh, please, try it on,' her mother persisted, pushing the jacket at her. 'Wait a sec, I'll find the trousers that go with it.' Turning to the wardrobe, she started pulling out garments willy-nilly and chucking them on the floor, not stopping until she emerged triumphantly with a pair of flared beige trousers. 'I knew they were in here somewhere. Come on, try them on.'

'No way!' Elma retorted. 'What were you thinking of, making me wear that? A fourteen-year-old girl in a beige trouser suit? Why couldn't I just have worn a pink dress?'

'You chose it yourself, Elma. Don't you remember?'

'I can't possibly have worn that voluntarily.'

'You and your friends all had them. Silja and Kristín both came along to your confirmation in the same kind of outfit. I've got a photo somewhere. Hang on, I'll find it.'

'No, for God's sake, Mum. Please, don't bother.'

'Well, anyway, I thought you all looked very smart,' Aðalheiður insisted, flicking invisible dust off the jacket. 'Have you heard from Kristín or Silja at all recently?'

'No, not a word.'

'You should get in touch with them. They still live here, you know. They didn't run away like you.' Although Aðalheiður's tone was light as she said this, Elma knew her mother had never been a fan of Reykjavík, dismissing it as too congested, too crowded and too far away. In fact, it only took forty-five minutes to drive there now that the Hvalfjörður tunnel had been opened, but it still seemed a long way to her parents, who were used to never having to drive for more than five minutes to get anywhere they wanted.

'I haven't spoken to them for years. It would be weird if I

suddenly rang them out of the blue, just because I've moved back home.'

'It doesn't have to be weird. People call their old friends. Who knows, they might be thinking the same thing?'

'Somehow I seriously doubt they're thinking the same thing.'

'Well, anyway, you were the one who took off. You moved away. They tried to stay in touch, didn't they? How good were you about ringing them back?'

Elma shrugged. She'd hardly given any thought to Silja and Kristín for years. The three of them had been inseparable all the way through school, but they had gradually grown apart after Elma moved to Reykjavík. 'I don't suppose I was good enough about returning their calls,' she admitted sheepishly, smiling at her mother. Sitting down on the bed, she started folding the clothes that Aðalheiður had thrown on the floor while searching for the trousers.

'It's never too late, Elma,' Aðalheiður said, gently stroking her shoulder. 'And now I insist you pop on the suit without another word. It cost me a fortune and you only wore it once. You owe it to me.'

A few minutes later, Elma was standing before the mirror in the beige velvet suit. The trouser legs and sleeves were too short and although she could just about button up the jacket, she couldn't zip up the flies at all.

'You haven't changed a bit,' Aðalheiður said, mouth twitching as she struggled to keep a straight face. Elma threw her an incredulous glance and they both exploded with laughter.

'What's going on?' Jón, Elma's father, put his head round the door and stared in surprise at his wife and daughter, who were wiping the tears from their eyes. 'Are you trying on clothes for your new job?' he asked Elma. When neither of them answered, he shook his head, muttering, 'Good, good,' and headed off in the direction of the TV room, where he would shortly nod off in his armchair with a book of sudoku puzzles on his lap.

'Right, we'll never get this done if we don't get started,' Aðalheiður said, once they had recovered. 'It's nice to see you laugh,' she added, with a good-natured glance at her daughter. 'I've missed that.'

Just over an hour later Elma stood there alone, surveying her handiwork. She had finished sorting through most of the clothes. One pile was to go to the Red Cross, another belonged to her sister Dagný, who was three years older than her and whose clothes had somehow found their way into the wardrobe as well.

Elma lay down on the bed and pulled the cover over her. The room had barely changed since she moved out. Still the same furniture and her old books on the shelves.

It was a peculiar feeling to be home again. After all those years in Reykjavík she felt as if she was back where she had started. But she wasn't angry, not anymore. The anger had only lasted a few days. Now she was just sad. And lonely. So desperately lonely. Would she ever get used to being single?

She sighed quietly and rolled over in bed. Anyway, here she was, having got through her first week at work. It was Saturday evening and, like so many other evenings before, she was lying in bed, waiting to hear her mother's voice calling to tell her that supper was ready. Somehow, time kept on passing.

She turned on her side and felt her eyelids growing heavy. There was something so comforting about the smell of the bed-clothes and the familiar sounds of the house: her parents' voices, the groaning of the plumbing when a tap was turned on, the creaking of the parquet floors.

She was finding it hard to sleep in the new flat. It took her ages to drop off and she kept starting awake in the middle of the night for no reason. It had nothing to do with her neighbours since the building was extremely quiet. Come to think of it, perhaps that was the problem. The silence. No sound of breathing at her side. No one turning over in bed.

Her old fear of the dark had reared its head again since she had moved into her new home. When she woke up in the night she invariably needed a pee, and on the way to the bathroom she couldn't shake off the feeling that someone was watching her. That someone was standing at the end of the hallway in the dark corner where no streetlights shone in. It took all her willpower not to run back to her room and pull the duvet over her head.

She had to remind herself that she wasn't a little girl anymore.

That the real evil wasn't to be found lurking in dark corners but in the human soul.

Magnea had got the email – she just hadn't read it. When she saw who had sent it, she knew immediately what it would contain. So she had deleted it without giving it a second glance. She didn't know how many emails that was now. They'd been arriving for weeks and they always said the same thing. Always contained the same plea. At first, the tone had been friendly, almost too polite, and she had begun to remember things that she had absolutely no desire to rake up. But now the tone had changed and the messages were despairing and increasingly aggressive. She hadn't met her since they were both little girls. That's why she had been so shocked when she saw her at the restaurant. Anyway, what could they possibly have to say to each other?

Magnea had come out for a run to clear her head, but it wasn't working. As she jogged, her thoughts kept returning to the messages, to what they had done. She just couldn't see the point of dragging it all up again. The past was past and nothing could change it now. She had done well for herself: she was happily married, lived in a beautiful house and went on regular foreign holidays – just for pleasure, because she could. She had no desire to change anything simply in order to achieve some kind of peace of mind, for which she felt no need.

Besides, Magnea knew that it would mean losing Bjarni and that was unthinkable. That's why she had deleted the messages without answering them, and hoped against hope that the woman would give up in the end.

She paused a moment to catch her breath, then carried on running. She needed to drop by the shop to buy a couple of ingredients for this evening's dessert. Bjarni was in charge of the roast; it was his speciality. Gylfi, Bjarni's childhood friend, and his wife, Drífa, were coming round for supper. Taking it in turns to invite one another to dinner was something they had done regularly over the years, though the invitations used to be much more frequent before Gylfi and Drífa had the twins, who were now five years old.

After picking up what they needed from the shop, she walked the rest of the way home. Physical tiredness sent currents of well-being through her body. She rarely felt as contented as she did after a good run. According to her watch, she had been going for nearly an hour at a brisk pace.

Bjarni was standing at the kitchen island when she came in, concentrating on cutting fine slices in the tops of the potatoes. The joint of beef was on the table, seasoned and ready to go in the oven.

'That looks good, love,' she said, kissing him on the cheek. Bjarni was so tall she had to stand on tiptoe to reach. She loved that about him. It made him seem so manly, so masterful.

'Good run?' he asked, without looking up from his task.

'Yes. I did a circuit of the town, past the forestry plantation, then down Innnesvegur. There was a fantastic view from the beach at Langisandur. It's perfect running weather – you should have come with me.' She turned on the tap and filled a glass, then drank it down in one go and leant back against the kitchen counter. 'Can I do anything to help?'

'No, I'm just going to stick these in.' Bjarni seasoned the potatoes and put them in the oven. 'Then I'm going to do this.' Turning to her, he gripped her by the thighs and lifted her up to sit on the counter.

'Well, well,' she said, laughing, and kissed him back eagerly, making no objection as he pulled down his trousers.

Afterwards she took a long, leisurely shower. Everything was more or less ready so she had plenty of time. The home help had come earlier and the place was shining clean. Not that she really understood why she needed a cleaner since there were only the two of them living there and the house rarely got dirty. There were no children to spill things or to tidy up after. But Bjarni insisted on the help. He had grown up with that arrangement and wanted everything cleaned once a week but saw no reason why Magnea should have to do it. She didn't object, but then she rarely did. After all, it was up to him how he spent his money – he was the main breadwinner, not her on her teacher's salary.

Magnea's thoughts returned to the email. She was so contented with her life, so perfectly happy with what she had. Why couldn't the woman understand that and leave her alone? Feeling the irritation building up inside her, she inhaled deeply several times. It didn't matter. The woman would give up in the end and go away and get on with her own life. It would be in her interest, after all.

By the time Magnea stepped out of the shower, she had succeeded in pushing away any unpleasant thoughts. First the run, then Bjarni, had left her feeling unusually relaxed, so she was quick to get into the right mood for the dinner party. While doing her hair and make-up she hummed along to the music Bjarni had put on. Then she dressed in a white chiffon shirt, black trousers and high stiletto heels. She swayed her hips to the music as she laid the table in the living room and lit the candles.

Shortly afterwards, the doorbell rang.

'I'll get it,' Magnea called to Bjarni and checked her appearance in the mirror before going into the hall. Putting on a wide smile, she opened the door, ready to show their guests her best side. But when she saw who was standing there, the smile was wiped off her face. A pair of dark-brown eyes stared at her anxiously.

'You didn't answer any of my emails,' the woman said, with a quick, on-off smile. 'You know we need to talk.' She sounded obstinate, as if determined to get her own way.

Magnea froze, staring at her, and prayed that Bjarni wouldn't come out. She didn't want to have to explain to him how she knew this woman. She had to get rid of her before he came to the door, but she knew the woman wasn't going anywhere until she had got what she wanted.

'All right, fine,' Magnea whispered. 'I'll meet you. We can talk. But not now, later. I'll meet you later this evening, but only if you leave now.' A car drove past and Magnea started to close the door. She didn't want the guests to arrive while she was standing here with this woman on the doorstep.

'Where can we meet?' the woman asked, wrapping her black coat tightly around herself.

'I'll be in touch,' Magnea hissed.

'You don't have my number. Do you want to write it down?' The woman's desperation was so palpable that Magnea almost felt sorry for her.

'By the lighthouse,' Magnea whispered. 'I'll meet you by the lighthouse.'

'By the lighthouse,' the woman agreed and walked away. She was still holding her coat tightly around her as she got into her car and drove off.

'Was that Mum?' Bjarni called from the bathroom.

'No, it was ... just some kids collecting bottles for the deposits,' Magnea replied, trying to sound normal. 'To raise money for the swimming club.' There was very little that could shake her composure these days, and this visit must be no exception.

Akranes 1989

She never knew exactly when it started. It happened so slowly. Like something you don't notice until afterwards, when you look back and realise that everything has changed. That's how Elísabet experienced it, at least. She remembered the time before everything went wrong, when her daddy was alive and she wasn't afraid. But the memory was so distant, it was like a dream.

If she were to try to pinpoint the time or place, it would probably be the day her little brother died. She remembered it so well. Her mother's screams and the people who came round afterwards; the same people as had come round after her daddy went away. Everyone in a hurry, their voices low, their eyes wet with tears. And she remembered the tiny body lying so still in the big bed.

But perhaps she had remembered wrong. Perhaps it had begun the day her daddy disappeared. Elísabet wasn't sure, and anyway it didn't really matter. Everything had changed because her mother had changed.

At first she thought her mother was ill. When she wouldn't get out of bed and just slept all day. All day and all night. Elísabet didn't know what she was supposed to do, and at first she had tried knocking on her mother's bedroom door and asking questions. What was for lunch? What clothes should she put on? Could she go out and play? But when there were no replies, she gave up knocking. When she was hungry and there was no food in the house, she simply went over to Solla's.

Then one day her mother got out of bed. Elísabet sat on the floor and played with her dolls while she watched her mother dressing up, combing her hair and putting on red lipstick. She was in a good mood, swaying to the music and winking at her. If Elísabet had known what this would lead to, she wouldn't have smiled back. After her mother had put her to bed and whispered to her to go to sleep, she had heard the front door slam downstairs. She had lain there quite still for a long time, listening. Had her mother gone out?

Elísabet had wriggled out from under the duvet and tiptoed downstairs, peeping into one room after the other, until in the end she was standing in the sitting room, calling her mother. First in a low voice, then louder and louder. No one answered: she was alone.

That was before she learnt that sometimes it was better to be on your own. Now she would give almost anything to be left alone.

Sunday, 26 November 2017

Aðalheiður sat hunched over the wheel, staring intently at the road in front of her. She held stubbornly to a sedate pace, ignoring the other cars that kept overtaking.

'Mum, you know the speed limit's ninety kilometres an hour here,' Elma protested and sighed as yet another car passed them, the driver flashing them an angry grimace as he swept by. 'Driving too slowly can be dangerous too, you know,' she added, but couldn't help being amused by her mother's look of fierce concentration.

'Ninety's the maximum speed in optimum conditions, Elma,' Aðalheiður replied, unfazed. 'Rain and wind don't count as optimum conditions, as you should know, being a police officer.'

Elma turned to look out of the window. Her mother was right. As so often, the weather, which had been fine back in Akranes, had deteriorated now that they were rounding the Kjalarnes Peninsula, in one of those bewilderingly fast changes for which the Icelandic climate was famous. Violent gusts kept battering the car, making her mother grip the wheel and slow to a crawl. Apparently this phenomenon had something to do with the way the mountains funnelled the wind. When Elma got up that morning a hard frost had covered the road outside her flat with glittering ice, yet now big, fat raindrops were falling out of a suddenly overcast sky and exploding on the windscreen.

Elma had woken early, despite having come home late the night before. To her surprise, Begga had rung her in the afternoon and invited her round to check out Tinder, as if this was a perfectly normal way to spend a Saturday evening. Unable to come up with an excuse, Elma had let herself be persuaded. Maybe it was all the wine they had got through, but she hadn't laughed so much in ages. She could remember little after crawling into bed later that night and had woken with a pounding heart, a heavy head and a churning stomach. She wasn't usually a big drinker and as she had sat on the side of her bed, trying to summon the strength to stand up, she'd remembered why.

It had been a beautiful morning and she had taken her hangover for a walk around town, stopping to buy a doughnut from the bakery, which she ate while strolling along the quay, reading the names of the fishing boats rocking gently on the calm sea. From there, her walk had taken her along Langisandur. It was low tide and the sun had come out, striking a glitter from the expanse of pale golden sand. If there was anything the town could be proud of, she had thought, it was this: the fine beach that on sunny days took on an almost Mediterranean atmosphere, with the townspeople basking on the sand and their children paddling in the sea. At the end of the bay, the cement factory stood idle, its white chimney towering above the town, while far away across the sea to the south, there was a glimpse of Reykjavík and, beyond it, the long, low line of the Reykjanes Peninsula, its mountains flattened out by the distance.

Elma was just passing her old school when her mother rang, telling her to be ready in ten minutes as they were going on a shopping expedition to Reykjavík. She had agreed reluctantly.

'Shall we grab a late lunch once we get there? It's no good shopping on an empty stomach,' Aðalheiður said cheerfully as they drove south. 'The shop has such a good restaurant these days – it's really excellent. We could even treat ourselves to a glass of wine.'

'That's the last thing I feel like right now,' Elma said ruefully. Her mother was in unusually high spirits that morning, humming along to the radio and shooting frequent glances at her daughter in the passenger seat beside her.

'So, you had a good night, did you?' Aðalheiður asked with a twinkle in her eye.

Elma shrugged. 'It was OK.'

'Well, I'm glad you had fun.'

Elma didn't answer. The thought of buying new furniture felt overwhelming, as if it marked the beginning of a new chapter in her life. It wasn't that long since she and Davíð used to go almost every weekend to buy something nice for their flat. Elma had moved to the capital at twenty, eager to stand on her own two feet, with no intention of ever returning home. Small-town life had never appealed to her. She had longed for the variety Reykjavík had to offer; the opportunity to meet new people and start again with a clean slate. But now here she was, back in Akranes and on her way to buy furniture for her new home. Or her old one, depending on how you looked at it.

'You're awfully quiet today,' her mother said, darting her another glance.

'I was just thinking.'

'I've heard that's a good thing. Thinking, I mean.'

'Maybe you should try it some time.' Elma grinned. 'I'm tired too. I didn't sleep well last night.'

'How's work going?' Aðalheiður asked.

She asked the same question every day but Elma never had much to say in reply. The majority of the cases that landed on the desks of West Iceland CID were road accidents, though she had been called out to a break-in on Wednesday. An elderly couple had noticed that the window of their garage had been forced open. Elma had gone to the scene with Sævar and met the couple, who were well into their eighties. Since nothing turned out to be missing from their garage, the case remained unsolved and would probably stay that way. All Elma could think was that the husband had forgotten that he had forced the window himself, judging by the way he seemed incapable of remembering anything for more than five minutes and kept repeating the same questions.

'Fine, nothing to report,' she replied.

'I hope Hörður's treating you well,' Aðalheiður said. 'It was kind of him to wangle this job for you. He and your father were good friends way back. Mind you, he was quite different in those days and could have drunk anybody under the table. But when he joined the police, he became a reformed character.'

'Hörður?' Elma exclaimed. She couldn't picture her boss drinking anyone under the table.

'Yes, indeed. He had quite a weakness for the bottle. But he's changed beyond recognition since he got the police job. Don't repeat this, but your father thinks he's become a bit of a pushover these days. He doesn't dare take on the more difficult cases because he's so terrified of putting people's backs up.' Aðalheiður grinned. 'Anyway, I'm glad to hear it's going well. You'll soon be one of the team. After all, it's not like you're an outsider.'

'It's OK, just a bit quiet. Very different from my job in Reykjavík. I just hope there'll be enough to do.' Elma gazed out over the island-dotted waters of Kollafjörður Bay. The grey sea was flecked with white where its surface was being whipped up by the wind.

'There's always something to do,' her mother said with a shrug. 'I expect you'll just have to get used to a different sort of case.'

Elma nodded. Perhaps something different was exactly what she needed.

'It stinks here.' Arna buried her nose in the big scarf she wore round her neck, trying to filter out the stench from the fish factory, which was blowing in their direction.

'You'll get used to it. Have a fag, then you won't notice it.' Reynir smiled and handed her a cigarette. Arna hesitated. She didn't really smoke. She'd tried once when her friend had stolen a cigarette from her grandmother, who smoked like a chimney. They had taken it down to the beach, where they'd had trouble lighting the thing, but in the end they had succeeded in inhaling a bit of smoke, before collapsing in coughing fits. After this experience, they had agreed that cigarettes were disgusting and promised each other they would never take up smoking.

But now, deciding to go for it, Arna accepted the cigarette. Reynir lit it for her and she puffed until it started burning properly. The car filled with smoke in no time. Arna did her best to suck it down into her lungs without coughing, then handed the cigarette back to Reynir.

He opened the window, letting in even more of the fishy smell, then turned up the volume and reclined in his seat. Arna watched entranced as he inhaled with his eyes closed, surrendering himself to the rhythm of the music. She didn't usually listen to this kind of stuff herself. She was a big Taylor Swift fan, though she'd never admit it to Reynir. He was so cool. She had butterflies in her stomach. It was so unlike her to be here with a boy she hardly knew. Her parents thought she was watching a film at Hafdís's house. They hadn't a clue that she was out with Reynir, who was three years older than her and had been a heartthrob all the way through school. All the girls had been crazy about him ever since the first year and, if anything, he'd seemed even cooler since he'd started at college. Anyway, he'd never so much as looked at any of them. That's why her heart had missed a beat when she'd seen the friend request from him on Facebook. Trembling with excitement, she had called Hafdís at once to tell her the news. Hafdís had been pleased for her, but at the same time Arna had heard a hint of jealousy in her voice. After all, it was Hafdís who had always had the biggest crush on Reynir.

'I'm going inside the lighthouse. You coming?' Reynir chucked the butt out of the window and got out of the car before Arna had time to answer. She hastily followed his example.

Although it couldn't have been more than 8.00 p.m., it was pitch dark outside. The last few days had been so wet and windy that Arna found it oddly quiet now that there was a temporary lull; the sighing of the waves seemed almost soporific. There was the odd spot of rain and a tang of salt in the air.

Reynir waited for her at the edge of the car park by the tall, new lighthouse, where the concrete ended and the rocks began.

The old lighthouse stood a little further off and to reach it they would have to clamber along the shore over the rocks. In contrast to the smooth, cylindrical lines of the new building, the old one consisted of a stumpy, square tower with peeling paint on the walls and a railing around the lantern room at the top.

'Hold on to me. It's slippery here,' Reynir ordered.

Arna obeyed, shyly taking his arm, and they picked their way together over the grey boulders with their clumps of yellow grass and unexpected, water-filled fissures, to the old lighthouse near the tip of the point.

Arna had often been out here with her father. He was a keen photographer and his enthusiasm had rubbed off on her. She enjoyed going out into nature and taking pictures herself and had developed quite an eye, but couldn't yet afford a camera of her own. Last summer, like so many Icelandic teenagers, she had taken part in a youth work programme, and her wages were now sitting untouched in her bank account, waiting until she had saved up enough for her dream camera. For now, though, she borrowed her father's. She and her dad would race outside when the Northern Lights were dancing across the night sky to try and capture their splendour on film, and the old lighthouse was an ideal spot for this. It made a brilliant subject, silhouetted against a background of sea and aurora. Her father had told her it was built in 1918, the first modern concrete lighthouse in Iceland. Recently it had attracted international interest and been voted one of the most picturesque lighthouses in the world. She was considering whether to share this information with Reynir when she lost her footing on the wet rocks.

'I warned you it was slippery!' Reynir grabbed her, flashing his gorgeous smile, and Arna, blushing, concentrated on looking at the ground in front of her until they reached the lighthouse.

The steel door was unlocked as always. The moment they stepped inside Reynir turned and pushed her up against the wall. Arna was taken aback but didn't say anything. His hands began roaming over her body. Breathing heavily in her ear, he squeezed her breast.

'Are you a virgin?' he whispered.

Arna nodded, unsure how to answer such a direct question, but Reynir seemed pleased and started kissing her on the mouth. One of his hands was propped against the wall above her head for support while the other stroked lower and lower, and his kiss became wetter and more urgent. Arna, unable to breathe, wasn't sure if she was enjoying this.

Of course she had been hoping to be kissed, but in her imagination, the kiss had been gentle and romantic. She had pictured it happening at the end of the evening, just before she got out of the car. Before that, they would talk about everything under the sun. Then he would give her a lift home (stopping at a discreet distance up the street, obviously) and she would open the car door, saying something like: 'Thanks for the drive.' He would seize her hand and say: 'Shall we do it again tomorrow?' And she would say: 'Maybe' – just to tease him. Then he might say: 'Do I get a kiss before you go?' She pictured herself hesitating, then giving in to persuasion, leaning towards him until their lips touched. Slowly, tentatively, perhaps with a little tongue at the end. Then she would break off the kiss and get out of the car without another word. She imagined him leaning back in his seat with his eyes shut, thinking about her, just like when he had been listening to the music earlier.

But this kiss was nothing like that. Instead, she was standing crushed uncomfortably against the icy wall while he groped her and stuck his tongue down her throat so she couldn't breathe. She was cold and wet, and it stank in the lighthouse.

'Did you hear that?' she asked, momentarily freeing her mouth. She thought she had heard a noise from inside the lighthouse but wasn't sure. It was probably her imagination, but she seized on this excuse to move away from Reynir.

'What?'

'I think there's somebody up there.' Arna peered up the staircase. She knew that kids often came here in the evenings, but they hadn't seen any other vehicles in the car park so had assumed they were alone.

'I didn't hear anything,' Reynir said, moving in to resume his wet kiss.

'I'm sure I heard something.' Arna quickly ducked her head to avoid another tongue-assault. Her jaws were already aching. Before he could start again, she wriggled away, pulled out her phone and switched on the torch. Then she started swiftly climbing the spiral staircase with its peeling green paint, the metal stairs clanging under her feet. She could see where the paint was flaking off the white walls. From the Coke cans and cigarette butts littering the place, it was obvious that this was a popular haunt for the town's teenagers.

Once she was at the top she opened the door out to the narrow gallery and leant against the hand rail. There was nobody there. Yet she could have sworn she had heard a noise. The moon cast a dim glow on the waves as they rose and fell against the rocks. Arna wrapped her jacket more tightly around herself and gazed down at the surface of the sea.

'I told you it was nothing, didn't I?' Reynir said, emerging at the top after climbing the staircase unhurriedly behind her.

'What on earth's that?' Arna peered into the darkness, pointing at the line of rocks that extended into the sea in the direction of the reef.

'What? I can't see anything.' Reynir followed her pointing finger.

'It looks like fur.' Arna shuddered. 'Do you think it could be an animal? We'd better go and see.'

'No way am I touching a dead cat.' Reynir pulled a face but Arna ignored him and ran down the stairs, then started picking her way carefully over the rocks to the place where she thought the animal was lying. Perhaps they could rescue the poor thing. She had seen a movement, hadn't she? Or had it simply been the waves moving the fur? She wasn't sure. The only source of light was the moon and the air was full of a cold spray that leaked down her neck inside her thin jacket.

Once Arna had clambered over the rocks to the shore, she stopped and peered down at the waterline just below. She could hear Reynir calling from some way off but his words were drowned out by the restless noise of the sea around her.

What she saw there was not the fur of an animal but a woman's hair, stirring gently with the waves.

The furniture shop was heaving. They trudged up and down the aisles, examining the showrooms. Aðalheiður paused by every display, picking things up and testing the sofas. A couple of hours later they had found a new sofa that hadn't been on Elma's list but which her mother had talked her into buying. Until then, Elma had been intending to make do with the old sofa bed from her parents' spare room. Other additions to the list included a bedside table and various other small items that her mother promised would make the little flat more homely. When it came to paying, Aðalheiður grabbed Elma's hand and held out her own card instead.

'Think of it as a small advance on your inheritance,' she said with a wink.

Elma felt herself welling up and quickly averted her eyes. She wasn't usually this sensitive but now she was having trouble swallowing the lump in her throat.

Her voice was still a little wobbly a few minutes later when she answered her phone. She was standing by the exit, loaded down with bags, waiting for her mother to reverse the car up to the door. It was past 8.00 p.m.

'Hi,' she said in an unnaturally reedy voice, having extracted her phone with difficulty from her pocket.

It was Hörður. 'Hello, Elma, something's come up. How quickly can you get yourself out to Breiðin?'

Akranes 1989

Elísabet had often seen the school before but it had never looked as imposing as it did now when she stood by the entrance, gazing up at the white building. On either side, the playgrounds and sports fields stretched out over what seemed like a vast area.

Gripping the red straps of her schoolbag, she entered the hall, where a crowd of children her own age were standing with their parents. She looked around her. Everyone seemed to be busy chatting. No one took any notice of her as she stood watching them. Then she met the eye of a little girl who was standing huddled beside her mother and she smiled at her, but the little girl turned her face away and took hold of her mother's hand. She was probably just shy. That was all right. Lots of the kids were shy like her. But some of the others were messing about and making such a racket that their parents had to turn round and shush them.

When the bell rang, the teacher came out and told the parents to say goodbye to their children. The pupils were to line up in front of him. Elísabet saw the shy girl resisting as her mother firmly pushed her into line. The girl wasn't crying but she bit her lip and stared down at her pink shoes that looked as if they had never come into contact with any dirt.

Elísabet's shoes were old and had once been white but were now more like grey or brown. They still had red stripes on them, though. Red was her favourite colour. She had got the shoes from the women who had come round the day before with some bags of clothes. The backpack had come from them too. Elísabet had been very impressed with it. Admittedly, it had a broken shoulder strap but that was all right because one of the helpful women had sewn it back on again. It was bright red with black seams and lots of pockets. But Elísabet had to admit that the other girl's bag was way cooler. It looked brand-new as well, like her shoes.

The teacher, an older man with small glasses, told the children to sit down in front of him in a carpeted corner of the classroom.

He started by reading out their names, and the children had to answer when it was their turn. While they were answering one after the other, Elísabet noticed two of the girls whispering and staring at her. Instantly guessing what they had seen, she tugged the sleeves of her jumper down over the bleeding sores on her fingers. She felt herself grow hot all over, and when the teacher called out her name, she couldn't make a sound. 'Elísabet?' the teacher said again, surveying the class. 'Yes,' she managed to croak, and the teacher nodded and put a tick by her name. Elísabet lowered her eyes to the grey carpet, oblivious to what the teacher was saying. When she finally raised her head, she saw the shy girl watching her. As their eyes met, the other girl smiled, showing milk-white teeth.

The girl's name was Sara, and when she smiled at her Elísabet knew that everything was going to be all right.

The building was almost empty, but Hendrik was still sitting in his office, contemplating his surroundings with a sense of satisfaction. He relished having all this space to himself, where he could close the door and even take a nap when he felt like it. Where he could work in peace, among the good furniture and expensive paintings, with an uninterrupted view of the ocean; nothing but blue as far as the eye could see. Though in fact it was black out there now – the Icelandic winter was so relentlessly dark. He leant back, his leather chair creaking, and stretched his legs.

Although he had finished the day's tasks, he couldn't face going home just yet. It was a pleasure to sit here alone and undisturbed for a while. And there was nothing waiting for him at home but Ása. Besides, this office would soon belong to Bjarni. Of course, it was high time. Hendrik had no intention of withdrawing entirely from the firm, despite having reached retirement age, but he would have to resign himself to handing over the management to his son.

Hendrik took a deep breath, then sat upright again. He heard a door opening. Footsteps. It must be the cleaners. Or cleaner, rather: the Asian woman who came in every day, after hours. He stood up, went into the kitchen and found the woman with her back to him, bending over and wringing out the mop over a bucket.

'Good evening,' he said blandly, reaching for a mug on the top shelf of the cupboard.

The woman returned his greeting in broken Icelandic, avoiding his eye. She was small and timid, like most of them. It was as if they instinctively recognised power when they saw it. Smiling to himself, he waited patiently for the coffee to percolate, his eyes resting absent-mindedly on the woman as she carried on mopping the floor. Then he took a seat at the table and unhurriedly drank his coffee.

He had certainly found his niche in life. In fact, you could say he'd had the good luck to be born in the right niche. Growing up in a small rural community had turned out to be a blessing in his case. He knew most of the locals. There were only around seven thousand inhabitants in the town even now, and the population had been much smaller in his youth. He could hardly go out to the shops without having to greet half the people he met. Sometimes he wondered what would have happened if he had given in to the urge to leave and try his luck somewhere else. But he generally came to the same conclusion: nowhere else would he have managed to make as good a life for himself as here. He'd been popular at school, a good student and a good sportsman too; a promising footballer, though it hadn't led to anything, but then he'd never been particularly interested in that sort of fame. While he enjoyed the comradeship associated with the sport, he wasn't prepared to make the kind of commitment necessary to achieve success as a footballer. Nor had it ever crossed his mind to abandon his local team. Akranes was his town. Here he was popular and well regarded. That was the advantage of living in a small community; those who had a good reputation reaped the benefits. Others were not so lucky.

He finished his coffee and got to his feet. His entire life up until now had been close to perfect. His schooldays had been carefree and fun. He had met Ása when he was in his mid-twenties and she three years his junior. As a young woman she had been a pretty, sensitive creature, who allowed him to wear the trousers. Women like that were hard to find these days.

Everything would have been perfect if it hadn't been for the little girl. She haunted him like a shadow. If he so much as thought about her, it was as if the wind had been knocked out of him – not that he let it show. To the outside world he was strong; powerful. But when dusk fell, the darkness took up residence in his soul and nothing seemed to matter anymore.

Elma drove past the quay where she had walked earlier that day. The boats that had been rocking gently against the dockside then were now being tossed violently back and forth by the churning waves. Turning right, she drove past the white buildings of the fish factory that had recently closed down, with the loss of so many jobs, then swung off the main road onto a gravel track. The streetlights illuminated part of the way but she had to drive the final stretch in darkness, guided only by her headlights. Breiðin, the westernmost point of Akranes, stretched out into the sea before her, the old lighthouse rising from the rocks near the very tip.

Elma drove to the end of the track and pulled up beside the police vehicles that were already parked there, along with an ambulance, a big four-by-four and a black BMW with its engine running. A yellow plastic tape marked 'Police' hung fluttering wildly across the car park by the new lighthouse, and in the distance she could glimpse members of the forensics team at work on the rocky point.

As she buttoned up her coat, she examined the smart new lighthouse that towered over the car park. The old one looked shabby and dilapidated by comparison. Almost sinister. Elma felt a familiar shiver run down her spine. She had been out there more times than she could remember, first as a little girl with her parents, and later as a teenager with friends who used to do their best to scare the hell out of each other with ghost stories. There was something so eerie about a building that had once performed such an important role but now stood derelict, abandoned to the elements.

As soon as he saw her arrive, Sævar came over to meet her, his black down jacket zipped up to the neck, his dark hair hidden under a thick woollen hat.

'Forensics are examining the scene,' he told her, sniffing, his nose running in the cold. He had to raise his voice to be heard over the gale.

'Have they been here long?' Elma asked. She'd driven back to Akranes as fast as she dared, her mother a bag of nerves in the passenger seat beside her, repeatedly grabbing her arm with terrified gasps.

'No, they're just setting up,' Sævar told her. 'They had to be called out from Reykjavík too.'

'Do we know anything yet?'

'It's a woman. Aged somewhere between thirty and forty. The officers who responded to the callout spotted the injuries as soon as they reached the scene, which is why we've got the whole shooting match out here now. That's all I know.' He nodded in the direction of the BMW. 'It was them that found the body. I told them to hang around so we could have a chat. I didn't want to do it alone. Hörður's only just got here as well. He was spending the weekend at his summer house in Skorradalur.'

Sævar walked over to the BMW and, bending down, tapped on the window. The door opened and a lanky boy stepped out. His dark hair flopped either side of his face, and he was wearing ripped skinny jeans and a baggy, pale-grey hoodie pulled up over his head. His hands were buried deep in the pockets of his black-leather jacket. The girl stayed in the car.

'Won't your friend come out and talk to us too?' asked Sævar.

'She's cold,' the boy answered. 'She hasn't stopped shivering since...'

Sævar bent down and tapped the window again. The girl, who was sitting staring into space, jumped as if she'd been in a trance. She looked up, hesitated, then opened the door and got out. Her blonde hair hung right down her back over her thin jacket. She was hugging herself and burying her chin in her big scarf in a futile attempt to keep out the cold.

'You lot had better hurry up before she's washed away,' the boy said, waving towards the old lighthouse.

Sævar opened the rear door of the police car, ignoring this unsolicited advice, and gestured to the two youngsters to get in.

'What were you doing out here?' Elma asked once they were all in the car, twisting round in the passenger seat to study them.

The boy lowered his eyes, then glanced up shiftily as he replied: 'Us? We were just sightseeing, you know. Checking out the lighthouse.'

'Were you alone?' Sævar asked.

The boy nodded, shooting a look at the girl, who just sniffed without saying anything.

'So, Reynir, you weren't aware of anyone else around – no cars, nothing like that?'

'No, nothing.' Reynir shook his head emphatically.

'I thought I heard something, though,' the girl said, suddenly finding her voice. 'That's why I climbed up the stairs and that's when I ... when I saw her.'

Sævar and Elma exchanged glances. 'What sort of noise did you hear?' Sævar asked.

'A thud. Like someone was upstairs in the lighthouse. But there was nobody there,' she replied, shuddering at the memory.

'Yeah, we only spotted her when we got to the top,' Reynir added. 'That is, Arna thought she saw something. I didn't.'

'What was it you saw?' Elma asked the girl. 'It must have been dark, and you can't see very far in these conditions. Could you really make out the body from up there?'

'Just the hair. I thought it was moving but that was probably the waves.' The girl's voice was so low that Elma had to lean closer to hear her over the noise of the wind that was walloping the car windows. 'I thought it was an animal. The fur of an animal.'

'And what did you do then?' Sævar asked.

'I just wanted to see if I could, you know, help it or something,' Arna said.

When she showed no signs of continuing, Reynir took over:

'We didn't have to get that close before we realised it wasn't an animal.'

'Did you touch anything on the rocks?' Sævar asked.

'No, we just got the hell out of there and called the cops. It's not the kind of thing you want to touch, you know.' The boy made a face.

The girl remained silent, her attention focused on scratching at the fabric of the seatback with her finger. Sævar looked at Elma, then took down their phone numbers and told them to go home and get warm.

Elma watched them drive away. 'Shouldn't we have kept them here a bit longer in case they were involved somehow? Do you think there's any chance they were?'

'Well, the woman's body was half submerged,' Sævar said, 'but their clothes were perfectly dry. So I didn't think there was any reason to keep them here.'

Elma nodded. 'OK.'

'The body's over there, right out on the point,' Sævar said. 'We'll have a bit of a scramble to get to it.'

Elma set off after him, almost losing her balance on the slippery rocks and inadvertently grabbing hold of him.

As they got closer, she spotted Hörður standing a little way off, his hands deep in his pockets, watching forensics at work. The technicians were dressed in blue overalls and one of them was holding up an LED light to illuminate the area. Under normal circumstances they would have mounted the light on a tripod, but Elma doubted this was possible on the rough terrain. Besides, the wind would have snatched it away in a matter of seconds.

The body lay at the foot of the rocks, caught between two boulders. Forensics had made no attempt to shield it with plastic sheeting or to erect a tent over it, presumably since it wasn't visible from the shore unless someone was right out on the point. Elma couldn't see the woman's face, just her hair, which was loose and swaying with the movement of the waves. She was wearing a black coat but her lower half was submerged in the water. Elma was so absorbed in examining the body that she jumped when a hand was laid on her shoulder.

'Sorry, I didn't mean to startle you,' Hörður said. 'It's not looking good. Seems like we're going to have quite a job on our hands.'

'Is there anything suspicious about it?' Elma asked, trying to ignore the cold. Her thin coat provided no protection and her hair was whipping around wildly in the wind. She looked enviously at Hörður, whose curly locks were neatly confined under his fur hat.

'It certainly looks like it, yes,' he replied. 'Unless she had a bloody bad fall.'

The technicians turned the body over, revealing a swollen face. The woman's eyes were closed and her skin was white, apart from patches of blue discolouration on her face and neck. Elma had seen enough corpses by now to know that the bruising was caused by lividity, or the pooling of blood after death, which meant she must have been dead for some time. One of the technicians brushed the dark hair aside, revealing conspicuous contusions on her throat.

'It doesn't look as if she fell,' Elma observed quietly.

'She can't have been in the water long, judging by the state of her body,' Hörður said. 'The sea fleas are pretty voracious around here.'

'Do you suppose there's any chance of finding evidence?' Elma peered around at the wet rocks, trying in vain to brush her hair from her eyes.

'It could prove tricky,' Hörður said. 'I'm afraid the location isn't going to make life any easier for forensics.'

After they'd been watching for a while, one of the technicians came over. 'We want to move the body as soon as possible,' he told them. 'There's no point trying to conduct any further examination out here. We need to shift her before the tide comes in.'

Some of the men brought over a body bag and helped to lift the woman carefully inside it. Once this was done, they set off, carrying her inert weight between them, picking their way precariously over the slimy rocks to the ambulance. Hörður, Elma and Sævar followed. The LED light had been moved, plunging the rocky point into darkness.

'Can you say anything else at this stage?' Hörður asked one of the technicians as they were making their way back towards the car park.

'I'm guessing she hadn't been there long,' the man replied. 'Her body must have been hidden by the sea and rocks for at least part of the time. Rigor mortis would have set in quickly as a result of the cold conditions and lasted longer than usual, so my guess is about twenty-four hours. The lividity on her face and neck indicates that she was lying face down the whole time. I don't think she's shifted or been washed up here from somewhere else. We'll have to let the pathologist establish the cause of death, but of course the marks on her neck suggest that she was dead before she ended up in the sea. One thing's for sure: it was no drowning.'

'Were there any other injuries?' Elma asked.

'Her left leg's broken. That's definite. And there's a cut on the right side of her head that could indicate a fall or a blow. It's impossible to say which at this stage or to state the actual cause of death.'

'Did she have any ID on her?' Hörður asked.

'No, we haven't found any clues to her identity,' the man said. 'Or anything of interest on the rocks around here either. The question now is how large an area we need to search. Seeing as there are a number of factors suggesting that she didn't die of natural causes, we'll need to cordon off a larger area.' They stopped in front of the new lighthouse, and the man turned to survey the scene. Judging by his expression, he wasn't looking forward to the task ahead. 'We'll be here for a while yet,' he added, wiping his forehead with his blue sleeve. 'I'm going to call out more officers from Reykjavík. There's nothing else for it.'

'Could she have been a tourist?' Elma asked, watching as the technician got into one of the nearby cars. 'Seeing as you don't recognise her.'

'Maybe…' Sævar furrowed his brow. 'But I find it unlikely, though I don't really know why. I can't put my finger on it but somehow she doesn't look like a foreign tourist.'

'It's impossible to tell at this stage whether she's a foreigner or an Icelander, but you can be sure she's not from Akranes,' Hörður said. 'I'd recognise her if she was.'

They were interrupted by a sudden squall that whipped up the waves, thickening the mist of spray with cold raindrops.

'Looks like we're in for a downpour,' Hörður said. 'I don't think we can do any more here for now. Let's get indoors before the wind really picks up.'

He considered the scene. The forensics team was still combing the area, and Elma noticed from the flickering lights in the windows that some of the technicians must be busy inside the old lighthouse. The ambulance drove off and they watched until it was out of sight. Elma had long ago given up trying to hold down her hair, which had been blown into a salty tangle, and her coat was now wet through.

'See you back at the station,' Hörður called as he climbed into the big four-by-four. Elma got into the car she had borrowed from her parents and switched on the ignition, rubbing her hands together and turning the heater on full blast. Water trickled down her face and the car shook, buffeted by gusts of wind. Although the seat soon started warming up, Elma knew it would be a long while before the chill left her body. It was getting on for 10.00 p.m. and the darkness beyond the lights was impenetrable as she peered towards the point, past the old lighthouse. The spot where the woman had been lying was now awash, the surf breaking over the rocks, no doubt snatching away anything loose that remained.

Akranes 1989

As the school week drew to a close and the weekend loomed ahead, Elísabet began to get pains in her stomach. Sometimes they were so bad that she had to go and hide in the toilets. She never told her teacher. She didn't like him much. He was strict and unwilling to talk about anything except what was in their textbooks, yet Elísabet enjoyed school in spite of this. She liked reading and had already graduated to thicker books than most of the other kids – books with fewer illustrations and more words. Books she could lose herself in, so she didn't even hear when the teacher spoke to her or the bell rang.

But what she enjoyed most was the time she spent playing with Sara. Ever since that first day at school they had been best friends. Elísabet had never had a friend before and she looked forward to school every day because it meant seeing Sara.

Sometimes, if she was lucky, she would be left to her own devices at the weekend. Her mother might or might not be home, but Elísabet would run over to Solla's house when she was hungry and be given supper and even biscuits if she asked nicely. She would play down on the shore or at the playground with Sara. At other times, she would spend the weekend hiding in her room while the people downstairs drank their disgusting booze. On those occasions she avoided going downstairs. She didn't like the look of her mother's friends or the things they got up to. One minute there would be loud quarrels, the next bursts of raucous laughter, and people would end up passing out on the sofa or floor. Anyway, her mother banned her from going downstairs when she had friends round, ordering her to stay in her room.

One woman, who was often there at weekends, used to come up to see her and would cuddle her and say all kinds of things that Elísabet didn't quite understand. She didn't mind, though. Sometimes, when she went downstairs, the guests would pull her over and ask her to sit beside them, and laugh at whatever she said, even though she wasn't trying to be funny. But when they started smashing things and raising their voices, she didn't dare venture out of her room. Then she would lurk upstairs until they quietened down and she could be sure they had fallen asleep.

One night she was woken by the squeaking of her door. When she looked up, she saw an unfamiliar face. It was a man who came and sat on her bed and started stroking the duvet. His breath was sour and his eyes seemed menacingly large as he stared at her in the gloom. When she woke up next morning, her nails were bitten down to the quick and there were streaks of blood on her pillow.

After that she stopped sleeping in her bed at weekends. Instead, she would drag her duvet and pillow into the cupboard under the sloping roof and sleep in there with the door shut. Although the cupboard smelled musty and she was sure there must be creepy-crawlies inside it, she felt safe; sure that no one could get to her in there.

Monday, 27 November 2017

Elma opened the fridge and took out a pot of *skyr*, then buttered herself a flat cake and topped it with a slice of smoked lamb. She took her snack over to the sofa, turned on the TV and started watching a programme without really taking it in.

It had been a long day. Despite having worked late the previous night due to the discovery of the body, she had gone into the station early this morning, as had Hörður and Sævar. It was rare for dead bodies to turn up in suspicious circumstances in Iceland, let alone in Akranes, and in most cases it was easy to work out what had happened. Murders were almost invariably committed at home, under the influence of alcohol or drugs, by someone close to the victim, who immediately confessed to the crime. But this was different, and the phones had been ringing incessantly with reporters on the hunt for information.

The problem was that the police had almost no information to give. They didn't even know the woman's name as she'd had no ID on her and didn't appear to have travelled to the scene by car, since no abandoned vehicle had been discovered in the vicinity. As a result, they were considering the possibility that the body had been dumped there; that someone had tried unsuccessfully to dispose of it in the sea. To lend support to this theory, forensics had discovered traces of blood at the scene. When they'd illuminated the area, the trail had been evident, leading from the gravel road by the new lighthouse and out across the rocks to the shore. The bloodstain-pattern analyst called in to examine the photographs was confident that the woman had been dragged from the car park to the shore where she had been found. For a more precise analysis of the cause of death, they would have to wait for the conclusions of the pathologist, who was due back in the country tomorrow. All in all, they had achieved little today other than to speculate about where the woman had come from and who she might be. No one had rung in to say she had disappeared. Currently, the only such notifications related to teenage girls who hadn't returned home since the weekend and had been reported missing by their anxious parents.

Elma put down the empty *skyr* pot and tucked the throw around herself. Everything had happened so fast: new job, new town, new life. It was at times like this that the longing to ring Davíð was almost unbearable. She yearned to hear his voice, to sense his presence. The evening he had gone was like a distant dream, and she kept having to remind herself that it had really happened – that he had really been capable of doing that to her. She was so preoccupied that she started when the phone rang.

'I hope you weren't asleep because I'll be outside your house in a couple of minutes.' It was Sævar. 'It looks like we've got a name.'

I

'A phone call came through this evening, reporting the disappearance of Elísabet Hölludóttir, a professional pilot, born in 1983. Apparently the reason we weren't notified earlier is that her husband thought she was in Canada for work. But when she didn't come home today, he began to get worried and rang the airline. It turns out she didn't actually take her flight; in fact she called in sick on Friday morning. No one knows where she's been since then.' Sævar slowed down as he reached the roundabout at the edge of town. They were on their way to visit the husband who lived right at the head of Hvalfjörður fjord, about half an hour's drive east of Akranes.

'It sounds like she had some kind of plan – to leave him, maybe?' Elma rubbed her hands together and checked that the heater was definitely on. She had dashed out of the house wearing only her cardigan, which wasn't nearly warm enough.

'Yes, that's what it sounds like, but you never know.' Sævar shrugged.

'Could someone else have made the call to say she was sick?'

'Good question,' Sævar said. 'We'll be able to contact her phone provider now we've got her name. They should have records of all the calls made to or from her phone. If it turns out she did make the call herself, that naturally raises certain suspicions.'

'An affair that ended badly?' Elma glanced sideways at him.

'Possibly,' Sævar replied. 'Apparently she lived in Akranes as a child, though I doubt that's relevant.'

'In that case I should recognise her, shouldn't I? Or, even if I don't, Hörður definitely should,' Elma said, remembering how the previous evening her boss had claimed to know all the inhabitants of Akranes by sight.

'Not necessarily. She moved away when she was about nine, according to her husband. He wasn't sure of the year. She's a pilot and he's a lawyer with an insurance firm in Reykjavík. Apart from that, he seemed to know next to nothing about her early life.' Sævar overtook a car that was crawling along the road at a snail's pace. 'But we'll soon know more.

'Are we sure it's the same woman?'

'Well, the age and description match. There aren't many women in their thirties who have recently gone missing in Iceland.'

They were both silent as they drove past the foot of Mount Akrafjall, then, leaving the Skagi Peninsula behind, turned off east to follow the great fjord inland. It was a long time since Elma had taken the road around Hvalfjörður. Until the tunnel under the mouth of the fjord was opened in 1998, cutting some forty-five kilometres off the ring road, getting from Akranes to Reykjavík used to be a far more time-consuming business. The townspeople had to choose between taking the ferry direct to the capital across the choppy waters of Faxaflói Bay or driving the long, slow loop around the fjord. Hvalfjörður was stunningly picturesque by daylight, but now, on a moonless winter night, the water was black and the mountains no more than dark shadows looming in the distance on either side. For much of the way, the drive was enlivened only by the occasional lights of a farm.

When they finally reached the head of the fjord, the house turned out to be a white, single-storey building with a flat roof and floor-to-ceiling windows. There wasn't much of a garden, just a lawn and some low posts that lit up the path to the front door. Unlike the other places they had passed along the way, there was no barn or cowshed to suggest that farming went on there. Instead, the house looked as if it had been designed for the upmarket suburb of Garðabær but then been plonked down in the depths of the Icelandic countryside. They parked in the drive behind a black Lexus SUV.

Elma rang the doorbell and, while they were waiting, read the small metal plaque on the letterbox, on which four names were engraved: *Eiríkur, Elísabet, Fjalar and Ernir.*

The man who came to the door was tall with short fair hair. The buttons of his white shirt were straining a little over his stomach and there were large patches of sweat under his arms. After introducing himself as Eiríkur and shaking them by the hand, he showed them into a sitting room that was as starkly modern as the house itself, with its blond-oak parquet flooring, black-and-white furnishings and several pieces Elma recognised from lifestyle magazines, which had probably cost more than all her furniture put together. Eiríkur invited them to take a seat on some armless black-leather chairs and sat down on the sofa facing them. From his expression, they could tell that he was in a bad way. He seemed to be waiting for them to start things off.

'Nice home you've got here,' Sævar said, looking around.

'Thanks,' Eiríkur replied distractedly. 'We got in an interior designer.' It didn't sound as if he was particularly happy with the result.

'Is that her?' Elma pointed to a photo on the sideboard behind them, of a heavily pregnant woman standing with her hands resting on her protruding stomach. She had long, dark, wavy hair, luminous dark eyes and a faint, almost invisible, smile on her lips.

'Yes, that's Beta. Do you think it was her they found?' Eiríkur's voice cracked and he coughed.

Sævar and Elma exchanged glances. It was hard to tell from the picture whether it was the same woman, as it had obviously been taken several years ago, but her long dark hair looked right.

'We'll soon find out, with your help,' Sævar said. 'It would be good if you could begin by telling us what happened. That's to say, when you last saw her and if anything unusual happened in the days leading up to her disappearance. I know you've already spoken on the phone to Hörður, the head of CID, but it would be great if you could repeat for us what you told him.'

'Of course. As I explained to him, Beta was due home this morning. She's usually back by seven or eight, but she hadn't arrived by the time I said goodbye to the boys. That wasn't particularly unusual, though, as flights are often delayed. I'm used to her working irregular hours. You can never rely on her being back by a certain time – that's just the way it is. I tried to call her during the day but her phone was switched off, which isn't out of the ordinary either as she generally sleeps until we get back. So I didn't think anything of it until I got home at around six and discovered that she wasn't here. That's when I started to get worried.' He leant forward on the sofa, his elbows on his knees, and Elma caught a powerful whiff of sweat under his aftershave. 'I rang the airline at suppertime, and that's when they told me she'd never turned up to work. That she'd called in sick.'

'Could she have been taken ill? Did you see her leave for work?'

'No, she didn't leave until after lunch, so we said goodbye to her on Friday morning. She hadn't been ill and looked fine when

I left to go to the office. You don't think there's any chance someone attacked her here, at our house?' Eiríkur asked, tensing up for a moment, then sagging again as he realised: 'No, that's impossible. Her car's gone and so's the suitcase she always takes with her on flights.'

'Did you notice anything unusual when you got home on Friday?'

'No,' said Eiríkur. 'The boys were home. Fjalar has a key. On the days when Beta's working, they're often alone here for half an hour or so until I get back. The only thing that was different was that Beta wasn't here when I came home today.'

'Did she usually drive to work in her own car?' Elma asked.

'Yes, it's a grey Ford Focus.'

'And I'm assuming she had a phone?'

'Yes, of course, she always has it on her. That's why I was so worried when I got home and she wasn't here. She always gives me a call before she goes to bed but I just assumed she must have forgotten because she was so tired. There's nothing strange about the fact she didn't call during her trip either. She's often exhausted and the time difference … But I should have guessed earlier that something was wrong – she always rings on her way home.'

Elma felt for Eiríkur as he sat there facing them, looking so bewildered. His eyes were unfocused, his face was pale and shiny, and there were red flecks on his cheeks. She wanted to give him an encouraging smile but was afraid it might seem inappropriate in the circumstances.

'I'm going to show you a picture,' Sævar said. 'This is the woman who was found by the lighthouse.' He drew a photo from an envelope and handed it to Eiríkur. 'Just take your time. Have a good look at it, then tell us if it could be Elísabet.'

The photo showed the woman lying with her eyes closed, her body covered with a white sheet, her dark hair forming a stark contrast to her pale face. She could have been asleep and, to

Elma's relief, neither the marks on her neck nor the wound on her head were visible.

Eiríkur took it and sat there examining it for a moment. Then he got up and put the picture down on the table, saying hoarsely: 'Yes, that's her. Please excuse me.' He disappeared into what Elma guessed must be the bathroom. Her eyes met Sævar's again. Breaking bad news like this was the hardest part of their job.

When Eiríkur came back he sat down on the sofa again and stared unseeingly in front of him, his jaw muscles clenched, his eyes red. 'I ... the whole thing's so unreal, I feel as if I'll wake up any minute,' he said in a hollow voice. 'Who ... what do you think happened?'

'We don't know yet but the nature of her injuries suggests we may be dealing with a suspicious death.'

'Suspicious?' Eiríkur gaped at them. 'Injuries? You mean ... you mean somebody deliberately killed her?'

'Like I said, we don't know yet,' Sævar replied in a level voice. 'But it's unlikely her injuries were self-inflicted. You can rest assured that we'll do all we can to find out what happened.'

Eiríkur frowned as if he was trying to process the information. When he raised his eyes again, his expression was angry.

'I thought...' He broke off and was silent for a while. When he started speaking again, his voice was shrill: 'Are you telling me she was murdered? It just doesn't make sense. Who would...?'

'Daddy...?' A small boy was standing in the hall in a pair of pyjamas decorated with yellow cartoon characters, blinking in the bright lights from the sitting room. 'I need to do a wee-wee.'

'Go ahead, son.'

No one said anything until the little boy had finished and scampered barefoot back to his room at the end of the hallway.

'We don't know,' Sævar said, when they were alone again. 'Were you aware of anything unusual in the days leading up to Elísabet's departure? Any phone calls? Did she seem different at all? Was she having problems at work? Anything you can remember?'

Eiríkur thought. 'No,' he said, shaking his head. 'I can't think of anything. Not a single thing.'

'Can you think of any reason why she should have failed to turn up to work and gone to Akranes instead?'

'No, that doesn't sound like Beta at all. She's so conscientious. She'd go to work even if she hadn't slept well, regardless of anything I said. There were times when I didn't think she was in any fit state to do her job but apparently it can't be helped in her line of business. Irregular or too little sleep is par for the course.'

'Did she know anyone in Akranes?'

'No. Nobody.' Eiríkur shook his head emphatically. 'But she lived there for several years when she was a girl.' He paused, then went on: 'She couldn't stand the place. Flatly refused to go there. We used to do our shopping in Reykjavík or Borgarnes, even though they're much less convenient. In fact, it was bizarre how much she hated the town. That's why ... that's why I just can't understand what she was doing there, of all places.'

'Do you have any idea why she hated the town so much? Do you think there was a specific reason?'

'To be honest, I don't know. She never explained, just said she had absolutely no desire to go there. She had bad memories of the place. I thought maybe it had something to do with being bullied at school, but I didn't ask. She made it clear she didn't want to discuss it.'

'Who did she mainly associate with? Apart from her colleagues at work.'

'Us,' Eiríkur said immediately. 'She doesn't have any contact with her family. Her mother died many years ago, before I came on the scene. There was an aunt, Guðrún, who she lived with after her mother died, but they're not on speaking terms anymore. And there's only one friend who visits regularly. Her name's Aldís. Apart from that, it's just me and the boys.'

'What about you? Where were you over the weekend?'

'Here at home with the boys. We didn't do much.'

'Can anyone confirm that?'

Eiríkur sighed and stared into space: 'Let's see ... on Friday I was at work and my colleagues should be able to confirm that. The boys had friends round in the afternoon and their mother picked them up at around seven. They live on a farm about ten minutes from here. On Saturday we stayed at home. No, actually, I gave the boys a lift to see their friends, and while they were there I did a food shop for the weekend. In the evening we had supper here, and Sunday was more or less the same, except that we went for a bit of a drive and got ourselves some ice-creams in Borgarnes.' He looked at them, adding wearily: 'Will that do, or do you want me to wake the kids to confirm my story?'

'No, there's absolutely no need for that,' Elma said quickly. 'But I'm afraid we will need to confirm your alibi. It's just a formality, though.' She gave him a brief smile.

'Right, well, I'm sure that's quite enough for you to be thinking about. We'll head off shortly and leave you in peace to deal with what's happened. But tomorrow it would be good if you could come and do a formal identification of...' Sævar hesitated. He had been about to say 'the body' but it sounded so cold. 'We offer trauma counselling for circumstances like this and I recommend you accept it. In the meantime, we've asked the local vicar to come round and see you, if you don't object. I'm afraid, given the nature of the case, we'll have to ask you further questions, so it would be helpful if you could keep your phone on you at all times. Also, do you have a recent photo of Elísabet you could give us?'

Eiríkur didn't immediately react, but after a few seconds he got up and found a photo of his wife for them. Elma wasn't sure he'd taken in everything Sævar had said but they both knew there was little point trying to ask him any more questions now.

Fortunately, they didn't have to wait long before the bell rang to announce the arrival of the vicar. Sævar went and opened the door for him. Elma hoped Eiríkur's family would be able to come and keep him company as well, despite the late hour. She got a lump in her throat when she thought about the two little boys sleeping, unsuspecting in their beds. Eiríkur was still sitting there, staring down at his hands, as she rose to her feet.

'Don't hesitate to get in touch if you think of anything,' Elma said before they took their leave, and she wrote down their phone numbers for him. She added, as she handed him the piece of paper: 'I'm really very sorry.' Eiríkur took the note in silence. They had started walking back to their car, leaving him with the vicar, when they heard his voice behind them.

'What am I to tell the boys?' he asked, looking from one of them to the other, his mouth hanging open in an expression of bewildered despair.

They had no answer to that.

Akranes 1990

Her daddy used to tell her stories. She knew most of them weren't true but that was what made them so fun. In her daddy's stories, anything could happen. The most unlikely things could come to life and her daddy was always getting into the funniest scrapes. He told her stories from when he was a little boy and used to get up to all kinds of mischief. He had been brought up on a farm, with sheep, cows, horses and hens. She used to listen enthralled, wishing that she could have grown up in the countryside like him, surrounded by all those animals. He promised to take her to the farm one day to visit them. Yet another promise he would never be able to keep.

One story kept running through her head. She didn't know if it was true or made up – perhaps nobody knew, as it had happened such a long time ago. He had told it to her as they were walking along the beach one mild, sunny day. The surface of the sea had been almost perfectly smooth and the Snæfellsjökull glacier had been clearly visible far away to the north-west.

'Do you know who lives in Snæfellsjökull?' her daddy had asked, smiling down at her. She had been writing in the sand with a long stick but paused to look at him, screwing up her eyes against the dazzling sunlight.

'Father Christmas?' she had guessed.

'No, not him,' her daddy had said. 'Bárður – Bárður Snæfellsás. They say he was so big that he must have been descended from both giants and trolls.'

'Was he dangerous?'

'Not at first, but then something happened to change him.'

'What happened?' she had asked and stopped writing in the sand. She knew he was going to tell her a story and she loved his stories.

He cleared his throat and sat down beside her on the sand.

'Well, you see Bárður had a daughter called Helga, who he loved

very much. And one day Helga was playing with her friends, Sölvi and Rauðfeldur.'

'Rauðfeldur,' she repeated, giggling.

'Yes, Rauðfeldur, because he had red skin. Don't you think it's a good name?'

She shook her head, laughing.

'Anyway, they were outside playing on the shore at Arnarstapi, near the boys' home. It was a foggy, windy day and the sea ice had come in close to land. They were having a competition, which turned into a fight, and it ended with Rauðfeldur pushing Helga out to sea on an iceberg. The wind was so strong that the iceberg floated away from shore, taking Helga with it.' He paused a moment before continuing: 'Do you know the name of the country that's our neighbour to the west? It's called Greenland. Well, the wind was so strong that it only took seven days for Helga to float all the way to Greenland on the iceberg.'

'Wow, seven days is a very long time,' she said.

'Yes, I suppose it is quite a long time,' her daddy agreed. 'But the story's not finished, because when Bárður heard what had happened to his daughter he went mad with rage. And that was bad, because he was from a family of trolls and giants, remember?'

She nodded.

'So, he went to Arnarstapi, picked up Rauðfeldur and Sölvi, one under each arm, and carried them up to the mountain. First, he threw Rauðfeldur into the big, deep fissure that's called Rauðfeldsgjá today – that means Redskin's Cleft. Then, he threw Sölvi off the high cliff which has been known as Sölvahamar, or Sölvi's Cliff, ever since. After that Bárður changed, and became silent and bad-tempered. He didn't feel he belonged in the world of men anymore so he went to live in the Snæfellsjökull glacier and that's how he got his name – Snæfellsás, the god of Snæfell. They say that he rescues people who get into trouble when they're climbing the glacier.'

'A bit like Superman?'

'Yes, a bit like Superman,' her father had said, laughing.

Sometimes, when she gazed at the glacier, rising from the sea like a pyramid on the horizon, she wished she could copy Helga – float on an iceberg to another country in only seven days. She knew now that seven days wasn't a very long time. And sometimes she told herself that if Bárður was the guardian spirit of the glacier, maybe her daddy was the guardian spirit of the sea. And, because of that, nothing bad would happen to her if she went to sea on an iceberg. She used to sit there for hours, remembering that day on the beach and daydreaming of a future in another country and of her daddy living under the sea. Soon she would be seven and then it would be a whole year since she had last seen him. She made up stories in her head about all the adventures she would have on her voyage. They were all nice stories, with happy endings.

Tuesday, 28 November 2017

By 9.00 a.m. Elma and Sævar were sitting at the table in the little meeting room, waiting for Hörður. He arrived a few minutes later, panting, his cycle helmet still on his head. He took it off and wiped the sweat from his forehead with a white handkerchief that he stuck back in his pocket. His hair was flattened down to his ears, below which it kinked out again in bushy curls. Drawing his glasses from his pocket, he stuck them on his nose.

'Beautiful morning,' he said, smiling at them as he took a folder out of his satchel and placed it on the table. He sat down, leafed quickly through the papers it contained, then got up again, asking them to hang on a minute. Sævar grinned at Elma, who raised her eyebrows. When Hörður came back, he was carrying a white cup that he put down carefully on the table to avoid spilling any tea.

'Right,' he said, having recovered his habitual composure, 'we've received confirmation that the body is that of Elísabet Hölludóttir, born 1983.' He wrote the victim's name on the shiny whiteboard with a red marker pen. 'Her husband Eiríkur formally identified her this morning. The verdict of the Identification Commission should be available in a couple of days.' Hörður turned, his face grave, and adjusted his glasses. 'The pathologist is due back in the country today and will start the post-mortem immediately, but the doctors who have already examined her are fairly sure that she was hit by a car.'

'Hit by a car?' Sævar asked, looking up from the picture he had been doodling on his pad. Elma, who had leant over to see what it was, also turned to Hörður with renewed interest.

'Yes, that's what the injuries to her legs and head suggest. The doctors don't believe they can have been caused by anything else. That doesn't necessarily mean she was run over at the scene. It's more likely that the culprit knocked her down, then moved her to the place where she was found in an attempt to dispose of her body.'

'Did she die as a result of the impact?'

'We don't know yet. As I said, I'm expecting the pathologist to get in touch as soon as he's completed the post-mortem. But we all saw the marks on her neck, which show that someone tried to strangle her, either before or after the collision. So the odds are that we're dealing with direct intention to kill.'

'So it can't have been an accident,' Sævar said.

'I sincerely doubt it.'

'She could have been chased there,' Elma suggested.

'Chased?' Sævar turned to her.

'Yes, given that she was found such a long way from the road. Maybe she was knocked down and tried to run away.'

'Towards the sea?' Sævar queried. 'It's not much of an escape route.'

'I doubt anyone would be thinking straight in circumstances like that,' Elma said, feeling that she was having to point out the obvious.

'Is it possible that someone could have knocked her down by accident, then panicked and tried to get rid of the body?' Sævar sat back in his chair. 'Then, when they realised she was still alive, they freaked out and finished her off?'

Elma shuddered. It sounded like a scene from a bad film.

'As we heard yesterday, forensics found blood on the gravel near the car park and on the rocks as well, so we know she received the injuries before she was moved. And don't forget that, according to the bloodstain-pattern analyst, she was dragged over the rocks.' Hörður sat down again. He fished the teabag out of his cup and put it on the saucer before continuing. 'You went round to see the husband yesterday. Anything of interest there?'

'He seemed shocked and told us he'd been at home all weekend with their sons,' Elma said, looking away from the greenish liquid that was leaking from the teabag to form a puddle on the saucer. 'But there's no one really to confirm his alibi, except maybe the parents of the kids who played with his boys at the weekend. Though of course Eiríkur could have gone out without the boys noticing. When they were asleep, for example.'

'Yes, that's possible. We'd better take a good look at the husband.' Hörður frowned. 'We'll need to ring his employer and check whether he turned up to work on Friday – and, if he did, when. The guys in forensics reckon Elísabet couldn't have been in the sea for more than twenty-four hours but we'll have to wait for the pathologist to confirm that.' Hörður broke off to leaf through the papers that lay in a neat pile in front of him. 'As you know, she called in sick on Friday, but Eiríkur claims he had no idea about that. Could she have been intending to stay somewhere else over the weekend while her family thought she was abroad on a flight?'

Elma leant back in her chair. 'Could she have been having an affair?'

'With someone here in Akranes, you mean?' Sævar asked.

'Not necessarily,' Elma said, 'though if her body was moved to the lighthouse, we can assume that it must have been done by someone who was familiar with the town. Or at least knew where to find somewhere quiet and off the beaten track.'

'Would you really describe Breiðin as quiet and off the beaten track?' Hörður sounded sceptical.

'Well, late in the evening or at night, yes, I would,' Elma said. 'According to Eiríkur, Elísabet couldn't stand Akranes and went out of her way to avoid coming here. He was also quite sure she didn't know anyone in the town, despite having lived here as a child. Which makes it extremely odd that her body should have turned up where it did. If she came here of her own accord, the question is what was she doing or who was she meeting?'

'Yes, she used to live here, apparently.' Hörður nodded thoughtfully.

'We know she had a car, a grey Ford Focus,' Sævar said. 'Since it hasn't turned up yet, the chances are she was driving it, so it's vital to track it down as soon as possible. We could start by checking if a car of that make is parked anywhere in or near the town.'

'Yes, that has to be our absolute priority. I'll get the officers on duty to start looking for it,' Hörður said. 'It could have been parked just outside the town, at one of the recreation areas like Elínarhöfði or Garðalundur. We'll need to check the local garages as well – see if anyone's brought in a vehicle with damage to the bodywork that matches the victim's injuries. It's unlikely the perpetrator would have taken it straight to a garage, but you never know. Sævar, you come out to Breiðin with me. I'd like to take a better look at the area now we know she was knocked down.'

'Did Forensics find any broken glass or other material from a car to indicate that the collision happened near the lighthouse?' Sævar asked.

'No, they didn't find anything like that at the scene. But conditions were so bad that I'd like to have the area carefully combed again by daylight, now that the weather's better, with the specific aim of searching for possible debris from a vehicle. The question is whether the boys from Reykjavík will agree.' Hörður turned to Elma. 'I'd like you to gather together all the information you can find about Elísabet and her past. Try to talk to the people she associated with. Someone must be sitting on information.'

'What about her phone?' Elma asked.

'I've sent a request to her provider for her phone records. Then we'll be able to see whether the call to the airline when she rang in sick definitely came from her phone.' Hörður replaced the papers in the folder and rose to his feet. 'See you back here this afternoon.'

Breiðargata had once been Akranes's main street, but the focus of the town had shifted away, relegating it to the outskirts. They drove past the abandoned fish-processing sheds and old wooden racks that had once been used for drying fish but now mostly served as climbing frames for the local children. Sævar parked by the information board next to the new lighthouse. A wooden walkway had recently been built out to the rocks and the paths had been surfaced with concrete. He wasn't sure what he thought of these developments. The place had lost some of its charm now that the lighthouse had become a tourist attraction.

They got out of the car and slammed the doors, breathing in the fresh sea air. The weather had improved since Sunday night, and by daylight it was much easier to see the rocks around the old lighthouse, which tapered into a long narrow reef at the very tip of the Skagi Peninsula. In rough conditions the surf could come right up to break against the old lighthouse. Here, at the westernmost point of Akranes, land, sea and sky seemed to converge. Looking back in the other direction, they could view the town at a slight remove. The foreground was dominated by disused oil tanks and the tall chimney of the derelict cement factory, which had once been white but was now showing its age. There was talk of demolishing it. Beyond it, the yellow curve of Langisandur stretched away towards the steep slopes of Mount Akrafjall, which looked like a crater that had collapsed in the middle. To the south, dimly visible across Faxaflói Bay, they could make out the buildings of the capital, while far off on the horizon the long line of the Reykjanes Peninsula reached away to the south-west.

Nearer at hand, a flock of seagulls was swooping and screeching over the rocks, as if they'd found something edible. In summer the birdlife was more varied, with sandpipers, turnstones, oyster catchers and eider ducks. Sævar liked to go for walks along the shore to watch them, though he wouldn't describe himself as a serious birdwatcher. Still, he found it soothing and his dog, Birta, enjoyed their outings too. The apartment block where he lived made him claustrophobic. The walls were thin, and there were families with children both above and below. One of the couples had such noisy rows that the sound of their shouting often kept him awake at night. When this happened, he would flee the building and walk down to the harbour, sometimes coming all the way out here to Breiðin. Telma was so used to it that she didn't make a fuss when he slipped out of bed in the middle of the night.

'Look at this,' Hörður called. 'These marks could have been made by someone braking hard.' He had been walking around the car park, taking photos. 'Mind you, it's hard to tell on this gravel.'

Sævar examined the marks Hörður had pointed out. He was right. The tyre tracks were just off the road, as if someone had swerved to the side and braked suddenly. The area had been cordoned off and kept under guard ever since forensics had undertaken the crime-scene investigation on Sunday evening, so it was unlikely that the marks could have been made since then. On the other hand, it was impossible to tell how old they were.

Hörður snapped a few more pictures. 'Perhaps there are fragments from the car around here. Forensics have scoured the area by the rocks where the body was found, but I'm not sure they've given the car park enough attention.'

'They extended the search area quite a long way,' Sævar pointed out. He straightened up from where he had been squatting over the tracks and scanned their surroundings. The area cordoned off by forensics stretched some way along the gravel road and down to the rocky shoreline around the two lighthouses. The technicians must have been working half the night to cover all that ground.

The two men wandered around without speaking for a while, peering at the ground without finding anything. Hörður put an empty beer can in a plastic bag. The wintry sun could do little to mitigate the chilly breeze blowing from the north. A car approached along the gravel road. Sævar held up a hand to shield his eyes and made out a grey jeep with a man and woman in the front and two children in the back.

'We won't find anything here now,' Hörður said. 'Let's get going.'

Sævar nodded and got into the car. He looked back towards the two lighthouses. The family had climbed out of their jeep and were staring curiously at the roped-off area. The man was carrying a large camera and the woman was holding the hands of the boys, who couldn't have been more than six or seven. By daylight the place had a tranquil, innocent air, but Sævar knew that once darkness fell it took on a creepier atmosphere. Not that he had ever been easily spooked. He was the down-to-earth type, who trusted in the evidence of his own eyes and nothing else. But even so he couldn't help seeing the woman's face every time he looked out towards the rocks.

Elma had been sitting at her computer, gathering all the information she could find about Elísabet Hölludóttir. From what she had discovered so far, Elísabet had been born in Akranes and lived there as a child, attending Brekkubær School. In 1992 she had moved to Reykjavík with her mother, Halla Snæbjörnsdóttir, who had died of cancer that same year, leaving her daughter behind to be cared for by her sister, Guðrún Snæbjörnsdóttir. Elma looked up the aunt and saw that she lived in the Reykjavík suburb of Breiðholt. She noted down her phone number.

Next, Elma rang Brekkubær School and asked them to email her a list of the children who were in Elísabet's form during the years she was a pupil there. Wondering what could have brought Elísabet back to Akranes, she'd thought perhaps it had had something to do with one of her former schoolmates. The helpful secretary sent over a scan of the file within minutes of her hanging up. The form had been called 1.IG, after the initials of the teacher, Ingibjörn Grétarsson, who had taught at the school throughout Elísabet's time there. Elma tried typing 1.IG into the Akranes Museum of Photography website and several images popped up, including a group shot of the entire class. Other photos showed the children engaged in a variety of activities, but frustratingly few of the captions included any names. Excited six-year-olds on their way to school, wearing over-sized anoraks and big backpacks; kids building a tower out of wooden bricks; two girls sitting at a square table, colouring in pictures. The caption of this last photo said: 'Pupils of Brekkubær School. Photo taken 1989'. One of the girls was looking straight into the lens with a happy smile; the other had strikingly dark hair and solemn brown eyes.

Elma peered at the picture, then held up a photo of the adult Elísabet to the computer screen. It wasn't the one provided by the pathologist but another, given to her by Elísabet's husband Eiríkur; a headshot, presumably a passport photo. There could be no doubt that the little girl on screen and the woman in the photo were the same person. Two pairs of arrestingly dark-brown eyes stared back at Elma.

She found two more images of Elísabet on the website. One was a group photo in which the children had been lined up in the classroom with their teacher beside them. The other showed a group of children in aprons, kneading dough. Four of them were splaying out flour-covered fingers. It was the only picture in which Elísabet was smiling.

Elma's thoughts went to the little boy who had emerged from his bedroom to go to the toilet when they were talking to Eiríkur. He had been the image of his mother, with his dark hair and eyebrows, differing from her only in that his expression had been far less grave. Elísabet didn't appear to have been a very cheerful child, but then you couldn't really judge from pictures. Perhaps the photographer had been a stranger, someone she found intimidating. Many children were shy about having their picture taken. Elma remembered that she hadn't been particularly keen on it herself. The photos in her parents' thick albums almost invariably showed a little girl with a sulky expression, while her sister beside her was beaming like a child model. The only shots in which Elma was smiling were those when she had been taken unawares, before she'd had time to put on a scowl.

Elma wondered if she should try to track down Elísabet's old teacher but decided that it could wait. Talking to her husband and anyone else she had interacted with recently was far more urgent than interviewing people from her past. Although Eiríkur's shock and grief had appeared genuine, murders were often committed by partners or other close family members, and there weren't many to choose from in Elísabet's case. None of her close relatives were alive apart from her aunt Guðrún, with whom she'd had little contact, if Eiríkur was to be believed. For the moment, the police weren't aware of any other family members.

Elma picked up the phone and dialled Guðrún's number. A hoarse voice answered almost immediately. 'Hello, is that Guðrún Snæbjörnsdóttir?' Elma asked.

'Yes, that's me?' It sounded like a question.

'My name's Elma and I'm calling from Akranes Police Station. I wondered if I could possibly meet you tomorrow for a chat?'

There was a brief silence at the other end. 'If it's about Elísabet, I've got very little to say. I haven't seen her for years, not since she walked out of here without so much as saying goodbye, let alone thank you.'

'Please accept my condolences for the loss of your niece,' Elma said, in spite of the cold indifference in Guðrún's voice. She hesitated, then said: 'If you don't mind my asking, how did you know I was ringing about Elísabet? Since you say you hadn't seen much of each other in recent years…'

'We certainly hadn't,' Guðrún said loudly. 'But her husband still had the manners to ring and let me know. At least my niece had the sense to marry well – that Eiríkur seems a very decent man. But I can't see why you want to meet me: I've nothing to tell.'

Elma paused. 'Nevertheless, it would be good if I could come round. I wouldn't take up much of your time. Would eleven o'clock tomorrow morning work for you?'

Again there was a silence, before Guðrún said grudgingly: 'Well, I don't know what good it'll do you, but you can come round. I'm busy until two, though, so you'll have to come after that.' She broke into a rattling cough.

Elma thanked her and rang off. It looked as if Eiríkur had been right about the strained relationship between aunt and niece. She put her finger against the second number he had supplied, which belonged to Aldís Helgadóttir, the only friend Elísabet had kept in touch with.

The phone rang and rang, and Elma was about to give up and end the call when a breathless voice answered.

'Yes,' the woman said brusquely, as if the call had interrupted something important. But her tone changed as soon as Elma explained what it was about. 'Of course I can meet you. God, if there's anything I can do...' She trailed off and Elma thought she heard a sob.

'Tomorrow, just after noon?' she asked, when Aldís didn't say anything.

'I've got a meeting at one, so midday would be good.'

Elma said goodbye after taking down the address of the hotel where Aldís worked as a manager. Then she sat there, phone in hand, thinking for a minute, before dialling the number of the National Register. An electronic voice informed her she would be put through to a customer-service representative as soon as one was available. She waited for several minutes before her call was finally answered, then she was put through to a woman who introduced herself as Auður.

'Let's see,' said Auður, and Elma heard the rattle of a keyboard. 'Yes, here it is. The address the mother and daughter were registered at in Akranes was number eight, Krókatún.'

'Thank you,' Elma said. 'I also wondered if you could possibly check if she ever had a patronymic and, if so, when she changed her name.' It had struck her as unusual that, where most Icelanders took their second names from their father, Elísabet had gone by her matronymic, 'Halla's daughter'.

'Let's see.' Again, Elma heard the sound of typing. 'Elísabet Hölludóttir never changed her second name. She's registered under her mother's name on her birth certificate. Her father was called Arnar Helgi Árnason. He died in 1989.'

'Is there any record of how he died?'

'All it says here is "accidental death", but it shouldn't be hard to find out the details by other means.'

Elma thanked her and rang off. Turning to the computer again, she opened the website of the newspaper archives and typed in Elísabet's father's name. The report came up almost instantly. It was dated 1989. Two men were reported missing after their fishing boat had sunk in a storm not far from the entrance to Akranes harbour on the evening of 16 February. A wave was thought to have broken over the boat, causing the five-tonne vessel to capsize with both crew members on board. Apparently, an area of low pressure had caused a sudden, unexpected deterioration in the weather, and conditions had been severe on the shallow coastal fishing grounds and in Faxaflói Bay. The report stated that Arnar was survived by his common-law wife and daughter.

Elma wrote the details in her notepad, then leant back in her chair. Elísabet had only been six years old when her father died, and it looked as if her parents had been cohabiting. So why had she been named after her mother instead of her father in the usual Icelandic manner?

Akranes 1990

The frost bit into her cheeks as she waded through the snow, trying to keep up with her mother. When she looked down she was momentarily dazzled; the snow was so incredibly white and sparkled in the sun like glitter. But it was bitterly cold too and it collected inside her boots, where it melted, soaking her tights. Raising her face to the sky, she put out her tongue, trying to catch the big flakes that were floating down lazily in the still weather.

'What are you doing? Hurry up!' her mother snapped.

Elísabet ran after her. Her mother was in a bad mood; her eyes were small and red.

A few snowflakes found their way into the neck of Elísabet's anorak and she felt them trickling down her spine.

'Mummy, I'm cold,' she complained, then immediately regretted it. Her mother had little patience for whining and, turning, she seized her arm and started pulling her along. Elísabet tripped and fell in the snow but, instead of stopping, her mother kept going, almost yanking her arm out of its socket as she dragged her along the ground. Elísabet could feel the tears squeezing out of the corners of her eyes but fought to hold them back. She didn't dare cry. Her mother had been in a foul mood recently. Often, Elísabet hadn't a clue what she'd done wrong: the blows arrived completely without warning.

Her nose was running and she tried to wipe it on the sleeve of her anorak with her free arm. She hoped nobody would see them. She could just imagine what the other kids at school would say if they saw her now, soaked to the skin, with snot leaking out of her nose. It was all her daddy's fault, she thought. If he hadn't gone out on the boat, her mother wouldn't be so angry and everything would be better.

They stopped outside a red-and-white block of flats and went to the middle entrance, where her mother rang one of the bells. There was no answer. Her mother didn't wait long before pressing the *button again, holding it down for a long time. Drips were falling from Elísabet's hair down her red anorak.*

'Yes,' a man's voice answered gruffly.

'It's me,' her mother said in a low voice.

Apparently the man knew her mother, because there was a loud buzzing. Her mother opened the door, then paused in the gap to look back. Bending down to Elísabet, she fixed her eyes on hers.

'Stay here,' she said firmly. Elísabet nodded and sniffed. Then the door slammed shut and her mother disappeared. She sat down to wait.

While she was sitting there, she saw Magnea coming out of the neighbouring stairwell with her mother. Magnea was in her class at school but they weren't friends. Elísabet sniffed hard, clenching her toes to get the blood flowing. Mother and daughter went straight over to a large, new-looking SUV and climbed in – no wading through snowdrifts for Magnea. She probably never got freezing toes. Elísabet watched enviously as the other girl put on her seatbelt, then sat there, cuddling a blonde doll on her lap.

Elísabet promised herself then and there that when she was grown up she would have a big car like that so her children would never have to suffer from frozen toes.

The day had passed with aching slowness. Magnea sat watching the clock on the wall, waiting for the hands to creep round. The children, sensing her indifference, were talking louder than usual and paying less attention to their work, but she couldn't be bothered to raise her voice to restore discipline. Instead, she sat at her desk, staring absently out of the window at the playing field, the sports hall with its mismatched roof panels, and the sea beyond. Visibility was clear enough today to make out Reykjavík on the other side of the bay. From time to time she dropped her eyes to the papers in front of her, read the simple answers and marked them right or wrong.

She laid a hand on her belly. It was still flat. No one would have guessed that there was a life growing inside it, however tiny. As tiny as a bean. She smiled to herself. They had been trying for so long, and now, all of a sudden, as if by magic, it had happened. It couldn't be a coincidence. She must have done the right thing. Somehow she must have done something right.

'Magnea, I've finished.' Agla was standing in front of her wearing a smarmy smile and holding out her white exercise book. She was the pupil most likely to sit there quietly obeying instructions and doing her tasks without complaint. Magnea took the exercise book with a perfunctory smile.

'What should I do now?' the girl asked after a moment, puzzled at receiving no further instructions.

Magnea sighed under her breath. 'Just sit down and read until the others have finished.'

Agla nodded obediently and returned to her seat, where she pulled out a book that looked far too thick for a nine-year-old and began to read. Magnea shook her head. Her own daughter was unlikely to turn out like that if she took after her parents. Of course, she didn't actually know the baby's sex yet but she was sure it would be a girl. A girl who was bound to be more like Gréta and Anna, who sat side by side, whispering together whenever they thought their teacher wasn't looking.

Magnea glanced round the class. Groups like this soon established an internal pecking order. She could point to the handful of children the others looked up to, the natural leaders, who dictated what the others should do and what was or wasn't cool. Most of the rest fell into the category of follower – the children who usually looked up to the leaders with admiration. Then there were the outsiders, the ones nobody wanted to be seen with, who were often the butt of whispers and bullying. Like Þórður, who was staring out of the window, in trousers that were too short, exposing his bony shins. Or Agla, who sat there immersed in her book when she wasn't glancing up to try and catch Magnea's eye.

Yes, it was a cruel world, even for nine-year-olds. Magnea was perfectly aware of the position she herself had occupied in the pecking order at school. She had been at the top. How she had revelled in her status and loved being in control. She missed that sense of power now. Life had become increasingly complicated over the years. She had watched impotently as her old power gradually slipped through her fingers and people became increasingly indifferent to who she had once been and what she had been capable of doing.

She stole a peek at the clock again. The day was almost over and she had a meeting after work; a meeting she had long been looking forward to.

A thermos of coffee and three mugs had been placed in the middle of the table, together with a basket containing *piparkökur* neatly arranged on a red napkin, which reminded Elma that Christmas was just around the corner. If this had been America they'd have had doughnuts, but here they had to make do with gingerbread biscuits, she thought, letting one dissolve in her mouth with the hot coffee. She was starving as she hadn't had time to go out and get lunch, and for once there had been no pastries in the kitchen. Hörður still wasn't back, though it was past five. Elma was gradually learning that, although her new boss possessed a number of virtues, punctuality wasn't one of them.

'Sorry! Apologies for keeping you waiting,' Hörður said when he finally arrived. 'I've just had the press on the phone.' Elma saw that Sævar was having trouble hiding a grin, but Hörður carried on oblivious: 'Eiríkur's employer has confirmed that he got into work at nine a.m. and left at half past four. In other words, there's nothing to suggest that he lied about that.'

'But that only covers Friday,' Sævar chipped in. 'If he found out that Elísabet had been seeing someone else, either later that day or at the weekend...'

'Exactly,' Hörður said, before continuing with what he had been planning to say. Elma noticed that he had made a neat list of bullet points in preparation for the meeting. 'None of the local garages say they've had any cars brought in with suspicious damage, either to the front or the back. But as Sævar and I spotted some deep brake marks on the gravel road in front of the lighthouse, I rang forensics in Reykjavík and they're going to go over the area again tomorrow. So it'll remain blocked off for now, and the officers on duty will just have to make sure that no one enters the area.'

'Does that mean we can work on the basis that Elísabet was knocked down by the lighthouse?' Elma asked.

'No, not at this stage,' Hörður said. 'We'll discuss it again after forensics have done a more thorough sweep of the area and, if we're lucky, found some evidence to confirm what happened there.'

Elma nodded and flicked a glance at Sævar. When he smiled at her, she felt inexplicably embarrassed and averted her gaze, though not before noticing that his brown eyes were like Davíð's.

'I've printed out Elísabet's phone records for us to go over.' Hörður picked up a few pages stapled together at the corner and laid them on the table in front of them. 'Here we can see all the calls made to or from her mobile phone over the last few weeks.'

Elma bent forwards over the table to try and read the telephone numbers and dates on the top page. It didn't look as if there were that many numbers. And Elísabet hadn't used her phone much during her last few days of life. Skimming the rest of the printout, Elma noticed that, in fact, her phone had been used very little during the entire period. The same two mobile numbers cropped up again and again. Elma guessed that one belonged to Eiríkur; the other was presumably the airline.

Sævar came round to sit beside her, and she could feel the warmth radiating from his body as he leant over her to pick up the printout. 'We need a computer,' he said after a moment and left the room, returning almost immediately with a laptop.

'Check these two numbers first,' Elma said, pointing to the top page. Sævar tapped them into the directory. The first produced no results but when he entered the second, Eiríkur's name popped up. Elma marked it on the list.

'Could the other number be the airline?' Elma asked. 'If it's a work extension that's only for staff use, it's unlikely to be listed.'

'Let's give it a quick check.' Hörður took out his mobile and punched in the number. 'Sorry, wrong number,' he said when someone answered, and hung up. 'Yes, that was the airline.'

'Right,' Elma said, marking that number as well. 'So the records show that she rang the airline at nine on Friday morning. That's shortly after Eiríkur left for work and the kids went to school.'

'She doesn't make any further calls after that,' Sævar said. He was still so close to Elma that she could smell the faint tang of his aftershave. 'It looks as if the last time she used her phone was on Friday.'

Elma sighed. It would have been too easy if the records had shown the perpetrator's number. But if Elísabet had got in touch with someone, she clearly hadn't used this phone. Turning the pages, Elma checked the phone calls further back in time but couldn't see anything of interest. There was also a list of text messages sent and received.

'There are a few old messages here,' she said. 'Most of them your standard sort of stuff: a reminder about a dental appointment, messages from Elísabet's friend Aldís and from Eiríkur. Nothing out of the ordinary.'

'What are the messages between her and Eiríkur like?' Hörður asked.

'Just the usual,' Elma said, reading them. 'Can you collect the boys; when will you be home; I'll pick up supper on the way. Nothing very personal. Nothing affectionate, no kisses.'

'Text messages tell you very little about the state of someone's relationship,' Sævar interjected. He couldn't remember the last time he had sent Telma anything but brief, impersonal texts. 'Especially when couples have been together for years,' he added, thinking that in fact they probably did tell you quite a lot about a relationship. After all, he couldn't claim that things were particularly good between him and Telma.

'Hang on, here's something,' Elma said. 'A message from Eiríkur. Listen to this: "I love you far more than you realise. But I don't believe you love me at all."'

'Well, well, well.' Sævar gave a low whistle. Now he read aloud: '"If you leave, you're on your own. The boys are staying with me."'

They exchanged meaningful glances.

'So she was planning to leave him,' Elma said. 'Though if you look at the date, you'll see that those messages are almost six months old.'

'Maybe she only went through with it now,' Hörður said. 'Maybe something happened to help her make up her mind. The question is, did Eiríkur find out?'

'But there's nothing to suggest that Eiríkur saw Elísabet on Friday,' Sævar pointed out. 'We've already examined that possibility, and there's no evidence that he followed Elísabet to

Akranes. On the contrary, he has a pretty solid alibi for that day.'

Hörður sighed and appeared to be thinking hard. 'We can't be sure about Friday evening or Saturday. We need to take a better look at his movements; get a water-tight alibi.'

Next, he turned to Elma and asked her to report back on what her research had uncovered.

Elma cleared her throat and glanced down at her notes. 'Right. Most of what Eiríkur told us turned out to be correct. Elísabet attended Brekkubær School during her time in Akranes, and she and her mother were registered as living at eight, Krókatún. Apart from that, Elísabet had virtually no social-media presence. She wasn't on Facebook, Twitter or any of the usual platforms, which fits with what we know of her character: that's to say, she was a very reserved person. I got in touch with her maternal aunt, Guðrún, who's agreed to meet me tomorrow. I also rang her friend, Aldís Helgadóttir. Although Elísabet doesn't seem to have had many friends, she'd kept in touch with Aldís since they were at sixth-form college. I was thinking of going into Reykjavík tomorrow to meet both the friend and the aunt. Perhaps they might have some idea about what Elísabet was up to on Friday.' Elma looked up from her notebook, adding: 'Or who she was meeting.'

'Fine, but wasn't she estranged from her aunt?' Hörður asked.

'Yes, that's right – according to Eiríkur, anyway. But maybe the aunt will be able to flesh out our picture of Elísabet and give us some background. I think it's important to get other opinions of her apart from her husband's, but there aren't many people we can ask. Eiríkur seems to know next to nothing about Elísabet's childhood in Akranes. Perhaps Guðrún can fill in some of the blanks.'

'Yes, I suppose that makes sense,' Hörður conceded, though he sounded unconvinced. 'OK, you go and talk to Guðrún and the friend tomorrow. Take Sævar with you and have another chat with Eiríkur on the way. Try to get more out of him – ask what their relationship was like. He must know more than he's letting on.'

'And there's another thing,' Elma said. 'I found out who Elísabet's father was. His name was Arnar Helgi Árnason and he died when the fishing boat he was working on went down in a storm in 1989.'

'In eighty-nine, you say?' Hörður sat up. 'I remember that. The whole town was in mourning. I was aware that one of the men had a child, though fortunately the other one was single and not that young. How strange.' He was momentarily silent, as if thinking back to those days, then said: 'As far as I remember, Arnar's girlfriend was heavily pregnant. Was there no information anywhere about Elísabet having a brother or sister?'

When she got home, Magnea saw that all the lights were off. Bjarni wasn't back from work yet and their big house was devoid of life. She parked in the drive and hurried inside. She still hadn't got used to living in a detached house. They'd lived in a terrace before, and there had been a degree of comfort in knowing that their neighbours were just the other side of the wall when she was alone at home in the evenings. She and Bjarni had long dreamt of building a place of their own, and their dreams had finally come true when they moved in during the summer. The house was exactly as they had planned, down to the last detail: it was light and airy, with big windows, high ceilings and a stylish white interior, furnished with expensive, quality pieces. In the summer Magnea had barely noticed how isolated she was, but now that the nights were drawing in, the house seemed suddenly cavernous. The keys echoed as she dropped them on the chest of drawers in the hall, and she quickly switched on the lights to banish her feeling of unease. Walking over to the high windows, she jerked the curtains across them, wishing they hadn't opted for such a large expanse of glass. There were no trees outside to shield them from prying eyes and she constantly felt exposed, as if someone was standing out there, watching her.

She turned on the television to drown out the overwhelming silence that filled the house. Then, with the comforting sound of voices babbling away in the background, she went through the bedroom to the walk-in wardrobe. After running her fingers along the row of clothes hanging there, she eventually pulled out a red nightdress with black lace at the hem and neck. To go with it she chose a black silk negligee and hung both on a hook in the bathroom. While the bath was filling, she studied her reflection in the mirror. Her face had hardly changed at all over the last decade or so. Her eyes were still beautiful, though the creases at the corners had deepened over the years; nothing that obvious, just a fan of fine lines. Her full upper lip still jutted a little over the lower one in a sensual pout. And there wasn't so much as a hint of grey in her long, blonde mane since she made sure she had the colour topped up regularly. She looked after herself and knew that Bjarni appreciated the fact. She loved it when he slipped his arm round her waist when introducing her to people, sensing his pride in having such a glamorous wife.

Winding her hair up in a knot, she pinned it on top of her head then dipped her toes cautiously into the hot, foamy water. As she lay back, closing her eyes, she tried not to dwell on the thought of how alone she was in this big empty house. Sometimes she imagined what would happen if an intruder came in and dragged her out of the bath. She played out the entire sequence of events in her mind, feeling every nerve in her body grow tense. There were times when she was so afraid that she prowled around, checking that all the doors and windows were definitely locked. Of course, locks gave one a false sense of security, but she tried not to think about that. If someone was determined enough to get in, they could easily break a window and no one but her would hear the crash. They were too secluded here; too far from their nearest neighbours.

After a while she heard the click of the front door opening, followed by footsteps. When she opened her eyes, Bjarni was standing there. He bent down and started kissing her, and she wrapped her arms round his neck, pulling him to her. Then she pushed him gently away and held him at arm's length for a moment, studying him. He was still just as handsome as he had been at school; the same boyish face, same clear-eyed gaze.

'I've got a little something for you,' she said, pointing to the sink.

He picked up the white plastic stick that lay on the bathroom unit beside the sink. The window in the stick showed two blue lines.

'Does this mean…?' He broke off to look at her.

A small smile curved her lips and she nodded serenely. Those two dark-blue lines would change everything. She could already hear the sound of childish laughter filling the house.

It was oddly peaceful wandering among the graves. The evening was foggy and the damp air hung perfectly still. The cemetery was situated on the opposite side of town from Akranes Church and had its own tall, pinkish-brown clock tower, built in the 1950s. This was a modern structure, designed to look like a spire pointing heavenwards, with jutting triangular windows on all four sides and, below each of these, three smaller windows with white frames. Rows of decorative pillars stood out in relief along two sides of the base. Elma could remember being slim enough as a child to squeeze into the gaps between them. The tower dominated the upper part of the cemetery, where the odd stunted tree grew in an otherwise bare field. The gravestones in this area were noticeably weathered and many of the names had been worn away by frost, wind and rain. The dates, where they could be read, were so old that the closest relatives of those lying there were probably dead themselves, which meant there was no one to tend to their graves.

'I should do this more often,' Aðalheiður panted at Elma's side. She was wearing a white raincoat and a black woollen hat bearing the logo of the Akranes Football Association. The town was proud of its local team, though Elma could never be bothered to follow its fortunes like her parents did. They still loyally attended all the home matches, sporting their yellow-and-black scarves and hats, although the team's heyday appeared to be behind it and recently it had been languishing near the bottom of the league.

'Yes, it blows away the cobwebs,' Elma agreed. She had been about to head over here alone on a specific mission, but when she opened her door she had come face to face with her mother outside, so she had invited her along for the walk.

'How's the investigation going?' Aðalheiður asked breathlessly. Elma had set a brisk pace on the way to the cemetery.

'We've not got very far as yet,' Elma replied. Frustrated by their lack of progress, her mind was like a broken record, constantly going over the same facts without being able to make any sense of them.

'It's strange that no one reported her missing earlier. Was the woman a bit odd? Had she been suffering from a mental illness?'

'No, not as far as we're aware. She was a pilot. She was supposed to be on a flight but rang in sick instead.'

'Really?' Aðalheiður exclaimed. 'Do you think it was the husband? Sadly, an awful lot of them batter their wives. Which reminds me: did you hear about Tómas Larsen? But what am I saying? Of course you'll have heard. Apparently, he beat the girl he's living with to a pulp. Do you think that kind of behaviour's acceptable?'

Elma shook her head. Given the Akranes rumour mill, the incident would be all over town by now.

'But then it was hardly unexpected,' Aðalheiður continued. 'That couple are nothing but trouble. Tómas has driven at least three families out of the block they're living in. Apparently, it's impossible to live next door to him, what with the rubbish and the constant noise. I'm surprised Hendrik didn't do something about it years ago.'

'Hendrik? Why should he intervene?'

'Because Tómas is his brother. Didn't you know? They're partners in the family business – the estate agent's – though I doubt Tómas has been involved in the management, not directly, anyway. He used to be responsible for collecting the rent, in his own unscrupulous way.'

'I didn't know that. I don't remember ever having seen Tómas,' Elma said. Her mind conjured up the bruised face of Ásdís, the young woman she'd met at her grandmother's house a few days earlier. But she didn't mention this to her mother, having trained herself to be discreet about her job.

'I'm sure you'll recognise him when you see him. He's very like his brother,' Aðalheiður said. Elma nodded, preoccupied. She had found what she was looking for. There it was, the grave of Elísabet's baby brother. A simple search had confirmed what Hörður had said: Elísabet's mother had been pregnant when Arnar died at sea, and had given birth to a boy a couple of months later. But the baby hadn't lived long. Elma had found the whereabouts of his grave by searching the cemetery website. He had been called Arnar Arnarsson and only lived for two weeks. She located the torch on her phone and shone it on the cross.

'It's always so tragic,' her mother said. 'Still, luckily there are very few cot deaths nowadays.'

Elma didn't answer. She bent down and picked up a small, black lantern that had been propped against the white cross. It looked fairly new: the glass was still clear and clean. 'He only lived two weeks,' she murmured, as if to herself.

'Is it anyone you know?' Aðalheiður asked.

Shaking her head, Elma straightened up. They moved on, making for the gravel track above the cemetery and the cluster of historical buildings belonging to the open-air folk museum, which were floodlit in the winter darkness. The first they reached was a yellow, late-nineteenth-century vicarage, which, despite its traditional appearance, had been the first residential house in Iceland to be built of concrete. Just beyond it was a red house, dating from around the same time, which was the oldest surviving timber building in Akranes. It used to be known as 'the Crystal Palace' on account of the unusual amount of glass in its windows, in contrast to the dark, poky turf houses in which most Icelanders had lived at the time. Although it was a little ironic to refer to such a tiny house as a palace, it was a charming building nonetheless. Mother and daughter walked on in the direction of the golf course, then turned into a street called Jörundarholt.

'Do you remember living here?' Aðalheiður asked as they passed a row of terraced houses, then immediately answered her own question: 'No, of course you don't; you were so young, you can't have been more than two.'

'I was seven when we moved out.' Elma smiled at her mother. She had good memories of the neighbourhood and had continued to play there even after they moved. Their new house wasn't far away, and this area had long been a popular spot for kids to congregate for outdoor games like 'it' or baseball, until they outgrew such pursuits and preferred to rove around town or hang out at the shops.

Her mother seemed to read her mind. 'It was a good place to live,' she said and Elma nodded. 'It'll be New Year soon, Elma love,' Aðalheiður went on, sounding suddenly serious. 'Time to put the old one behind you.'

Elma nodded again, well aware of what her mother was getting at. If only it was that simple. If only she could just forget, everything would be so much easier. But, although she had no intention of burdening her mother with the fact, she doubted she would ever be happy again.

Akranes 1990

'Shall we have a sleepover?' Elísabet suggested to Sara one day. They were sitting with their dolls in Sara's bedroom, digging into a large bowl of popcorn.

Sara smiled and nodded eagerly. 'But I need to ask Mummy first,' she said, getting up and running out of the room. A minute or two later Sara's mother came in. She was small and kind but much older than Elísabet's mother, so old that Elísabet thought she could just as well be Sara's grandmother. She must be getting on for forty.

'Do you think your mother would let you stay over?' she asked.

Elísabet nodded. 'I'm sure she wouldn't care,' she said. She knew this was true, and the thought made her sad for a moment.

'Then I'd better give her a call,' Sara's mother said and asked for their telephone number.

'We don't have a phone,' Elísabet said quickly. 'I'll just ask her.'

Sara's mother didn't seem entirely happy with this suggestion. 'I'd rather talk to her myself,' she said, in a kind but firm voice, and Elísabet knew there was no point arguing. Sara's mother was strict. She always insisted Sara was home by a certain hour and that she finished her homework before going out to play. Sara envied Elísabet because she never had to ask permission for anything and could stay out as late as she liked. Elísabet just smiled and pretended that this was a good thing.

'But…' she began.

Before she could say any more, Sara's mother interrupted: 'Why don't we go round to your house now?' she said. Elísabet nodded reluctantly. She normally avoided inviting Sara round to play.

They put on their coats and shoes and set off in the direction of Elísabet's house. She walked slowly, lagging several paces behind Sara and her mother. She wasn't sure if her mother would be home – or who would be there with her.

'What a beautiful house!' Sara's mother exclaimed when they got there.

It was true: their house was beautiful – in Elísabet's opinion, anyway. It was big, with three storeys and a triangular dormer window in the roof where her bedroom was. There was a pretty garden round the house too, with trees and a swing she played on a lot in summer, and a pink rosebush.

'I'll go and check if Mummy's in,' she said and took the steps in a couple of bounds.

'I'll come and say hello as well,' Sara's mother said, following her.

Elísabet sighed. She opened the door and was met by a stale fug. She was so inured to the smell that she rarely noticed it, but after spending all day round at Sara's, with its faint, pervading scent of soap, she couldn't help but be conscious of the difference.

'Mummy!' she called out apprehensively once she was inside. There was no answer. Sara and her mother stood in the hall, silently taking in the state of the place. Elísabet knew what they were thinking. Why did her house always have to be such a mess?

She went upstairs and knocked tentatively on her mother's bedroom door. When no one answered, she opened it and went in. There she lay, sound asleep, her chest slowly rising and falling, and her hair in a wild tangle on the white pillow.

'Mummy,' she whispered, gently pushing at her shoulder. Her mother stirred and opened her eyes to slits. 'Can I go for a sleepover at Sara's house?' Elísabet asked.

Her mother waved her away and turned over on her side. Elísabet stood there for a while, at a loss, then crept out and closed the door.

'Mummy's asleep but I'm allowed to stay over,' she announced when she rejoined the others.

'Are you sure?' Sara's mother asked. 'I'd rather talk to her myself.'

'She's asleep,' Elísabet said stubbornly. 'She doesn't want to be disturbed.'

'I see.' Sara's mother wrinkled her brow. She hovered uncertainly in the kitchen for a moment or two before eventually smiling. 'All right, we'd better go then. We can stop and buy some ice-cream on the way home. How would you both like that?'

'Are you asleep?' Sara whispered later that evening. They were sharing a mattress on the floor of Sara's room.

The mattress was supposed to be for Elísabet, but Sara had insisted on joining her, saying it was much more fun than sleeping in a bed.

'No,' Elísabet whispered back and giggled. The duvet smelled so nice that she pulled it right up to her nose until all that could be seen of her was her dark hair and brown eyes.

Sara stopped laughing and turned her big, blue gaze on Elísabet. 'Why does your house smell so funny?' she asked.

'I don't know.' Elísabet couldn't understand why her mother never cleaned and hardly ever opened a window although she smoked all the time.

'Where's your daddy?' Sara asked.

'He's under the sea,' Elísabet answered. 'He was in a boat at sea when a storm came.'

Sara was quiet for a while, gazing pensively at the ceiling. 'I wish he'd been on the boat instead,' she said, just as Elísabet was dropping off. 'I wish he'd died instead of your daddy.'

Elísabet turned her head to stare at her friend in surprise. Who was she talking about? Whoever it was, that wasn't a very nice thing to say. She was about to respond when Sara turned over, pulling more of the duvet over herself. Not long afterwards they were both sound asleep.

Wednesday, 29 November 2017

From the pronounced purple shadows under his eyes, it appeared that Eiríkur had hardly slept. But, in spite of that, his hair was carefully styled with gel and he was neatly dressed, in jeans and T-shirt. Rather too neatly, Elma thought. She couldn't imagine having the patience to stand in front of the mirror and style her hair at a time like that. Her own appearance certainly wouldn't have been top of her list of priorities. Studying him in daylight, she was also fairly sure he had applied fake tan to his face, as there was a conspicuous yellowish-brown line under his chin.

Eiríkur showed them into the kitchen, where the older boy sat eating his cereal. Elma was struck yet again by his close resemblance to his mother: the same dark hair and naturally dark lashes. He was the complete opposite of his father, who was so fair that his eyelashes and brows were almost invisible.

'Fjalar's off school today,' Eiríkur said. 'I know I should probably have kept both boys at home but Ernir asked if he could go in and I thought it would do him good to get out of the house. It'll distract him. Otherwise they'll both be stuck here with me all day, and I'm not exactly a bundle of laughs at the moment.' His smile was almost a grimace. 'My younger boy can't really grasp what's happened,' he added. Fjalar looked up, eyeing Elma and Sævar suspiciously. Elma gave him a reassuring smile, but he averted his gaze and went back to studying the picture on the cereal packet.

They took seats at the breakfast bar in the kitchen and Eiríkur offered them coffee. Elma accepted; Sævar asked for a glass of water. Once Eiríkur had given them their drinks, he leant over to Fjalar. 'Go and get dressed now, there's a good boy.' His son put down his spoon, rose to his feet and walked reluctantly to his room without giving them another glance.

'They seem to be taking it very differently,' Eiríkur said, once the boy was out of sight. 'Fjalar's so quiet; it's as if a light has gone out inside him. Ernir keeps asking what's happened: where's Mummy now, why isn't she coming home?' Eiríkur's eyes strayed to the window, then returned to them. 'I don't know which is worse.'

'I think they'd both benefit from talking to someone,' Elma said. 'To a professional.'

'Well, we've talked to the vicar, and it's the same thing then: Ernir keeps asking questions; Fjalar won't say a word. I'm more worried about Fjalar, actually. He and Elísabet had a special bond – a bond I never really understood. That's not to say she didn't love them both equally, but she and Fjalar were so alike. They had that same aloof manner that can seem off-puttingly cold to people who don't know them.'

'Do you have family who can support you? I know that every-day tasks probably seem beyond you right now: shopping for food, doing the school run…'

'Yes, my parents have been coming round every day. My mother seems to think we can eat our way out of our grief.' Eiríkur gave them a faint smile.

Sævar took out a small notebook and cleared his throat. 'All the same, we'd like to ask you a few questions about Elísabet, if that's OK?' he said. When Eiríkur nodded, he went on: 'Did she have any contact with her aunt? Or her cousins?'

Eiríkur snorted. 'No, none at all. Her aunt, Guðrún, is a total cow, but I rang her anyway to let her know what had happened, because I felt it was only right to break the news to Elísabet's re-maining family members. But the truth is she never cared about Elísabet; she only took her in out of a sense of duty. I don't know if she had any children herself, as Elísabet never mentioned them.'

'Elísabet went to live with Guðrún after her mother died, didn't she?'

'Yes. She was nine or ten at the time.'

'Cancer, wasn't it?'

'Yes,' Eiríkur said, pulling a face. 'Horrible disease, but I gather Halla didn't exactly live a healthy life; she was a heavy smoker and drank a lot. In fact, from the little Elísabet let slip, it sounds as if she had a serious drink problem. Apparently, there were always people partying round at their house when Elísabet was small. And Halla can't have been more than thirty when she was diagnosed.'

'Was that why she took Elísabet to live in Reykjavík?' Elma asked. 'To be closer to family when she found out she was ill?'

'Yes, I suppose so.' Eiríkur scratched his head. 'Though I don't actually know much about it. Maybe Guðrún could tell you more. I suppose Halla wanted to give Elísabet a chance to get to know her aunt before she died, as she knew Guðrún would take her in. But Elísabet never wanted to talk about it.'

They heard a sudden blast of music from one of the bedrooms and a singer's voice started booming out. Eiríkur stood up with a sigh and left the room. The volume was abruptly turned down and he came back to the kitchen and took a seat at the breakfast bar again.

'Was Elísabet still in touch with anyone in Akranes?' Sævar resumed.

'No, not really,' Eiríkur replied. 'Like I said, she never wanted to go to Akranes. The only time she did was to meet some old woman, and that was very rarely.'

'Some old woman?' Elma repeated. 'Would you happen to know her name?'

'No, I'm afraid I've totally forgotten.' Eiríkur shook his head. 'Actually, I don't think her name ever came up.'

'Any idea how Elísabet knew her?'

'No, I asked her once but she would never properly explain, just said she'd been a friend of the family. That was all.' He was silent for a moment or two, then said: 'I just don't understand it. Don't understand who could have done this to her.' He looked at them both in turn. 'I've been trying to think who could have had a grudge against her; who could have wanted to harm her, but I can't come up with a single name. The only person I know Elísabet definitely didn't like was her aunt Guðrún, but she's so old and frail that she could hardly have attacked her.'

'We're doing our best to find out what happened,' Sævar assured him.

'How was your relationship?' Elma asked. 'Had you had any problems recently?'

Eiríkur appeared disconcerted and a note of irritation entered his voice as he answered: 'We had a perfectly normal relationship. Of course we had our disagreements but nothing major.'

'We read a text message you sent her,' Sævar said, fixing Eiríkur with a stern look. 'A message sent about six months ago, which suggests that your problems were a bit more serious than that.'

Eiríkur glanced towards the children's room, then said in a lower voice: 'For God's sake, that was just a row. We've been fine since then.'

'And you're quite sure Elísabet wasn't seeing someone else?' Elma asked, not taking her eyes off him.

He opened his mouth to speak, then closed it again. When he eventually answered, he sounded defeated: 'To tell you the truth, I don't know. I never really knew what Elísabet was thinking. We'd been together for nine years but there were times when I felt I didn't know her at all.'

Elísabet's friend Aldís was a big woman, tall and heavily built. She wore a slash of bright-red lipstick and her dark hair was drawn back severely in a high bun. She sat at the desk in her office at the hotel, very erect in her black trouser suit, fixing her large, round eyes on Elma and Sævar in turn.

'When I first heard that it was Beta...' Shaking her head slowly, she closed her eyes for a moment. 'I literally couldn't move. I was on my way to a meeting that I couldn't postpone, so I just had to sit there in total shock. I didn't take in a word, don't remember a single thing that was said.' She leant towards them and Elma caught a powerful waft of perfume. 'I mean, who would do something like that? You hear about that sort of thing on the news and read about horrible murders happening abroad, but that's all so far away, so unreal.' Her lips pursed, she straightened up again, still staring at them with those wide, unblinking eyes.

'So you knew each other well?' Elma prompted.

'Yes. We met at sixth-form college and stayed in touch, though less so over the years.'

'Did you meet up often?'

'No, I wouldn't say that. Elísabet had a family, of course, and lived in the middle of nowhere. I haven't had time for that yet … starting a family, I mean. I work too hard.'

'Do you remember the last time you met?'

'Let's see.' She thought. 'Yes, it must have been a couple of weeks ago – no, three, I think – when I went round to see her one evening. We had some wine and chatted. Nothing out of the ordinary.'

'Do you know what her relationship with Eiríkur was like?'

'Oh, I always got the impression it wasn't that close. As if Beta was never really in love with him. I mean, look at them: Beta was gorgeous; she could have had any man she wanted, but she went and settled for Eiríkur – Mr Average. I could never understand what she saw in him.'

'Did she ever talk about leaving him?'

'No, never.' Aldís examined her red fingernails, then raised her eyes to them again with a defiant expression. 'Look, you have to understand one thing about Beta: she was an extremely reserved person; it was hard to read her. She could come across as a bit arrogant, but I always thought she was very misunderstood and that's why not many people liked her. Not that they actively *dis-*

liked her, but it was difficult to get close to her. Being Beta's friend was always a challenge because she never let you into her inner-most thoughts. It was like you were always opening up far more than she did.'

'Do you know what made her like that?'

'No, I don't. People are just different.' Aldís shrugged. 'Beta was your classic introvert. She never had much need for company. Never needed recognition from other people.'

'Do you think Eiríkur was like that too?'

'I think Eiríkur was just happy that someone as stunning as Beta so much as looked at him,' Aldís retorted a little sharply, then went on: 'Look, I'm not saying Eiríkur was a bad husband, just that I never understood their relationship. It was so lacking in chemistry. If I didn't know better, I'd have thought their parents had set them up, like in one of those Muslim marriages.'

'One of those Muslim marriages?' Elma repeated, raising her eyebrows, and Aldís made a dismissive gesture and laughed apologetically.

'Don't get me wrong. I just mean it was like an arranged mar-riage – on Elísabet's side, anyway. Eiríkur was absolutely crazy about her. But she never even mentioned him, then suddenly they were a couple, and next minute they were married and she was expecting a baby.' Aldís shook her head in disgust. 'They didn't even have a proper wedding, just went to the magistrate and got hitched, just like that.'

Elma nodded. 'So there was nothing that struck you last time you talked? Nothing that suggested their relationship had changed?'

Aldís thought again. 'No, nothing like that. It was all just the usual stuff.'

'Do you know if she had any friends or acquaintances in Akranes?'

'No, though of course she used to live there. But surely you must have known that already?' Aldís asked in a tone of disbelief, her large eyes opening even wider. When they nodded, she continued: 'She never said much about Akranes. Just that she had no interest in moving back there. Though she did mention something about going to visit the house she grew up in. Apparently it came on the market recently.'

'Do you think that could have been what took her back to Akranes? To see her old house?'

'I haven't a clue what she was doing there. Maybe she did go to see the house. Who knows? All I can tell you is that she didn't have any friends there anymore. But then she never did have many friends, full stop,' Aldís added impatiently, then glanced at her watch and announced that she was going to be late for a meeting. She got to her feet and picked up her bag with her manicured hand, then paused, as if struck by an afterthought: 'But … to be honest, it wouldn't surprise me if she had been seeing someone else. I would quite understand.' She gave them a brief, impersonal smile before showing them out of her office.

There was silence in the car as they drove out of Reykjavík, heading north. It was past four and the rush-hour congestion was predictably bad, with car after car stretching into the distance in an unbroken line. Elma closed her eyes, feeling drowsiness creeping up on her.

Little of interest had emerged from their conversation with Elísabet's maternal aunt, Guðrún. The old woman had invited them into her tidy flat, in special housing for pensioners, which was located in the eastern suburb of Breiðholt, an area of big apartment blocks stretching up the hillside overlooking the city. The flat was full of heavy, dark furniture and the walls were hung with embroidered artworks. Everywhere they looked there were wooden carvings of cats in all shapes and sizes, so Elma shouldn't have been as shocked as she was when a tabby suddenly jumped down from one of the cupboards, landing right in front of her.

Guðrún had little to say about her niece except that she had been a bit of a loner, preferring to spend her time shut up in her room rather than with the rest of the family. Guðrún's own two boys, who were older than Elísabet, hadn't been particularly interested in getting to know their little cousin when she had suddenly been foisted on them. 'And I don't blame them,' Guðrún said, her face screwed up with distaste. 'The girl didn't exactly encourage friendship. She was sullen and standoffish, and spent most of her time reading books. If you ask me, she was just bone idle and that's all there was to it.' She muttered the last sentence, as if afraid Elísabet might overhear her from beyond the grave. Elma noticed that she didn't seem in the least distressed by her niece's untimely end. She spoke of it matter-of-factly, as if it had nothing to do with her.

'What sort of relationship did Elísabet have with her mother, Halla – your sister?' Elma asked. 'For instance, do you know why she took her second name from her mother rather than her father?'

Guðrún sighed disapprovingly. 'Yes, then there was that too. They never wanted to get married and, as far as I know, they weren't even officially living together. I'd always assumed Halla was registered as a single parent so she could claim benefits. But of course it backfired on her later, when he died.' Elma could have sworn that the old woman was actually gloating a little as she said this.

Guðrún had made coffee and laid the table when they arrived, so they felt they had no choice but to sit down and accept the cake she offered them, a traditional *randalína* made of layers of sponge and jam. When they asked if she thought someone might have had it in for Elísabet and wanted to harm her, she exclaimed and looked at them in astonishment. 'Harm her? No, what on earth do you mean? The only person who might have wanted to harm her was Elísabet herself.' When they asked her to explain, she went off on a rant about Elísabet's antisocial behaviour and how some people just chose to cut themselves off.

'Claiming it's some kind of illness – that shutting yourself in your room for days on end is anything other than sheer bloody idleness – it's beyond belief,' she said, her voice harsh. 'No – if I know Elísabet, she just gave up. Typical. I always had the feeling that she'd simply throw in the towel one day. It was as if nothing could make her happy. How she managed to hold down a job as a pilot is beyond me,' she said scornfully, slurping her coffee while watching them over the rim of her cup.

Elma had left the flat with a bad taste in her mouth, which wasn't entirely due to the stale *randalína*. Several times she'd had to take a deep breath and bite her lip to stop herself from contradicting Guðrún's ignorant comments about depression or her implication that women had no place on a flight deck.

They had learnt almost nothing of interest from the interview, and Elma hadn't even bothered to point out to Guðrún that Elísabet's injuries were totally inconsistent with her theory that her niece had killed herself.

Elma thought back over what they had discovered. Guðrún and her sister Halla had grown up in the countryside in the East Fjords, where their parents, Snæbjörn and Gerða, had a farm. They were born only a year apart and, as teenagers, the sisters had moved across the country together to study in Reykjavík and had never returned to live in the east. Guðrún had met a man who she had later married and had two sons with, while Halla had a daughter, Elísabet, and the little boy who had died at two weeks' old. Halla had been employed at the Haraldur Böðvarsson and Co. fish factory in Akranes until Arnar, the father of her children, had died in the accident. After the loss of her baby boy, Halla had never gone back to work, just lived on benefits, as far as Guðrún knew. The sisters had fallen out not long after they moved to Reykjavík, but Guðrún flatly refused to discuss the reason why, saying it was none of their business and that there was no need to reopen old wounds.

Elma was so lost in thought that she didn't hear what Sævar said until he turned down the radio and repeated his question.

'I said: are you hungry?' He threw her a glance. 'Or just tired, maybe?'

'Can I say both?' Elma asked, yawning.

Sævar smiled. 'Why don't you get a bit of shut-eye while we're driving back to Akranes, then we can go and get something to eat.'

'After the meeting?'

'Yes, of course, after the meeting,' Sævar said. 'Can you wait that long?'

'Sure.' Elma yawned again and closed her eyes.

Next thing she knew, the car was pulling up in front of Akranes Police Station and she became aware of a draught of cold air as the window rolled down. 'What are you doing?' she asked through her yawn, hugging her coat around herself.

'Time to wake up: we're here,' Sævar replied.

'Why do I always sleep so well in cars?' Elma rubbed her eyes and tried to stretch her limbs in the cramped space.

'It's the noise,' Sævar said. 'That's why you sleep well in planes too. The noise is on the same frequency as your mother's heartbeat when you were in the womb.'

Elma looked at him in surprise and started laughing. 'I wasn't actually expecting a scientific explanation but I'm glad to know there is one.'

'Right, so, we've got the preliminary findings from the pathologist. Our case was given top priority.' Hörður's gaze moved from Sævar to Elma and back as he sat facing them, the deep lines in his forehead accentuated by the fluorescent ceiling lights. His pale-blue eyes seemed to have sunk deep into his face. He ran a hand through his hair, flattening his curls which immediately sprang up again. 'Elísabet was dead before she was dumped in the sea. According to the pathologist's report, the cause of death was a heavy blow to the head and she died sometime between ten and twelve on Saturday night. An unsuccessful attempt had also been made to strangle her. Her injuries confirm that she was hit by a car with considerable force, which may explain the braking marks that Sævar and I found yesterday, which forensics analysed this morning. Her left leg had been smashed, and her hip may have left a dent in the car's bodywork, judging by the point at which the bumper caught her legs. The trauma to her head probably occurred not when she landed on the car but when she bounced off and hit the ground. At that point she sustained a fractured skull and a brain haemorrhage.' Hörður took off his glasses and rubbed his eyes before continuing. 'Other than that, there were no injuries on her body apart from the marks on her neck. The pathologist confirmed what forensics said: the body couldn't have been in the sea long and would only have been submerged for part of that time. That rules out the theory that she was thrown in the sea somewhere else and drifted to where she was found. According to the experts, it would have taken several days for the currents to carry her to land if she'd been dropped in the sea in, well … in Hvalfjörður, for example, or on Langisandur.'

'So we're working on the basis that she was knocked down by a car in the vicinity of the lighthouse?' Sævar asked.

Hörður nodded. 'Everything points to that. Forensics took samples of blood and hair found at the scene and sent them for analysis. But no fragments of glass turned up, so the car's headlights are unlikely to have been damaged.'

'She must have been dragged to the sea after the car hit her, then,' Elma said, picturing the slippery rocks. 'That can't have been easy.'

'No,' said Hörður.

'But why would the perpetrator have tried to strangle her if she'd died from the blow to her head? Could the strangling have happened before she was knocked down?' Elma asked.

'It's possible she didn't die instantly but showed signs of life following the collision,' Hörður said.

There was a brief interval of silence while they considered the implications of this.

'Has her phone been traced yet?' Elma asked at last, unzipping her coat, which she still hadn't taken off. She was feeling invigorated after her nap in the car and listened with interest to what Hörður had to say. Not that the information came as much of a surprise: it merely confirmed what they already knew.

'Her phone was switched on until around eight o'clock on Saturday night,' Hörður answered. 'No further signals were received from it after that.'

'Could her killer have taken it?'

'Yes, I did wonder about that,' Hörður said, 'so we'll carry on monitoring it in case it's switched on. But my guess is that it's at the bottom of the sea. Either that or in her car. At present they're going through Elísabet's laptop and we're hoping something useful will emerge from that. In the meantime, we'll make every effort to find her car. Cars don't just disappear, damn it – it has to be somewhere.' Hörður stroked his chin, then lowered his eyes to the papers on the table in front of him. 'The marks on her neck are believed to have been made by a small pair of hands.'

'A woman's hands?' Sævar asked in surprise.

'Or a man with small hands,' Hörður said. 'Did you happen to notice her husband's?' They shook their heads. 'No, you wouldn't have had any reason to.'

Having ascertained that nothing earth-shattering had emerged from their interviews with Guðrún and Aldís, Hörður asked them to postpone their report until the following day's progress meeting as he had an urgent phone call to make.

After the meeting was over, Elma couldn't help thinking that it hadn't provided many answers. Though at least they now knew that someone had run Elísabet down with their car, then tried to strangle her before leaving her in the sea to die. Who, she wondered, could possibly have hated her that much?

'I can always walk home,' Elma told Sævar as they were on their way out. 'You're going in the opposite direction, aren't you?'

'Hey, don't be like that – I promised to buy you supper, re-member?' Sævar pointed firmly to the car. Elma dithered on the pavement, aware that if she went home she'd probably end up eating nothing at all. It was days since she had last been to the shops, and the only things in her fridge were bound to be well past their sell-by date. 'OK, I'll come,' she said at last. 'But isn't there a takeaway nearby where we can grab something quick?'

'You do realise there's a top fast-food place right next door?' Sævar nodded towards the kiosk in the neighbouring building. 'I'm sure I heard the "yacht-dogs" calling me just now. Didn't you?'

Elma laughed. 'God, I haven't had a yacht-dog for … You know, I can't even remember the last time. Probably not since I was in my teens.'

'Elma, Elma, you're missing out.' Sævar shook his head in mock ruefulness. 'What a good thing I'm here to educate you.' Elma grinned but let herself be persuaded and got in the car, and they drove the short distance to the kiosk.

The Akranes speciality, a deep-fried hot dog, tasted exactly as she had remembered. And the melted cheese, chips and burger sauce more than satisfied all her junk-food cravings. Then, almost before she knew it, they were pulling up outside her flat.

'Well, thanks,' she said, wiping the sauce from the corners of her mouth.

'You're welcome. Thanks for letting me educate you,' Sævar said with fake solemnity.

Elma hesitated before getting out. 'I've got a couple of beers if you'd like a night cap.' She tried to sound casual but could feel herself blushing. She didn't really know what she wanted but told herself that she was just after a bit of company. She was always alone in her flat; her parents were her only visitors, though it wasn't as if she didn't have any friends. Over the last few weeks she had found herself thinking a lot about the girls who had once been such a big part of her life; the friends she had made at university and later at police college. She realised now that she could have been better at keeping in touch with them in recent years, but then most of the friends she did have were so busy with their husbands and children that they hardly had any time left for her. Of course, she had talked to some of them after what happened with Davíð, but they hadn't called her first: she'd had to ring them. To be fair, they'd probably thought she wanted to be left alone, especially since she'd left town and moved to Akranes. But Elma knew it wasn't only that. Their relationship had changed since they were twenty and used to meet up every weekend and ring each other on a daily basis to chat about everything under the sun. It was more impersonal these days – just a coffee now and then or dinner with their partners. She no longer shared her secrets with them, but that hadn't bothered her because she'd had Davíð. But now that she was alone, she sometimes felt as if she'd burst with all the things she wanted to say. Often she just wanted to ring him and tell him everything that had happened, how she was feeling and how much she missed him. But then, with a jolt, she would remember that he wouldn't answer her calls.

She noticed Sævar's hesitation, but after a moment he switched off the engine and got out of the car.

'So this is where you live,' he said once they were inside. Elma was relieved that the flat smelled OK and there weren't any knickers lying on the floor. Sometimes she came home from work to be met by the stink of neglected rubbish or sour milk. Just to be sure, she went into the bathroom, snatched up the clothes that were lying on the floor and chucked them into the bedroom.

Sævar walked around, examining the flat. 'You've certainly made yourself comfortable. It's not that long since you moved in, is it?'

'No, only a few weeks,' she said, fetching the beer from the fridge.

'You should see my place.' Sævar ran an appreciative hand over the decorative carving on the chest. 'I've lived there for three years but haven't managed to make it nearly as homely as this.'

He sat down on the sofa and Elma covertly studied him as he sipped his beer. His dark hair, usually so neatly combed at work, was dishevelled from where he had run his hands through it, and his eyebrows almost met in the middle.

'We must have come across each other before,' she said suddenly. 'There can't be a single person in Akranes that I haven't run into at some time or another, and I'm very good at faces. I never forget them,' she added, when he looked at her in surprise.

'I'm not,' he said, grinning. 'I couldn't remember a face if you paid me. I once went to a job interview and was in there nearly an hour and was feeling pretty good about it. Afterwards I bumped into a man outside the building and asked him the way without realising it was the same guy who had been interviewing me five minutes earlier. You should have seen the look on his face when I didn't recognise him.'

Elma burst out laughing.

'Needless to say, I never heard from him again.'

She was still laughing.

'It must be strange,' Sævar said, when she had finished.

'What?'

'Being back here.'

'A bit, I suppose.' She shrugged. 'Not as strange as I'd expected, actually.'

'You can't kid me that you missed Akranes that much,' Sævar said. His smile was infectious.

'What do you mean?' she asked with mock indignation. 'Are you implying that there's no chance I could have missed the flat landscape, the cracked pavements, the potholed streets and the lovely smell of fish?'

'Oh, when you put it like that...'

'No, you're right,' she said, dropping her gaze. Sævar waited. She couldn't make up her mind. She hadn't said it aloud once since she'd got here. She hadn't even discussed it with her parents. Her heart started pounding and she could feel herself breaking out in a sweat. No doubt the red blotches were spreading under her jumper. But then she chickened out and just said: 'I ... my relationship ended,' and shrugged as if it didn't really matter.

'Ah.'

Before Sævar could say any more, Elma interrupted. 'What about you? Any dirty secrets?'

'No, I don't have anything to hide. I like living in Akranes. I know the people here and they know me. I reckon I'd feel a bit lost anywhere else.'

'Does your family live here?'

'My brother,' Sævar said, taking another sip of beer. He seemed distracted and glanced at his watch. 'Anyway, I should probably get going. Big day tomorrow and all that. You can drive the car back to work in the morning, can't you?'

Sævar passed her the keys, then opened the door to the deck, grimacing when a chilly gust of wind tried to snatch it out of his hand. After zipping up his jacket and ramming his hat firmly over his ears, he raised a hand to her in parting. Elma got up to close the door and watched him dash across the road and disappear behind the houses on the other side.

The cake looked good but didn't actually taste of anything. Magnea ate some of the cream filling and felt overwhelmed by nausea. Putting down her fork, she pushed the plate away. Even the soda water couldn't get rid of the buttery taste.

'How are your studies going, Karen?' Sigrún asked, pouring milk into her tea and stirring it. The four friends were sitting at the white varnished table in Karen's kitchen. From the sitting room came the unmistakeable sounds of a football match, punctuated from time to time by cheers or curses from her husband.

'Oh, don't even mention it,' Karen said, rolling her eyes. That autumn she had enrolled in a distance-learning course in business studies at the University of Bifröst. 'I should be finishing a report this evening. I'd forgotten how awful studying is – there's always something hanging over you. Not to mention when you're working more or less full time and have children as well.'

'God, I don't blame you for finding it too much,' Brynja said. 'Still, I think you were amazingly brave to try.'

'I haven't given up,' Karen said, rather huffily. 'I'm just going to ask for an extension for this project. The good thing is that the teachers are very flexible, especially when you're stuck at home with a sick child – like I am this evening.' She winked at them and they laughed. 'This is just what I needed,' she continued. 'This week has been unbelievable. We found silverfish in the bathroom on Monday.' Her friends gasped. 'I mean, we've only just put in a new bathroom and now these pests turn up. We'd have done better to build a new place from scratch than try and restore an old house.'

'But you've got it looking so beautiful,' Brynja protested. 'And silverfish are perfectly harmless; you just need to put down some insecticide.'

'There's no point.' Sigrún finished her tea in one gulp. 'They turn up where there's damp and won't go until you're rid of it.'

'We should have gone for a new-build, like you, Magnea.' Karen sighed. 'You must be free from all creepy-crawlies and other problems.'

Magnea nodded without listening.

'Are you all right, Magnea? You're awfully quiet.' Karen was looking at her searchingly.

'Yes, I'm fine,' she said, smiling. 'Really,' she added, when her friends appeared unconvinced.

'Apparently there's some horrible bug going round,' Brynja said.

'There's always something going round,' Sigrún retorted.

Cheers were heard from the sitting room, followed almost immediately by swearing and loud exclamations that it wasn't bloody offside. The women exchanged grins.

'Christ, he'll wake the kids.' Karen glanced anxiously towards the children's rooms. 'Well, they're his problem if he does.'

The friends all knew this was a lie. Karen took care of the children and the house while her husband, Guðmundur, looked after nothing but himself. They had witnessed this during the various visits to summer houses and camping trips that the group of friends had undertaken over the years. He invariably lounged on his backside, beer in hand, while the children ran around shrieking or bawling, with Karen on their heels.

'I've never understood how they can get so worked up over football,' Sigrún said disgustedly, shaking her head. 'It's only a game.'

'Don't let Gummi hear you say that,' Karen said. 'Seriously, I tried it once and I'm not doing that again in a hurry.'

They all laughed.

'By the way, did you hear that they found a body by the lighthouse?' Karen looked round at the others, her expression part scandalised, part excited. 'Apparently they've identified the woman and she was local. Or, at least, she lived here as a child.'

'Seriously?' The other women leant forwards eager to hear more. 'Who was she? It's so awful. I heard she'd been murdered. Is that true? It seems unbelievable.'

Magnea could feel herself beginning to sweat. She took another sip of water and ate some chocolate raisins, but it didn't help.

'Yes, apparently. She's ... or rather she *was* called Elísabet. She went to Brekkubær School, but recently she'd been living in the Hvalfjörður area with her husband and kids. Two boys.'

'Elísabet...' Sigrún lingered over the name. 'I don't remember any Elísabet. Was she our sort of age?'

'Yes, she was in our year. I looked up a picture of her and recognised her face, though I don't remember much about her. Apparently she was very young when she moved away.'

When the noise from next door suddenly ceased, Karen glanced at the clock. The game was over and the TV had been switched off. Shortly afterwards they heard the sound of the shower.

'It's absolutely terrible. Her poor children.' Brynja put a hand to her cheek. 'I just can't understand what sort of person would do a thing like that. Was it the husband? It often is, isn't it?'

'Would her body have turned up here in Akranes if it was him?' Karen asked. 'I don't understand why she was here. What on earth could she have been doing out by the lighthouse?'

'Maybe she was drunk and wandered out there, and was unlucky enough to run into the wrong guy.' Sigrún yawned.

'Who, though? Wouldn't we know if there was somebody living in Akranes who was capable of doing a thing like that?' Karen asked.

'You think so? Would it be that obvious?' Sigrún looked doubtful. 'Mind you, there are some pretty dodgy types living in this town.'

'Yes, dodgy, sure, but murderers ... I doubt it,' Karen said.

Magnea bent forwards and took a deep breath.

'Are you sure you're all right, Magnea?' Karen looked concerned.

Magnea raised her head. Her breathing was coming fast, she felt dizzy and could smell herself sweating under her perfume.

'No,' she said finally. 'No, I'm not feeling too good.' She hoped they wouldn't notice that she swayed slightly when she stood up. Saying a hasty goodbye, she headed for the door. Karen got up and followed her.

'You must be coming down with something, darling. You're as white as a sheet,' she said, fetching Magnea's coat from the cupboard. 'Shall I give you a lift home?'

'No, there's really no need.' Magnea tried to smile, then said goodbye and hurried out, avoiding Karen's eye as she closed the front door.

She felt better as soon as she was out in the cold, damp air and her nausea receded further with every step she took away from the house. She drew a few deep breaths, then stroked her belly. It was becoming a habit, although her stomach was still flat. It was so reassuring to sense the life growing inside her and know that she was no longer alone. But now, as she placed a hand on her belly, all she could feel was emptiness, and she had a sudden premonition that it would all go wrong; that the child would be made to pay for what she had done.

Akranes 1990

She had a premonition that something was going to happen before she even opened the door. Every step she had taken away from school and closer to home had amplified the feeling. Although it was only April, the sun was shining brightly, the breeze caressed her cheek and there was a sweet smell in the air – the scent of new grass peeping up through the soil. But she was numb to these harbingers of spring. The sounds around her receded into a distant hum. She was no longer aware of the cars, people's voices, doors opening and shutting or the cries of the birds. All were drowned out by the deafening silence inside her. She could sense that something was going to happen.

The concrete steps leading up to their house were crisscrossed with cracks and there was moss sprouting in the gaps. She sat down and started tearing it up until she had reopened the sores on her fingers. Her hair fell forwards, almost covering her face. She was wearing the brown anorak and red-and-white trainers given to her by the women who sometimes came and visited her mother.

The women were OK. They brought her clothes and looked her in the eye when they spoke to her. How are you feeling? they asked. How are you getting on at school? Do you have many friends? What happened to your hands? All questions to which she had answers. Well – I'm getting on well, I've got a friend called Sara, I fell over when I was playing. Yes, Mummy's good to me. They took her hands and their faces grew concerned as they examined her nails, or what was left of them. She rarely noticed until they started bleeding. She had bitten her nails ever since she could remember. And she scratched at things too. Clawed at stones or concrete until the skin of her fingers split and they bled even more.

Like now. Blood mingled with the dirt and moss on the concrete steps. The wounds on her fingers were swollen and angry. Sometimes they developed a white or greenish tinge. At school she went around with her fists clenched so no one would see what she had been doing. She couldn't stand the looks on the other children's faces when they saw her hands. After the first day at school, she had been careful always to hide her fingers, but sometimes it just wasn't possible. Disgusting, she read in the other kids' faces. But the expressions on the adults' faces were even worse. In them she could read pity. Concern.

There was nothing for it. Elísabet opened the front door and was relieved to find there was nobody home. The floorboards creaked as she went into the kitchen. Their house was old. This had never occurred to her until she started going round to Sara's. She hadn't noticed before how dirty everything was either. Perhaps she had ceased to see it because it had always been like that, ever since she was a little girl. She didn't feel like a little girl any more, though. Soon she would be seven but she had long ago stopped thinking of herself as a child.

Their house was big too; they had all three storeys to themselves. She had never stopped to wonder how they could afford to live there until one evening her mother told her they would have to move. That the rent was too high. But something must have changed, because they hadn't moved out after all, although her mother never had a job and there was never any money.

She found a yoghurt in the fridge and mixed it with breakfast cereal and brown sugar – lots and lots of brown sugar. Then she sat down at the kitchen table and gazed out of the window as she ate. The sea was calm and the sun cast a yellow-white streak across its blue surface. As always when she looked out to sea, her thoughts drifted to her father.

She was still thinking about him when the front door opened and she heard her mother's voice. It was shrill and she was laughing loudly. Too loudly. Elísabet heard a deep male voice too and immediately started glancing around for somewhere to hide. There was a larder leading off the kitchen and she stood up, but before she could dart in there, they were both standing in front of her.

'Elísabet,' said her mother. Her expression was remote, her eyes

glazed. She was so thin that her jeans hung off her. 'Go up to your room. Now.' There was a man beside her. Unlike the other men who sometimes came to visit her mother, he was neatly dressed, in a shirt and tie.

'What's your name?' he asked. His eyes were a stony grey, his hair dark.

'That's Elísabet,' said her mother. She took him by the hand and tried to pull him away. 'And she's to go to her room,' she added in a stern voice, narrowing her eyes.

But the man lingered.

'You're a pretty girl, Elísabet,' he said. He smelled nice and he was smiling at her.

'Say thank you,' said her mother.

'Thank you,' Elísabet said, her head drooping.

'He owns our house,' her mother added, smiling up at him. 'So you'd better be nice to him.'

Elísabet nodded. She could feel the man's eyes following her as she climbed the stairs.

Thursday, 30 November 2017

Elma got to work early the following morning. She had lain awake for much of the night, her mind buzzing with thoughts about the case, the people she had met that day, and Sævar. She was troubled by a nagging sense of guilt because of Davíð. It was too soon. Too soon to be interested in someone else. Yet her thoughts kept returning to Sævar. She got up, fetched a cup of coffee and tried to clear her head and focus on the case. Chewing the cap of her pen, she stared at the wall, going back over the conversations she'd had the day before.

Guðrún had done little other than confirm what Eiríkur had said. Nothing she had told them could explain why Elísabet had been found dead by the old lighthouse in Akranes.

Elísabet puzzled Elma. She had been beautiful in spite of her sombre, verging on sullen, air. With that dark, almost black, hair and luminous skin. Why had she been so serious? Was she naturally made that way? Just as some people were always smiling for no obvious reason, wasn't the opposite possible as well? She seemed to have been well set up in life, with a husband and two children; both she and Eiríkur had had good jobs, and it was a long time since she had broken all ties with Akranes. Apparently she hadn't been in contact with anyone who lived there, apart from an old woman whose identity had not yet been established. Yet her body had turned up there. Nearly thirty years after she had sat in a classroom in Akranes, gazing solemnly into the camera, she had been found on the shore near the town. Murdered.

Had she been meeting a man? Had Eiríkur found out? Statistically speaking, the average Icelandic murder victim was not a mother of two in her thirties. Since 2000, around twenty men and ten women had been murdered. Most of the male-on-male killings were linked to alcohol. When the victims were women, on the other hand, it was usually the result of domestic abuse. Elma knew that violence in the home was often well hidden, existing even among the expensive designer furniture in luxury apartments, so it would make sense to take a closer look at Eiríkur.

Elma recalled the look on his face as they were leaving. She didn't for a minute doubt that his grief was genuine, but there had been something else there too: anger. Elma was sure that was what she had seen. For some reason he had been angry.

Eiríkur hadn't made a particularly good impression on her. He was far too slickly presented, too conscious of his own behaviour and appearance. It made him come across as insincere. All his movements had a rehearsed quality, as if he were putting on a performance. Yet there was nothing to suggest he had wished Elísabet any harm. On the contrary, he had clearly been crazy about her. But what if she had been planning to leave him? The police hadn't found any confirmation of this other than the text messages, but then Elísabet didn't seem to have had any confidantes, apart from her friend Aldís. Perhaps her computer would provide more clues. Forensics were currently going through the contents, searching for anything that might hint at what had happened. Elísabet could have entered some search term, for example, that would demonstrate conclusively that she had been considering leaving her husband.

Then there was the house. Aldís had mentioned that Elísabet had talked of wanting to visit her childhood home on Krókatún, so it was perfectly possible that this was what had drawn Elísabet back to Akranes. Perhaps it had been part of an attempt to come to terms with her past. From the descriptions they had been given, it sounded as if there had been something weighing on Elísabet. Perhaps something had happened at school or at home that had caused her to become so withdrawn and unsociable.

Elma closed her eyes and tried to think logically. It didn't help that ever since Elísabet's body had turned up, the town had been alive with curiosity. People kept dropping into the police station on the off-chance, sniffing around for information on the pretence of having some other business. The phones were constantly ringing too, with reporters asking for information. The fact was, the clock was ticking and it wouldn't look good if the police didn't throw the press a titbit soon. It was understandable at first, but as time wore on it would begin to look as if they were clueless. Which was right, of course. It was more than three days since the body had been found but they still had no leads.

All they had so far was a report from the pathologist, but they still didn't have a suspect. The progress meeting was due to start in a few minutes, and Elma wasn't holding out hope that anything substantial would emerge from it.

Hörður's grey-streaked fringe was standing on end and his eyes, peering over his glasses, were weary.

'They've gone through her computer but her search history doesn't show anything of interest. Just the usual browsing; no suspicious search terms or anything like that. In fact, she doesn't seem to have spent much time online at all.' He paused and lowered his eyes to his notes. 'But what they did find was an email showing that she had an appointment with a lawyer last Friday. His name's Sigurpáll G. Hannesson and he works at a solicitor's office in Reykjavík. We'll need to get in touch with him and find out what she wanted.'

'Do you think she was applying for a divorce?' Sævar asked, arching his spine in the hope that it would alleviate his backache. He was tired and stiff from having sat hugging Telma all evening until she had finally fallen asleep. Despite his cramped position, he hadn't dared move for fear of disturbing her and, as a result, he had woken up in the middle of the night with a numb arm and a crick in his neck. At that point he had taken her to bed, where she had gone back to sleep, pressed against him. Her sobs had continued sporadically even after she had dropped off, keeping him awake for hours.

'Yes, I was wondering that too,' Hörður said. 'Eiríkur could have discovered that she was cheating on him. Or just that she was seeking a divorce. Though, of course, that doesn't necessarily mean there was another man involved.'

'When Sævar and I talked to Eiríkur, he insisted they weren't having any problems,' Elma pointed out.

'Of course he did,' Sævar said.

'What about the aunt, Guðrún?' Hörður asked. 'Did she know more than the husband's letting on?'

'Guðrún was no help,' Elma said, picturing again the shrunken little woman who had seemed so devoid of feeling or pity. 'I got the feeling that Guðrún wasn't particularly happy about having to take Elísabet in back then. She described her as ungrateful and insisted that she was antisocial and lazy. They hadn't spoken for years, so she could tell us next to nothing about her recent circumstances. Whereas Elísabet's friend, Aldís, gave us the impression that Eiríkur was a bit obsessed with her. That he was much more in love with Elísabet than she was with him. I don't know how much weight we should place on her opinion but I think we should take a closer look at him anyway.'

'He's got an alibi, if his kids are to be believed.'

'Is it watertight, though?' Sævar asked. 'How long would it have taken him to drive to Akranes? Half an hour? If the boys were asleep, they wouldn't have noticed him going out.'

'Is there anything to indicate that she was planning to leave him?' Hörður asked. 'We have very little real evidence to support that theory.'

'There's the fact she called in sick without telling Eiríkur and then stayed away overnight,' Elma pointed out. 'We still have no idea where she was. Not only that but she had a meeting with a lawyer. Mind you, I think that could have been connected to something completely different. To events in her childhood maybe, or to someone she knew before she moved away. According to her friend Aldís, she was talking about going to see her childhood home, which had recently come on the market.'

'The house on Krókatún?'

'That's right. It's been sold but I think we should drop round and see the new owners. Find out if they had a visit from her at the weekend.'

Hörður nodded. 'OK, you take a look at the house, Elma. Sævar, you check what kind of car Eiríkur owns and see if you can find any holes in his alibi: was he caught on CCTV somewhere he shouldn't have been? That sort of thing.'

Elma stood up and glanced at Sævar, who gave her a brief smile. She got the impression he'd been avoiding looking at her ever since they arrived. She noticed the dark circles under his eyes. He had left so abruptly the previous evening that she was worried she'd done something to scare him off.

Elma pulled up outside the house in the west of town. There was a bare lawn around it; no fence, just wind-blown trees and a lone swing rocking gently to and fro in the breeze. The front of the house facing the road was clad in white-painted timber and had triple-casement windows. The other side looked out over the sea, and in good visibility it would have a clear view of the Snæfellsnes Peninsula to the north-west. The place was obviously in need of maintenance as the concrete at the base of the walls was crumbling, and stained here and there with streaks of rust.

Elma climbed the cracked concrete steps to the front door, thinking that it was exactly the sort of old house that Davíð would have appreciated. She knocked at the door. After a short interval it opened and a woman in a baggy light-blue shirt and torn jeans gave her a cheerful welcome. Her fair hair was tied back in a pony-tail with a few strands hanging loose around her face.

'Do come in,' the woman said after Elma had explained what she wanted. She introduced herself as Gréta. Elma followed her into the kitchen while she was talking. There were cardboard boxes all over the place, some open, others yet to be unpacked. 'We've just moved in,' Gréta explained. 'We're going to do the place up and convert it into an Airbnb. It's far too big for the two of us and I've been dreaming of opening a guesthouse for ages, so I finally decided to go for it.' She motioned to Elma to sit down at the small kitchen table. 'I've recently got divorced,' she added.

'I hear that Akranes is becoming ever more popular with tourists,' Elma remarked, accepting the cup of coffee Gréta offered her.

'Exactly,' said Gréta. 'Anyway, you were asking if I'd had any visitors, weren't you?'

'Yes, it's to do with a case we're investigating,' Elma said. 'This may sound a bit strange but you didn't by any chance have a visit last weekend from a woman who used to live in this house as a child?'

'Yes, I did,' said Gréta, nodding eagerly. 'She was very nice. Not pushy at all. She just asked politely if she could take a look round. She'd been meaning to come earlier, when the house was on the market, but hadn't been able to for some reason.'

'Was she alone?'

'Yes, it was just her. I spotted her from the window. It was quite odd, actually.' Gréta laughed. 'I'd just got out of the shower and saw her standing behind the house, on the wild bit of garden down by the sea, just staring at the view. When I came out to see what she wanted, she was rather embarrassed and apologised. But as soon as she explained what she was doing there, I understood perfectly. You often feel a strong connection to the place where you lived as a child. I myself grew up in a blue house in Hafnarfjörður and I sometimes take a detour past it just to say hello, if you know what I mean.'

'What did she say?' Elma interrupted quickly, before Gréta

could go off on a tangent about her own childhood. It was clear she enjoyed talking.

'Oh, she didn't say very much, actually. Just mentioned that she'd lived here with her mother and had always wanted to see the house again. She asked if she could be alone for a minute in her old room in the attic, which is Nói's room now. I let her, of course, but you can picture Nói's face when he was forced to look up from his computer for once. Then she just wandered round the house. I offered her a coffee but she said no thanks. She was very enthusiastic about the changes we're planning to make. Very enthusiastic...' She trailed off and Elma waited patiently for her to resume.

Gréta coughed and laughed awkwardly. 'Sorry, it's just ... after she came downstairs from the attic she seemed in a strange mood. I got the feeling it had stirred up bad memories or something because she seemed so ... sad. I asked if she'd been happy here. You know, it matters to us. Every owner leaves an aura behind, which helps to create a good atmosphere in the house. But she didn't answer, just said thanks and left almost at once.'

Elma was sceptical about auras, good or bad, but nodded anyway. 'I couldn't possibly take a look at the attic myself, could I?' she asked.

Gréta shrugged. 'Sure, but there's nothing there now except Nói's stuff. He's hardly lifted a finger since we moved in. The only thing he's unpacked is his games console.' She rolled her eyes, then yelled 'Nói!', so suddenly that Elma jumped. She looked towards the stairs and after a minute or two a gangly teenage boy appeared at the top of them, in skinny jeans and a baggy hoodie that reached almost to his knees. He came slowly downstairs in obedience to his mother's impatient summons.

'Nói, this is Elma. She works for the police and just wants to take a quick look at your room.' Gréta put a hand on his shoulder. Nói looked at Elma then back at his mother. He opened his mouth to protest, then groaned and flopped down on the sofa.

Gréta went upstairs, beckoning Elma to follow her. 'It's such an old house that everything's a bit cramped, but that's part of its charm,' she said, once they were on the landing.

Elma examined the attic room. She didn't know exactly what she was doing up there or what she hoped to find. There was old parquet on the floor and a built-in cupboard running the length of the wall at the foot of the sloping ceiling. The floor was stacked with boxes. On one side of the room was a bed and opposite it a table had been set up with a TV and games console. Remote controls littered the crumpled duvet and on the bedside table was a half-full glass of some fizzy drink. Gréta reached up to the skylight and opened it wide.

'Phew, it's a bit stuffy in here,' she exclaimed. 'That cupboard would be good for storage but I can't bring myself to put Nói's clothes in there.' She opened the door of the cupboard under the sloping roof. 'Look how filthy it is. I still haven't got round to cleaning it out.'

'Mind if I have a look?' Elma asked.

Gréta shrugged. 'There's nothing in there. At least, I hope not. Though I wouldn't be surprised to find a dead mouse or even a rat.'

Elma used the small torch on her key ring to illuminate the interior. She had to crouch down to see inside as the cupboard roof was low and the space became more cramped the further back it went. The walls inside were grimy and sticky. There was a thin layer of dust on the floor and as it was stirred up Elma had to pinch her nose to suppress a sneeze. But there was nothing inside the dark cubbyhole. No sign of a dead rat or anything that could have belonged to the former owners. She was about to shut the door again when she noticed marks on the inside of it. She ran her fingertips over the rough wood.

'Yes, I'd noticed that,' Gréta said. 'There must have been a mouse problem. It'll take a while to restore the cupboard.'

Elma nodded absently. The inside of the door was covered in

irregular scratches: circles and lines and something that looked like a picture or letters, which made it impossible that the marks could have been made by an animal. In places the wood was stained by something that had dripped down it. Although the scratches were shallow, the dark streaks were conspicuous on the light-coloured wood.

'What do you think that is?' Gréta bent down and peered at the marks.

'Nothing in particular,' Elma answered as she stood up again. She banged the dust from her trousers. 'This must have been a child's room.'

'That would have been a while ago then, because the couple who lived here before us didn't have any kids.'

'Yes, I expect the marks are old,' Elma agreed. She felt suddenly overwhelmed with depression. Perhaps it was the effect of the airless room but, whatever it was, she needed to get out of there as quickly as possible.

Hendrik had decided that they should meet at the office as it seemed more appropriate in the circumstances. His brother was late as usual, and Hendrik reclined in his chair, waiting patiently.

He had always felt protective towards his little brother. Ever since they were boys it had always been Tómas who got into trouble. He went looking for fights and quarrels, never happier than when he was in the thick of the fray. And it was always Hendrik who had to bail Tómas out when he'd managed to turn everyone else against him. Hendrik had always been popular and enjoyed respect from the group, and Tómas had reaped the benefits. If it hadn't been for Hendrik, Tómas would probably have had a rough ride.

Their father was Danish. He had met their mother when she was studying at the Folk High School in Denmark, and moved to Iceland with her, where they had eventually settled in Akranes.

When Hendrik was ten, however, their father had moved back to Denmark and met a Danish woman with whom he went on to have three children. He never came back to visit his sons in Iceland. Tómas had only been six at the time, and Hendrik was sure that his younger brother had been much worse affected by their father leaving than he had been himself. Hendrik had always been their mother's favourite, whereas Tómas and their father had been very alike. They had understood each other. Their mother hadn't been particularly surprised when their father walked out on them. He was just made that way – impulsive, thinking only of himself – and Tómas was the same. Sometimes their mother had looked wearily at Tómas, shaking her head, and said that it was as if their father had never left: Tómas was the spitting image of him.

But Hendrik wasn't sure that all Tómas's faults could be blamed on their father. He had been the same as far back as Hendrik could remember: mischievous, restless and irresponsible – and their father couldn't be blamed for bringing him up that way. Nowadays he would probably have been diagnosed with some kind of behavioural disorder but at that time such things were unheard of. Nevertheless, Hendrik couldn't go on letting Tómas off the hook forever; his youthful escapades had given way to crimes that were far more serious.

Hendrik was not happy about the rumours currently doing the rounds: it seemed that everyone had heard about the way Tómas had treated that girl. Hendrik had forgiven his brother a lot over the years; he'd even turned a blind eye to his methods of collecting the rent on their properties, reasoning that at least it meant the women didn't have to pay and could use the money for something else instead. Yet his conscience had always bothered him and belatedly he had put a stop to it. By then, people had started talking too. Those rumours were never proved, but it was different in this case, with the girl's injuries so glaringly obvious.

'Hiya,' Tómas said, sauntering into his office without knocking, as usual.

Hendrik didn't answer, just nodded and motioned to him to sit down.

'What's up?' Tómas asked. His shirt could have done with an iron and he was unshaven. The rank smell of stale sweat carried to Hendrik across the desk. Once, Tómas had played an active role in running the company. He used to turn up to work every day, neatly presented, and had been an active business partner. But that was long ago and it had ended badly. When the company had gone through a rough patch, Tómas had skipped off so quickly that he couldn't be seen for dust, and Hendrik had the feeling that he had never truly come back.

'There's no easy way to say this,' Hendrik began, his face grim, 'so I'll just go ahead: I want to buy you out.'

'Out of the company?' Tómas asked.

Hendrik nodded.

Tómas looked grave for a moment or two, then, to Hendrik's consternation, he began to smile. The smile widened until his yellowing teeth were exposed and he burst out laughing, his guffaws booming around the office.

'I thought you'd never ask,' Tómas said, once he'd finally got himself under control again. 'I've been waiting for you to say that for years but you never did. You don't need to worry about me any longer, big brother; I can take care of myself.'

Hendrik was speechless. He had already prepared the contract, so he silently pushed it across the desk, showing his brother the sum of money he had in mind. Tómas merely nodded and signed without bothering to read the rest of the document.

As Tómas was leaving, he turned in the doorway, his face momentarily grave. 'Are we quits now, bro?'

'What do you mean?' As he stared, frowning, at his brother, Hendrik was transported back to the days when they were little boys. When Tómas was always getting into scrapes and Hendrik had to clear up the mess. He could still remember his little brother's guileless gaze as he said he was sorry. But he never apologised to his victims: he always left that to Hendrik.

Instead of explaining, Tómas merely smiled enigmatically and left. Hendrik sat in his office, his eyes resting unseeingly on the door, recalling long-forgotten memories of two little boys who had once been inseparable.

Elma decided to have a coffee while she was waiting for Sævar and Hörður. In the kitchen, she found Begga and Kári sitting round the table with Grétar, a uniformed officer Elma had only met in passing. She noticed that Begga was conspicuously less smiley than usual. She was staring out of the window but glanced round when Elma came in. Elma assumed her sombre mood was due to the case until Begga heaved a sigh and explained that her cat had got out two days ago and still hadn't come home. 'You haven't seen him, have you?' She held out her phone to show a large, ginger cat curled up in a brown armchair. Elma remembered the animal from when she had gone round to Begga's flat. She had tried to push him away as politely as possible when the cat had rubbed against her legs, then jumped onto her lap uninvited. As soon as she got home, she had chucked her fur-covered clothes in the washing machine.

Elma shook her head. 'No, sorry.' In fact, she was fairly sure she wouldn't recognise it if she encountered it on her way to work as she didn't usually pay any attention to the cats that crossed her path. But she couldn't say this to Begga when she was looking so dejected.

'Pass me the picture, Begga.' Kári leant over the table, holding out his hand. He examined the photo closely. 'I think I saw a cat like that in my garden yesterday. Since we both live on Vesturgata, it could well have been him. If I were you, I'd check the area around the barber's shop. I live behind it, as you know.'

Begga's face brightened. 'I'll go and give Dad a call and ask him to drive past just in case. Thanks, Kári.'

'You're welcome.' Kári posted an entire biscuit into his mouth.

'It's so awful,' Grétar remarked, after they'd been silent for a while.

'About Begga's cat?' Elma enquired, finding it hard not to smile.

'No, about Elísabet,' he said, frowning. 'I remember her from school – we're around the same age; she was in the year below me. I didn't even know she lived just down the road in Hvalfjörður. I thought she'd moved away years ago. To be honest, I'd totally forgotten about her. She's not on Facebook, so I didn't really come across her at all.'

'Why didn't you mention this earlier?' Elma asked, taking a proper look at Grétar. He had joined the police fairly recently, in spite of being older than her. She wondered why he had decided on the career change and what he had done previously. Perhaps she'd ask him when she got a chance.

Grétar shrugged. 'I didn't realise at first, but then it didn't matter. It's not like I really knew her.'

'Do you remember what she was like at school?' Elma asked. 'Who she hung around with and so on?'

'I can hardly remember who I hung around with myself,' Grétar said with a laugh, but quickly grew serious again when he saw Elma's impatient expression. 'But I do remember that Elísabet was a bit strange.'

'How do you mean?'

'Only that she wasn't like the other kids. She was different, somehow.'

'There's nothing wrong with being different,' Elma snapped. It came out rather more sharply than she'd intended. 'We get the impression she didn't have much support at home.'

Grétar thought for a moment. 'I remember that her mother was a headcase.'

'A headcase?' Elma repeated, taken aback by his choice of language. She wondered what had prompted him to use such a word about Elísabet's mother. Was that how people had talked about Halla in Akranes? If everyone knew she had mental problems, why had nobody intervened?

'Yes, she was a bit mental,' Grétar said, looking rather shame-faced. Reddening slightly, he added: 'Some kids just never have a chance.'

'You can say that again,' Elma agreed. She drank the rest of her coffee, ignoring her rumbling stomach, and left the kitchen in a thoughtful frame of mind. Her phone began vibrating in her pocket the moment she sat down at her desk. The number that flashed up on the screen didn't ring any bells but she answered anyway. She'd hardly had any calls in the last few weeks, except from her parents or on work-related business. She had the feeling people were avoiding her after what had happened.

'Elma?'

She recognised the voice immediately.

'Hi, Lára. What can I do for you?' She could hear how cold her voice sounded; how distant, as if it didn't belong to her.

There was a brief silence.

'Oh, Elma … I should have rung before.'

'Don't be silly, I'm fine,' Elma said, trying to force herself to sound breezy.

'I can't believe what happened.' Lára hesitated. 'The thing is, I heard you'd left town and I wanted to give you time … Maybe it was wrong of me. But it's been difficult for me too. I wish there was something I could say…'

Elma was silent. She could feel a lump forming in her throat and knew if she said anything her voice would break. Damn it, she'd become far too sensitive.

'You may not want to talk to me but I'm here when you're ready. Call this number, Elma. Any time.' She sounded sincere. 'I'm so sorry.'

Elma mumbled a reply and hung up.

'I got hold of the lawyer,' Sævar announced. Elma looked up from her desk. 'He couldn't tell me much because of the duty of confidentiality but he did say that Elísabet had a lot on her mind when she came to see him.'

Elma nodded. 'So now we know. On Friday she leaves home, calls in sick at work, then goes to meet a lawyer in Reykjavík.'

'Right,' said Sævar. 'The fact she hid it from her husband has to mean that the meeting had something to do with him.'

'Yes.' Elma paused. 'Unless it was about something else, something she'd been keeping quiet about, which may not have had anything to do with her husband.'

Sævar came and sat down facing her, his eyes fixed on her face. As she carried on talking, Elma tried to ignore the blush that she could feel stealing across her cheeks. 'We still don't know where she spent Friday night, but I've established that she visited the house on Krókatún on Saturday. You know, the house where she used to live with her mother.'

'Ah, so she did, did she?'

'Yes, and apparently she behaved quite oddly, according to the woman who lives there. Especially after she'd been up to the attic to see her old bedroom. Perhaps something bad had happened to her up there.'

'Like what?'

'There were some strange scratches inside the bedroom cupboard. Of course, I can't be sure, but it looked as if someone had been clawing at the door. There were dark streaks, like ... well, as if blood had dripped down from the scratches.'

Sævar frowned. 'There could—' he began, but Elma interrupted.

'I know there could be any number of other explanations for them but I was just wondering if we should widen our focus beyond the husband. Nothing's emerged yet to suggest he's done anything wrong and we haven't found any proof that Elísabet had a lover. Whereas it does appear that she had a difficult childhood and that she overcame her distaste for Akranes enough to go and visit her old home.' Elma paused again. When voiced aloud, the idea sounded more far-fetched than it had in her head. In her opinion, what they'd learnt about Elísabet's behaviour seemed a strong indication that she'd suffered some kind of trauma in her youth. Whether that had any bearing on her death, however, was another matter.

'Why did she go and see a lawyer, then?' asked Sævar. 'Surely it must be linked to her husband?'

'I don't know,' said Elma. 'She could have been checking her legal situation in relation to some incident in her youth.'

'If you're talking about sex abuse, it would probably still be within the statute of limitations. But, remember, there was no man in the house when she was growing up.'

'No, that's true,' Elma conceded. 'But if her mother was an alcoholic, who knows how many strange men were coming and going?'

Sævar sighed heavily. 'Well, if she was going to report a crime, I suppose it's possible that someone wanted to silence her. I can't believe it was just a case of bad luck – that she was in the wrong place at the wrong time. But why now, after all these years?'

Elma shrugged. 'It's common for victims of sexual abuse to tell their story long after the event. Especially if the incidents happened when they were kids. I'd like to build up a better picture of her childhood. I could talk to her old teachers, classmates and neighbours. That way we might also find out if she'd been meeting someone here in Akranes.'

'Would you be doing that purely from curiosity or do you really think it's relevant to the case?' Sævar asked with a grin.

'I admit I'm curious,' Elma said, returning his grin. 'But I still think it could be relevant or I wouldn't have brought it up. Don't you find it a bit suspicious that she'd always avoided the town, and then, when she does finally come back, someone kills her? Was it the town she was avoiding or somebody who lives here?'

Sævar shrugged.

'I doubt the murder was premeditated,' Elma went on. 'It was too messy – too amateurish. But I do think she knew her killer. The location's too out of the way. Someone has to have known that she'd be at the lighthouse.'

'Yes, I'll give you that. It certainly doesn't look well organised,' Sævar said. 'But...'

Before he could finish, Hörður stuck his head round the office door: 'The car's turned up.'

Akranes 1990

The man owned their house and Elísabet was to be nice to him. That's what her mother had said. He came round regularly but never stayed long. Elísabet didn't know what he did while he was there, but her mother always told her to go up to her room. Or to go outside and, better still, stay out.

Her mother always dressed up for his visits. Put on lipstick, drank out of a long-stemmed glass and smoked one cigarette after another. Elísabet liked to sit and watch her getting ready but her mother couldn't stand it. 'What are you gawping at?' she used to ask, blowing smoke in her direction.

Although Elísabet was only seven, she knew her mother didn't love her. She'd read about mothers in the books she borrowed from the school library and knew what they were supposed to be like; how they were supposed to behave. They were supposed to be like Sara's mother: telling you to do your homework, making sure you had a bath, brushing your hair. Mothers were supposed to be kind and loving. Her mother wasn't like that. She did none of those things. Elísabet couldn't even remember her mother cuddling her, back before everything changed. It had always been her daddy, never her mother.

One day in December her mother drank too much. Elísabet found her lying on the floor in the sitting room, a broken bottle and a large wet patch beside her. At first Elísabet was frightened, but then she saw that her mother's ribcage was moving. She stood there at a loss, staring at her, wondering if she should fetch Solla or leave her mother alone. She had just decided to leave her to sleep it off when the doorbell rang. Elísabet answered it to find that it was him: the man who sometimes came round, the man who owned their house.

'Hello, Elísabet,' he said.

Elísabet didn't answer. She didn't know why he was always visiting her mother but she did know that it had a bad effect on her.

After he left, her mother would sit there for ages, smoking and staring vacantly at the wall. Her eyes and face seemed to change with every month that passed, and Elísabet was sure that in the end there would be nothing left of her; nothing resembling the mother she had once known.

'Is your mum home?' the man asked, peering inside.

Elísabet shook her head and made to close the door, but the man put out a hand to hold it open. Then he came in and closed the door behind him.

'Elísabet,' he said gently and squatted down. He stroked a strand of dark hair back from her face and gazed into her eyes. 'You're a beautiful girl. Did you know that?'

Elísabet was silent. He owned their house. She had to be nice.

'I can't for the life of me understand how the car got in here.' The man was standing, looking perplexed, one hand on his hip, the other scratching his head. Beside him was his wife, dark-haired and tanned, in a white chiffon top and tight jeans. They ran a fashion boutique in town and had just returned from Tenerife, where they regularly spent time in November, before the Christmas rush began at the shop.

'Were the garage doors closed when you got back?' Hörður asked.

'Definitely. Closed and locked,' the man confirmed.

The woman pursed her lips, shooting her husband an irritated glance. 'You must have forgotten to lock them. I just hope nothing's missing.'

The man snorted. 'There's not exactly much of value in there. I doubt burglars would be interested in stealing tools or old children's clothes.'

'Does anyone else have keys to the house?' Hörður asked.

'No,' said the woman. 'Well, except for the kids, but I doubt they'd have left a strange car in there.'

'Perhaps they came round and forgot to lock up after themselves,' Hörður said. 'Can you get into the house from the garage?'

'Yes, but that door was locked and we can't see any sign that an intruder's been in the house.'

Hörður nodded, surveying the garage. 'Has anything else been touched?'

'No, not as far as we can tell.' The woman tried and failed to hold back a yawn. 'It just doesn't make any sense. What was the owner thinking of, parking their car in our garage? I mean, was it snowing outside and they couldn't be bothered to scrape their windows or something?'

Hörður didn't reply. He picked up a cloth and used it to try the car door.

'We've already tried to open it. It's locked,' the man said.

Hörður sighed but didn't comment. How were they to know that the car was linked to a murder investigation?

'There's sand on the tyres,' Elma pointed out. She had been hanging back with Sævar, letting Hörður take charge of interviewing the couple. Hörður bent down and peered under the dirty car.

'Can't we push it out?' the man asked. 'I can't be doing with a strange car in my garage. There's supposed to be a frost tonight and I need to get the jeep under cover.'

Hörður straightened up and gave the man a level look. 'We need to investigate further so I'm afraid your jeep will just have to remain outside for the moment.'

'Investigate...?' the man asked, annoyed. 'What kind of bullshit is this, Hörður? Can't you just tow the car away?'

'No, I'm afraid not. Though I hope we'll be able to soon.' Hörður didn't elaborate.

'Well, in that case I'm off to bed,' the wife said in a resigned voice. 'Come on.' She took her husband by the hand and led him away before he could say another word.

'The number plate matches,' Hörður said, once the couple had gone indoors. 'The car's registered as belonging to Elísabet.' He took out his phone to call forensics, walking off to one side.

'There's something inside the car,' Elma said. She pressed her face against the window. 'Clothes of some sort, rubbish and a pile of papers. She must have been quite a slob, which is odd when you think of how spotless their house was.'

'She didn't have any car keys on her when she was found,' Sævar said thoughtfully. 'Which suggests someone else hid her car here.'

'But why here?' Elma said. 'It's not like it wouldn't be discovered eventually.'

'Yes, but it's hard to hide something as big as a car. The killer must have known that the couple who lived here were abroad.'

'And had a key to their garage?' Elma asked sceptically. Could the killer simply have been buying time? She had to admit that the trick had succeeded in holding up the investigation for several days. Could he or she have used the time to disappear – to leave the country, even?

'Maybe.' Sævar shrugged. 'Unless the wife was right and her husband simply forgot to lock it.'

'Forensics will be here in an hour,' Hörður announced once he'd finished his phone call, 'so we can examine the car then.'

It began to rain. Heavy drops started landing on the roof with a loud drumming that echoed around the garage.

'Well, we don't all need to wait here,' Hörður said, zipping his coat up to the neck and pulling on his fur-lined hat. 'I'm going to nip back to the office, but call me when forensics turn up.'

Once Hörður had gone, Elma pulled out a small stool from by the garage wall. She yawned and huddled into her coat, saying: 'What I wouldn't give for a coffee right now.'

'Hey, why don't I run out and buy us some?' Sævar offered. 'It's not far to the Olís garage.' He pulled up his hood and dashed out to the car.

Elma remained behind in the garage, listening to the booming of the rain and the hissing of the hot-water pipes. Sævar was his usual self again and she felt silly for thinking that yesterday evening could have affected their relationship. It wasn't as if anything had happened. There was no reason to believe his hurried departure had had anything to do with her. After all, she was hardly the sort of temptress who was constantly having to push men away.

A cold draught sneaked under the garage door as the wind gained strength. When she walked to work that morning, it had been perfectly still and there had hardly been a cloud in the sky. You certainly couldn't complain about the monotony of the weather at the moment. She got to her feet and began pacing around the garage to keep warm.

The place was a mess. Stuff was crammed into shelves, cupboards and boxes, as if the owners never threw anything away. Few of the boxes were labelled. Elma opened a large cupboard and discovered that it was filled with what looked like dozens of shoes and coats. The place was littered with outdoor gear too: skis, snowboards, fishing rods and waders. None of it showed much wear and it had clearly been lying there untouched for a long time.

What must all this gear have cost? Millions, no doubt. She knew the couple who lived there were well off. In addition to fashionwear, the wife sold all kinds of designer goods, sports gear and so on. This was often the way in country towns: shops couldn't afford to specialise too much as the market wasn't large enough to support outlets for individual types of goods. The couple had two kids, one of whom, the son, was the same age as Elma and had been at school with her. Yet there had been no sign that they recognised her – not that she had expected them to. She hadn't exactly been friends with their son. He'd been one of the cool gang, always dressed in the latest fashions and tanned from frequent holidays abroad. The family had never made any attempt to hide their wealth; in fact, she suspected them of acting as if they had more money than they really did.

The son's name was Hrafn, but he had always been known as Krummi. When she was younger, she'd had a crush on him, like most of the other girls in her class, but as she grew older she had begun to see him with new eyes. She'd realised he was arrogant and incredibly cruel to the vulnerable kids in their class. Thinking back now, she remembered how he used to talk about one of the other boys, a shy, unattractive kid. Krummi used to go on loudly about what an ugly loser he was, even when the kid was only sitting a few feet away, and Elma had watched the boy slumping ever lower in his seat until eventually he had leapt up and run out of the classroom, followed by the jeering laughter of Krummi and his mates. She also recalled the time he had be-friended Eyrún, a girl who was generally considered a bit weird, and promised that, if she sang a song she had made up herself in front of the whole class, he would invite her to the school disco. Naturally, he hadn't been serious. The girl's performance had brought the house down. Even the teacher had struggled to hide a smile. Elma could still remember the girl's expression when she realised that everyone was laughing at her; that her fairy-tale prince would never take her to the dance.

By the time Sævar returned, Elma's stomach was tied up in knots and she felt as if a black fog had descended over everything. It was the effect that remembering her schooldays always had on her.

'Coffee for the lady,' Sævar announced, handing her a paper cup. 'Black and sugarless. I'm getting to know your requirements.'

Smiling at him, she took a sip. It felt good standing there in the garage with Sævar while the raindrops drummed on the roof. When she was younger, she used to fantasise about living in a cave, like the character from an Icelandic folktale. She would gaze dreamily towards Mount Akrafjall and imagine how she would live there all alone in her dark lair, observing the world from a safe distance.

'Why do you think Elísabet didn't want to come back?' she asked, after they'd stood there in companionable silence for a while, sipping their coffee.

Sævar raised his brows enquiringly: 'Where?'

'Here – to Akranes.'

'I don't know. Maybe she was unhappy at school – got bullied. Or suffered some kind of abuse at home, like we discussed. Or perhaps she just had no reason to come here.'

'It's got to have been more than that. Her husband said she hated the town. What would make a person hate a whole community? That's putting it quite strongly, isn't it?'

'Yes, hate's quite a strong word. Maybe she connected the town with something bad that had happened to her as a child. Perhaps there are people here she didn't want to meet. I don't know – it could be so many things. People tend to associate bad experiences with particular places.'

Elma glanced up at him, raising an amused eyebrow.

'I'm not joking,' Sævar said, reluctantly giving way to laughter. 'There's a name for it. What is it again? You know, like the child and the cat? Or the dog being made to drool?'

'The child and the rat, you mean?'

'Yes, or the rat. You studied psychology, you should know.'

'You mean the Little Albert experiment. They managed to associate a rat with fear in the baby's mind by making a scary loud noise every time he touched it. In the end the presence of the rat alone was enough to make the baby cry. He associated his fear of the noise with the rat and ended up being afraid of all furry animals. It's called classical conditioning.'

'That's it. Isn't that often the reason why people develop phobias?'

'Yes, possibly. Though it's a bit far-fetched to feel fear or hatred for a whole town.' Still, Elma thought, Sævar's idea was actually quite plausible. She thought about her own reaction to her old school building. About how she was filled with the same sense of dread every time she passed it or set foot inside. About how she felt when she bumped into any of those people – Krummi and his gang, her former classmates.

'Well, I wouldn't know. People often behave irrationally and Elísabet seems to have had a number of issues.' Sævar drained his paper cup and put it down on one of the shelves. 'But it stands to reason she must have had a friend or acquaintance in Akranes, given that she was here. She has to have spent the night somewhere and it's pretty suspicious that no one's come forward.'

Elma nodded. He was right. Someone knew something but was keeping quiet. Over the booming of the rain they heard the slam of a car door: forensics had arrived.

Hörður was holding up a clear plastic bag between finger and thumb, inspecting its contents. Elma had watched for a while as the forensic technicians got down to work. Her stomach had stopped rumbling and she was fairly sure that she had started digesting her own insides, but that didn't matter. What mattered was that Elísabet's car had turned up and forensics were busy combing through it. With any luck they would soon find out if there had been another person in the car with the victim.

'I'm still thinking,' Sævar murmured in her ear, 'that someone must have been aware that the couple who live here were abroad. The person who hid the car in their garage knew they were away and when they'd be back.'

'In other words, it must have been someone who knew them well,' Elma said, still watching Hörður as he squinted at the small plastic bag. The rain had temporarily eased up and the garage door was open. The street consisted of detached houses, many of them new-builds of grey concrete and dark wood, with double garages and large decks. Now that darkness was falling, the neighbours were clearly visible, silhouetted against the light, as they watched curiously from their windows. A few had come out to speak to Hörður.

'That's the trouble with Akranes – everybody knows everyone else's business,' Sævar said. 'That's why it's no good just checking the neighbours or close family members. Most people in town are acquainted with this couple since so many of them shop at their boutique, so any number of them would have been aware that they spend time abroad every year. On top of that, he plays golf and she teaches spinning, which means an even wider group would have known they were away that weekend.'

Elma had to admit he was right. On the other hand, there couldn't be many people in town who had a key to the garage, and there was no evidence of a break-in.

'Anyway, perhaps none of that matters,' Sævar said. 'We're bound to find something in the car.' But he didn't seem any more optimistic than Elma was about the chances of that happening.

'Hörður,' Elma said, going over to her boss.

'Hmm?' Hörður looked up. He appeared bemused, as if he'd been lost in thought. Elma nodded towards the bag he was holding.

'Did they find anything?'

'Well…' Hörður hesitated. 'This note. I don't really know how I'm to…' He broke off and they both glanced round at a sudden blast of loud music.

The music, which was booming from a car that had just drawn up by the pavement, was abruptly cut off. Out stepped a man who Elma immediately recognised as Krummi. He was oddly unchanged, almost as if time had stood still: as boyish as ever, with the same nonchalant walk and piercing stare. All that had changed were his clothes and hair. He no longer wore ripped jeans that hung low on his hips and his hair no longer had blond highlights. Today he was dressed in a black shirt, dark-blue trousers and a black coat. He gave Elma a brief once-over as he walked up to Hörður. Seeing from his expression that he didn't recognise her, she emitted a silent sigh of relief.

'What's up?' he asked, slapping Hörður on the shoulder. It was obvious they knew each other. 'I hear the police have taken over our garage.'

Hörður smiled, slipping the plastic bag unobtrusively into his pocket. 'Nothing to worry about. It's just a precaution as the car may be linked to a case we're investigating.'

'The murder case?' Krummi asked, bending to see inside the garage.

Hörður nodded. 'Tell me, do you have a key to your parents' house?'

'Yes, of course,' Krummi said. 'But I didn't come here while they were away. I've had too much on.'

'Yes, right, I'm sure,' Hörður said. 'Still coaching the football team? I only ask because it doesn't look as if anyone has broken in or tampered with the garage door. So maybe it was left unlocked. You haven't by any chance mislaid the keys or forgotten them somewhere?'

'No, they're where they should be. The door must have been unlocked,' Krummi said, frowning. 'I'd be surprised, though. Mum's always so anal about locking everything. There's enough junk in there, after all. Of course, you never used to have to lock your doors but times have changed.'

'Do you know if anyone else had keys to the house?'

'No, you'd have to ask the old folks. As far as I know, it's only us kids – me and my sister Hanna – who have keys,' Krummi said. 'Anyway, mate, I won't hold you up. I just came round to catch up with my mum and dad.' He waved and went into the house. As he passed he threw Elma another glance and this time grinned in a way that caused her stomach to lurch. Against her will, she dropped her eyes, feeling the red blood rising to her cheeks.

Hörður wasn't himself when they got back to the police station. He seemed distracted and there was an uncharacteristically deep furrow between his brows. Elma had never seen him out of his depth before. He'd always given the appearance of having everything under control. Although at times she felt like an awkward teenager in his presence, she appreciated his positive attitude and imperturbable manner. Her boss in Reykjavík had been a very different type, the kind who believed that a man in his position should maintain a certain distance from his subordinates. She had always been a little scared of him and insecure about how to behave in his presence, and was sure that had been exactly the way he wanted it. Much as she missed her old colleagues, she didn't miss her boss at all.

'Gulla, would you be a dear and make us some fresh coffee? It would be great to have a thermos in here,' Hörður said, holding open the door for Sævar and Elma. As soon as forensics had finished going over the car, they had gone straight back to the station, where their colleagues in uniform were eagerly awaiting news. Hörður wouldn't answer any questions right away, however, merely told them that he'd hold a progress meeting later. He, Sævar and Elma took seats in the small meeting room, placing the box forensics had given them in the middle of the table.

'Right,' Hörður said, stroking his chin pensively before taking out the small plastic evidence bag that Elma had seen him studying earlier. 'This was found in Elísabet's car.' He put it on the table and Elma and Sævar leant over to examine it.

The bag contained a small note with only two things written on it: an address and a telephone number.

'This is a lead, isn't it?' Sævar asked, looking enquiringly at his boss. 'Presumably it's someone Elísabet was intending to meet.'

Hörður nodded but Elma got the feeling he wasn't happy about the contents of the note. There was a knock on the door and Gulla came in carrying a large thermos of coffee and a bowl of biscuits. 'Don't mind me,' she said, but none of them uttered another word until she had left the room.

'This is the address of Bjarni Hendriksson and his wife Magnea,' Hörður said, once the door had closed and they were alone again.

'The number belongs to Bjarni too,' said Elma, who had quickly looked it up on her phone. 'What do we know about Bjarni Hendriksson? I mean, obviously I'm aware that he and his father run an estate agent's here. I remember him from school, of course, but otherwise I don't know much about him.'

'Yes, the business belongs to the brothers, Hendrik and Tómas, though I understand Bjarni's about to take over the management,' Hörður said. 'Surely you must know who Bjarni Hendriksson is? How long is it since you lived here?'

'Quite a while.'

'Everyone here knows Bjarni,' Sævar explained. 'He's a promi-
nent figure in local business and politics, and used to be a
promising footballer too.'

'Like Hendrik,' Hörður chipped in.

'He's married to Magnea, who teaches the younger classes at
Grundi School,' Sævar added. 'Happily married, I'd always
assumed.'

'Now, now, don't let's jump to conclusions,' Hörður said. 'There
has to be some reasonable explanation – I'm sure of it.'

'But Elísabet didn't make any calls to Bjarni,' Elma said. Bjarni's
number hadn't been listed in Elísabet's phone records, and Elma
doubted she would have called him from any other phone.

'If she wrote down his address and phone number, there's a
chance she went to see him,' Sævar reasoned. 'Won't we have to
talk to them?'

He and Elma both looked at Hörður, who nodded reluctantly.

'Yes. I suppose we have no choice,' he said heavily, then
coughed and rose to his feet without another word. He went out,
leaving them alone in the room.

Hörður sat in his office, his arms folded, staring out at the rain
that had started falling again after a brief let-up. Taking a deep
breath, he picked up his desk phone, but at that moment his
mobile started vibrating in his pocket and he put down the receiver with a sigh of relief.

'I just wanted to check when you're coming home.' It was his
wife Gígja. There was a lot of noise going on in the background.
He glanced at the clock: it was almost six, so she must be at the
supermarket.

'I'm not sure. Late, probably.' But, then again, perhaps the call
to Bjarni could wait until tomorrow morning. He longed to go
home and take a shower. Relax in front of the news.

'You won't be back for supper, then,' Gígja said, without waiting for an answer. 'You can just eat the leftovers when you get home.'

He rumbled something that sounded like agreement and said goodbye.

Hörður picked up his work phone again and tapped in the number he had scribbled down on a piece of paper. He didn't have to wait long for it to be answered.

'Magnea,' said a woman's voice.

Hörður was a little flustered as he'd been expecting Bjarni. 'Is Bjarni there?'

'Hang on, he's around here somewhere,' Magnea said. He heard rustling and a muffled conversation, then a deep voice at the other end said:

'Bjarni.'

'Hello, Bjarni, it's Hörður.' He knew Bjarni would immediately realise who it was.

'Oh, hi, Hörður. How are you doing?' The deep voice sounded warmer.

'Good. I'm well,' Hörður said, then hesitated.

'How's the little girl? It was a girl, wasn't it? Magnea said she was a bit premature.'

'Yes, that's right. Both mother and daughter are doing very well, thank you. She arrived four weeks early but it all went smoothly.' He coughed. 'Actually, I'm ringing about another matter. I need you to pop round to the station. You see, your name's come up in connection with a case we're investigating.'

There was silence at the other end.

'If you could make it soon that would be very helpful,' Hörður added.

'Of course, if there's something I can help you with. Which case is it regarding, if you don't mind my asking?' Bjarni's tone was still light, but he couldn't hide his curiosity.

'I'll tell you all about it when you get here,' Hörður said. 'But don't worry, it's just an informal chat and I can always come round to yours if that would be more convenient.'

'No need. I'll come over,' Bjarni replied quickly.

'Good, then I'll see you in a minute,' Hörður said and rang off.

Ⱡ

'Wouldn't it be more usual to go round to his?' Elma asked, when Hörður rejoined them.

'No, it's better like this,' Hörður said firmly. I'd rather not involve his wife in the unlikely event that there was something going on between him and Elísabet. That wouldn't do anyone any good.'

Elma refrained from comment. It was better not to ask why Hörður regarded the possibility as so unlikely. Or why he wanted to protect Bjarni. She remembered her mother saying that Hörður was too concerned about being liked by the locals. No doubt it was like that in most small communities, she thought. The intimacy of small-town life made conducting investigations like this fraught with difficulty since the police had to tread carefully to avoid arousing hostility.

When Bjarni arrived, Elma could immediately see why he was so popular. His charm extended to both his manners and his appearance: he had grown up to be tall and muscular, with fair hair and neatly trimmed stubble on his otherwise clean-shaven face. Under his thick, well-defined eyebrows, his gaze was good-natured but determined. He bestowed a polite smile on Elma and Sævar when he entered the room, then greeted Hörður like an old friend. Elma found herself instinctively returning his smile when he shook her hand and introduced himself.

'Well, what's it all about?' Bjarni asked, once they were seated. 'I'm dying of curiosity.'

'This is your number, isn't it?' Hörður asked in a casually friendly voice and read it out.

'No, that's Magnea's number,' Bjarni replied in surprise. 'She answered when you rang earlier, didn't she?'

'But … the number's registered in your name,' Hörður said.

'Yes, true. But that's the phone Magnea uses. Is that why you wanted to talk to me? What's this all about?'

Hörður cleared his throat and lowered his eyes to the paper he was holding.

'The phone number turned up in the course of an inquiry,' he said after a moment. 'And your address too.'

'The murder at the lighthouse?' Bjarni was quick to make the connection.

Hörður nodded.

'And you think … what? That my wife had something to do with that?' Bjarni laughed incredulously.

Seeing Hörður's awkwardness, Elma intervened. 'Naturally, we need to talk to everyone the victim may have been in contact with in the days leading up to her death,' she said in a reasonable voice. She didn't like the way the balance of power had shifted in the room: Hörður was tiptoeing around this man as if terrified of offending him. Whereas she couldn't care less about his status in the town.

'This is a pretty strange way of going about things, Hörður,' Bjarni said, as if Elma hadn't spoken. 'It's like I'm under suspicion.' He laughed again. 'You can hardly think there was anything going on between me and that woman?'

'We're simply trying to find out what happened,' Hörður said in a placatory tone.

Bjarni got to his feet without once taking his eyes off Hörður. His smile had turned distinctly chilly.

'Well, it's obviously silly season for the police,' he said. 'Are you seriously telling me that's all you've got to go on?'

'It's just one of the leads we're duty bound to follow up,' Elma answered coolly, before Hörður could get a word in. 'I'm afraid we can't reveal any further information about the case at this stage.'

Still ignoring her, Bjarni addressed Hörður: 'Should I send Magnea round to see you, then, or do you want to come home with me now and talk to her there?'

'Sævar and I will come with you,' Hörður said hastily, dropping his eyes to avoid Bjarni's stinging look.

Elma would have given anything to be able to ask Hörður to stay behind while she went with Sævar to interview Magnea. Apparently, Hörður's son was a close friend of Bjarni's, and she was afraid that their acquaintance would prevent the necessary questions from being asked. But she was in no position to tell her boss what to do and had to settle instead for going through the rest of the material that forensics had found in Elísabet's car.

She pulled on a pair of latex gloves. The box turned out to contain a collection of papers and other stuff that had been recovered from the car. On top was a knitted scarf, a black child's mitten and a bottle of mascara. Elma leafed through the papers, skimming the contents: bills and documents relating to the car, including a service report and a log recording when the oil was changed. There were only two things that might potentially be of interest. One was a large envelope addressed to Eiríkur, bearing the logo of Sigurpáll G. Hannesson, Solicitor. The moment she opened the envelope, she realised what it was: divorce papers. So they'd been right: if Elísabet had gone to see a lawyer about getting a divorce, it must be because Eiríkur had refused to grant her one. Normally, when both parties agreed to divorce, it was enough for them to go and see a magistrate. No doubt she had been thinking of the children too. Was it possible that she hadn't wanted Eiríkur to have joint custody? Or had she been afraid of losing custody rights herself?

The other envelope was unmarked, small, made of thin white paper, and appeared to be empty. She tore it carefully open.

Inside was a photograph. A creased, blurred image, taken with one of those old Polaroid cameras that printed the photo instantly. It showed a girl with her head bowed and her face obscured by her long, brown hair. Although the picture was rather dark, Elma recognised the room at once. It was the attic bedroom she had visited earlier that day; there was the parquet flooring and the cupboard under the sloping roof in the background. The girl couldn't have been more than eight or nine. She was standing with her arms at her sides, in nothing but a pair of white knickers, her eyes lowered to the floor. Her knees turned in a little and her back was slightly hunched, as if to make herself as inconspicuous as possible. What struck Elma immediately was the girl's vulnerability. Whoever took the picture was someone she was frightened of. There was no doubt in Elma's mind: the child's attitude conveyed abject fear and misery.

▌

Bjarni and Magnea lived in a large, detached house on the outskirts of Akranes, near Garðalundur, the local forestry plantation. As yet there were few other houses in the area, just the odd new-build standing on a patch of dirt. But now that the financial crisis was in the past and the good times had returned, Sævar thought, they would probably soon be joined by others. Sure enough, he saw signs that foundations were already being excavated in several places.

Bjarni had driven on ahead and by the time they reached the house he had already gone inside to warn his wife. This annoyed Sævar, though he refrained from saying so to Hörður. Personally, he felt it was important to observe the initial reactions of the subjects they interviewed. An evasive glance, unnaturally fast breathing or hesitation when answering – they all told their own story about the person's state of mind. But, in this case, Magnea would have had time to recover and prepare what she wanted to say.

Before they could knock, the door opened and there she was, smiling a welcome, in a loose, pastel roll-neck jumper and black leggings. Her hair was drawn up in a high knot, with a few loose curls artfully framing her face. She looked quite different from the times Sævar had seen her before. Usually, she was so smartly dressed that she gave the impression of working in a bank rather than a school.

Magnea greeted them and invited them in. Having wiped his wet shoes conscientiously on the mat, Sævar followed her through the hall. Inside, the ceiling was high and the house smelled of newly varnished wood.

'We only moved in recently,' Magnea said, as if reading his mind. 'That's why it's not finished yet. I keep nagging Bjarni about the skirting board, but you know how it is. There's always so much to do, but for some reason it doesn't seem to bother him as much as me.' She laughed.

Sævar hadn't noticed any unfinished touches but now saw that the skirting board hadn't yet been attached in the kitchen.

'Coffee?' Magnea looked at them both, her eyebrows raised enquiringly.

'I wouldn't mind, if it's not too much trouble,' said Hörður. Sævar merely nodded. He didn't usually drink coffee in the evening but today seemed like it was never going to end.

Magnea reached up to a glass-fronted cupboard and took down two cups. No one spoke while the coffee machine was grinding the beans, then filling the cups. Magnea poured herself a glass of water and sat down facing them. 'Bjarni told me my number had come up in connection with the inquiry into Elísabet's death.'

'That's right. We found her car earlier today, and the thing is, it appears she wrote down your and Bjarni's phone number and address,' Hörður said. 'Or, rather, your mobile number. So we were wondering if Elísabet had tried to get in touch with you.'

Magnea nodded composedly. 'Yes, she did. Elísabet came round here last Saturday. She'd emailed me. I kept meaning to answer but forgot. I hadn't heard from her for years.'

'You used to know her, then?' Sævar asked. He wondered how the team going through Elísabet's computer could have failed to notice the email or emails. Was it possible she had sent them from a different address? From another email account that Eiríkur wasn't aware of?

Magnea shrugged. 'I wouldn't exactly say I knew her. We were in the same class at school but we were never friends.'

'Then why did she get in touch with you after all these years?'

'She wanted to meet me. She seemed worked up about something.' Magnea glanced down the hallway as a television was switched on loudly in another part of the house. 'I didn't have time to talk to her, though, because we were having a dinner party that evening.' Magnea turned her gaze back to the two policemen. 'But she came round anyway, uninvited, and knocked on the door.'

'What did she say?'

'Not much. I mean, she wanted to talk but I'm afraid I was a bit short with her, and I regret it now, after what … happened to her.' Magnea took a mouthful of water.

'And she just went away again?'

'Yes, I told her I'd talk to her later in the evening. She wanted to meet me by the lighthouse, of all places.' Magnea shook her head and took another drink of water. 'I was expecting our guests to arrive any minute, so I just said OK.'

'And did you go and meet her?' Sævar asked.

'No, of course not,' Magnea snapped, then smiled apologetically when she realised how sharply she had spoken. 'I'd drunk a couple of glasses of wine by then and didn't want to drive. And, anyway, dinner went on so late that, to be honest, our meeting completely slipped my mind. It only came back to me when I heard she'd been found dead.'

'I see,' said Hörður. 'Do you know what she wanted to talk to you about?'

'No. I've absolutely no idea.'

'What was Elísabet like at school?' Sævar asked, changing tack.

'God, it's been so long – almost thirty years,' Magnea said. She drew a deep breath and her gaze strayed to the window. 'She was very quiet. I don't remember particularly noticing her. Except maybe because she was so scruffy. And she always stank of smoke.'

'Cigarette smoke?'

'Yes, she always stank of cigarettes. Of course, it was more common for people to smoke in those days. I mean, my parents used to.' Magnea smiled. 'But they were careful not to do it indoors. I imagine Elísabet's parents didn't even bother to open a window. The poor kid smelled like an ashtray.'

'Times have certainly changed,' Hörður said. When the TV abruptly went silent, he shot an uneasy glance into the hallway.

'What about friends?' Sævar asked. 'Did Elísabet have any friends that you can remember?'

'No, none. She always seemed to be alone.' Magnea dropped her eyes to her glass as she answered. From the evasiveness of her gaze, Sævar had the feeling she wasn't telling them everything she knew.

'Well, how's it going?' Bjarni came into the kitchen. 'I hope we've been able to help you.'

Hörður cleared his throat and rose to his feet. 'We're about done here,' he said, and shook hands with both Magnea and Bjarni. Reluctantly, Sævar followed his example.

'Just one more thing,' Sævar said as they were going to the front door. 'Why didn't you let us know she'd come round? You must have heard our appeal for information.'

'I'm afraid it just didn't occur to me that it was important,' Magnea replied, with an unnaturally forced laugh. 'I mean, I spoke to her for all of two minutes, then I never saw her again.'

Sævar merely nodded and said goodbye. He didn't believe a word she'd said.

'Well, that wasn't much use,' Hörður remarked, once they were back in the car.

'At least we now know she had something on her mind that she wanted to talk about.' Sævar stared distractedly out of the window. 'Actually, I reckon Magnea knows more than she's letting on. Elísabet can't have come round to her house for no reason.'

'Oh, I'm not so sure.' Hörður turned the key in the ignition. 'Going by what we've heard about Elísabet, she doesn't seem to have been very stable.'

Sævar mumbled a noncommittal reply but on the way home he couldn't help thinking that maybe Elma was right after all; maybe the case had nothing to do with the husband or a lover but with something else entirely.

Magnea felt sick. The moment the police had gone, she hurried to the bathroom, turned on the shower and threw up in the toilet. Then she sank down to sit on the floor, leaning her head against the cool wall tiles as the room gradually filled with steam. She wished she'd had the courage to confess to the police about the secret that had been weighing on her conscience all these years. But she wasn't brave enough. She knew that if she did, she would lose everything. It would mean moving and starting a new life somewhere else, where nobody knew who she was.

It had been hard enough finding an explanation that would satisfy Bjarni. He hadn't been aware that Elísabet had come round that evening and had been perplexed and suspicious about her failure to mention it. She shouldn't have lied to him; it always looked worse. She didn't know why she always lied. Ever since she was a little girl she had got herself into trouble by telling little fibs. She had embellished her stories, lied to her friends about what she'd done at the weekend, made up stuff about people she didn't know. It wasn't a cry for attention because she'd always been the centre of attention. The words just came out before she could stop them.

But there was one lie she would have to live with. One lie that she would never be able to shrug off.

She stroked her flat belly and felt the warmth spreading through her as it always did when she thought about her unborn child. She knew she would never be able to tell anyone. Bjarni would never forgive her. And Akranes society certainly wouldn't. No, she couldn't reveal her secret. She'd have to take it to her grave. But at least now she no longer had to be afraid that someone else would tell, since the only other person who had shared the secret was dead. And her own lips were sealed.

Akranes 1990

Sometimes she did bad things. She didn't know why and couldn't possibly explain it but she knew there was something wicked inside her.

She thought about this as she watched the spider venture out of its lair under the stones by their house and start to crawl up the wall. Then she picked it up between finger and thumb and began tearing off its legs, one by one. When she had finished, she put what was left of the spider on the step and watched it jerking feebly.

It was a Saturday and she was going round to Sara's later but it was still too early and everyone was asleep in the house. She wondered if it was too early to go to Solla's. Her stomach was rumbling and Solla often had something nice to eat at weekends: freshly baked bread or cinnamon rolls sprinkled with sugar. She was fond of Solla. She didn't know what she'd do if Solla wasn't next door to look after her. Putting her finger on the spider's abdomen, which had almost stopped twitching, she squashed it until there was nothing left but a small black mark on the concrete step.

Sara was unbelievably lucky. She lived nearby, in a big house with a beautiful garden, and her mother was always home. She baked cakes and made delicious food and sometimes gave them money for ice-cream. Then they would run out to the Einarsbúð grocery or the kiosk to buy ice lollies.

Sara's long, blonde hair was perfectly straight and smooth, unlike her own unruly mop that stuck out wildly in all directions. Sara always wore new, clean clothes too and came to school with a packed lunch so generous that she used to share it with Elísabet. They walked home from school together almost every day and played together well into the evenings. Sometimes they played outside, but best of all was when they went round to Sara's house. She had a pretty, pink bedroom and an enormous doll's house full of furniture and dolls, which they used to dress up. Everything Sara owned was pink and smelled nice. Her bed, her clothes, her room.

She herself smelled of such nice shampoo that Elísabet used to furtively sniff her hair when she wasn't looking.

Elísabet had never had a friend before. It changed everything. But she was terribly afraid that if she told Sara the things she did and how wicked she was, Sara would stop being her friend. So she said nothing and kept her secret, even though she wanted to tell her so badly that she thought one day she might burst if she didn't.

Elma couldn't get the photo of the little girl out of her mind. She squinted at the glowing computer screen. According to the Icelandic land registry, the house on Krókatún had changed hands four times since 1980. Up until 1982, it had been owned by one Sighvatur Kristjánsson. Elma's eyes opened wide when she saw that Hendrik Larsen had bought the house from him and owned it until 2006, but she soon realised that this didn't necessarily mean anything. Hendrik owned a lot of rental property in the town through his estate agent business, Fastnes Ltd, so it was unlikely he had ever actually lived in this particular house himself. Besides, he had no daughter, only a son, Bjarni.

A couple called Andrea Fransdóttir and Haraldur Traustason had bought the house in 2006 and owned it until 2009, when it was repossessed by the Housing Financing Fund, the government-owned mortgage lender. When Elma searched for Sighvatur Kristjánsson's current residence she drew a blank, but Andrea and Haraldur were both living in Reykjavík, though at different addresses. Elma wondered if their financial difficulties had led to the breakdown of their marriage, as was so often the case. After checking their Facebook pages, she was sure that they couldn't have had any offspring together. The children with them in the pictures were too young to have been born before 2009.

She entered Sighvatur Kristjánsson's name in the search engine. The results included an obituary, obviously for the right man, reporting that he had died a little under ten years ago at the Höfði Nursing Home in Akranes. He had been born in 1926, lived in Akranes all his life and had four children, three boys and one girl. They had all written obituaries in which they praised their father, describing him as hardworking and a loving father and grandfather who used to take them on fishing trips on his boat in the summers, letting them cast out lines and sell the fish they caught. The photograph showed a weather-beaten, middle-aged man, clad in a traditional *lopapeysa* jumper and smiling into the sun. It wasn't the usual sort of obituary portrait and had obviously been taken years before he died, but perhaps it was the picture that best captured his character. His children concluded their memories of him by saying that he was now with their mother in the afterlife, whatever that might mean. Elma looked up Sighvatur's daughter and saw that she was so fair that there was no chance she could have been the girl in the photo.

It could only have been Elísabet. She had lived in the house during the period when it belonged to Hendrik, so, logically, her mother must have been renting from him. Bearing that in mind, could it be a coincidence that his son's name had cropped up in the course of the investigation?

Elma called up Hendrik's Facebook page. His profile picture showed him in the act of swinging back a golf club. He was wearing light khaki trousers, a dark-blue polo-neck and a peaked cap. Elma remembered seeing him around town in her youth, but from what she could see of his face now, he appeared to be in his sixties and had the sort of tan you only get from expensive holidays in the sun. Judging by the palm trees in the background, the photo must have been taken in some tropical paradise.

She scrolled down the page, pausing at a family picture taken on some special occasion. There was Hendrik in a suit, standing next to a petite woman who was staring unsmilingly at the camera. Beside her was a stunning younger woman with a thick mane of blonde hair, her white teeth bared in a dazzling smile. She was tagged as *Magnea Arngrímsdóttir* – the woman Sævar and Hörður were interviewing at this very moment. Bjarni had his arm around her waist. He was very like his father: tall and tanned, wearing the same smile, though he was fair where Hendrik was dark. Elma had recognised him immediately when he came to the station. Although he was several years older than her, she remembered him well from her youth.

Elma closed the website and sat back in her chair, thinking. She recalled the face of the young woman she had visited just over a week ago, marred with bruises where her much older boyfriend had taken his fists to her. Tómas, Hendrik's brother, was a partner in the family business. And it wouldn't be long now before Bjarni took over.

Hunching over the keyboard again, Elma opened the Akranes photography archive and tracked down the picture of Elísabet with a couple of her classmates in 1989. Yes, there could be no doubt: it was the same girl in both pictures. Not many people in Akranes possessed such dark hair or such long, naturally dark eyelashes. Elma rested her chin on her hand as she studied the old Polaroid of Elísabet in her underwear. Who had taken it? Who had been with Elísabet in her room that day?

Elma sat in the kitchen waiting impatiently for Hörður and Sævar to get back from interviewing Magnea. She toyed with the crispbread she had buttered herself but found she had no appetite, in spite of her empty stomach. She had finished going through all the material from the car but had discovered nothing else of interest, only the divorce papers and the photo. The image was etched on her retinas; she couldn't stop thinking about the child and what she might have suffered.

'What's this?' Sævar asked, taking the papers she held out to them the moment they walked through the door.

'I reckon we've solved the mystery of her visit to the lawyer,' Elma said. 'It turns out she was applying for a divorce through the courts.'

'Meaning what?' Sævar asked.

'Basically, that they hadn't agreed to a separation before a magistrate,' Elma explained. 'Usually that's because one of the couple is resisting a divorce.'

'So,' Hörður said, 'in other words, Eiríkur must have refused to grant her a divorce, as we originally suspected. Yes, that has to be it.'

'I found this too,' Elma said, before Hörður could get too

excited about the news. She placed the Polaroid of the girl on the table.

'Is that Elísabet?' Sævar sat down and examined the picture.

Elma nodded. 'I think so. Of course it's impossible to say for sure, but it definitely looks like her. See, here's a photo of her aged six, taken at school.' Elma pointed to the picture on her computer screen. 'The girl in the Polaroid is a little older but I don't think there's much doubt it's Elísabet. And I recognise the room – it's the attic in the house on Krókatún.'

'Who do you think took the photo? Could someone have...?'

'I think the photographer was someone the girl was afraid of,' Elma said. 'Look at the way she's standing. It's clear she's uncomfortable. If you ask me, the person behind the camera had done something to her.' Elma met Hörður's eye. 'I think we should at least consider the possibility that this is why Elísabet came to Akranes. That she wanted to confront the person who took that picture. There has to be a reason why she brought it with her.'

'Couldn't her mother have taken it?' Hörður asked. He bent forwards and examined the photo.

'I very much doubt it,' Elma said. The truth was, she hadn't even considered the possibility. 'Mothers don't take pictures like that,' she added, but, even as she said it, she was no longer sure. Could Elísabet have been that frightened of Halla?

'Quite aside from that, we can't be sure that it's Elísabet,' Hörður pointed out.

Elma silently replaced the Polaroid in the envelope. She was positive she was right and in that moment was filled with a determination to pursue this line of inquiry. But she didn't tell Hörður that, merely changed the subject and asked instead: 'What did Magnea have to say?'

Hörður told her about the visit and what had emerged.

'And you really believe Magnea didn't know anything? She must have some idea what Elísabet wanted to talk about,' Elma objected. 'No one would come to see you after so many years without a very good reason. And, if not, why wasn't Magnea interested? Why did she just tell Elísabet to go away? I know I'd have been dying of curiosity if some long-forgotten classmate had come round urgently wanting to talk to me.'

'I agree,' Sævar said. 'I definitely got the feeling she wasn't being straight with us.'

'Magnea knew Elísabet was at the lighthouse,' Elma persisted, trying unsuccessfully to catch Hörður's eye. 'She may have been the only person who knew.'

Hörður nodded reluctantly. 'Yes, you're right – at least, she's the only person we're aware of. Though someone could have followed Elísabet and seized their chance while she was standing there alone. It's quite an isolated spot at that time of night, as you said yourself.'

Elma sighed. Although they now had a clearer picture of Elísabet's movements and had established who she had visited shortly before she went out to the lighthouse, they were still none the wiser about her killer's identity or motive. The case just kept throwing up more questions than answers. Elma's stomach chose that moment to growl loudly in the hushed meeting room, and she took a quick bite of crispbread. She was reassuring herself that no one had noticed when she caught Sævar's lips twitching.

'At any rate,' he said, 'we need to talk to Bjarni and Magnea's friends and confirm that they spent the evening with them.'

'Yes, right. And we'll call Eiríkur in tomorrow,' Hörður said. 'Even though there's no real evidence to suggest he was with Elísabet that evening, their marriage was clearly rockier than he's willing to admit.'

Hörður's frown had been deepening ever since they'd got back to the police station. He sat leafing distractedly through the case file, pausing from time to time to read a line or two, then continuing dispiritedly to turn the pages. Finally, he seemed to pull himself together. He closed the file, straightened his back and said with sudden decision: 'I think we've missed a trick in relation to Eiríkur. His only alibi is his boys, but they were almost certainly asleep at the time. He must have found out that she was planning to divorce him. You know, I have a feeling we're on the verge of a breakthrough.' He rose, picked up his jacket and walked out of the meeting room, humming.

Elma and Sævar looked at each other. Neither of them shared Hörður's confidence that the solution was in sight.

As Elma was approaching her building, she noticed a young man get out of a car parked outside and head to the front door. Although she had lived there for several weeks, she had never seen him before. He was wearing a tracksuit and had a backpack slung over one shoulder. 'Have you just moved in?' he asked, holding the door open for her.

'Yes,' Elma said, smiling. 'Several weeks ago, actually.' He must be slightly younger than her; in his late twenties, no more.

'Sorry not to have said hello before but I've hardly been home. I work on a freezer trawler and I'm usually away for a month at a time.'

So not all her neighbours were pensioners. The thought cheered Elma up. Since moving back to Akranes and renting this flat, she hadn't known what to feel. Sometimes she felt as old as her pensioner neighbours; at least, her life seemed to follow the same pattern as theirs: long evenings spent alone at home, interspersed with walks at weekends. But another part of her felt like a teenager again, hardly ever cooking for herself, just going round to her parents' house, where she lay on the sofa and watched the news with her father while her mother got the meal ready. Just like she used to fifteen years ago.

'Do you get a good break between trips?' she asked, once they were inside.

'Yes, I've got a month off now. But I use the time to study, so it's not much of a holiday.' He paused in the corridor, smiling. 'What do you do? You haven't just finished work, have you?'

'Yes, I'm in the police. It was a long day today,' she said, yawning as if to prove how tired she was.

The young man nodded and, pausing before entering his flat, which was opposite hers, he told her to knock on his door if she ever needed any eggs or sugar. Not that he had either, but it was always nice to have a visitor, he added with a wink.

Once Elma had closed her door behind her, she became acutely aware of the silence. But in no time she had banished it with the sound of running water as she filled a bath for herself. Pulling off her clothes, she chucked them on the dark tiles of the bathroom floor. The pile of dirty laundry was growing by the day but she didn't care: the flat was already such a tip that a few more clothes were neither here nor there. The bags from the furniture shop were still in the kitchen, waiting to be unpacked. The milk in the fridge hadn't even been opened, though it had passed its use-by date several days ago. There had been no time this week to get her life in order.

She lowered herself carefully into the hot water and felt the tension flowing out of her limbs. She couldn't resist the urge to dip her head under the water, then immediately regretted it. If she went to sleep with wet hair, it invariably stuck up in wild tufts, like a badly tended lawn, when she woke up next morning.

The plan was to bring Eiríkur in for a formal interview tomorrow. Hörður had seized on the divorce papers as confirmation of his guilt, but Elma was sceptical. For one thing, they still couldn't explain how he could have parked Elísabet's car in the garage since he had no known connection to the couple who owned it. Elma was clinging to the hope that forensics would find some clue in the car that would help to clarify what had happened. She was also haunted by the Polaroid of the little girl, who she was convinced was Elísabet. Had the mysterious person behind the camera been the reason for Elísabet's unwillingness to visit the town? Did he or she still live in Akranes?

Elma's eyelids grew heavy and gradually she ceased to be

aware of her body. As her breathing slowed, the bath water became almost perfectly smooth.

She was lying in a soft bed, tucked up in white sheets embroidered with flowers. The heat in the dark room was suffocating. He was sitting on the edge of the bed, his back to her, his head turned to the window. There was nothing to see out there but darkness and the glow of the streetlights reflecting off the black tarmac. She sat up in bed and reached out to touch his bare back. 'Davíð,' she whispered, but her hand caught at thin air.

She opened her eyes with a jolt. The white wall tiles screamed at her. The bathwater had gone cold. She stood up clumsily and wrapped her soft dressing gown tightly around herself to stop her shivering. When she finally fell asleep, the night passed without dreams but when she awoke next morning the sense of loss was almost more than she could bear.

The evening began much as it usually did. Ása followed Hendrik up to the dark-blue house and before they could ring the bell the door opened and Þórný was standing there with a wide smile of welcome on her lips. As ever, Ása immediately felt inferior. Þórný was always so elegant, dressed this time in a perfectly fitting blouse, tasteful skirt and high heels. Ása's own clothes had cost a fortune but however hard she tried, she would never be as glamorous as Þórný. She knew Hendrik thought so too. As usual, they clashed cheeks, then went inside and took off their coats.

'Something smells good,' Hendrik said hoarsely, inhaling appreciatively. He'd drunk a whisky before coming out and the alcohol had deepened and thickened his voice. But the whisky hadn't deterred him from driving and Ása had long ago given up objecting. As if the police would ever dream of pulling over Hendrik Larsen. The very idea was preposterous, he said. But Ása secretly hoped they would stop him one day. Every time they passed a white police vehicle she would stare pointedly at the officers inside, only to be infuriated when they did nothing but nod a respectful greeting to Hendrik. He was never stopped.

'Haraldur's in the kitchen, Hendrik. Do go and find him. Us girls have got some catching up to do.' Þórný winked at Ása. Taking her by the arm, she led her into the better sitting room and waved her to the sofa. 'What news of the family?' Þórný took out two crystal glasses from a large cabinet and half-filled them with port. Then she sat down close beside Ása on the sofa as if creating an air of cosy intimacy and fixed her with her grey-blue eyes.

'Not much,' Ása replied, sipping her port.

'How's Hendrik been since he stopped work? He must be impossible around the house – a man like him, used to working hard enough for three people.' Þórný crossed her legs and demurely pulled down her skirt.

'I hardly see him. He's always on the golf course.' Ása took another sip and felt the warmth spreading inside her.

Þórný gave a tinkling laugh. 'Darling, you need to find a hobby. Come out with my walking group. It's not just about the exercise, though we all need that, of course. It's about company.'

Ása sighed under her breath. Þórný had been pestering her to join this group for years. As far as she could work out, they only walked half the time and spent the rest guzzling cake and coffee. So much for the benefits of exercise.

'I'll see,' Ása said noncommittally. She knew from long experience that there was no point arguing with Þórný.

'It would do you good. It's so important to have a hobby,' Þórný persisted, giving Ása an encouraging smile. 'Now, where's your glass? I'll get you a refill.'

Ása looked down. She hadn't realised how quickly she'd polished off the port. She drank so rarely and when she did, she usually only had a drop. Perhaps it was from habit. She had always held back to compensate for the amount Hendrik put away, because someone in the house had to be sober. But these days who did she have to worry about but herself? She had no children, nothing … The port made her head feel pleasantly fuzzy, lending everything a vaguely unreal air. It made a welcome change. Recently, the world had been only too grimly real. All she wanted was to retreat and forget everything for a while.

'I always used to go to a sewing group in the evenings,' she piped up suddenly. And, as she said it, those days came back to her so vividly: the needles, the brown canvas chairs, the companionable sound of women's voices. 'Now I just knit alone at home.'

And she remembered why she had stopped.

'Why did you stop?' Þórný asked cheerfully.

'Hendrik used to be home in the evenings to babysit. But later he started working so late that I had to be there to take care of the children.' Ása relaxed against the back of the sofa. She yawned and sank deeper into the dark-brown leather, picturing the evenings she had spent away from home. The house they had lived in, with the carpeted sitting room and the beams in their attic bedroom. Waves breaking on the black sand. And she saw in her mind's eye a blonde head and a pair of blue eyes. For a moment she felt an unfamiliar pricking in the corners of her eyes. She hadn't cried for years; not since the accident. Afterwards, she had done nothing but cry for months, but in the end there had been nothing left. It was as if she had drained the well of tears dry. Poured out enough for a lifetime. She didn't cry now either; this feeling was different.

It began like a numbness in her fingers, a numbness that travelled up her arms and back. She felt her skin prickling, then the pain struck, sharp, like a sudden blow. She heard her name being called a long way off until the voice faded into silence like everything else.

Akranes 1990

'What have you done?' Sara looked from her to the cat and back again.

'It was only a stray, Sara,' Elísabet said, rooting in the sand with her stick. 'No one will miss it.'

Sara didn't answer. She didn't need to.

They walked on in silence. Elísabet had begun to regret what she had done. Not because she felt sorry for the cat but because she couldn't bear the accusing note in Sara's voice. Or the way her friend was staring at her as if she was weird. She was filled with a cold fear that Sara wouldn't want to be her friend anymore, now that she knew how wicked she was; the things she was capable of.

But the cat had been more dead than alive when she found it among the rocks on the beach. There had been a big gash on its face, half its ear was missing and it was dragging one leg. It had stopped and hissed when it saw Elísabet; a loud, threatening hiss, baring its sharp little teeth.

Without stopping to think, Elísabet had stooped and picked up a stone. The stone had caught the cat right between the eyes. Elísabet had walked calmly over to its feebly twitching body. As she drew near, it had tried to hiss again but this time when it opened its mouth hardly any noise had come out. Elísabet had picked up another stone, aimed at its head and struck. The cat hadn't moved any more after that.

She had been standing there, contemplating its body, when Sara appeared without warning behind her.

'Shall we dig a grave for it?' Elísabet asked, with her sweetest smile. 'Then at least it'll go to heaven.'

'Elísabet, you...' Sara sighed with an expression of motherly reproach. 'You mustn't do things like that. If anyone found out...'

Feigning shame, Elísabet lowered her eyes to the sand. Then she raised them again and nodded, as if she agreed. As if she wasn't really a bad person. 'I promise never to do it again,' she said meekly.

Sara was regarding her gravely. 'Do you promise?'

Elísabet nodded vehemently.

After a moment Sara smiled. 'All right, then. Where shall we dig the grave?'

Relief flooded Elísabet. It was dawning on her that it would be wiser to keep quiet about some of the things she thought and did.

Friday, 1 December 2017

Eiríkur arrived punctually at the police station, his black Lexus SUV pulling into the car park a few minutes before ten. Elma watched from the window as he sat for a minute in his car before opening the door, climbing out and walking briskly towards the building.

Once he was inside, Eiríkur shook hands with them all, smiling politely. Hörður gestured to him to take a seat in the meeting room, facing them across the table. He sat down and waited patiently for one of them to begin. His features were finely etched in the harsh glare of the ceiling light and Elma thought he appeared much younger than he was. He was neatly dressed as before, in a light-blue jumper and dark-blue trousers.

Hörður cleared his throat. 'To start off, I'd like to update you on the progress of the investigation. Yesterday we found Elísabet's car.'

'Where was it?' Eiríkur sat up.

'It turned up in a garage belonging to a couple here in Akranes. They discovered it yesterday when they got home from a holiday abroad.'

Eiríkur was staring at them, his eyes wide. 'In their garage? Doesn't that mean they must be involved?'

'No. Like I said, they were abroad at the time Elísabet died.' Hörður read out the couple's name. 'Do you know these people or did Elísabet have any contact with them that you're aware of?'

Eiríkur shook his head. 'No, I've never heard their names before. But then I'm not familiar with Akranes. I even had to use sat nav to find the police station.'

'You must have come here at some point, surely?' Elma said, though she knew that few people from Reykjavík bothered to visit the town. Stuck out at the end of the Skagi Peninsula, Akranes wasn't on the way anywhere and most Icelanders simply passed it by, continuing north to Borgarnes or south to the capital.

'No. Except when I was younger and came to the swimming pool. I once attended a football tournament here too, I think. Apart from that, I just can't remember ever having any reason to come here. Did you find anything in the car?'

Hörður glanced down at his notepad, then back at Eiríkur. 'I know we've already asked you this, but could you describe your relationship with Elísabet for me?'

'Our relationship?' Eiríkur echoed. 'What do you mean? We were married and had children, with all that goes with it. One minute sunshine, the next showers.' His smile was unconvincing.

Without a word, Hörður slid the divorce papers across the table to Eiríkur, who skimmed them quickly, then sat back, his lips stretched in a humourless grin that gave Elma an uneasy feeling in the pit of her stomach. 'I hadn't a clue she'd gone that far,' he said. 'She mentioned something a while ago about wanting a divorce but then said no more about it.'

'Did you refuse?'

Eiríkur snorted. 'Refuse? Yes and no. I thought we should give it another go, but it's not like I'd have refused if she'd been serious. I just knew she wasn't. Elísabet was … well, she could be a bit up and down. Her moods changed from day to day.'

'What was her mood like in the days before she left?'

'I didn't notice anything out of the ordinary or I'd have told you,' Eiríkur replied. 'Look, are we done here?' He pushed back his chair and stood up.

Elma intervened before he could go anywhere: 'In light of this information I'm afraid we need to take a closer look at your relationship.' Eiríkur's head swung round to her and she went on: 'We may need to talk to the school, your employers and anyone else you both had dealings with.'

'For Christ's sake, is that really necessary?' Eiríkur threw up his hands.

'May I remind you that we're doing everything in our power

to find out who killed your wife,' Elma said coolly, and could hear how provocative she sounded. 'Surely you don't have any objection to that?'

Eiríkur dithered for a beat, then sat down again, his eyes resting on Elma as if mentally reviewing his options. After staring across the table for a moment or two, he seemed to make up his mind. With a shrug, he leant back in his chair and ran his hands through his hair. 'OK. Fine, I admit it. Our relationship could have been better. But I don't know why that should matter. I didn't do anything to her,' he said flatly.

'Was Elísabet cheating on you?' Hörður asked.

Eiríkur was silent, his gaze fixed on the papers in front of him. Then he looked up and shook his head. 'No, I'm the one having an affair. Her name's Bergþóra. We've been seeing each other for a while. She's a single mother, with two boys the same age as Fjalar and Ernir.'

This wasn't at all what Elma had been expecting. Eiríkur's voice didn't betray an ounce of regret and he met their eyes coldly as he told them.

'Has the relationship been going on long?' Elma asked, recovering from her surprise.

Eiríkur shrugged. 'A year. Maybe longer. I can't quite remember.'

'Was that why Elísabet wanted a divorce?' Hörður asked. 'Because she found out you were cheating on her?'

'No, she was totally unaware of that, as far as I know. And even if she had known, I'm sure she wouldn't have cared.'

'Then why did you object to giving her a divorce?' Elma asked.

'Because I loved her,' Eiríkur said, and Elma caught the bitterness in his voice as he added: 'But she never loved me. I'm not sure she ever loved anyone.'

'Busy?' Sævar asked, taking his eyes off the road to smile sideways at Elma. They were on their way to see Eiríkur's mistress, Bergþóra, who lived on a farm in Hvalfjörður.

Elma had been absorbed in typing something on her phone but she glanced up and returned his smile. 'What do you think?' The low sun shone into the car, lending a golden sheen to her pale skin. Sævar noticed that her grey eyes had a hint of green in this light.

'Any plans this evening?' he asked.

Elma didn't immediately answer. 'I don't know,' she said after a pause. 'I suppose it depends how long we have to work.'

Now that she had looked up from her phone, she saw that they were halfway down the fjord, with the long sheet of blue water to their right and low, smooth-topped mountains stretching green and brown on either side. Ahead, in the distance, the four distinctive peaks of Botnssúlur came into view, standing out starkly white against the darker fells. Closer at hand, on the shores of the fjord, the road was passing through an area of hayfields, dotted with white farm buildings with red roofs.

'I think we want that turning.' Belatedly Elma pointed to the left.

Sævar stamped on the brake so hard that she was thrown forwards and was only saved by the seatbelt from bashing her head on the dashboard.

'Sorry,' Sævar said.

'No problem.' Elma rubbed her breast where the seatbelt had tightened uncomfortably across it. 'I'll get my revenge later.'

They parked outside a single-storey house clad in white corrugated iron. Unlike most of the others they had seen, its roof was blue rather than red. Not far off they could see what must be sheep sheds but the paddock in front of them was empty. When they walked up to the gate, an Icelandic sheepdog ran out barking to greet them.

'There's no need for a doorbell with him around,' a cheerful female voice called, and a woman came striding towards them, shielding her eyes from the sun. Her shabby anorak, big wellington boots and grimy gloves all showed that she'd been busy working. Pulling off a glove, she introduced herself and shook their hands. 'Would you like to come in?' she asked, opening the front door of the white bungalow. 'I assume it's me you're here to talk to.'

Bergþóra was a robust-looking woman with fair hair, a weather-beaten face and red-veined cheeks. Elma thought Eiríkur could hardly have found a woman less like Elísabet. Bergþóra obviously wasn't surprised or remotely abashed by their visit, and immediately set about making coffee and getting out some cinnamon buns.

'It must be tough taking care of the farm and the children alone,' Elma remarked.

'Yes and no,' Bergþóra boomed as she placed mugs and plates on the table. Speaking loudly seemed to come naturally to her. 'I've got a good arrangement going with the neighbouring farm. We share the sheep shed, and I only have a small number of animals myself.'

Elma nodded. She hadn't noticed the other farm, which was tucked away at the foot of the mountain, out of sight of the road, but she could see it now from Bergþóra's kitchen window.

'It's beautiful here,' Elma said, taking in the browns, greys and pale greens of the surrounding mountains, the gleaming sheet of water below. She indulged in a momentary fantasy of what it would be like to live in the midst of this dramatic scenery.

'If you ask me, Hvalfjörður's the most beautiful place on earth,' Bergþóra said cheerfully. 'I've always lived here and I expect I always will.'

'The reason we're here is to ask you about Eiríkur,' Sævar intervened, feeling that the civilities had gone on long enough.

'Just a mo.' Bergþóra stood up. 'You've come all this way to see me and no one leaves my house without a coffee inside them.'

She took their mugs, filled them, then pushed the plate of cinnamon buns in their direction. She seemed suddenly flustered and Elma wondered if the coffee was a diversionary tactic to buy her time to think.

'Thanks very much,' Sævar said, sipping the scalding coffee warily. 'About Eiríkur – I gather you've been seeing each other for quite a while.'

Bergþóra nodded matter-of-factly. 'It's not something I'm proud of,' she said. 'Especially since I've been the victim of that sort of behaviour myself. My husband had an affair with another woman, which is one of the reasons why I threw him out and live here alone now with my two boys.' She didn't sound as if she had any regrets. 'Eiríkur and I met through the kids. They often play here together. They're exactly the same age, so it's very convenient.'

'Then presumably you'll know that the boys' mother died last weekend,' Elma said, watching Bergþóra's reaction closely.

'Yes, I know,' Bergþóra replied. 'It's an absolute tragedy and I really hope the person who did it is caught soon. God knows, whatever it might look like, I didn't wish her any harm.'

'Were you aware that Elísabet had asked Eiríkur for a divorce but that he was refusing to grant her one?'

Bergþóra's mouth fell slightly open. 'No, that's the first I've heard of it.'

'Are you surprised?' Elma asked, noting that she seemed dazed, as if the information had completely wrong-footed her.

After a few moments' silence, Bergþóra said flatly: 'Yes. Yes, I have to say I am.' Then she sighed. 'We've talked so often about living together. About making it serious. He was always promising he'd … end it. But he didn't want to hurt her – he said she was so fragile. And I can believe it. I mean, you never met her while she was alive but she came across as terribly vulnerable. That's why I didn't put any pressure on him.' Her face hardening, she dropped her eyes to the coffee cup she was cradling. 'If I'd known…'

'If you'd known, what?' Elma asked, looking at her searchingly.

'If I'd known it was him who was putting up obstacles to getting a divorce, I'd never have opened the door to him yesterday.'

Sævar's and Elma's eyes met. Elma's opinion of Eiríkur, which hadn't been that high to begin with, now took a nosedive. Bergþóra, on the other hand, struck her as a very different, much more straightforward type, and Elma wondered what on earth she saw in Eiríkur. They appeared to have so little in common.

'Where were you on Saturday evening?' Sævar asked.

'I was at a reunion. We meet up once a year – our old class from the agricultural college at Hólar, that is,' Bergþóra replied, her voice as muted as it ever got. 'I stayed the night with friends – they can confirm that.' Without their having to ask, she fetched a pen and paper and wrote down a phone number for them. 'Here, you can ring them if you need to check.'

Elma accepted the piece of paper with a nod. 'Tell me, did Eiríkur ever say anything to you that suggested he hoped something bad would happen to Elísabet?'

Bergþóra had been staring out of the window, her coffee forgotten, but now she turned to Elma. 'Not that I remember. We never talked about Elísabet. He tried to sometimes but I stopped him. It made me so uncomfortable to think about her when we were together. I know I sound like a terrible person but I liked pretending everything was above board.' She smiled in embarrassment and Elma noticed the heightened colour in her cheeks.

Once they had finished their coffee, Elma and Sævar rose to their feet and took their leave of Bergþóra. Elma could see how upset she was by their conversation and guessed that this would be the end of her relationship with Eiríkur.

'There's something I've been wondering about ever since I heard that Elísabet had been found dead,' Bergþóra said, as they were standing in the hall. 'You know how it is ... children are always talking nonsense, but ... now I'm wondering if it might be important.'

'What?'

'Oh, it was just something Fjalar said to me when he was round here several days ago. He said his mother had told him she had to go away for a while because there was something she needed to sort out.' Bergþóra's voice grew suddenly husky as she added: 'This was only a few days before she died.'

Ása had dressed in her clothes from the night before and was sitting on the visitor's chair by the bed, waiting for Hendrik to come and pick her up. When she had come to her senses yesterday evening it was to find herself lying in a white hospital bed with tubes sticking out of the back of her hand. She hadn't immediately been able to work out what had happened, although she'd remembered the dinner party and felt an uncomfortable sensation deep inside her. She'd wondered if she were dying; if her time had finally come. When she tried to sit up, she'd felt a stabbing pain in her head. There had been some kind of dressing on her forehead and she'd thought perhaps she'd had a fall. The last thing she had been able to remember was sitting, drinking port with Þórný. It had occurred to her that she might have been involved in a car accident on the way home.

She had read that people sometimes lost their memory of the preceding days or even months after a severe head trauma. But she'd reasoned that she couldn't have been that badly injured if she could remember her conversation with Þórný. Unless that had happened weeks ago. She had peered around her, searching for some clue to tell her what day it was. It was dark outside but that didn't help much. It was almost always dark at this time of year.

A cheerful, fair-haired nurse had bustled into the room. 'Hello, how are you doing?'

'I ... I'm fine,' Ása had said, from habit. In truth, she had been feeling far from good, but it wasn't like her to give in to self-pity. 'What happened? Did I have an accident?'

'Well, sort of. You fainted earlier this evening.' The nurse had glanced at the clock. 'It's only twenty minutes since you came in. We took a blood test and sent it off for analysis, but it looks as if you just experienced a sudden drop in blood sugar.'

'Oh,' was all Ása had been able to think of to say.

'Your friend was quite worried about you. She's waiting outside.'

'Þórný?' Ása had asked.

'Yes. Your husband's here too. Do you want me to send them in to see you?'

Ása had nodded and the nurse had turned on her heel.

'Darling, we were so worried about you.' Þórný had hugged her. She'd still been wearing the same skirt as earlier. Ása had been relieved to discover that she hadn't been unconscious for long. 'I almost had a heart attack when I saw you collapse on the floor like that. How are you feeling?'

'Tired,' Ása had said truthfully. She was finding it hard to keep her eyes open.

'I spoke to the doctor,' Hendrik had said bracingly. 'He doesn't think it's anything serious. And you can come home tomorrow.' When he'd smiled at her and taken her limp hand in his, Ása had snatched it away, closing her eyes to block out their astonished expressions.

She had spent the night in hospital and now Hendrik was due any minute to pick her up. But Ása didn't want to go home. She would give anything not to have to go back there.

'Twenty-eight … twenty-nine …' Elma drove slowly down the street, ducking and peering through the windscreen in an attempt to spot the house number. She stopped in front of a de-tached house and parked by the kerb. The house was white with a green edging round the roof and there were two cars in the drive: an SUV and a hatchback.

After briefly dropping into the police station, where Hörður had waved them away with an uncharacteristically preoccupied air when they told him about their meeting with Bergþóra, Elma had decided to start making serious enquiries into Elísabet's childhood. To this end, she had found the address of Elísabet's old form teacher, who still lived in Akranes but now taught at the local community college. Sævar had agreed to come with her. Following their interview with Eiríkur and visit to Bergþóra, he was increasingly coming round to the view that Elma was right. There was no evidence to suggest that Eiríkur had been responsible for Elísabet's death. Not only that, but Sævar was convinced that Magnea was mixed up in it somehow.

The garden was neat and carefully tended although it was December and the grass was turning brown. There was a rake propped against the wall and a pair of gardening gloves lying on the path. To the left, a large deck ran the length of the house. The front door was round on the right-hand side, where the drive led to a garage. Elma pressed the bell and they heard it ringing inside. They weren't kept waiting long before the door opened to reveal a tall, short-haired woman in her sixties, wearing a black shirt. She invited them inside, introducing herself as Björg.

Björg led them into the kitchen where Ingibjörn Grétarsson sat immersed in the local paper. He didn't immediately acknowledge them, as if he wanted to finish the article he was reading first. Only then did he remove his thick glasses and close the paper. He was stout with greying hair and a short, snub nose, and wore a diamond-patterned jumper. From her research, Elma knew that he was in his sixties and taught Icelandic, but his staid manner made it hard to picture him teaching young children. He stood up, greeted them formally, then pointed to a couple of chairs facing him.

'Excuse us for disturbing you just after work like this,' Elma began.

'You're not really disturbing us, dear,' Björg assured her, her friendliness making up for her husband's off-putting manner. 'Would you like some coffee?'

'No, thanks. But if I could have a glass of water...' Elma was still feeling a little queasy after Bergþóra's powerful brew.

'I'd be grateful for a glass of water too,' Sævar said with a smile.

'Of course.' Björg ran the tap for a while before filling two glasses. 'Is your visit to do with the woman who was found by the lighthouse?' she asked, her eyes alight with curiosity.

'Yes, it is, actually,' Elma told her. 'I understand she was in your class around thirty years ago,' she added, turning to Ingibjörn.

He coughed. 'Hmm, yes, that's right. I couldn't place the name at first but when they published her picture in the papers, it came back to me. I hadn't seen her for years, though. To tell the truth, I'd forgotten all about her. So many children have crossed my path during my career. Some of them stay here in Akranes all their lives, others leave and you tend to forget those ones.'

'I see.' Elma nodded. Before she could carry on, Björg cut in: 'Wait a minute, I haven't seen you before. Are you new here?' She had drawn up a chair beside Ingibjörn and was studying Elma with interest.

'Yes, I recently moved here. Before that I was in the Reykjavík police.'

'Oh, really? So you decided to have a change and come out here to the sticks?' Björg clasped her fingers on the table. Her nails were long and painted with pale-pink polish.

'Yes...' Elma hesitated. 'Actually, I grew up here.'

'Oh, did you?' Then came the inevitable Icelandic question: 'Who are your parents?'

'Jón and Aðalheiður,' Elma replied, feeling as if the tables had been turned and she was the one being interrogated.

'Jón and Heiða? Heiða who works for the council?'

'That's right,' Elma said and Björg nodded, obviously pleased to be able to slot her into place. 'I wanted to ask...' Elma began, but got no further.

'I recognise you, though,' Björg interrupted, smiling flirtatiously at Sævar. He didn't answer, merely nodded, but Elma saw that his eyes gleamed with amusement. Ingibjörn appeared oblivious. Elma coughed politely and returned to her question: 'Anyway, about Elísabet: I understand she was a bit of a loner as a child – she didn't have many friends. Is that correct?'

'Oh, it's so hard to remember,' Ingibjörn sighed. 'But yes, she was an unusually serious child, that's true.'

'Do you know if there were problems at home?'

'I seem to recall that there were, yes. I remember her mother, Halla. I gather the woman wasn't well. She lost her husband in that shipwreck. It was a terrible thing. A storm blew up out of nowhere and the fishing boat turned over with both men on board. Neither of them survived.' Ingibjörn took out a cloth and wiped his glasses methodically before putting them away in a velour-covered case. 'But that wasn't what tipped her over the edge. It was the baby she had not long afterwards. The poor little boy only lived for a couple of weeks. Cot death, they said it was.'

'I remember Halla,' Björg chipped in. 'I hadn't realised she was Elísabet's mother. I knew she drank. She did nothing else after the baby died. Drank and partied till all hours. Everybody knew but no one did anything about it. I dread to think what that little girl must have gone through.' Björg shuddered. 'I'm afraid Halla must have neglected her terribly. But … in those days we didn't like to interfere.'

A silence fell. Outside the wind was growing stronger and there was a patter of small raindrops on the kitchen window. In the utility room off the kitchen, a washing machine began to spin with a loud rumbling.

'Did you notice if Elísabet was picked on?' Elma asked.

Ingibjörn sighed. 'I wasn't aware of any trouble the first year. She had a friend and seemed happy enough. It wasn't until the second year that I noticed she was spending a lot of time alone. Or was it the year after that? I can't remember. But she wasn't the only one. Some kids simply prefer to play alone and I can't see what's wrong with that. I myself have always enjoyed my own company. I regard being self-sufficient as a sign of intelligence and a healthy mind.'

Elma nodded gravely and pretended not to see as Sævar looked down at his lap, struggling to keep a straight face. 'So you didn't notice any bullying?' she asked, surreptitiously kicking Sævar under the table.

'No, not in my classroom,' Ingibjörn said with blithe confidence. 'But if you want to know what went on in the playground, you'll have to talk to the break supervisors. They kept an eye on things during play time. I concentrated on maintaining discipline during lessons – something I feel is sorely lacking in the school system these days. Now teachers have to mind their p's and q's if they don't want a pack of parents on the warpath. It used not to be like that: pupils used to respect their teachers. But times have changed and not necessarily for the better.'

'You've since transferred to the community college, haven't you?' Elma said.

'Yes, many years ago. It must have been not long after Elísabet moved away. Yes, that's right, in about 1992. The teaching at the community college suits me better. Those who want to apply themselves do so. The others, well … they have no place in my classroom. I don't hesitate to throw them out. The students who want to learn shouldn't have to put up with disruption from the rest.'

Elma nodded. Ingibjörn had a reputation for being strict – strict and eccentric. According to Sævar, he made latecomers stand up in front of the class to explain and apologise. Students were rarely late. Absences were more common.

'Who did Elísabet go around with?'

'I didn't pay much attention, to be honest. The girls were always forming little cliques. That's how it is at that age. But they didn't get to choose who they sat next to in my class. Lessons were for learning, not mucking around,' Ingibjörn went on. He blew his nose vigorously into a handkerchief, as if to emphasise his words, then folded it neatly and put it away in his pocket. 'Is all this really relevant to Elísabet's death?'

'Not necessarily. I'm just trying to get a better picture of what she was like as a child – how she got on here in Akranes. She doesn't seem to have had very positive feelings towards the town, according to her husband. That's why we're interested in finding out why she died here. We're trying to establish who, if anyone, she could have been meeting.'

'Well, I doubt I can help you with that. Though there is one thing that springs to mind when I think about Elísabet.' Ingibjörn scratched his head. 'She was a vicious little thing. She got into a fight with a boy at school.'

'A fight?'

'Yes, apparently she just went for him. His name was Andrés; one of the special-needs kids. He works at the local library these days.'

'Do you know why Elísabet went for him?'

'No, I don't. Though I seem to remember that it was unprovoked. As I said, you should talk to the break supervisor or headteacher. They handled the matter without involving me.'

Elma nodded. She was surprised by how little Ingibjörn seemed to have cared about anything except imparting knowledge to his charges. She found it incomprehensible that a man like that would ever have applied to teach young children.

'I'm afraid I'm not much help,' Ingibjörn said with a grunt when Elma was silent.

'Is there any chance it could have been an accident?' asked Björg, who had been listening quietly, examining her nails while Ingibjörn was talking.

'We haven't ruled anything out yet,' Elma replied. 'Was there no one in town who was close to the family or had any sort of dealings with them?'

'No, no one,' Ingibjörn said. 'I didn't meet Elísabet's mother often, just once or twice at parents' evenings. Then suddenly they were gone. I don't remember getting any advance warning that they were planning to move and that Elísabet would be leaving the school. One day she just didn't turn up.'

'Was there any particular reason why they moved away?'

'I wouldn't know,' Ingibjörn said, heaving another sigh, as if he was losing patience with their questions. 'But I very much doubt Elísabet's death has anything to do with the past. Surely it was just an accident? A tourist who was speeding in dangerous conditions, for example? It wouldn't be the first time something like that had happened.'

Elma found it extremely unlikely that a tourist would, after knocking Elísabet down, first attempt to strangle her, then dispose of her body in the sea in the hope that it would be washed away. But she decided to protect him from the details. Turning, she caught Sævar's eye. He read her mind and they both stood up simultaneously and thanked their hosts.

'So *that* was her teacher,' Sævar said as they got back into the car. 'What on earth made him want to work with young children?'

'Search me.' Elma shrugged. 'He doesn't seem to have enjoyed it much.'

'Why do you think she attacked the boy?' Sævar asked.

'I don't know,' Elma said. 'It needn't have been for any particular reason – they were only kids, after all.'

'I got into a fight once,' Sævar said.

'What, only the once?' Elma grinned.

'Yes, only the once. I was ten and another boy made fun of my headband.'

'Your headband?' Elma burst out laughing.

Sævar nodded. 'I'm afraid so. I have to admit it – I walked around in a headband and matching tracksuit and thought I was seriously cool.'

'Well, if you think that's bad, I used to wear popper trackie bottoms.'

'Oof, now I've lost all respect for you.' Sævar pretended to be scandalised.

It was pitch-dark outside as it was getting on for seven o'clock. Elma's mother had already sent her a message asking whether she'd be home for supper since her sister Dagný and family were coming round.

'Are you … er … are you doing anything this evening?' she asked, trying to sound casual.

Sævar glanced at her, his eyebrows lifting slightly, then turned back to the road. 'I'm going to dinner,' he said, adding after a short pause: 'With my girlfriend's parents.'

'Oh,' Elma said. 'No problem.' She could feel her cheeks burning. They drove on in silence. It was a relief when Sævar said goodbye and got out. Somehow she had missed the fact that he had a girlfriend.

On the way home, she wondered why he had never mentioned it; never said a single word about her. 'What was I thinking of?' Elma thought, embarrassed that she might have said something inappropriate. But she was even more mortified by her awkward reaction when he'd mentioned his girlfriend's parents. She stopped the car outside her flat and looked up at the black sky. The glare of the streetlights and heavy banks of cloud blocked out the stars. Cold raindrops landed on her hot cheeks. For a few seconds she felt as if she could stand there like that forever. But the feeling didn't last and she hurried inside when a car came past, breaking her reverie.

Akranes 1991

The child wasn't yet two years old. A little girl who ran around the place giggling. She could hardly talk yet and the ice-cream she was holding dripped onto her clothes, but even so the grown-ups couldn't take their eyes off her. They all wanted to cuddle and make much of her, and talked to her in baby voices, cooing about how adorable she was. They smiled and scooped her up in their arms, and Elísabet watched them sniffing her hair appreciatively and kissing her sticky cheeks.

Elísabet was filled with loathing for her.

They were round at Sara's house and Sara's mother had a friend visiting, a blonde woman with big curls who laughed at everything the little girl said and did – even when she threw the ice-cream on the floor and it made a big mess.

Sara's mother had called them over. 'You're such big girls now you're seven. Won't you take Vala to play in your room? You can show her your toys and practise babysitting.'

Sara nodded obediently.

'Make sure she doesn't put anything in her mouth,' the little girl's mother said. 'She's so young, just a baby still.' She picked up the toddler and set her on her feet, then gently wiped off the ice-cream that was smeared all over her face right up to her forehead. The child wailed and tried to push her mother away, then ran after the two bigger girls on her unsteady legs, giggling excitedly, as they went into the bedroom.

Elísabet sat down on Sara's neatly made bed and watched the toddler. She had no interest in babysitting. 'Look at the doll,' Sara said, handing the little girl one of her Barbies. The child took the doll and babbled something incomprehensible, then threw it on the floor and started pulling out the furniture the older girls had been arranging in Sara's big Barbie doll's house.

Sara sighed and looked at Elísabet. 'I need the loo,' she said. 'Can you make sure she doesn't break anything?'

Elísabet nodded. She was still lying on the bed, her eyes resting broodingly on the toddler. She thought of the little girl's mother laughing all the time. It was as if the child could do no wrong. As if she could get away with anything and no one would mind. Elísabet got up off the bed and went over to her. 'Look,' she said, 'it's a doll.'

'Do',' the little girl repeated, revealing her tiny front teeth in a smile. She grabbed at the doll with her sticky fingers. She had soft, milk-white arms and her fingernails, though delicate, were intact. Elísabet compared them to her own bitten-down nails. The sores on her fingers were obvious now. She had spent the night in the cupboard. Lain there listening to the wind as it forced its way through the cracks in the wooden panelling, trying to distract herself from thinking about the people downstairs. Would this little girl ever have to sleep in a cupboard? Would she ever know what it was like to be frightened? Elísabet doubted it. She felt over-whelmed by the injustice of it all. She didn't know why she was so angry. Taking hold of the toddler's plump arm, she bent and, without even stopping to think, bit it as hard as she could.

The child opened her eyes wide; she had probably never felt such pain before. Never known what it was like to be deliberately hurt. Elísabet recoiled as the deafening screams filled the room. Big tears poured down the fat cheeks. 'Shh, it's all right,' Elísabet said, des-perately trying to hug the child. She heard the door opening. Felt eyes boring into the back of her head and her cheeks beginning to burn.

She glared at the little girl with an even fiercer loathing.

'What was Davíð's uncle called again?' Aðalheiður asked. Elma was sitting at the table, chopping vegetables for supper; her mother was standing by the cooker. 'You know, the politician,' she added, almost managing to make the question sound casual.

'Höskuldur,' Elma answered, without looking up from the paprika she was slicing.

There was a brief silence in the kitchen apart from the low hissing of the radio that no one had bothered to retune, although the voices were hard to hear through the interference. The kitchen was small, with dark-wood units, a fitted table and leather-upholstered benches. Elma's parents had often talked about replacing the kitchen but they had never got round to it and Elma was glad. She had always loved sitting at this table. It was where she used to do her homework, her hair in pigtails and her yellow schoolbag beside her, while her mother was cooking. She had lost count of the waffles and the thick pancakes known as *skonsur* that she had eaten at this table, the quiet hours she had whiled away there, safe from the hustle and bustle of the world outside. It was usually peaceful in the kitchen at home and always cosy.

'Have you talked to Davíð's family at all?' Aðalheiður asked, holding the pan by the handle as she broke up the mince with a spatula. Elma shook her head. 'Elma, love,' Aðalheiður said, without looking up from her task, 'surely you can talk about him? You behave as if you'd never been a couple, as if he hadn't been a part of your life all these years.'

'Not yet,' Elma replied in a clipped voice, feeling her chest tighten.

'All right, darling. You take your time,' Aðalheiður said. 'But it often helps to talk to professionals. We've got some good therapists here in Akranes. If you like, I could...'

'*Mum!*' Elma interrupted. 'No, thanks. The last thing I'd do is talk to a therapist, particularly here in Akranes.'

Aðalheiður's mouth shut in a tight line. Elma sensed how difficult her mother found it to say nothing. She was someone who stuck her nose into everyone's business and felt compelled to sort out everyone's problems. It must be destroying her that she couldn't help her own daughter.

Elma sighed. She really hadn't meant to sound so rude. 'It's not that I'm in denial or anything,' she said after a moment, 'I just don't see how it's supposed to help. It happened and nothing can change that. He left me. He betrayed me and all his promises to me. I just … I just need a bit more time.' She smiled at her mother, who returned her smile, though she still looked troubled. Aðalheiður was about to say something else when the front door opened and a child's voice called out:

'Granny! Granny, do you know what?' Alexander came tearing into the kitchen in his wet boots and gazed at his grandmother with big eyes.

'No, I don't know what,' Aðalheiður said cheerfully, bending down to him.

'Alexander, shoes off!' Dagný bellowed from the hall.

'I'm getting a spaceship for Christmas,' Alexander announced, ignoring his mother.

'A spaceship? Do they sell them at the toy shop?'

'Yes, you can get it at Toy Story,' he said, opening his eyes even wider.

'Alexander,' barked his mother, 'it's called Toys 'R' Us and I don't know if you can buy spaceships there. Take your shoes off right now. You'll make Granny's floor all wet.'

'It doesn't matter,' Aðalheiður said, smiling at Alexander as she helped him off with his boots. 'And I'm sure they sell spaceships at Toy Story. Don't they sell everything there?'

Alexander beamed and nodded eagerly.

'Today it's a spaceship; yesterday it was a dinosaur and the day before that it was a flying car like the one in Harry Potter.' Dagný rolled her eyes. 'He's not asking for much this year!' She gave her mother and sister quick kisses. Viðar, Dagný's husband, followed her in with Jökull in his arms.

Alexander was five and Jökull was one. They were polar opposites: Alexander had a blond mop and blue eyes like his father;
Jökull had his mother's light-brown hair and plump cheeks that
showed no signs of disappearing, although he was now one and
a bit.

'Do you want to come to Auntie Elma?' Elma held out her
arms to Jökull who spread his own and reached out to her. She
kissed his round cheeks and cuddled him, but the moment
Aðalheiður put the toy box on the floor, he started struggling to
get down.

'That smells good, Mum,' said Dagný, sitting down at the
kitchen table. 'Is there any coffee?'

'Work wearing you out?' Aðalheiður asked, putting a cup
under the coffee machine.

'No, not really. It's just the shifts I find so knackering.' Dagný
accepted the coffee. In the glare of the ceiling lights Elma noticed
the dark circles under her eyes, which she had tried to disguise
with concealer.

Dagný was only three years older than her but in spite of that
they had never been close. They were very different and Elma
always had the feeling she was getting on Dagný's nerves,
without being able to put her finger on why. Elma had envied
her sister ever since she could remember. Dagný had always been
popular, effortlessly drawing people to her with her genuine
smile and easy manner. She also had the knack of putting people
at ease and of appearing interested in everything. When listening, she would lean forwards, hardly blinking, and nod eagerly.
Though, here, Elma was the exception. Dagný always looked at
her as if she was her little sister, not with affection but as if she
thought Elma was a bit slow. The sister who never understood
anything. The sister who had to be prevented from embarrassing
her. Who needed to be told that her top didn't go with her skirt
and that her eye-make-up was uneven. Elma had lost count of
the times she'd had to listen to what a 'beautiful girl' or how

'lovely and clever' her sister was. She doubted Dagný had ever been forced to listen to similar praise of her.

They had never played together, as far as Elma could remember. When Dagný had her friends round, they used to shut themselves in her room, all leaning against the door to keep her five-year-old sister out. Elma could remember standing, crying outside and banging on the door until her mother came and found some way to distract her. Later, she wouldn't have dreamt of wanting to hang out with Dagný and her friends – a bunch of girls whose reaction to everything, however funny or horrible, seemed to be to giggle foolishly.

Dagný had always known her own mind and had a clear idea of what she wanted to do in life. On the wall of their parents' house hung a picture of Dagný at six years old in a nurse's uniform: today she worked at Akranes Hospital as a midwife. She had got together with Viðar when they were both fourteen and had never seemed to have a moment's doubt about their relationship or herself. They were still together, all these years later, with two kids, a detached house, a jeep and everything else you'd expect of the average family. Elma could hardly believe she and Dagný had come from the same gene pool.

'How's life in the police, Elma?' Viðar asked, accepting a cup of coffee from his mother-in-law. Elma opened her mouth to answer but Dagný got in first.

'God, you'll never guess who's pregnant!' Without waiting for an answer, she went on: 'Bjarni's Magnea!' She looked round expectantly. The duty of confidentiality had never prevented Dagný from discussing her patients outside work.

'No!' Aðalheiður exclaimed. 'I'd begun to think there must be something wrong. Physically, I mean. Though you don't dare ask these days, as you have to be so careful not to offend people.'

'No, not a bit of it. She's eleven weeks gone,' Dagný said. At that moment there was a commotion from the floor. Alexander had snatched a toy car from Jökull who began to wail. Dagný nudged Viðar, shooting him a look that told him to take care of it.

'I'll do it,' Elma said hurriedly and got up. She lifted Jökull's solid little body into her arms and started walking around the room with him. His silky hair smelled sweet. His crying subsided as soon as he had his dummy in his mouth. He leant his cheek against Elma's chest and closed his eyes.

'Of course, you mustn't tell a soul; it's still absolutely hush-hush,' Dagný continued.

'We won't breathe a word,' Aðalheiður promised.

'Oh, don't let him go to sleep now or we'll never get him down this evening,' Dagný exclaimed irritably, noticing Jökull's closed eyes.

'But he's so sleepy,' Elma said, hugging him tighter. 'See how happy he is with his auntie.'

'Elma, seriously. He won't sleep this evening if he drops off now. All it takes is a five-minute nap, then it's like he's had an adrenaline jab in the bum.'

'In the bum?' Alexander echoed fearfully, looking up from the cars he had been absorbed in lining up. 'Who's having a jab in the bum?'

'No one's having a jab,' Viðar reassured him.

'He still hasn't forgotten his vaccination when he was four,' Dagný whispered, once Alexander had turned back to the cars. 'Honestly, I don't think he'll ever get over it.'

Saturday, 2 December 2017

When Begga rang to invite Elma to share a bottle of red wine on Saturday evening, she had accepted the invitation with alacrity. She appreciated Begga making the move as she would never have dared to ring herself; she didn't feel they knew each other well enough yet. Elma had always found it hard to make friends as she was too shy to take the initiative. But Begga, it seemed, had no qualms on that score. Nor did Elma have to make much effort to keep the conversation flowing when they were together since she was lucky if she could get a word in edgeways. Begga, who was on good form now that she'd got her beloved cat back, talked more or less nonstop. When Elma finally got home, she realised that she'd knocked back rather too many glasses. For the second weekend in a row, she welcomed the numbness and temporary release from care that went with being drunk. She smiled foolishly as she searched for her house keys in her pocket. It took her several fumbling attempts to insert the front-door key in the lock, and before she managed to turn it, the door was opened from the inside.

'How're you?' The young man from the flat opposite hers was grinning.

'Fantastic!' Elma answered, beaming back at him. She'd thought she would sober up on the walk home but the corridor was moving up and down and she was finding it hard not to sway. The wine made everything seem a little unreal, which was welcome right now.

'Good evening?' he asked, looking Elma up and down.

'Yes. Yes, actually, it was a lot of fun.' Elma laughed. 'Thanks for letting me in.'

'Do you need help with your own door too?' the young man asked.

'No, thanks, I think I can manage.'

'OK,' he said but showed no signs of budging. Instead, he stood and watched her.

Elma got the key in the lock of her flat door at the first attempt this time. But before she could open it, the young man said quickly:

'I've got some beer in the fridge if you're interested.'

Elma turned. 'It's so late,' she said, with a rather exaggerated yawn. In her imagination she was already in the bath she'd been planning to run for herself.

'It's exactly … twenty past eleven,' the young man said, grinning again.

'Really?' Elma peered hazily at her watch. 'That early?'

The young man laughed. 'The offer's still open, if you're interested.'

Elma hesitated. 'Weren't you going out?'

'Yes, but only to buy some Coke. It can wait.'

'All right, maybe just one drink.' She smiled at him uncertainly. Perhaps she just needed to do something different, something out of character.

'Great,' he said and led her into his flat. Elma watched him open the fridge and take out two beers. He was younger than her but very good-looking. Better-looking, in fact, than anyone who had ever shown an interest in her before. Her mind strayed briefly to Sævar and his dinner with his girlfriend's family. To Davíð too, but she managed to push this thought away. All she asked was to be free of him for one evening. To have one evening where she wasn't tortured by thoughts of what she could have done differently.

The young man handed her a beer and sat down opposite her on the sofa. She still didn't know his name. She had only taken one sip when he put down his beer, got up and came over.

Akranes 1991

The two of them sat side by side on the edge of the sandpit, burrowing their feet in the wet sand. One dark haired, in an anorak that was too small for her and scuffed trainers; the other blonde, in a shiny new raincoat and boots. Neither said a word. Two eight-year-old girls, sunk in their own thoughts.

They had always found it easy to be quiet together. Ever since they first met at school it was as if they had tacitly understood that words weren't always necessary. Unlike most children their age, they felt little need for inconsequential chatter in each other's presence. The hours they spent together offered a brief respite, a momentary lull from the constant barrage of stimuli that went with being eight years old.

The blonde girl suddenly stood up. She looked at the other girl and sniffed dolefully. 'I can't be your friend anymore,' she said, meeting her eye. Elísabet had been so deep in her own thoughts that she stared at her friend uncomprehendingly for a moment. 'Mummy says I'm not allowed to play with you,' Sara continued. She hovered there for a while as if uncertain what to do next, then finally turned on her heel and ran away from the playground. A few moments later she was out of sight.

The dark-haired girl in the wet trainers was left staring down at the sand. Small drops of rain fell from the sky and mingled with the salty tears that were rolling down her cheeks.

Sunday, 3 December 2017

One of the former break supervisors from Elísabet's school, a woman called Anna, had agreed to meet Elma early on Sunday morning. She had retired and now lived in sheltered accommodation near the Höfði Old People's Home. She invited Elma to take a seat at a small kitchen table covered in a flowery plastic cloth and put some of the doughnut twists known as *kleinur* and a cup of coffee in front of her.

'I only worked at Brekkubær School for a few years,' she said, once she'd sat down opposite Elma. 'After I left, in around 1995, I got a job at the Einarsbúð grocery and stayed there until my Bússi died last year. Then I gave up work and moved here.'

'Which years did you work at Brekkubær School?' Elma asked, taking a small mouthful of coffee. She had woken up feeling sick and headachy for the second time in a week. She didn't intend to make a habit of it.

'I started at the school in 1989, so ... er, that would have been six years, wouldn't it? It was never meant to be permanent but there you are – it just goes to show what a long time you can spend doing something that was never part of the plan. Be careful you don't get stuck in a rut like that,' Anna said with a chuckle. 'Oh, it was all right. In fact it was fine. There were two of us break supervisors and we kept an eye on the kids at play time, mopped the corridors and so on. It doesn't sound too exciting but it had its moments. I got to know the kids, especially the naughty ones – the troublemakers.' She gave another low chuckle.

'Do you remember a girl called Elísabet?' Elma asked. She instinctively warmed to this old woman, who sat there smiling and rubbing her bony hands together. Her home was clad in dark wood panelling and the walls were covered with pictures. Children, grandchildren – and great-grandchildren, she had announced proudly as she pointed to the most recent photo, of a little boy with a single tooth who sat holding a ball. Elma had also noticed the small glass table in the sitting room on which were arranged the photo of a man in a gilded frame, a glass candleholder and a small book with a cross on the front.

'Elísabet?' Anna frowned. 'Elísabet … no, I don't remember anyone of that name.'

Elma took out her phone and showed her the photo of Elísabet as a child from the Akranes photography archive.

'Oh, you mean little Beta,' Anna said, her face lighting up when she saw the picture. 'Do I? Poor little mite, she had such a tough time. I always felt sorry for her. She came from a broken home, you know: her father was dead and her mother … she wasn't well. A neighbour used to look after her most of the time – Solla, quite a good friend of mine. But in spite of everything Beta was always so calm and level-headed, like she was untouchable somehow. Of course she wasn't, but she seemed different from the other kids. Looking back, I suppose she was more grown up because of what she'd had to go through. She always seemed like she was older than the other kids.'

'When you say "what she'd had to go through", are you talking about the deaths of her father and brother?'

'Well, yes, there was that too, which of course can't have been easy. But that happened before she started school. She was always a serious little thing but she was still a child. She used to laugh and play and watch the other kids. It was only after her friend died that she – how shall I put it? – she seemed totally lost. She used to turn up to school but she didn't watch the other kids anymore, let alone take part in their games. She kept herself to herself mostly, and the other kids picked up on it and made fun of her. Poor little thing.'

'Her friend died?' Elma asked.

'Oh, yes, it was terrible. They used to spend all their time together. I saw them walking home from school almost every day. They were like chalk and cheese: Sara so blonde and Elísabet so dark. You can see them in that picture. That's Sara, behind Elísabet and Magnea.'

'How did she die?' Headache and nausea forgotten, Elma studied the picture on her phone with new interest. Behind Elísabet and Magnea was a fair-haired girl who was looking up at the camera. She was lying on her stomach with a sheet of paper in front of her and crayons scattered all over the floor.

'Yes. Surely you must remember it? The whole town was in shock. I've never known anything so tragic.' Anna shivered. 'The girl just vanished. All they ever found were her trainers on the beach at Krókalón.' Anna gazed out of the window, her eyes sorrowful. Her house was near Langisandur and had a view of the sea, but as it was high tide, hardly any of the yellow beach could be seen. 'They began the search when she didn't come home at suppertime. But it wasn't until several days later that a raft they thought had something to do with her disappearance washed up on the beach where they'd found her shoes.'

'What about Sara herself? Did they never find her body?'

'No.' Anna's voice grew huskier. 'She was never found.'

Elma was silent, a chill running through her flesh.

'Ása and Hendrik were inconsolable,' Anna added, and took a mouthful of coffee.

'Ása and Hendrik?'

'Yes,' Anna said. 'Sara's parents. They never really got over their loss.'

The shift was changing when Elma got back to the police station. Weary officers were saying goodbye and preparing to go home while the new shift took over and switched on the coffee machine.

Sævar was sitting at his desk, staring intently at his computer screen. He seemed tired. His hair was a mess and he had shadows under his eyes. Elma paused in the doorway and leant against the doorpost. 'Is Hörður in?'

'No, I haven't seen him.' Sævar glanced at the clock. 'He should be here any minute.'

Elma bit her lip. She had no idea what to do with the information she had just received or how it might be significant. 'OK, maybe I should wait for him.'

Sævar shrugged and she turned to leave, hovered in the corridor for a moment, then went back into his office. When he didn't notice her, she coughed.

'Do you remember Sara – Hendrik and Ása's daughter?' she asked. When Sævar shook his head, she sat down facing him across the desk. 'Sara Hendriksdóttir died when she was nine. Her shoes turned up on the beach at Krókalón but her body was never found. They believed she'd been playing on a raft that was swept out to sea.'

'Oh, yes. Now you mention it, I do remember hearing about the case, but I didn't move to Akranes until I was in my teens, several years after her disappearance. But of course you couldn't avoid hearing about it; it was on the national news. A tragic accident. If I remember right, they found biological traces on the raft – a hair caught on a nail or something.'

Elma nodded. 'Right. I was so young when it happened, only just six, that I only have a very vague memory of it. According to a break supervisor who worked at Brekkubær School at the time, Sara and Elísabet used to be inseparable.'

'Where are you going with this?' Sævar asked.

Elma sighed. 'I don't know. It just strikes me as a bit odd. Why did so few people know that they were friends? Neither Elísabet's aunt Guðrún nor Eiríkur mentioned Sara's disappearance when we asked them about Elísabet's childhood in Akranes, yet it must have been a traumatic experience for her. Do you suppose she never told them about it?' Elma leant her elbows on his desk and began massaging her temples. 'I'm puzzled about the fact that Hendrik's family keeps cropping up in connection with the investigation. I was thinking of talking to Sara's parents, Ása and Hendrik…'

'I don't think that's a very good idea,' Sævar interrupted. 'Making them rake up a family tragedy when we don't even know if it's relevant.'

'No, maybe not.' Elma stared pensively out of the window behind Sævar. She knew he was right. 'But what about Magnea? Didn't she mention Sara at all?'

Sævar shook his head. 'No, but then we didn't ask her much about her time at school. She said that she and Elísabet weren't exactly friends.'

'Anna, the break supervisor, said that the woman who lived next door to Elísabet used to take care of her. She was called Solla, or Sólveig. Do you reckon she could be the woman Eiríkur mentioned? He said the only time Elísabet went into Akranes was to visit some old lady.'

'Yes, that sounds likely. It's bound to be the same woman,' Sævar agreed. He yawned and turned back to the sports news on his computer, apparently unaffected by Elma's excitement. 'I just find it hard to see how it can have any relevance to what happened to Elísabet,' he added, after a pause, looking back at Elma.

She nodded. Although she didn't agree, she didn't say so. For her, this latest detail sounded like too much of a coincidence. There had to be a link. She didn't know what but she had every intention of finding out.

'Elma?'

'Yes?' Snapping out of her thoughts, she saw that Sævar was grinning.

'Was there anything else?'

Elma shook her head and left his office.

It turned out that Hörður remembered Sara's disappearance well. 'Hendrik and Ása reported her missing when she didn't come home that evening. We searched the nearby playgrounds and knocked on doors but no one had seen her. We soon started combing the beaches and that's when we found her shoes. It was only really then that we began to suspect the worst.' Hörður frowned at Elma, puzzled. 'Why are you asking about that now?'

Elma repeated what she had told Sævar, but Hörður was obviously unimpressed; he shrugged and muttered that it was highly unlikely to have any connection to the investigation. 'Though it might be one reason why Elísabet avoided coming to Akranes,' he conceded. 'There were obviously too many ghosts here. Still, that doesn't explain why she was found dead by the lighthouse.'

'I was thinking of sounding out Sara's parents,' Elma began, 'Ása and Hendrik, but—'

'You will do nothing of the sort!' Hörður snapped. 'You're talking about an incident that happened thirty years ago; we're not going to start digging that up now.'

'I know it's a delicate subject,' Elma hastened to assure him. 'I just thought maybe Sara's parents could tell us more about Elísabet's situation, seeing as she was close friends with their daughter. Don't forget that Halla rented the house from them as well.'

Hörður frowned. 'No, the whole thing's too far-fetched. We've already interviewed Bjarni and Magnea; it'll start to look like we're persecuting the family if we go on like this.' Squaring his shoulders, he added: 'To be honest with you, the situation's not looking hopeful. We found nothing in the car, no DNA, except from Elísabet and her children; no blood; nothing. The only remotely interesting find was some strands of wool on the driver's seat.'

'Strands of wool?' Sævar asked. 'You mean, like from a *lopapeysa*, or a scarf or something?'

'Exactly. But Elísabet owned a *lopapeysa* herself, like most people, and forensics are currently checking if the fibres in the car could have come from her jumper. Her phone records haven't turned anything up either. She called in sick herself and there's nothing to suggest she wasn't in Akranes of her own free will. We know she was seeking a divorce from Eiríkur but we don't know why she came here. Perhaps she just wanted some breathing space before having to face the fight with her husband. Perhaps she came back to her childhood home in search of closure. As you've discovered, Elma, she had a lot of bad memories associated with this place. We know she went to the lighthouse to meet Magnea, who didn't turn up – Bjarni and Magnea's friends have confirmed that she was with them all evening.' Hörður looked from Elma to Sævar, his face grim. 'The fact is, we don't have any other leads to go on and it's pretty clear that we're not going to solve this case unless new evidence comes to light. My guess is that someone knocked Elísabet down by accident and tried to dispose of her afterwards. The culprit was probably drink-driving and the whole thing ended in disaster.'

'But they still had the presence of mind to hide Elísabet's car in the garage belonging to a couple who were abroad?' Sævar interrupted.

'Sure, why not?' Hörður retorted. 'It's a small town; everyone knows everyone else's business. I don't have to tell you that.'

'So? What do we do now?' Elma asked.

'We carry on with our investigation, of course, and keep searching for a lead,' Hörður said. 'But we mustn't neglect our other business. A number of things have been stuck on the back-burner for the last week. Anyway, I'm going to spend the rest of the day at home, though I'll keep my phone on. I suggest you two do the same.'

'What do you think?' Sævar asked as they stood in the corridor outside his office. 'Have we hit a brick wall?'

'I thought I was getting somewhere, but of course it may be a dead end. Maybe I'm just digging up secrets that have nothing to do with the murder.' Elma shrugged. Hörður's speech had taken the wind out of her sails. She heaved a sigh, then hurriedly closed her mouth, afraid Sævar might smell the alcohol on her breath. Her headache had subsided but her empty stomach was crying out for food. 'We can't just give up, though. I'm going to see what I can find out about Sólveig, Elísabet's old neighbour, just as soon as I've had some lunch. Do you fancy coming along?'

'No, I've got some stuff to do,' Sævar answered distractedly. Only now did Elma notice how tired, dispirited and unlike himself he seemed. She had been so preoccupied with the case that she hadn't registered the fact.

She had woken at the crack of dawn and crept back across the corridor to her own bed. She blushed every time she thought about what had happened, though she remembered only snatches. But she had no reason to be ashamed. She wasn't tied to anyone. She was a woman in her thirties who was free to sleep with anyone she liked. She didn't judge other women who chose to live like that, so why should she be so harsh on herself?

'No problem,' she said lightly, avoiding Sævar's eye. Was it her imagination or was he avoiding her gaze too? Once she was outside in the fresh air, it occurred to her that it wasn't exactly that she was ashamed of herself, more that she simply wished she'd slept with someone else.

In the event, it wasn't difficult to track down Elísabet's childhood neighbour. Only one woman fitted the bill: Sólveig Sigurðardóttir had lived in the same house on Krókatún for forty years. She was now eighty-six and a resident at the Höfði Old People's Home. When Elma arrived to talk to her she was sitting on a bench in the garden with her eyes closed. Her walking stick was propped against the bench beside her and she was wearing a dark-blue headscarf knotted under her chin. One of the staff, a girl with a ring through her nose and thick, black eye make-up, pointed her out to Elma. 'She's always out there,' the girl said in a long-suffering voice.

Elma walked unhurriedly over to where Sólveig was sitting. The old woman was holding her face up to the cold rays of the wintry sun. She wore a thin, light-brown anorak and plastic covers on her shoes. Elma sat down beside her and coughed without eliciting any response. 'Sólveig?'

The old woman opened her eyes and squinted at Elma for a long moment before answering in a high, threadbare voice: 'Yes, that's me.'

'My name's Elma. I'm with the police. I was wondering if I could ask you a few questions?'

The old woman laughed quietly. 'The police want to talk to me? Yes, that shouldn't be a problem.'

Elma smiled. 'Am I right that you used to live on Krókatún?'

'For most of my life, yes. Why do you ask?'

'Do you remember a girl called Elísabet? She would have been a child when she lived there. Her mother's name was Halla.'

'Of course I remember Beta and Halla. Beta comes to see me sometimes.' Sólveig smiled at the thought.

'Has she been round recently?'

A flock of seagulls was swarming not far off, making a harsh cackling. The old woman's attention was distracted by the noise and Elma had to repeat the question.

'Has who been to see me recently? Oh, Beta? I remember Beta. She lived next door to me for years. I used to look after poor Beta.'

'You looked after her?'

'I fed her. Kept an eye on her and made sure she had clean clothes.' Sólveig's hands were covered in liver spots. Her skin hung in loose wrinkles over the fragile bones and Elma felt a momentary impulse to stroke them.

'Why did you take care of her? Where was her mother?'

'Oh, Halla didn't mean any harm, but life's unfair, you know.

Some people are just born weaker than others.' Sólveig didn't explain, but then she didn't need to. Going by what Elma had heard, Halla must have had a serious drink problem. The screaming of the gulls grew louder. They must have found something edible on the shore.

'Do you remember if Elísabet had any friends?'

Sólveig took her time about answering this and, when she did, spoke slowly, as if remembering. 'She used to play with Sara, Ása and Hendrik's daughter. Sara was the only girl I remember going round to visit her. Then she disappeared. It was terribly sad.'

'So you don't remember a girl called Magnea going round to see her?'

Sólveig shook her head. 'No, I don't remember any Magnea. Who was she again? Mind you, I can hardly remember what I did yesterday ... but I do remember Sara. A sweet little thing. Always a bit shy but very sweet.'

Neither of them spoke for a while. Sólveig leant back against the bench and closed her eyes, her expression serene. Elma had begun to think she'd fallen asleep, when she continued: 'She hauled her away, you know. Ása came and hauled her away one morning. I saw from the window. It was early. Sara was on her way round to Beta's when Ása appeared and dragged her off crying.'

'Do you know why?'

'No, but Halla had a bad reputation in town,' Sólveig said. 'She used to get a lot of visitors. The town's undesirables, mostly. Unlucky souls, people with problems. I don't suppose Ása wanted her daughter spending time in company like that. Sometimes Elísabet would come round and stay with me when things were too chaotic at home, but not always. I'd have liked to go over and fetch her but I never did.'

'Do you think Elísabet was at risk in that house?'

Sólveig seemed to reflect for a while, then said: 'I saw her in the garden once. She was holding a stick and there was a bird in front of her. The bird was injured – it was still moving but it was clearly suffering. Elísabet watched it for a while, then started hitting it. Again and again. I remember thinking that she was putting it out of its misery. Some wretched cat had probably been playing with it and she'd found it in that state. But she didn't show any emotion.' Sólveig looked pained. 'I don't know what happened round there when they were all drinking and carrying on. But I noticed the change in the child. Her eyes changed. All the happiness went out of them. But she was still beautiful. I suppose that's why no one else noticed.'

'Noticed what?'

Sólveig fiddled with the hem of her anorak, then went on: 'She had to go through so much: first her father, then her baby brother, and lastly her friend. I suppose it was hardly surprising if she changed and stopped showing any emotion. Something had to give.'

'Did you never suspect that she was being abused at home?'

'Abused?' Sólveig frowned. 'What are you saying? Is there anything to suggest that?'

'I was just wondering. There was so much going on: strangers coming in and out, drinking and possibly worse. Could you be sure she was safe?'

Sólveig seemed to be having trouble breathing. She gave a low moan and the breath whined in her nose. 'The poor, dear child,' she said at last. 'I just don't know. I remember wondering sometimes, but you don't want to believe it. I didn't want to believe it.'

'You couldn't point me towards any of the crowd who used to visit Halla?'

'The crowd, you say...' Sólveig sniffed and wiped away a tear. 'People like that don't live long, I can tell you. Stjáni used to spend a lot of time round there but he died several years ago. Drank himself to death. Then there was Binna, who killed herself. I can't remember all of them, but Rúnar may have hung out with them. He's still alive. You should try talking to him.'

'Do you remember his second name?'

'No. But he works as a bin man; has done for years. He used to come and say hello sometimes when I was still living at home. This…' She gestured at the white-and-blue building of the old people's home '…this will never be *home* to me. It's just a waiting room. I can't wait to leave.' Sólveig was smiling but her expression was defiant. Elma decided to call it a day and leave the old woman in peace. But there was one more question she needed an answer to.

'Do you remember how long it is since you last saw Elísabet?'

'I feel like it could have been yesterday, but it could have been months, even years ago. My memory's going, you know,' Sólveig said apologetically. 'It's much easier to remember the old days. They're crystal clear. The rest is all a bit hazy.'

'Right, well, I won't disturb you any longer. Thanks so much for talking to me.' Elma got to her feet.

'Give Beta my love,' Sólveig said in parting.

Elma nodded, deciding there was no call to tell her what had happened to Elísabet. She didn't want to upset the old woman and doubted she would remember it for more than a few minutes anyway. 'It's a beautiful day,' she said instead, and took her leave.

'Come with me,' Aðalheiður said, the moment Elma walked through the door. 'Come and see what I've found.'

Elma obeyed and followed her mother into the garage.

'I went up to the loft to look for the boxes of Christmas dec-orations. I've been trying to get your father to bring them down, but you know what he's like.' Aðalheiður snorted, but Elma could hear the affection in her voice. Her parents had met when they were children. They had got together at the Akranes Primary School, which had later become Brekkubær School. Elma often had to listen to them nagging each other, but there was no anger behind it. It sounded more like the good-natured bickering of two people who knew each other too well.

In the middle of the garage were some open boxes, from which protruded a variety of mostly red-and-green Christmas decorations. Plastic fir branches, plump Father Christmases and homemade angels. Elma was familiar with it all. Not much had been replaced since she was a girl, when she used to wait impatiently for Advent to arrive so she could take the shiny objects out of their boxes and arrange them around the house.

'I was just wondering when you were going to start putting up the decorations,' she said, picking up a carved angel holding a gilded star.

'Yes, I don't know what I've been thinking,' Aðalheiður said. 'Anyway, look what I found – your box.' She pointed to a small cardboard box. 'It's got all your books and paper dolls in it. There are the diaries you kept all those years too – I've been very good and haven't looked at them. And your scrapbooks and drawings.'

Elma crouched down and peered inside the box. 'You kept all this, Mum?' she asked, picking up a yellowing watercolour.

'Of course,' Aðalheiður replied, as if nothing could be more natural. 'You sometimes complain that I never throw anything away but there are times when it can be a good thing, you know. Even when the things aren't valuable in themselves, they have so many memories attached to them.' Stooping, she began to take out the Christmas decorations.

Elma pulled over the small box. There should be eight diaries, she thought, sealed with tiny locks and decorated with flowers and teddy bears. Sure enough, there they were.

'No, I can't read this,' she said as she leafed through one of them. 'It's too embarrassing. I was such an idiot in those days.'

'It's up to you, of course. I just thought you'd be pleased to have them.' Aðalheiður lifted one of the boxes to carry it into the house. 'Come and help me decorate. You were always so good at it.'

'All right, I'm coming,' Elma said distractedly. A photo fell out of one of the books. It showed the three of them: her, Silja and Kristín sitting together on a bunk bed. Elma remembered that trip. They had gone to a summer house with her parents. They couldn't have been more than eight years old and all that had mattered to them in those days was what game they were going to play next. Elma smiled reminiscently and put the picture back in the box. She felt a sudden wave of nostalgia. Would life ever be as simple again?

There were the old school newspapers too, not just from Elma's alma mater but from Brekkubær School as well, which were published at the end of every year. She picked up one and leafed through it, stopping when she came to a picture of Bjarni. He had been voted the school hunk and most promising sportsman of his year. There was an interview with him, tracing his football career and asking him about his future ambitions. Glancing at the date, Elma saw that it was a year after his sister had died. He had answered that he wanted to be captain of Akranes football team, then work for his father's company. It seemed Bjarni had realised his dreams.

Elma went on turning the pages and eventually came to the class photo she had been looking for. There was Magnea aged ten, smiling broadly in the middle of the group. She was so dominant that it looked as if the picture had been arranged around her, though of course it hadn't.

Elma went on rooting around in the box but couldn't find the paper from the previous year. On the other hand, she did find the one from the year before that. It didn't take her long to find the class photo for 1:IG. There had been two more pupils in that one: Sara and Elísabet were standing next to each other in the front row. They weren't looking at the camera and neither of them was smiling. Magnea was standing behind them but, unlike them, she was staring straight into the lens with a broad grin, just as she was in all the other photos Elma had seen of her.

Elma went on looking through the pictures of school life. There was the same photo she had found in the online archives, with Elísabet and Magnea sitting side by side, while Sara lay on the floor behind them, drawing. Elma's eyes suddenly widened when she saw what the little girl was drawing. She hadn't paid any attention to the picture before but now she saw what it was. Sara was drawing a man. He had large eyes and was baring his big teeth in a smile. He was holding something black too – a small black box. Was it supposed to be a camera? Elma's thoughts flew to the photo she had found in Elísabet's car. Was this the same man? Had he taken pictures of Sara as well? Sara had drawn the man with thick black lines and big, glaring eyes, and behind him stood a figure that looked like a girl. The girl had no arms, but what drew Elma's attention most was her mouth.

It was wide open in a big 'O'.

Akranes 1991

Some days he took photos. 'You're so beautiful,' he said and told her to smile. He ordered her to face this way and sit like that and she did everything he said. Obeyed everything he told her to do. Except that she never smiled and she refused to look at the pictures afterwards.

He put them in his pocket and took them away with him. She didn't know where he lived but imagined him alone in a big, black house. Perhaps it wasn't black, but she felt that would be appropriate. Perhaps he took the photos out and examined them as he sat alone in the evenings, smoking his cigarettes, but she tried not to think about that.

When he came, she trained her mind not to dwell on what was happening. She thought about the book she was reading. She fantasised that she lived in the countryside or could open a wardrobe and find a door to another world. She thought about dwarfs and elves and trees that could talk and horses that could fly. Anything but her room and the man who wanted to take pictures of her.

One day she found a photo under her bed. She picked it up and studied it. Was that really her? She hardly recognised the girl who stood there, her eyelids lowered. She seemed so alone. So frightened.

She felt her eyes growing hot, but before the tears could spill over, she got a grip on herself and slid the picture into a crack in the cupboard, pushing it all the way in until it was completely hidden, then put it out of her mind.

Monday, 4 December 2017

The engine coughed into life after several attempts. Elma put the heater on full but immediately turned it down when cold air started blasting out. There wouldn't be time to warm up the car during the short drive to the police station. She knew it would probably be quicker to walk but it was so bitterly cold that she didn't want to spend any more time outdoors than was strictly necessary.

She was terribly late. Usually she turned up to work punctually but she hadn't gone to sleep until the early hours as she had been too busy obsessing over Sara and Elísabet, and the possible identity of the mysterious man. She knew what that sort of drawing meant. The two years she had spent studying psychology had taught her enough to know that children's drawings often reflected something they couldn't express in words, such as fear or dread or their feelings about something that had happened to them. She had sat up late, studying examples of drawings by victims of sex abuse. Sara had shown the man with his teeth bared in a grin. Elma knew that it was common for children to depict their abuser with an oversized mouth and sharp teeth. In these pictures the perpetrator was often drawn smiling, while the children's own mouths tended to be either turned down or wide open. There was often something missing in the picture too, symbolising the victim's powerlessness. Like the girl's missing arms in Sara's picture. Elma was surprised that no one had noticed what she had drawn. To her, it was glaringly obvious that it had been a cry for help. The girl was trying to say something but no one had understood the message. Then again, recalling that Ingibjörn had been her teacher at the time, Elma wasn't so surprised. She couldn't picture him trying to read any particular meaning into his pupils' drawings. For him, school was nothing more than a seat of learning, where children's heads were to be crammed full of information.

She wasn't yet ready to explain this to Hörður. And she still had no idea how it related to the case, but she was determined to find out. She suspected Elísabet might have come back to Akranes because of the man who had abused her as a child. If so, the man in question would have had good reason to want to silence her.

Elma switched off the engine and half ran into the building. To her surprise, Sævar wasn't there.

'Begga, have you seen Sævar?' she asked in the kitchen.

Begga shook her head. 'No, he hasn't come in yet this morning.'

'Really, he's not here? ... What?' she added, when she noticed the look Begga was giving her.

'Nothing,' said Begga. 'I didn't say a word.' She grinned, her dimples becoming even more pronounced. When Elma showed no signs of rising to the bait, Begga added: 'Did I mention that I'm clairvoyant?'

'No, you didn't,' Elma said, giving her a puzzled smile as she left the kitchen.

'I know exactly what you're thinking, Elma,' Begga called after her, and burst out laughing.

Elma rolled her eyes. She didn't have a clue what Begga was insinuating. But she was getting used to her ways and had given up trying to analyse all the nonsense she came out with.

She debated with herself whether she should go and talk to Hörður. His coat was hanging in the corridor, which meant he was probably in his office with his headphones on. She drank her coffee, warming her hands on the hot mug. There weren't many witnesses she could talk to. You could count on the fingers of one hand the people who had known Elísabet. She flicked through the little notebook she always carried. After the meeting with Sólveig, she had made a note of Rúnar's name, as possibly one of Halla's old drinking pals. Of course she could go and talk to him, but what was she supposed to say? What she really wanted was to talk to Ása but she didn't like to defy a direct order from Hörður. Besides, she agreed with him. It must be indescribably awful to lose a child, especially like that, and she would rather not compel the old woman to rake up the memory unnecessarily. Though in fact she doubted that Ása would need to think too hard to remember – incidents like that didn't fade over time. They became part of you. Not simpler, not more bearable; just something you learnt to live with.

Elma ran through the list of pupils in form 1.IG again, pausing at Magnea's name. She had never met her and knew little about her apart from what Hörður and Sævar had told her – and, thanks to Dagný's indiscretion, the fact that she was pregnant. Magnea was probably at work now but it couldn't hurt to check if she had time for a quick chat. Elma called Magnea's mobile number on the off-chance. A cheerful voice answered after the first ring. By a stroke of luck, it turned out that Magnea wasn't at work today as she was feeling unwell. But she was willing to talk, if Elma could give her half an hour to jump in the shower first. Elma thanked her and hung up. She wondered if she ought to pop home for a shower herself but decided to go via the shop instead and grab a bite to eat.

She put down her mug and stood up. Hörður could hardly object to her having a brief chat with Magnea – surely? She darted a shifty glance in the direction of his office as she was sneaking out and heaved a sigh of relief once she was safely out of range. Although she'd half expected to bump into Sævar as she was leaving, there was still no sign of him, so she got into her chilly car and drove off alone.

Magnea was so impeccably dressed that it made Elma feel acutely self-conscious. She started pulling down her bobbly jumper where it had creased up at the front and trying in vain to hide the embarrassing coffee stain she had failed to notice that morning. To her chagrin, it was situated just below her left breast, so there was no way of covering it up without having to adopt an unnatural pose.

'Can I bring you something – coffee, water?' Magnea asked, after inviting Elma to take a seat on a white sofa in the sitting room because the home help was cleaning the kitchen.

'No, thanks, I don't need anything,' Elma said.

As on the phone earlier, Magnea hadn't seemed particularly surprised by Elma's request for a chat; she'd just smiled and invited her in, without asking what she wanted. Since Magnea was wearing a tight jumper and neatly pressed black trousers, Elma couldn't help noticing that her stomach was still perfectly flat, betraying no sign that she was three months pregnant.

'If you don't mind, I'm going to get a glass of water for myself,' Magnea said.

'Sure.'

While she was away, Elma took in the elegant sitting room. A large, imposing canvas hung on one wall, featuring insubstantial figures among a swirl of moss and lava. A Kjarval, Elma saw from the signature at the bottom. That figured: although she didn't know much about art, she did know that Kjarval was Iceland's most important painter. There was no television to be seen, just two big leather sofas and an armchair with curved arms. A large, old-fashioned chandelier was suspended from the ceiling above a coffee table with a glass top, supported on curved stone legs. The black-stained parquet floor formed a striking counterpoint to the white walls and furnishings.

'So,' Magnea said, once she had sat down again, 'what did you want to ask me?'

'I wanted to ask you about Elísabet.'

'Elísabet? Sævar and Hörður have already been round to talk to me about her.' Magnea revealed her teeth in the same brilliant smile that Elma had noticed in the school photos.

'Yes, I know,' Elma replied. 'But still, I'd be very grateful if you could answer a few questions. People often don't realise they know something that could turn out to be important.'

'Of course,' Magnea said. 'But, like I told them, I hadn't spoken to her since we were girls, then she suddenly appeared on my doorstep the other day.'

'Didn't it strike you as odd that she should have knocked on your door that evening?'

'Yes, I have to admit I was a bit thrown. I'd never expected to see her again. I only recognised her when she told me who she was. It wasn't as if we were ever really friends.'

'How did she look?'

'She looked good. But then Elísabet was always very beautiful, with her dark hair and dark eyes. I remember how I used to envy her.' Magnea laughed. 'Of course she was older, but just as stunning. She seemed a bit on edge, though.'

'On edge?'

'Yes, as if she was stressed or nervous about something. She kept looking round and … yes, a bit stressed.'

'Do you think she might have been afraid of someone?'

'You mean that someone was following her? The murderer, maybe? God, that hadn't even occurred to me. Do you think that could have been it?' Magnea appeared shaken.

'What did she say to you?' Elma asked, instead of answering her question.

'At first I thought she'd just come to see me for old times' sake and I found that kind of strange. I mean, you don't just go round to someone's house thirty years after you last saw them and have a cup of coffee as if nothing had happened. I told her that unfortunately I couldn't invite her in as we were expecting guests for dinner, but we could meet another time.' Magnea took a sip of water. 'But Elísabet said it couldn't wait and asked if I'd meet her later that evening. I said the next day would be better but she wouldn't hear of it. I thought that was rather rude, actually, but she wouldn't take no for an answer, so in the end I gave in and agreed. She insisted on meeting at the lighthouse.'

'But you didn't go?'

'No, it completely slipped my mind. Now, of course, I wish I'd gone. She might still be alive if I had.' Magnea looked suitably sorrowful at the thought. Yet Elma couldn't help thinking that everything Magnea said and did was a well-rehearsed act. Her smile and her sadness, the expressions she adopted, the way she tilted her head on one side and crossed her legs were all part of a performance. 'Do you think it would have changed anything?' Magnea asked.

Elma shrugged. 'Impossible to say.' Which probably wasn't the answer Magnea had been hoping for. 'Have you any idea what she wanted to discuss with you?'

'Well, obviously I've been wondering that ever since it happened. There's only really one thing I can think of that she might have wanted to discuss.' Magnea broke off and took a deep breath. 'When we were at school we knew each other slightly through a mutual friend. We were so young – just little girls, you know. At that age you don't realise the consequences of your actions – the effect they can have on other people. That's why I'd totally forgotten until now...'

'What?' Elma prompted, when Magnea didn't immediately continue.

'We used to pick on a boy in our class. He was tall and thin with sticking-out ears. We used to bully him and call him names and were really horrible to him.'

'And you think that was what she wanted to talk about?' Elma asked.

'Well, it's the only thing I can think of. Perhaps her conscience had been bothering her all these years.'

'Do you remember the boy's name?'

'He's called Andrés. He works at the library.'

This was consistent with what Ingibjörn had said about Elísabet attacking Andrés. Elma made a note. 'Do you remember Sara?' she asked.

'What? Sara?' Elma could see how the blood rushed to Magnea's cheeks under the thick layer of make-up.

'Yes, she was in your class, wasn't she?'

'Yes, of course I remember Sara.' Magnea definitely wasn't smiling now. 'Sorry, but I'd rather not talk about her. What happened to Sara is too personal. Not only because we were school friends but because she was my husband's sister.'

'Yes, I'm aware of that. It must have been a terrible blow for the family.'

'You have no idea.'

'I understand that Elísabet and Sara were close friends.'

'Yes,' Magnea replied curtly. 'They were.'

'I know you were only a child at the time, but did you ever get the impression that there was something else bothering Elísabet apart from her difficult home life?'

'What do you mean?' Magnea frowned.

'I'm just wondering what went on at her house. If something could have happened to her there.'

'If you're asking if I think she was abused, I doubt it. Not physically, anyway. She never struck me as … a victim. She was self-confident. Almost arrogant. And she never, ever let anyone push her around.'

Elma bit back the urge to explain to Magnea that children could react to abuse in very different ways; they didn't necessarily behave like victims. 'Do you remember any incidents in which she herself was violent, at school or outside it?'

Magnea shrugged. 'No, I can't say I do. But she was imaginative and got up to all sorts of mischief. The other kids didn't like her much but she got away with a lot. All she had to do was blink those big eyes of hers at the teachers and they'd forgive her.' Magnea's laughter was unusually shrill.

'What about Sara, what was she like? Was she as determined as Elísabet?'

'No, not at all. Sara was the small, sensitive type.' Elma could have sworn she detected a note of anger in Magnea's voice, although her expression didn't change. 'There was something about Elísabet that made you wary. I didn't particularly dislike her but I could never understand why they were friends.' And from the way she said it, there was no doubt at all in Elma's mind that Magnea had loathed Elísabet.

Elma was no reader. She hadn't set foot in the town library since she was a little girl. In those days it had been in a completely different place, near Brekkubær School and the hospital, but now the old library had been converted into flats. She remembered clearly what it had been like inside: the smell of books, the brown carpet, the big wooden shelves. She also remembered the librarian, a small woman with curly hair and a friendly face, who had always made her feel welcome.

She was aware of mixed feelings when she thought about the library. It had been a refuge of sorts; a place she went to forget herself, to wander from shelf to shelf, searching for exciting-sounding titles. It was somewhere to go when she was unhappy. She used to cycle there after school and often spent the whole day there at the weekend. Perhaps that was why the thought of it made her feel so melancholy now. Had she really been that unhappy as a child? She had never stopped to consider it at the time or to analyse her feelings. She had simply escaped into the world of books.

Akranes Library was now housed in a new building on what had once been a marsh where they used to skate in freezing weather. Inside it had a high ceiling, a grey floor and white walls. Modern chairs and light-fittings were lined up in the middle of the space and the girl at the desk, a young blonde with her face buried in a magazine, didn't even look up when Elma walked in. There was little trace of the old library's faded charm.

She walked over to the desk where the girl was turning the pages of her magazine.

'Is Andrés working today?' Elma asked when the girl finally bothered to look up.

The girl shook her head. 'No, he went home early.'

Elma thanked her and was on her way out again when suddenly she paused. Since she was here, she might as well look around. She remembered what a soothing effect the old library had had on her and how much pleasure she used to derive from wandering among the stacks, breathing in the smell of the books. Perhaps she could recapture that feeling now. She walked slowly back to the shelves and spent a while scanning the titles. She had just found a book she liked the look of when she heard someone say her name.

'Elma?'

It took Elma a moment or two to recognise the woman.

'Kristín?' she asked hesitantly.

For a brief interval, neither of them said a word, as if they didn't know how to behave in each other's presence. Then Elma went over and gave Kristín a quick hug.

'Nice to see you,' she said. 'I was hoping I'd bump into you now I'm back in town.' She only realised something was wrong when Kristín raised her eyes.

'God, what's the matter with me?' Kristín said in a strangled voice and sniffed.

'Are you OK?' Elma asked. She studied her old friend. Kristín's face was pale and bare of make-up. Her hair was tied back in a pony-tail and she was wearing tracksuit bottoms. This wasn't the Kristín Elma had seen on social media. There, she was invariably photographed beaming, surrounded by her three children, living what appeared to be the perfect life.

Kristín drew a deep breath and seemed almost too choked up to speak. 'Are you ... busy?' she asked.

'No, of course not. Shall we get a coffee somewhere?' Elma suggested, and Kristín nodded gratefully.

⚓

She hadn't spoken to Kristín for years, probably not since they finished sixth-form college. Their friendship had gradually petered out, without Elma really noticing. Now, as she sat face to face with Kristín, she wondered why that had happened. She remembered all the secrets they used to share; the in-jokes that only they had understood.

'I'm sorry,' Kristín said, with a watery smile. They were sitting in Garðakaffi, the café attached to the open-air museum. Inside, the wooden beams and furniture gave the place a homely, rustic feel. 'I don't know what came over me. It was just so good to see a familiar face.' She nursed her steaming coffee cup in both hands. Kristín had always been a little on the plump side. Not fat, but not thin either. But now, in spite of the thick knitted jumper, Elma could see that she had lost weight. The tracksuit bottoms hung loose on her thighs and her face looked different. Her cheeks, which had always been so round and rosy, now looked haggard and pale. She met Elma's eye. 'I know we haven't talked for a long time, but there's something special about child-hood friends – it's like they always know you best. New friends can never know you as well as the old ones do.'

'No, I suppose you're right,' Elma said. 'To be honest, I haven't been good about keeping up my friendships over the last few years.'

'I heard what happened, Elma,' Kristín said. 'I'm so sorry. How are you?'

Elma smiled. 'Getting there,' she said, wondering if everyone knew about Davíð. 'Anyway, what about you? What's your news?'

Kristín heaved a sigh. 'I'm divorcing Guðni and suddenly it's like the whole of Akranes has turned against me.'

'Why do you say that?'

'You know who Guðni is, don't you? He's Krummi's best

friend. One of the in-crowd – that we were never part of.' The flicker of a smile touched Kristín's lips. 'Well, anyway, after we decided to split up, all our friends, all the couples we knew, sided with Guðni. Everywhere I go, I meet closed doors.'

'What about Silja?' Elma asked.

'Silja?' Kristín said, and sighed again. 'Silja's changed. I'm not good enough for her anymore. She started hanging out with Sandra and her mates. They invited me along while I was with Guðni, but after we separated they dropped me and I haven't heard from them for months.'

Elma didn't know what to say and sat sipping the cocoa she'd ordered while Kristín went on talking, pouring out the whole story. How they had defriended her on Facebook, how lonely she was. 'I've been wondering if I should just move,' she said finally, in a resigned voice.

'Absolutely not,' said Elma. 'Don't let them drive you away. You have to show them you're stronger than they are.'

'But I'm not,' Kristín said, a catch in her voice. 'Not that it matters anyway because Guðni would never let me move. That's not the worst thing, though – the worst thing is that he wants sole custody. The weeks he has the kids are unbearable. I have nothing to do but sit there missing them, and no one comes to see me. I've taken to spending my days in the library.' Her attempt at a smile came out as a grimace.

'I'll come round and see you,' Elma said quickly. 'And don't worry, there's no chance of him getting custody.'

'I know that really … Thanks, Elma,' Kristín said. 'Thanks for letting me dump on you. You know, I've missed you, and I'm not just saying that because of the mess I'm in.'

Elma smiled awkwardly and regretted not having got in touch first. She'd been so preoccupied with her own problems that it hadn't occurred to her she might not be the only one suffering.

The pictures were in an old shoebox, buried among the socks and underpants at the back of the wardrobe. She didn't know exactly what she was looking for. She had been wandering aimlessly around the flat all day, alone at home as so often, with no idea where he was. But then she rarely knew and never asked. It was his business. He could come and go as he pleased, but it was different with her. She had to account for every trip and phone call. Sometimes he seemed to realise how he was behaving. Then he would hold her in his arms and she could, if she liked, pretend to herself that they had only just got together. That none of the ugly stuff had happened. Once, when he'd drunk too much, he had tried to explain why he behaved like that, opening up about his difficult childhood – about the rejection he'd experienced and his constant fear of abandonment. She tried to be understanding but it was often hard. He could be so unfair, she thought, rubbing the new, violet bruise on her sore arm.

Sometimes she wondered how she had ended up in this situation. It hadn't been deliberate, absolutely not. She just hadn't realised what was happening until it was too late. And now she was trapped in a relationship with a man she simultaneously loved and feared. She used to read about women like that and wonder why they didn't just leave. It wasn't that simple, though. It was far too complicated for her just to walk out and disappear. The trouble was, she loved him.

She had to admit that it was nice to have money too. She didn't need to work unless she wanted to and could have almost anything she wanted. Life had never been like that at home – just a perpetual struggle to make ends meet, always waiting for the next pay cheque. She'd never known her father and never wanted to look him up, so it had only been her and her grandmother since her mother died. And her grandmother never wanted to spend a króna unless it was absolutely necessary: the old lady was forever scrimping and saving.

The few friends she had made as a girl used to say they didn't feel comfortable coming round to her house: the furniture was shabby and the place was full of the kind of creepy silence that you only got in old houses. A silence that seemed impossible to fill, as if words were unwelcome and fell, muffled, into the deadening hush.

She sometimes felt as if that pall of silence had followed her and hung over her wherever she went. Like now, alone in the empty flat. Perhaps that was what had attracted her to a man like him: things were never quiet when he was around. Not only that, but he loved to buy her expensive presents; to spoil her with nice clothes and meals at smart restaurants. She couldn't say no; she didn't want to.

Besides, she had no wish to bring up his child alone.

She took out the shoebox and opened it, expecting to find some old junk like letters or postcards – the kind of stuff people keep in shoeboxes in the wardrobe – which was why she got such a shock when she saw the photos. She dropped the box on the bed as if she'd been burnt.

A shiver ran through her and her chest felt so tight she could hardly breathe. She bent over, leaning on the bed, eyes closed, trying to absorb the shock. Then, after a few moments, she picked up the box and emptied it carefully. There must have been at least twenty photos, most of them of the same child, a beautiful, dark-haired girl of maybe ten years old. She was standing in an awkward pose, all skinny arms, bare stomach, knock-knees and that cloak of hair reaching right down to her waist. She'd never seen the girl before. But there were also several pictures of a fair girl, and she recognised her immediately.

She stared at the photos for a while and the girls seemed to stare back. In the end, she stuffed them back in the box with trembling hands, closed the lid and returned it to the wardrobe. She could feel her gorge rising and only just made it to the bathroom before she threw up.

Akranes 1991

Of all the kids in her class Magnea was by far the most popular. She was always surrounded by a large group of friends and admirers who followed her around the school, playing with her during break and vying with each other to be allowed to hang out with her after school. Elísabet had been watching her from afar but couldn't understand what was so special about her. Magnea wasn't particularly bright, nor was she particularly funny or nice. But she was self-confident and never seemed to suffer from a moment's doubt. She talked the most, laughed the loudest and strutted around the playground as if she owned it and everyone in it.

Up to now, Elísabet hadn't taken much notice of the other children in her class. It had been enough to have Sara as her friend. Ever since she started school two years ago, it had been the two of them united against the rest of the world, best friends forever. She had told Sara everything. Well, nearly everything: Sara didn't know how she felt when she did bad things. Hadn't a clue about the suspense beforehand, the way all her nerves tensed, or about the rush of well-being that flooded her afterwards. Elísabet had always pretended to be ashamed. She knew what other people looked like when they were ashamed; knew how to arrange her features to mimic them. Look down, don't smile, and sometimes, if she'd done something very bad, shed a few tears.

Sara had always forgiven her ... until now. Now she had gone too far. The toddler's wounds had been so deep that she'd needed stitches. And now Sara wouldn't speak to her. Wouldn't even look at her.

Elísabet sat down on the wet grass and stared across the playground. She felt her trousers growing damp but it didn't matter. She was watching Sara. Sara was holding Magnea's hand and they were walking around the playground together, pointing and laughing. Elísabet could feel the rage building up inside her. She was alone now. No one was bothered about her. No one cared. No one in the whole wide world.

Elísabet didn't cry. She wasn't the type. She'd long ago realised that it didn't do any good; that no one would ever come to comfort her.

'What do you know about Andrés?' Elma was sitting at the kitchen island, watching her mother roll a haddock fillet in breadcrumbs. Aðalheiður was wearing the red apron that she must have owned for thirty years. The colour was fading and there were spots of fat on the front.

'Andrés who works in the library, you mean? He's a bit peculiar, poor thing, but perfectly harmless. He lived with his parents until they died a few years back. Since then he's been living in supported accommodation. Why do you ask?'

'Just curious. I went to the library today.'

'You used to spend so much time there as a child,' Aðalheiður said, smiling reminiscently. 'Did you find any books?'

'I don't have time to read.'

'Nonsense, there's always time to read. I read every evening before I go to sleep. I can't drop off without a book.'

'And you leave the light on until all hours,' Elma's father commented as he came into the kitchen and took a can of malt drink from the fridge. Her mother just smiled and carried on stirring the onions that were sizzling in the pan, giving off a deliciously savoury smell.

Without warning the front door opened.

'Hello!' Dagný's voice boomed from the hall. 'Is there any coffee?' she asked once she was installed at the kitchen table, her feet up on a chair.

'Are you on your own?' Aðalheiður asked, pouring a mug for her.

'Viðar's taken the boys to football practice,' Dagný said, yawning. 'We'll grab some pizzas on the way home. I've had it for today.'

'What nonsense, there's plenty of food here,' Aðalheiður said. She put the mug on the table in front of her elder daughter and went back to her cooking.

'Oh, I promised them pizza. I'll never hear the last of it if I go back on my word.'

'Do you remember Andrés?' Elma asked.

'Weird Andrés? Sure, I do,' Dagný said. 'Why do you ask?'

'Because I was at the library earlier,' Elma said.

'He once gate-crashed a party at Bjarni's,' Dagný said, shaking her head. 'He'd got hold of a whole bottle of moonshine and was totally wasted. A few minutes later his mum stormed in wearing her dressing gown and curlers, and dragged him off home. I've never seen anything so ridiculous.'

'You went to parties at Bjarni's place?' Elma asked in surprise. Bjarni Hendriksson was at least five years older than her sister.

Dagný shrugged. 'Yes, years ago. Everyone went to his parties. Or at least they did until his dad put a stop to them.'

Elma had never been to those parties. Of course she'd heard about them but she'd never been invited. 'Why did he put a stop to them?'

Dagný glanced incredulously at her. 'Where were you, Elma? Do you really not remember?'

Elma shook her head, trying not to let her sister's contemptuous tone get to her.

Dagný sighed impatiently. 'There was a girl who turned up pissed out of her skull and probably high as well. She passed out in one of the bedrooms and when she woke up she started coming out with all these accusations.'

'What kind of accusations?'

'Oh, she claimed she'd been assaulted. As far as I can remember she was going to press charges, but nothing ever came of it because she didn't have any proof. She'd been totally out of it at the party.'

'Who was she assaulted by?'

'She didn't know and I expect that's why it didn't go any further.'

'Do you think she was making it up?'

Dagný sighed again. 'I don't think anyone did anything to her, not deliberately, at least, but maybe she slept with some boy and regretted it afterwards. Those parties often got out of hand, and people could easily have got up to stuff in that state, and then regretted it later.'

'What were you doing at those parties, Dagný?' Aðalheiður exclaimed.

Dagný tutted in exasperation. '*Mum!* I don't think I went along more than two or three times and I never got wasted like so many of the others.'

'Who was the girl?' Elma asked. She doubted her sister had been quite as much of an angel as she was implying.

'I have a feeling her name was Vilborg. I don't think she lives in Akranes any longer. In fact, I think she moved away not long afterwards,' Dagný said, and began flicking indifferently through the newspaper.

'Do you remember her second name?'

Dagný shook her head without looking up. 'No, but she was two years older than me, so it shouldn't be difficult to find out.'

Elma studied her sister. There were times when she still wished they could be closer. They only ever met at their parents' house. When Elma was younger she'd looked up to her so much and wanted to copy everything she did – to be like her. But Dagný only ever spoke to her to snap at her or accuse her of having mislaid something. She had blamed herself for the fact that Dagný didn't want to be her friend but over the years she had realised that they were simply very different and in their teens her admiration of Dagný had turned to anger. She was fond of her sister and loved her nephews but she wasn't sure she could ever forgive Dagný for the way she had treated her when they were kids.

'Right, I'd better be off,' Dagný said, finally looking up from the paper. She finished her coffee and got to her feet. 'Bye, Mum,' she called from the hall.

Elma rolled her eyes and called as loudly as she could: 'Bye, sister dearest.'

They heard the front door slam and Elma grinned at her mother who groaned but couldn't quite hide a smile.

They'd been invited round to dinner, which didn't happen very often. It was rare for them all to get together, except on special occasions like birthdays, Christmas or Easter. Of course, Ása saw Bjarni almost every day, either when she dropped by the office bringing lunch for her husband and son, or when Bjarni popped in to see her on his way home from work. Bjarni took good care of his mother; she certainly couldn't fault him as a son. But Magnea seldom came with him and then only under pressure. Which was why Ása had been so surprised to receive the invitation. A dinner party for no obvious reason! That was something new, she'd thought to herself as she put down the phone that morning.

When Hendrik came home, she was waiting on the sofa in the sitting room, putting the finishing touches on a pale-pink romper suit with mittens and bootees attached. She had laid it on the sofa to admire it and drifted into a reverie as she stroked the soft wool and tried different buttons against it. When Hendrik finally appeared, he made do with changing his shirt and slapping on some aftershave. Not that he needed any more. Ása thought she would be asphyxiated by the overpowering smell in the car but instead of winding down the window, she sat there without moving or speaking.

They tapped lightly on Bjarni and Magnea's door. Bjarni never knocked when he came round to their house; he had his own key and came and went as he liked. Of course, they had keys to Bjarni and Magnea's house as well, but they wouldn't dream of using them. Not on an occasion like this.

Bjarni came to the door. As usual, Ása couldn't help feeling proud when she saw him. He was so handsome. He'd been a beautiful child, a cute boy and was now a handsome man, tall and broad-shouldered, with fair hair and pale-blue eyes.

'Hi, Mum,' he said, giving her a hug, then shook hands with his father. He helped her off with her coat and hung it in the wardrobe.

'I'm perfectly capable of doing that myself, you know,' Ása protested. 'I'm not completely past it.' Her grateful smile vanished the moment Magnea appeared in the hall.

'Hi,' said Magnea, her cheeriness sounding a little overdone as usual, which always made Ása doubt her sincerity. Magnea kissed them both on the cheek, and it drove Ása up the wall the way Hendrik seized the chance to slip his arms round her waist. 'Can I offer you something?' Magnea said. 'Water, coffee? Or wine?'

'Would you get me a drop of whisky, sweetheart?' Hendrik asked, in the voice he always used with Magnea. He settled into the armchair in the formal sitting room. Hendrik always made himself at home wherever he was. Ása, in contrast, perched stiffly on the edge of the sofa.

'What about you, Ása? Can I offer you something?' Magnea asked, having taken Hendrik his whisky.

'No, thank you,' Ása said, trying to smile politely.

Magnea sat down too and an awkward silence fell until Bjarni joined them. He had a way of lightening the atmosphere and getting those around him to relax. Perhaps that was why people were drawn to him. When he was young, the house had always been full of boys. The doorbell had rung incessantly, and at one time it had become such a nuisance that Ása had been forced to put her foot down: no one was to come round until after four o'clock and everyone must have gone home by half past six.

Some people were born leaders, Ása knew that. She'd known it ever since Bjarni was two. He was born in July and his star sign was Leo, a fact that had always seemed symbolic to her. Bjarni sometimes reminded her of a majestic lion, the way he swaggered around, keeping a possessive eye on his pride. Even at nursery school he'd had his pick of friends and later he'd had his pick of girls too. Ása had never understood why he'd had to go and fall for Magnea.

Bjarni sat down beside Magnea and put an arm round her shoulders. He looked expectantly from Ása to Hendrik, then, apparently unable to contain himself any longer, said: 'It's no good, Magnea, I can't wait until the end of the evening like you wanted.' He laughed, his eyes bright with excitement.

Ása glanced, puzzled, at Hendrik, then back at her son. What did the boy have to tell them? What was going on?

'Magnea's pregnant,' Bjarni announced. 'We're expecting the patter of tiny feet in June.'

Ása opened her mouth, then closed it again. Hendrik got straight to his feet and hugged them both delightedly. After a moment, Ása followed suit, then sat down again, as if in a daze.

'Are you all right, Mum?' Bjarni asked, his face concerned.

Ása realised she still hadn't said a word. Finally she smiled and, to her astonishment, felt a tear trickling down her cheek. She hastily wiped it away, laughing in embarrassment. Bjarni's and Magnea's eyes met and they smiled.

'Oh, Ása darling, we didn't mean to upset you,' Magnea said, getting up and going over to sit by her mother-in-law.

Ása laughed again, feeling foolish. All eyes were on her; she wasn't used to being the centre of attention. 'I'm sorry,' she said. 'I don't know what came over me. It's wonderful news. Wonderful.'

'Now we'll finally have a use for all those clothes you've knitted,' Bjarni said.

Ása nodded and bit her lip. She managed to prevent any more tears from spilling over but felt as if something had broken loose inside her. A sensation that she hadn't felt for a long time made itself known. Excited anticipation. For the first time in years she actually had something to look forward to.

Elma was on her way home when Sævar rang. He asked, apparently casually, whether she'd like to grab some supper. 'It's past eight, Sævar,' she pointed out. 'I've already eaten.'

'What about a drink, then? My shout,' Sævar suggested. Elma could tell over the phone that he was smiling and felt she couldn't very well refuse.

She'd never been to Gamla kaupfélagið – the Old Cooperative – before. A bar, restaurant and a popular party venue at weekends, it stood on the high street in an attractive, white gabled building. Ironically, although the town had grown since Elma was young, there were fewer pubs and restaurants than there used to be. Ever since the Hvalfjörður tunnel had been built, the locals had tended to head into Reykjavík when they wanted to go out and the nightlife in Akranes had suffered as a result. Still, the quality of the places on offer had generally improved. When Elma went in, she was pleased to discover that the bar had a simple but tasteful interior. The lighting was cosily dim and there were few other customers in there, as you'd expect on a Monday evening.

Sævar was sitting at a table at the back of the room and had already ordered her a beer. He was wearing a T-shirt, which revealed the thick pelt on his arms, and his hair was tousled. Elma's thoughts went inadvertently to Davíð, who used to spend ages styling his hair in the mornings, standing in front of the mirror, making sure not a single hair was out of place. She had always found it rather endearing, taking it for granted that he wanted to look good for her. Sævar hadn't even shaved. His beer had left a moustache of foam on his upper lip and Elma felt an almost irresistible urge to reach out and wipe it off with her thumb. Sævar took another good swig, wiped his lip, then put down his glass.

'It's over,' he said abruptly. 'I've split up with Telma.'

'Oh,' Elma said, taken aback. Sævar's expression conveyed neither relief nor pleasure and she hadn't a clue how she was supposed to react. She took a sip of beer to fill the awkward pause.

'She'd only just told me her mother had cancer and what do I do? I go and dump her.'

Elma choked on her beer and couldn't stop the ensuing bout of coughing which had changed into laughter before she knew what was happening. Her whole body shook with the effort to suppress it.

'Are you OK? Have you got something stuck in your windpipe?' Before Sævar could come round the table and do the Heimlich manoeuvre on her, she waved him away. Tears were rolling down her cheeks. 'Are you laughing?' he asked, astonished.

'Sorry,' she gasped. 'I don't know why I'm laughing. Of course it's not remotely funny.' She concentrated on taking deep breaths and took another mouthful of beer, careful to make sure it went down the right way this time.

'Are you losing it, Elma?' She was relieved to see that he seemed amused, in spite of her inappropriate reaction.

'I don't know. Probably.' She dried her eyes and adopted a serious face. 'Sorry, I've stopped now. What were you saying – is it over between you?'

'Yes, it's over,' Sævar said.

'And is that a good thing or…?'

'Yes, it's a good thing, Elma. It's such a relief, but at the same time I feel like a total shit. I mean, she'd only told me a few days ago that her mother was ill.' Sævar pulled a face. 'And don't start laughing again,' he added, shooting Elma a warning look.

'So she took it badly?'

Sævar shrugged. 'She cried. But I don't know – it can hardly have come as a surprise to her. It hasn't been working for at least a year now.'

Elma nodded and took another gulp of beer. She was beginning to get that familiar heady feeling.

'I don't really know how I feel,' Sævar went. 'It's as if a chapter of my life has closed and I'll miss it in a way. But I'm more than ready to end it and, to be honest, I feel guilty that I don't feel worse. I mean, I should feel bad, shouldn't I? After all, we're talking seven years of my life. Seven years is a bloody long time.'

Elma nodded.

'Elma...' Sævar's gaze was fixed on his glass now. 'I always meant to apologise for the way I ran out on you that time. I don't know why I left like that.'

'Don't worry about it,' Elma said lightly.

'You were saying your relationship had recently ended. Is it long since you broke up?'

'Nearly four months.'

'And that's why you moved home?'

'Yes,' Elma replied. 'It was never the plan but somehow it worked out that way.'

'So it was a bad break-up?'

Elma nodded. Judging from the silence that followed, Sævar was waiting for her to elaborate. 'Yes, it was. Very bad. Davíð was my best friend and...' She trailed off, afraid her voice would break and reluctant to burst into tears in front of him. Part of her wanted to tell him everything but she couldn't bring herself to. She just couldn't.

Sævar signalled to the waiter to bring them more drinks. 'Do you miss him?' he asked.

'Yes,' Elma said, her voice emerging in a whisper. She cleared her throat. 'I've just been so angry that I haven't been able to miss him properly. But now it's coming home to me how much I do. I just ran away.'

'To Akranes, of all places,' Sævar said with a grin. 'Who would have imagined?'

'Not me, anyway.' Elma heaved a sigh. 'But what about you, what originally brought you to Akranes? You said your brother lived here. What about your parents?'

'My brother has a learning disability and lives in a group home. Maybe I'd have moved away if it weren't for him,' Sævar said. He sipped his beer and stared down at it as he spoke. 'My parents died in a car accident five years after we moved here. I'd just turned twenty at the time. My brother was sixteen and very happy in the group home. I couldn't abandon him. There's only the two of us left now.'

Elma nodded.

'What is it about this town that you dislike so much?' Sævar asked, after a brief silence.

Elma was disconcerted at how well he could read her, since she couldn't remember having told him about her negative feelings towards Akranes. 'Maybe it was never the town that got to me,' she said slowly. 'I suppose it was more about who I was. I didn't particularly like myself when I lived here.'

'Oh? I reckon I'd have liked you a lot.'

'Oh, really? I'm not so sure.'

'Want a bet? Go on, tell me everything – all Elma's dirty little secrets.'

Elma laughed, then began to talk.

Akranes 1992

The bathroom mirror was so dirty that she could hardly see her reflection. She'd wiped it with water but that didn't help much. She spat the toothpaste into the sink and stood on tiptoe to drink from the tap. Then she dried her face on her sleeve and studied herself in the mirror.

Elísabet was nine and well aware of how beautiful she was. Even the smeary mirror couldn't hide that. Her dark hair reached down to her waist and her dark-brown eyes were large and entrancing. She knew it was desirable to be beautiful. People praised her, smiled at her and exclaimed over her eyes and her thick hair. The children in her class didn't pick on her like they did on the boy with the sticking-out ears. But no one wanted to play with her. They said she was weird. That her house stank.

She'd never really fitted in. She'd always felt like an outsider among these people. Her little brother had been lucky. Lucky never to have to find out what it was like to grow up. She used to visit him in the graveyard. She'd sit there for a long time, gazing at the white cross, pulling up the grass around it and stroking the black plaque with his name on it.

Her father lay buried beside her little brother and she visited him too. But it was becoming increasingly difficult to summon up the few memories she had of him. She could hardly picture his face anymore: it was lost in a mist. She couldn't remember the shape of his nose or the colour of his eyes. But she would never forget his hand; her daddy's big, rough hand. 'Working hands,' he used to say. She had a faint memory of what it had felt like when he hugged her. How she'd been engulfed in his arms, how his bearded cheek had rasped against her hair. The thing she remembered most vividly, though, was his voice. She could hear him talking, even though she could no longer recall his features.

She could hear his voice amidst all the noise and also in her quieter moments.

They were at the playground; both dressed the same, with their hair in matching plaits.

'Hi, Elísabet,' said Magnea when she noticed her. She glanced at Sara and they both grinned, as if they knew something Elísabet didn't.

Elísabet didn't answer. She had resigned herself to being alone. Life was simpler when it was just her. But this conviction was belied by the way her heart missed a beat when they invited her to play with them. They'd whispered to each other for a while, before eventually turning to her and asking if she wanted to join them. Elísabet had trouble hiding her happiness.

Later that evening she bounded up the steps, light as air, and collapsed exhausted into bed. She was asleep before she could even undress and didn't wake up until morning.

Tuesday, 5 December 2017

It didn't take Elma long to track Vilborg down once she got into work the next day. All she had to do was go back through the old school newspapers. It transpired that there had only been one Vilborg born in 1980 at Grundi School and her patronymic was Sæmundsdóttir. Elma typed her name into the search engine and found both a Facebook page and an entry in the telephone directory. The sight of Vilborg's address elicited a silent groan from her: it wasn't far from where she and Davíð used to live. She toyed with the idea of ringing her instead but concluded that, given the sensitive nature of the case, it would be better to talk to Vilborg in person. She dialled her number and Vilborg answered after the first ring. When Elma told her what it was about, Vilborg immediately agreed to see her. Elma grabbed the car keys.

'Where are you off to?' Hörður asked, meeting her in the doorway.

'Just popping to the dentist's,' she lied, privately berating herself for not having come up with a more original excuse, but Hörður seemed to accept it without question. Elma hurried out of the building before he could see through her. She was a useless liar.

Several minutes later, she put her foot down on the accelerator and watched Akranes receding in the rear-view mirror. The late-winter dawn was breaking and the shrivelled grass gleamed in the cold rays of the sun. Elma turned up the radio and sang along to the tune that was playing. She was still in high spirits from the evening before when she and Sævar had sat in Gamla kaupféla-gið until closing time – which wasn't actually that late since the bar closed at ten, but during that time they had talked nonstop. Perhaps the beer had helped to loosen her tongue because, once she'd got started, she had found she couldn't stop, though she had avoided saying too much about Davíð because the pain was still too raw.

They'd also discussed the case and she'd told him about Sara's drawing, her conversation with Magnea and what Dagný had said about Vilborg. 'When children are abused, the culprit is usually somebody close to them. Someone with easy access to them,' Elma had said. 'Don't you find it an extraordinary coincidence that a sexual offence should have been committed during a party at Ása and Hendrik's house? At Sara's home? For all we know, it could have been the same person?'

Sævar had been sceptical. 'You have to take into account how many people used to go to Bjarni's parties,' he'd countered. 'We're talking dozens. And, to be honest, I wouldn't be surprised if your sister was right. I'm not saying the rape didn't take place, I just find it more likely the perpetrator was someone her own age, who was as drunk as her.' At that moment, the lights had come on and the waiter had started collecting the glasses from their table. They had walked home together, turning to lighter subjects. Elma couldn't recall exactly what they'd talked about but she did remember laughing helplessly in a way she had hardly done for months.

Vilborg was expecting her and opened the door of her basement flat as soon as Elma rang the bell. She was wearing a loose smock with an elaborate, swirly pattern. The flat reeked of incense but even that couldn't disguise the sickly smell of cannabis. Vilborg invited Elma to sit down on a curry-yellow sofa and offered her some tea, which she accepted. After making two cups, Vilborg settled herself in a dark-green armchair and waited for Elma to begin.

Elma noticed that the furniture was old and there was no sign of the typical designer items one would normally expect to find in an Icelandic home. Everything was a bit shabby, and Vilborg obviously had a penchant for decorating in bright colours, judging by the dark-green walls in the sitting room and wine-red ones in the hall.

Elma decided to come straight to the point. 'What happened that evening at Bjarni's house?' she asked.

'I suppose you'll have heard the stories?' Vilborg said.

'Actually, I've heard very little. Only that you accused someone at the party of assaulting you while you were asleep.'

Vilborg put down her teacup and laughed bitterly. 'Assaulting me? That's putting it mildly. And I wasn't as drunk as people say; I'd only had three beers but they went straight to my head. I was just sixteen, after all, and I'd only recently started drinking. I felt so dizzy that I went to lie down and must have fallen asleep. The next thing I remember is being woken up by a sharp pain. He'd pulled down my tights and forced himself inside me. I tried to scream but couldn't make a sound. He was pinning me down with one arm and forcing my head into the pillow with the other.'

'Did you see who it was?'

'It was so dark that I never got a good look at him. After he'd finished, he left me lying there on the bed. I didn't dare look up. I just lay there crying until I couldn't bear it anymore and ran home.'

'Do you think you could describe him?'

'He was older than me. At least, that's the impression I got, though I couldn't see anything. He held something over my face – I think it was a woollen hat. He was heavy and it felt as if he had a beard – not much, just stubble, you know. None of the boys at the party were that heavily built so I thought ... I thought it must have been an adult.'

'An adult?'

Vilborg nodded. 'I told my parents. Not immediately – I couldn't. But they saw the change in me and kept pestering me until I told them. In the end I admitted what had happened and who I thought had done it to me.'

'And who did you think it was?'

'Bjarni's father, Hendrik,' Vilborg said, after a moment's hesitation. 'Of course, I can't be sure, but I met him later and he smelled the same. Of the same aftershave.'

'What did your parents do?'

'Dad went mental. He went storming round to Hendrik's, demanding to know who had done it. I don't know what happened but I don't think it can have ended well because we moved away from Akranes shortly afterwards. Mum and Dad just said we could all do with a change of scene.'

'Did you go for a medical examination the night it happened?'

Vilborg shook her head. 'It never occurred to me at the time. I just got straight into the bath and washed the horrible stuff off me. Later, of course I wished I'd gone to hospital so they could have caught the disgusting creep, but it was too late when I finally told people what had happened. Now I'll probably never know for sure who it was.' She reached for her teacup again. 'Why do you think it's connected to the woman who was found by the lighthouse? Had she been raped too?'

'No, she hadn't been raped. Not then, anyway.'

'Oh? Had she been raped before?'

Elma quickly shook her head. It wouldn't do to say too much. 'Do you think I could talk to your father? I'd like to know what passed between him and Hendrik.'

Vilborg's face grew sad. 'No, sorry. Mum and Dad are both dead.'

'Oh, I'm sorry. My condolences.'

'It's all right. They were both getting on and they'd had long, happy lives.'

Elma spent the drive home brooding over what she'd learnt. She was shaken by Vilborg's story. If Hendrik really had been her rapist, it would come as a major shock to Akranes society. A man as powerful and well respected as him. But, of course, she would have to give him the benefit of doubt, since Vilborg's accusation, although serious, was based on almost nothing more solid than the smell of aftershave. How many men had used that same aftershave? Nevertheless, this was yet another element linking Hendrik's family to Elísabet's death.

Her thoughts went to Sara and Elísabet. Had the same man been responsible in all their cases? Of course, she couldn't know if Sara had really been the victim of sexual abuse. After all, how much was it safe to deduce from a drawing by a six-year-old? It was different in Elísabet's case as the photo was clear evidence of some level of abuse. And a lot of dubious types had had access to Elísabet's house – far too many, in fact. Darkness fell as Elma reached the Hvalfjörður tunnel. She wondered what kind of person would be capable of taking another person's life simply in order to protect their own reputation.

The doorbell rang shortly after midday. Magnea sighed under her breath when she saw her mother-in-law standing outside. When they had told Ása about the pregnancy the night before, her attitude to Magnea had undergone a transformation; it was as if they were suddenly best friends. Magnea was surprised that Ása couldn't see for herself how transparent her behaviour was, but instead of confronting her with the fact, she merely put on a smile and opened the door.

'I thought you might be hungry,' Ása said, wiping her shoes on the mat. 'Bjarni told me you were off sick today and I've just baked some bread.'

'It smells delicious,' Magnea said, accepting the loaf. There was a few seconds' awkward silence until it dawned on Magnea that Ása was waiting to be invited in. 'Would you like to have some with me? ... Or have you already had lunch?'

'Oh, no, thank you, I wouldn't want to disturb you,' Ása said, from force of habit.

'Of course you're not disturbing me,' Magnea assured her, well trained in her role. 'Why don't we have lunch together? I could do with some company.'

Ása followed her inside and took a seat at the kitchen table. She always sat as if she were uncomfortable, poised to get up in a hurry, her hands folded in her lap and her elbows pressed to her sides. Ása's primness and inability to relax never failed to get on Magnea's nerves.

She laid the table for them both, then cut some slices of the warm bread and arranged them neatly in a napkin-lined basket. They exchanged polite small-talk as they ate. Although Ása wasn't the chatty type, if there was one thing Magnea was good at it was making conversation. Bjarni used to say she'd be capable of keeping up a conversation with a broom handle. Once they had finished eating, Magnea cleared the table, noticing out of the corner of her eye as she did so that Ása had opened her bag and was taking out something pink. Naturally she knew that her mother-in-law was always knitting – she'd seen the wicker baskets full of yarn and half-finished knitting projects in the sitting room but had never mentioned the fact. Never asked who they were for. She knew, like everyone else, that they weren't for anyone except Ása herself.

'I … It occurred to me that you might like to have this,' Ása said. Her lips trembled slightly as she smiled and Magnea felt a little moved in spite of herself, sensing the pain behind the smile. 'I made this for Sara.'

Magnea gasped. 'I couldn't…' she began.

Ása forestalled her. 'Of course, I don't know the child's sex, but if it's a girl, I'd like her to have it.'

Magnea took the jumper from her. Although it was a little worn, and had obviously been used, it was still soft and pretty.

Ása stood up, smoothing down her skirt. 'It would mean the world to me to see the jumper used again.'

Magnea nodded without a word. She accompanied Ása to the door and said goodbye to her. As soon as she had gone, she opened the wardrobe and put the jumper behind a pile of bed-clothes where no one could see it.

A little over forty minutes after leaving Vilborg, Elma pulled up in front of Ása and Hendrik's house. On the drive back from Reykjavík she had made up her mind. In spite of Hörður's orders, she simply had to speak to Ása. She couldn't let Hörður's relationship with Hendrik's family get in the way of the investigation. She had to find out if her suspicions about Hendrik were correct.

She was struck by the beauty of Ása and Hendrik's house with its cream-coloured walls and the large dormer windows with their distinctive dark frames. It was situated at the bottom of a cul-de-sac with a view of the Höfði Old People's Home and, beyond that, of the beach at Langisandur and of Reykjavík on the other side of the bay. There was no car in the drive in front of the double garage and the lights were off, but in spite of that Elma took hold of the brass knocker in the middle of the mahogany front door and let it fall twice.

'Good afternoon,' said a high voice behind her, making her jump. 'Sorry, I didn't mean to startle you,' Ása added.

'Oh, that's all right,' Elma said, hurriedly extending her hand. 'My name's Elma and I'm from the local police. I wondered if I could have a quick word.'

'What about?' Ása asked, regarding her in astonishment.

'Elísabet Hölludóttir. You knew her, didn't you?'

Ása hesitated before inserting the key in the lock and beckoning her wordlessly to come inside. Elma followed her into an attractive sitting room with high windows that looked out over the garden. Ása invited her to take a seat on the dark-brown leather sofa, then sat down opposite her and waited, her red-lipsticked mouth no more than a thin line in her pale face. Ása was unquestionably a lady; the type who knew all about table manners and who went to the hairdresser every two weeks, judging by the way her short white hair had been elaborately blow-dried. Elma's gaze, travelling around the room, fell on a wicker basket beside the sofa, which was overflowing with balls of wool and what appeared to be baby clothes.

'What a beautiful home you have,' she began, smiling.

'Thank you,' Ása replied, with no answering smile. 'We haven't lived here that long. I preferred our old place; I had such a lovely garden there. We used to win prizes for it.'

Refusing to let herself be thrown by Ása's coolness, Elma continued in a friendly tone: 'As you probably know, we're investigating Elísabet's death. I ... we're trying to build up a better picture of her.' She paused. 'To be honest, we don't have much to go on and the investigation's not making much progress, so we need to make sure we examine every angle as closely as possible. She was a friend of your daughter Sara, wasn't she?'

Ása merely nodded, but her expression changed infinitesimally at the mention of Sara. The corners of her mouth twitched faintly and her body tensed. Elma sensed that she was on her guard.

'Were they close friends?' Elma asked.

'They were inseparable, believe me. I tried...' Ása gave a slight shake of her head.

'Why did you want to separate them?'

Ása took a deep breath. 'I once went round to Elísabet's house. Of course I'd heard the rumours, the gossip. I was aware that Halla was one of the ... Well, she hung around with the town's undesirables, but I'd never have dreamt it was possible to live in such squalor. Cans and bottles all over the place, rotting food, the floor black with dirt. But the worst thing was the smell – a repulsive stench of cigarette smoke mixed with the reek of all the rubbish and other filth.' Ása wrinkled her nose at the memory.

'Did it never cross your mind to report the situation to social services?'

'Of course I reported it,' Ása shot back. 'For all the good it did. I think she was given some second-hand clothes. That was about it.'

'What was Elísabet like as a girl?'

'She was just a child. A little girl who'd never been taught any manners or discipline, and was allowed to run wild. It was as if she couldn't stay still. She always struck me as a bit strange. Of course, she was stunning but she was … odd. As if something wasn't quite right.' Ása paused, choosing her words with care. 'The worst thing about Elísabet wasn't her mother or her home life, it was that she … how shall I put it … she had a wicked streak. She was beautiful, that's true, but there was something evil there. That's what I always sensed.' Ása didn't look at Elma as she talked but focused on the shrubs outside the sitting-room window as their branches swayed gently in the breeze.

'Evil? What do you mean by that?'

'Once we had some friends visiting. They brought their two-year-old daughter with them and we let her play in Sara's bedroom with the girls. Next minute the child was screaming her head off and we ran in to find out what was wrong. When we got there, she had an ugly bite mark on her arm. It was bleeding. Of course, Elísabet wouldn't admit she'd done it, but it was obvious: she'd been alone with the child at the time.

'So your daughter wasn't in the room when it happened?'

'No, she'd stepped out for a minute,' Ása said. 'After that, I wouldn't let Sara play with Elísabet anymore. I used to collect her from school myself and made sure they didn't spend any time together. I told Sara to play with the other girls, who weren't such a bad influence.'

'And did it work?'

'Elísabet didn't come round to our house again, you can be sure of that.' Apparently realising how cold this sounded, Ása added: 'Please, don't get me wrong. I felt very sorry for her, given her situation, but I had to put my own children first. I was thinking of Sara. I was only trying to protect her.' The final words emerged in a whisper.

'Is it true that Elísabet's mother, Halla, rented her house from you and your husband?'

'You'll have to ask Hendrik about that. I had very little to do with the business side of things. But yes, we owned the house, and I assume she must have been paying rent. Though, having said that, I never understood how she could afford such a big place. I know she worked at the fish factory before her husband died, but after that she was on benefits. I didn't get involved, though.'

'I see,' Elma said. How, she asked herself, had Halla been able to pay the rent on a large detached house if she'd had practically no income? 'Did you ever see Elísabet after Sara died?' she asked.

Ása smoothed invisible creases from her skirt. Elma noticed that her hands were shaking slightly and when she spoke her voice was hoarser than before. 'She turned up to the memorial service. That's the last time I saw her. She was sitting with Sara's school friends at the reception afterwards and I remember being amazed at how calm she was. She just sat there, completely expressionless, and didn't shed a single tear.'

Ása seemed so small and vulnerable as she sat there facing Elma. Her dainty hands were hardly more than skin and bone. Her hair was thin, despite the bouffant style, and her face was drawn. Perhaps it was her imagination, but Elma felt as if she was still marked by the loss of her child; as if it had been slowly but steadily eating away at her all these years.

'Sara was afraid of water,' Ása said suddenly, meeting Elma's eye. 'Terrified, ever since she was tiny. It was difficult even getting her into the bath. If she got water in her eyes, you could hear her screams next door.' She smiled reminiscently but the smile vanished when she added: 'She would never have got on that raft voluntarily.'

'What do you mean?' Elma asked, regarding Ása in surprise.

'I told them. But nobody believed me.' Her voice was so low now that Elma had to lean closer to hear her.

'What do you think happened?'

Ása looked out of the window again. 'What do I think? When has it ever mattered what I think?'

Akranes 1992

'I fancy Beggi or Palli, how about you?' Magnea leant against the rough wall, hands in her pockets, her eyes fixed on Sara.

Sara pulled her sleeves down over her fingers, avoiding Magnea's gaze. 'I don't know,' she said so quietly that the words were almost inaudible.

'And your brother's totally fit.' Magnea emitted a heartfelt sigh. Sara's brother, Bjarni, was several years older than them but they sometimes bumped into him in the school corridors. Magnea always did everything she could to attract his attention.

Sara glanced up at her with a grimace. 'But he's so old.'

'I know, that's why I'd rather fancy Beggi. Or Palli. Do you know who you fancy, Elísabet?' There was something about Magnea's smile that made Elísabet uneasy. She shook her head. She'd never been particularly interested in boys, unlike Magnea, who could talk endlessly about who was fit and who wasn't.

'Do you fancy weirdo Andrés then?' Magnea said mockingly. Andrés was a boy in their class who most people wouldn't be seen dead with. He was tall and thin with sticking-out ears and his trousers were always too short for him. He tried to compensate for his height by walking around with his shoulders hunched, which made him look even more of a freak.

'No,' Elísabet said. It was a week since the two girls had invited her to hang out with them and she was already fed up with Magnea. What's more, she could have sworn that Sara was too.

'Hi, Andrés!' Magnea called, waving to him as he stood in the playground, boring his toe into the gravel. When Andrés waved uncertainly back, Magnea grinned at the other girls. The bell rang and the children ran into the classroom.

By the time second break began, Elísabet had made up her mind to talk to Sara. She was going to ask if they could meet up later – just the two of them, like they used to. But she had no sooner set foot outside than he came running up to her, flung his arms round *her, held her head in a tight grip and kissed her on the face. Again and again. Elísabet wasn't sure what happened after that – everything was hazy. She struck out as hard as she could, not stopping even when he fell to the ground and put his arms over his head. She didn't stop until someone seized her from behind and dragged her away.*

The sand was black in Krókalón bay. Seaweed swayed at the water's edge and there was a sharp tang of salt in the air. As Elma walked slowly along the beach, a chilly breeze ruffled her hair. She zipped her coat up to her neck, shoved her hands deep in her pockets and gazed out over the surface of the sea. How far out would she have to wade before the current swept her away? The water was almost black now, like the sand. On the horizon, she could see the faint, dome-shaped outline of the glacier rising from the sea at the end of the chain of peaks that marked the Snæfellsnes Peninsula. Every year, its white cap seemed to shrink. A few more and the glacier would have vanished altogether.

Had Sara been playing here twenty-seven years ago? Had she found a pallet on the beach and built a raft out of it? Alone?

It was getting on for four o'clock and the sun that had been shining brightly all day was setting. The light was already fading and Elma gradually became aware of a skin-crawling sensation that she wasn't alone. She stole a quick glance around. The beach was empty but there were lights on in the houses lining the shore and she could hear the distant drone of traffic.

Elma was still trying to work out her next move. She had wanted to believe Ása when she said that Sara would never have gone out on the raft voluntarily, but at the same time she was aware that children could be drawn into various escapades with their friends that they wouldn't dream of if left to their own devices. It was this that convinced her that Sara couldn't have been alone. Elísabet had almost certainly been there with her.

Elma turned to look at the house that had once been home to Elísabet and her mother. It was clearly visible from the beach. The lights were on, so the mother and son who lived there now must be home. Could the house have been the catalyst for the whole chain of events? Had Elísabet seen the advert on the estate agent's website and been overwhelmed by memories? Elma pictured her standing there, staring at the house while everything came back to her with a brutal clarity. She wondered whether all Elísabet's memories had been bad or if her life had been better before her father died. Would everything have turned out differently if he hadn't gone out to sea that day?

Elma knew these questions were unanswerable. She had wasted far too much time going over her own life and asking the same kind of thing: would everything have turned out differently if only...? She knew it was utterly futile.

Without warning, the sea seemed to wake from its slumbers and a large wave came rolling up the beach, scattering Elma's thoughts. It left behind a layer of scum on the sand after it had retreated again, and Elma realised that she was cold. At that moment the last rays of the sun disappeared below the horizon and darkness closed in. There were no lights on the beach and Elma shivered. She walked rapidly back to the road without looking over her shoulder, conscious all the time of that feeling of being watched.

The photographs were in a white envelope that had been pushed through the letterbox. There was no stamp, no sender, nothing but her name: *Ása*. All the envelope contained were the photographs of two little girls.

One of them was her daughter.

The moment Ása realised, her hands began to shake so badly that she dropped the pictures on the floor. Overcoming her reluctance, she bent down to retrieve them. She recognised the other girl too: it was the dark-haired woman who had come to see her recently. Ása had never forgotten the squalor of the house where she had lived as a little girl.

She could feel herself growing hot and cold in turn. Her whole body seemed to have gone numb, as if she were no longer part of this world. She didn't even stop to wonder who had sent her the photos; there was no point.

She started pacing around the empty house, pausing by the window to stare out at a world that had suddenly changed. The sitting-room wall was covered with family photos, taken on various occasions. She lifted one of them down and gazed at the face of the little person whose presence she had only been allowed to enjoy for a few brief years. She remembered what beautiful fingers she'd had as a baby, long and delicate like the hands of a future pianist. Ironically, she had never been particularly good at the piano, though Hendrik had insisted she take lessons and practise for an hour every day. And she had done so, as she had done everything, with a good-natured smile on her face. Sara had been such a cheerful child. Happy by nature. When the change came, Ása had put it down to her age. It was only natural for children to become moodier as they neared adolescence; an inevitable consequence of growing up and losing their innocence. Or so she had consoled herself.

She hung the picture back on the wall and walked into the kitchen as if in a daze. When she had found what she wanted, she went into the bedroom. There she sat down on the bed they had shared for the last forty years and waited.

It was late by the time Elma got back to the office. Since her phone hadn't rung all day, she assumed no one had missed her.

'So, what did the dentist have to say?' Sævar asked when she came in.

'What?' Elma replied, having completely forgotten the lie she had told earlier.

'Weren't you at the dentist's?'

'Oh, yes, right...' Elma said. 'To be honest, I didn't really have a dental appointment.'

'Aha, I suspected as much. You were away so long I'd begun to wonder if you'd had all your teeth pulled out. So, what have you been up to, then?'

'I went to see Vilborg.'

'Really?'

'And Ása.'

Sævar's brows drew together in a frown.

Elma took a deep breath. 'I had to talk to her. You see, I suspect that Sara was being sexually abused as well. And I have a hunch that she wasn't alone when she vanished.'

'Surely you didn't say that to Ása?' Sævar asked, horrified.

'No, of course not,' Elma hastened to assure him. 'It's just that I suspect Elísabet and Sara were victims of the same man. Vilborg too, possibly. I believe Elísabet came back to Akranes because she wanted to report him. And I think she met the man – the mysterious photographer.'

'And you reckon you know who he was?'

Elma nodded. 'Think about it for a moment, Sævar. We've got Sara, Elísabet and Vilborg. Vilborg was raped at Hendrik and Ása's place. Hendrik owned the house that Elísabet's mother rented, and Sara was his daughter.'

'You don't seriously believe he'd be capable of … I mean, sexual abuse is one thing, but to murder someone just to shut them up…?'

'From what I've heard, Hendrik is very concerned about his reputation in town,' Elma said.

Sævar flung himself back in his chair, running a hand through his dark hair. 'Bloody hell, Elma. If you're right…'

'Of course, I can't be sure,' Elma said. 'But you have to admit that it doesn't look good for him.'

Sævar groaned. Outside the office they heard Begga's infectious laughter followed by Kári's guffaw. The coffee Elma had fetched before sitting down with Sævar had gone cold and she still couldn't shake off the chill that had entered her bones during her walk at Krókalón.

In one swift movement, Sævar swung round to his computer and began tapping away on the keyboard. After a short interval, he looked back at Elma.

'There are two cars registered in Hendrik and Ása's names. A jeep and a family car. Shall we check if they're both parked in their drive?'

'Yes, let's.' Elma smiled at him gratefully. 'But there's another person I'd like to talk to as well: one of the gang who were always visiting Elísabet's mother, Halla. Do you know Rúnar Geirsson, alias Rabbi?'

Sævar nodded. 'He's an old friend of the law. But we haven't had any dealings with him for several years so I'm guessing that means he's finally managed to turn over a new leaf. Temporarily, at least.'

Elma had a bad conscience where Hörður was concerned. She hadn't informed him of what she'd been up to over the last few days and was worried about how he'd react when she came clean. She knew he would never have given her the green light to go and talk to Ása. All she could hope was that by the time Hörður found out, they would have got hold of some hard evidence; some clue that would connect Hendrik to Elísabet's death.

'You said earlier that you didn't believe Sara was alone when she went out on the raft. Why's that?' Sævar asked.

'Because, according to Ása, Sara was terrified of water, and had been ever since she was tiny. I'm not saying anyone forced her onto the raft but I do find it unlikely that she was alone,' Elma said. 'I've examined the case files and I have to say that the whole thing looks pretty suspicious to me. The idea that the girl would have simply climbed onto the raft at the water's edge and drifted out to sea; sure, she was only nine, but she must have known how dangerous it was.'

'It can happen so quickly,' Sævar pointed out. 'The currents are hard to predict and the waves can be powerful. Perhaps she miscalculated.' He slowed down and turned into Ása and Hendrik's road. Their house appeared to be empty. There was no car in the drive and all the lights were off.

'Could they have gone somewhere in separate cars?' Elma found that she was whispering, though she didn't really know why; no one could hear them as they were still sitting in the police car.

'Looks like it,' Sævar said. 'Unless one or both cars are in the garage, of course.'

'Let's leave ours here,' Elma suggested.

The shrubs in the garden were too low to hide behind, which made Elma grateful for the darkness. She remembered Ása saying how much she missed the garden at their old place. Here, it would be many years before the trees attained any sort of height. Elma walked resolutely towards the front door, pretending not to notice Sævar's expression, and knocked. She was sure there was nobody home, and when no one answered, she went round to the garage. The door was locked and the windows were so high up that she couldn't reach them to peer inside.

'Sævar,' she called in a low voice, beckoning him over.

'I'm not going to lift you up if that's what you think,' Sævar said. He scanned their surroundings nervously.

'No one will see,' Elma said confidently. 'Quick, give me a leg up. I just need to check if the car's in there.'

Sævar sighed, but gave in and bent down with his fingers clasped so Elma could step on his hands. 'Hurry up then. I've no idea how we're going to explain this if we're spotted.'

Elma slipped off one shoe and placed her foot in Sævar's big, warm palms. Then she hauled herself up to the window and tried to peer inside. 'I can hardly see a thing – it's too dark. There's a car in there but I can't see the front.'

She got down and slipped her shoe back on.

Sævar straightened up. 'Then let's get out of here,' he said, heading off smartly with Elma on his heels. He flinched when a car drove past and Elma laughed.

'You're not much of an adrenaline junkie, are you?' she teased.

'Well, I am a police officer,' Sævar retorted. 'I'd have thought that made me quite enough of an adrenaline junkie.'

'In Akranes?'

'There's been plenty going on since you arrived,' Sævar said in his defence.

'True, though I wouldn't exactly call this business as usual for Akranes CID.'

It wasn't yet 5.00 p.m., so they decided to postpone their visit to Rúnar until they could be sure of catching him at home, rather than disturbing him at work. Elma lay back in the car seat, feeling suddenly tired. Soothing music was playing on the radio and she closed her eyes for a minute.

'I don't know what it is about this car,' she said, yawning, 'but I feel sleepy the minute I recline my seat.'

'Shall we stretch our legs?' Sævar suggested. The car stopped and Elma opened her eyes to discover that they were at Breiðin. She hadn't noticed that Sævar had been driving out towards the point.

'A breath of sea air will soon revive you.' The way he smiled at her made Elma feel warm inside. Her thoughts flew inadvertently to the young man who lived opposite her. Recently she had taken to dashing in and out of her flat in an effort to avoid bumping into him.

They walked past a pallet on which the opening times of the new lighthouse had been written in black marker pen in both English and Icelandic. It had recently become a popular tourist spot and the picture attached to the pallet showed the new plan for the area. When Elma was a child, the point had been untouched and beautiful in spite of its flaws: no tourists, nothing but sea, birds and the two lighthouses.

'These days it's better to visit in the winter,' Sævar remarked, as if reading her mind. 'When there's hardly anyone about.'

'But it's so dark at this time of year. Only five hours of daylight if you're lucky.'

'The darkness can be beautiful too,' Sævar said. 'I like the short days and long nights – they don't bother me. What drives me nuts is when the sun starts shining round the clock.'

'I agree,' said Elma. 'Most people love it, but I hate trying to go to sleep in broad daylight. Having said that, I miss the sun. I wouldn't mind breaking the winter up a bit and going on holiday somewhere warm.'

They sat down on a bench by the new lighthouse and gazed out to sea. The lights of Reykjavík were twinkling across the bay. Elma lost herself for a while in the pleasure of watching the waves and breathing in the salty air. It was such a lovely, tranquil spot that it was almost impossible to believe that something terrible had happened there. Yet Elísabet's body had been found only a few metres away. Elma pictured again the dark hair spread out over the rocks, the puffy face and swollen eyes. The eyes that had once belonged to the lovely little girl in the photos.

She was positive that Magnea knew more than she was admitting. And there was no doubt in her mind that something had happened to Elísabet when she was a child. Someone had taken that picture.

She mentally reviewed the family. There were Hendrik and Ása, in whose house the atmosphere of grief seemed almost palpable – unless the feeling emanated solely from Ása, who still seemed so weighed down with sorrow. Although Elma had only ever seen Hendrik from a distance, he had an aura of self-confidence, just like his son. Bjarni obviously found it easy to adapt his manners to the circumstances. After all, even she had been charmed by him originally. Finally, there was Tómas, the black sheep of the family. Elma knew little about him, apart from the fact that he hadn't hesitated to beat his girlfriend to a pulp and seemed to live off his brother's success.

Elma was roused from these thoughts by the feeling of Sævar's warm hand touching hers where it was resting on the bench. At first, she wasn't sure if the touch had been accidental. But Sævar didn't move his hand. She went on staring straight ahead, relishing the warmth that radiated from him. They sat there like that for a while, until Sævar eventually withdrew his hand and got up.

'Shall we make a move?' he asked. 'You must be cold.'

Elma nodded, though she felt as if the ice inside her had melted away as she sat there beside him.

They drove in silence. Elma longed to say something but didn't know what. Several times she opened her mouth, only to close it again because the words wouldn't come. She felt acutely aware of Sævar's presence beside her. It was hard to stop herself gazing at him, at his hand on the gearstick; hard to suppress her longing to reach out and touch it. But by the time they parked in front of a dreary-looking block of flats, the moment had passed and it was too late to say anything.

'He should be home by now,' Sævar said, peering up at the building.

The white paint was dirty and flaking here and there, while the garden, encircled by an old fence, contained nothing but a slide and a sandpit full of withered grass and nettles. They went into the lobby and found Rúnar's name on the bell. A hoarse voice answered and, after they had explained who they were, buzzed them in.

Rúnar, or Rabbi as he was known, was a scrawny figure with a face deeply lined from years of substance abuse. He still stank of the rubbish he had just finished removing from the town's bins but it didn't seem to bother him. His flat stank too – of cigarettes and of something rank that Elma couldn't identify. They followed him into the living room, where he invited them to take a seat on a battered leather sofa that looked as if it was about to fall apart. There wasn't much else in the room, only a coffee table covered in junk and a TV on a small shelving unit. The floor was littered with books, magazines and electrical cables, but the walls were bare apart from a small cross hanging over the sofa.

When they asked Rúnar if he remembered Halla, his eyes grew distant and rested on the wall as he was talking. 'Those were the days.' He smiled reminiscently. 'That was when I was just having fun, you know, before I got into the hard stuff. Before everything went to pot and it took over my entire life. I had a job in those days. I used to go out on the trawlers for tours lasting several weeks, so I had plenty of time to let my hair down when I was back on shore.'

'Do you remember Halla's little girl?' Elma asked. She was perched on the edge of the sofa, trying to touch as little as possible. 'Her name was Elísabet.'

Rúnar nodded and coughed. Rubbing his fingers together, he lowered his eyes unseeingly to the dark-brown parquet.

'Do you remember her being there?' Elma continued, when Rúnar didn't say anything. 'While you lot were partying, she was probably in her room upstairs. Didn't you ever see her? Didn't she come down sometimes?'

'Yes, sure. I saw her but I don't remember … I couldn't say how often.'

'Did you ever speak to her? Did you go up to her room?' Sævar's eyes were boring into Rúnar's face.

Rúnar looked up, confused. 'What the … what do you mean? Are you accusing me of something?'

'Do you know if anyone else went up to her room while you lot were partying?' Elma asked.

Rúnar's mouth twisted in a grimace and he shook his head. His eyes darted to the window, then back to them.

'Are you sure?'

Rúnar didn't answer. He fished a cigarette out of his pocket and lit it without opening a window. The poky flat was soon filled with smoke.

'She was found dead several days ago,' Elma said. 'Murdered.'

'I heard about it. Saw her picture in the papers,' Rúnar said. 'But you don't think it could have had anything to do with that, do you?'

'To do with what?' Sævar leant forwards, his eyes fixed unblinkingly on Rúnar. 'To do with what, Rabbi?'

Rúnar was obviously having trouble sitting still. He took several deep drags of his cigarette and blew them to one side, as if that would prevent the smoke from reaching Elma and Sævar. Elma noticed that beads of sweat had begun to break out on his forehead.

'Will you promise it won't go any further?' he said at last. 'You didn't hear it from me.'

'I'm afraid we can't promise that. But if you knowingly conceal information that could be important, that would be a crime and you could go to jail.'

Rúnar heaved a sigh, stubbed out his cigarette and wiped his forehead with the sleeve of his jumper.

'Oh, well, it's not like I have much to lose,' he said. 'Anyway, I doubt it's relevant. She was the woman found by the lighthouse, wasn't she? I thought I recognised her. You don't forget a face like that. Such a pretty little girl.' He was silent a moment before resuming. 'The thing is, I just don't know. It's not like I have any proof of my suspicions – of what we all suspected – but the fact is he often went up to see her. He used to come round while we were partying and go upstairs. We couldn't hear anything because the music was so loud. I don't know how long he spent up there, or what he got up to. It's hard to keep track of time when you're having fun. Well, it used to be...' His smile didn't reach his eyes. 'But we all knew he went up there. Halla knew too, but she didn't do anything about it. I reckon she told herself there was no harm in it. That he wasn't hurting her...'

'Who was it? Was it Hendrik who went up to her room?'

'Eh? Hendrik?' Rabbi gaped at them both in astonishment and shook his head vehemently. 'God, no, it was Tommi – Tómas,

Hendrik's brother. And if he finds out I told you, I'll get a much worse beating than his old lady. You have to promise not to let on that it was me. Please, I'm begging you.'

The house struck Hendrik as unusually quiet when he got home from his day on the golf course. He didn't often come back to an empty house and didn't particularly like it. Ása was usually sitting there knitting those infernal baby clothes that they would finally have a use for. Though now that he stopped to think about it, she'd been behaving oddly for several days. Ever since she came home from hospital she'd been sitting around empty-handed, and he kept catching her staring out of the window, though at what he couldn't tell. Perhaps at something that no one else could see.

He walked around the house, trying to spot any clues as to where she could have gone. The alarm hadn't been switched on, so she couldn't have gone far. Her handbag was in its place, hanging from the radiator in the hall, but he couldn't see her shoes. Maybe she was in the garden. In summer, when Ása wasn't inside knitting, she was usually to be found outside, pottering in the garden. He went over to the sitting-room window and looked out at the rather bleak view of brown grass and bare branches. Thinking he spotted a movement, he peered towards the bushes. It was probably yet another bloody cat. He couldn't stand the creatures – always slinking around and popping up when you least expected them. They gave him the creeps.

The kitchen tap was dripping. Hendrik tried to turn it off more tightly, but the drops kept on coming, falling with loud smacks onto the shiny steel. Hearing a sudden creak from the parquet floor behind him, he jerked round his head. But there was no one there; he was alone in the house. So why did he have the feeling that someone was watching him? He scanned his sur-roundings for anything untoward, but everything was in its place. Nothing had been disturbed. He cleared his throat and coughed loudly, only to break off abruptly when he thought he heard a rustle from the sitting room. He walked noiselessly back down the hallway, his nerves taut. His heart was beating so fast he could feel his head throbbing and his breathing was laboured and shallow.

There was no one in the sitting room. What a fool he was. He felt stupid for letting his imagination run away with him like that. Burglaries weren't unheard of in Akranes, but he doubted thieves would be about at this time of day. Still, it was a fact that the townspeople could no longer leave their doors unlocked. Several had learnt the hard way, which was why he'd had an alarm installed.

He paused, his gaze arrested by one of the family photos on the sitting-room wall. It had been taken at their old house in 1989. In the background, there was a glimpse of pale-pink curtains and the white pelmet Ása had crocheted. He stood there for a long moment, gazing at the picture, and felt his breathing grow laboured again as he was hit by a wave of grief. He missed Sara so much that the pain was sometimes physical.

He tried to calm his breathing, afraid that his heart was on the verge of packing up after decades of grief and loss. It couldn't take much pressure anymore. That was one of the reasons why he had decided to give up work. He had already undergone two angioplasties and any kind of strain was difficult for him. He had first been diagnosed with an irregular heartbeat shortly after Sara's disappearance, when the grief hadn't yet fully sunk in. He could remember little from that time, only the gulf he had been aware of between himself and other people. He hadn't been there for Ása and she hadn't been there for him. But at least she'd had her friends. People had gone out of their way to comfort her whereas they had made do with slapping him on the shoulder – as if a mother's grief was more profound, more heartfelt, than a father's. He remembered clearly that Tómas hadn't shown his face for days, and although Hendrik had never revealed the fact, his brother's betrayal had hurt.

He had always been there for Tómas.

There was another creak from the parquet, closer to the kitchen this time. He walked quickly back into the kitchen, but there was nobody there and nothing had been touched.

He dropped into a chair by the round table, bending forwards over his knees and wiping the sweat from his forehead with his sleeve. When he looked up, the sweat sprang out again: one of the kitchen drawers was pulled right out. He rose slowly to his feet, leaning on the kitchen worktop, and closed the drawer with a trembling hand. Now he was quite sure that something strange was going on. The drawer had been closed a few minutes ago, surely? Or had it? Suddenly, he wasn't sure. The tap was still dripping but apart from that all was quiet.

He started moving slowly from room to room. There weren't that many. One contained a desk and bookshelves, another a made-up spare bed and the third was his and Ása's bedroom. As soon as he opened the door, he saw that the bed was unmade and the curtains hadn't been opened. Had Ása gone out without making the bed? Impossible. He knew his wife and knew she would never have left their room in that state. Only then did it dawn on him that something might have happened to Ása. It was only a couple of days since she'd had a turn and fainted. Perhaps it had happened again. But, if so, where was she?

The only room left to check was the en-suite bathroom. When he opened the door he was met by his own face in the mirror above the sink. But it wasn't alone: there was another face there too.

Before he could say a word or turn, the cold blade of a knife was driven into his neck.

Akranes 1992

They were all looking at her with the sort of concerned expression that she couldn't stand. She felt as if she ought to be crying. As if they were waiting for her to. She almost wanted to do them the favour. To cry her eyes out so they could comfort her and tell her that everything would be all right, but she couldn't; the tears wouldn't come, so she simply stared out of the window and tried not to think about anything.

'We've called your mother and she's on her way,' the headteacher said. Elísabet didn't answer. She hadn't said a word since she sat down in his office.

'Andrés's parents are coming to pick him up too. He'll probably need stitches.' The headteacher's tone was accusatory. The woman next to him gave him a look and sighed. Then she leant over the table.

'Elísabet, can you tell us what happened? I know Andrés shouldn't have grabbed you like that but...' The woman's voice was soothing. She had said she was a psychologist. No doubt many people would have been won over by those observant eyes and that persuasive voice, but not Elísabet. She merely continued to stare out of the window, though she did wonder if she should report that she'd seen Magnea whispering in Andrés's ear before he came running over to her. That she had almost certainly egged him on, in the same way that she ordered everyone else around. But Elísabet knew it was pointless: they wouldn't listen. Grown-ups never listened.

'How are things at home?' the woman continued. 'Is there something you'd like to tell us?'

The door opened and there stood her mother, her hair tied back in a pony-tail to hide the bald patch at the back of her head. Apart from her usual heavy, black eye make-up she looked quite presentable. And the stink of smoke was only obvious when she came closer.

The headteacher and psychologist greeted her mother and offered her a seat. While they were filling her in on what had happened, she nodded impassively, without so much as a glance at Elísabet.

'Given the violence of her over-reaction, we were wondering if the root of the problem could lie elsewhere,' the psychologist said. 'Do you think there could be something bothering Elísabet at school, or at home, maybe?'

'Well, I don't know,' her mother said. She looked so small sitting there in the chair by the desk, almost as if she had shrunk. This absurd idea made Elísabet smile, and the headteacher noticed.

'She doesn't seem to be taking it very seriously,' he remarked.

Elísabet lowered her eyelids as if ashamed.

The psychologist, ignoring his comment, gave Elísabet a friendly smile. 'I recommend that Elísabet comes for an appointment with me. She might find it helpful to speak to someone neutral. A stranger.'

'If you ask me, that's completely unnecessary,' her mother said quickly. 'And, anyway, we can't afford to pay for that sort of thing.'

'It would be part of the service offered by the school,' the psychologist assured her. 'What do you say, Elísabet? Don't you think that would be a good solution?'

Elísabet met the psychologist's eyes for the first time. She took care to keep a straight face as she nodded.

'Right, that's that then,' the psychologist said, standing up as a sign that the meeting was over. Elísabet's mother smiled coldly and laid a hand on Elísabet's shoulder.

As they were leaving, Elísabet saw Sara and Magnea standing a little way off, watching them. She was sure they were both grinning.

When they got home, her mother slammed the door behind them, then grabbed Elísabet by the arm and shoved her so hard that she *fell on the floor and grazed her elbow. She could feel her mother's eyes burning into hers and hurriedly looked away.*

'How dare you do that to me?' her mother hissed. She took out a cigarette, lit it and sat down at the kitchen table. Drumming her fingers, she sucked the smoke deep into her lungs.

'Go to your room,' she said, without even looking at Elísabet. She just sat there, her face turned to the window, smoking.

Elísabet got up, rubbing her elbow. She went upstairs to her room, as usual avoiding the stair that creaked loudest.

The cord of her bedside lamp was long enough to reach into the cupboard under the sloping ceiling. She pulled the duvet off her bed and pushed it into the cupboard along with her pillow. The yellow glow of the lamp lit up the cramped space, making her feel strangely safe in there, almost as if she were in another world. She sat down and started running her fingers over the scratches on the door. Sometimes she imagined she was in a cave. They had learnt about cavemen at school. Her teacher had shown them the pictures they had scratched on the walls, pictures that told whole stories.

But the scratches in her cupboard didn't tell any stories, except perhaps her own, which no one but her would understand. She wrapped her duvet tightly around herself and eventually drifted off to sleep to the sound of the wind whistling in the gaps between the boards.

She didn't wake up until evening, when she was disturbed by the familiar creaking of the top stair.

A dim light now showed inside the house and there was a black jeep parked in the drive. If it hadn't been for the ambulance and police cars outside, they would have assumed it was an evening like any other. And so it was for most people. Weary parents were standing by stoves, stirring saucepans. The smell of cooking was beginning to emerge from the houses to mingle with the odour of wet tarmac. The rush-hour traffic was thinning out with every minute that passed. Everywhere they looked, windows were illuminated by flickering television screens. Elma pictured children sprawled on sofas, transfixed by the antics of colourful cartoon figures, their jumpers stained, their hair, which had been so tidy that morning, a tangled mess. The only times Elma could remember her sister voluntarily spending with her were those hours in front of the TV while supper was bubbling away in the kitchen. She wondered if the family who owned the house in front of her had ever enjoyed such times. Whether the little girl had sat beside her brother, watching cartoons while her mother was cooking. Had they been happy before disaster fell?

Kári and Grétar were standing outside the house, Grétar on the phone, Kári at his side, his hands buried in his pockets. His small eyes looked even blacker than usual in the gloom.

'What the hell happened?' Sævar asked. The phone had rung just as they were leaving Rúnar's, and after that things had happened quickly. They had run down the steps, driven through town as fast as they dared, and Elma had opened the door and leapt out before the car had even stopped moving.

'She stabbed him,' Kári said. 'She just went and stabbed him.'

'What … Why did she do that?' Elma asked, but Kári merely shrugged in bewilderment. 'Where is she now?'

'She's in there with Hörður. I gather they're going to take her to the station.'

The house was as tidy as it had been earlier that day when Elma had gone round to see Ása, apart from the dirt trampled over the floors. The smell was different too. Instead of the scent of freshly baked bread, a strange, metallic odour hung in the air. She could hear Hörður talking somewhere in the house and the sound of low voices issued from the bedroom where forensics were at work. Sævar followed the voices but Elma remained in the hall. The tiled floor was largely covered by a Persian rug. The walls were hung with paintings and a collection of objects were arranged on an imposing sideboard: figurines, a silver bowl and a vase on a crocheted white doily. There was a framed photo of the siblings – a little girl and an older boy. It was summer in the picture and the children's blond hair was almost white. The boy had his arm around his sister. She was beaming from ear to ear; he wore a knowing smirk. Elma flinched when the grandfather clock emitted a hollow chime. One stroke. It was half past six.

When Elma peered into the sitting room she saw Hörður sitting on the sofa beside Ása. They hadn't switched on the lamps and the only illumination came from the outdoor lights on the decking. Ása was sitting bolt upright with a knitted shawl over her shoulders. Her eyes were blank and she didn't react to Elma's approach. Hörður rose to his feet, beckoning Elma to go back into the hall with him.

'She still hasn't said a word,' he whispered. 'Of course we'll wait until we get to the station before we question her, but she's just sitting there, staring into space. I think she must be in shock.'

'Is it definite that she stabbed Hendrik?'

'She called emergency services herself,' Hörður confirmed. 'She said Hendrik was lying unconscious on the floor and that she had stabbed him. Apparently she sounded very calm on the phone, and when Kári and Grétar arrived, the door was unlocked and they found her sitting in the bedroom, holding out a blood-stained knife to them.'

Elma glanced disbelievingly into the sitting room. The petite woman sitting in there looked barely capable of standing up, let alone of stabbing a man so much bigger than herself.

'Apparently the scene was horrific,' Hörður went on. 'Hendrik was lying on the bathroom floor bleeding heavily, while she just sat on the bed and watched. There was no sign that anyone else had been there. But still, I find it hard to believe she could have done it. I mean, I know them both so well. It's completely incomprehensible.'

'Is Hendrik alive?'

Hörður shrugged. 'He was alive but unconscious when the paramedics arrived. I haven't heard any news since then.' He drew a deep breath and looked back towards the sitting room. 'I just can't work it out. What in God's name happened here?'

'Why hasn't she been taken to the station?' Elma asked, regarding Hörður in astonishment.

He shrugged again and sighed. 'I'll get Kári and Grétar to do that now. You stay with her while I'm gone.'

He left and Elma went into the sitting room and sat down warily beside Ása on the sofa. She didn't know how to behave or what to say. Ása didn't look round, just adjusted her shawl a little, wrapping it more tightly around her shoulders. Her hair, which had been fussily blow-dried when Elma first met her, now hung limply on either side of her pale face. Yet in spite of this she seemed oddly dignified.

'We'll have to take you down to the station in a minute,' Elma said, after a short silence.

Ása turned slowly to look at her, and Elma was taken aback when she smiled a cold, sad smile. 'I didn't believe her.' As Ása said it, her expression grew stony and her lips tightened. Her face, which up to now had been blank, suddenly contorted and Elma felt an urge to put an arm round her shoulders. When Ása spoke again her voice was choked and her eyes were fierce. 'I didn't believe it when she told me. She came and told me what he'd done. She told me everything but I didn't believe it.'

'Who told you everything?' Elma asked in dawning surprise. 'Are you talking about Elísabet?'

Ása nodded, then reached down and drew a small envelope

from under the rug. She handed it to Elma, who took it, casting an uncertain glance towards the hall before cautiously opening it. Inside were three photographs, similar to the one from Elísabet's car. Elma saw immediately that one of them was of Elísabet as a child, standing in nothing but her knickers, with an unmade bed in the background. A duvet without a cover and a ragdoll. Elísabet was looking directly into the camera. Her hands were clasped behind her back and her long hair fell over her bony chest. The picture must have been taken at the same time as the one found in her car. It was the same room, the same setting.

But the other two pictures showed a blonde girl lying on a large bed, her knees drawn up to her chest. She had both arms clasped over her bare ribcage and her eyes were lowered. Elma became aware of a bad taste in her mouth and could feel her face growing hot.

'Who gave you these pictures?' she asked. 'Did you find them here?'

'Hendrik did that to her,' Ása whispered, dropping her gaze to her hands that were lying in her lap. Elma noticed that she kept stroking her finger and remembered that she had been wearing a ring earlier.

'He did that to my girl. To my little baby.'

Her weeping continued to echo in the house even after she had gone, rending the silence, piercing to the bone. Elma knew that the sound would pursue her into the night.

When Ása had finally stood up she was so weak that Elma had to support her. Kári and Grétar had escorted her down to the station where she would spend the night before formal questioning began in the morning. This evening she would have to undress and submit to a body search, as well as giving various samples and having her mugshot taken. Elma felt genuinely sorry for her. She had helped her into her beautiful black leather coat, wrapped the shawl round her neck and eased her feet into her shoes, while the whole time Ása had kept up a quiet, heart-broken sobbing, like a small child.

Elma had shown the pictures to Hörður and Sævar, after which neither of them had said much. They needed time to take in the implications. Hörður spent the rest of the time there either talking on the phone, speaking to the forensics team in the bedroom or walking round the house in search of goodness knows what. Large patches of sweat stained his light-blue shirt.

'She needs to rest. We'll talk to her properly tomorrow,' he told them later in the evening.

'Ása said that Elísabet came to see her,' Elma said. 'Apparently, Elísabet told her about Hendrik and what he had done to her and Sara.' In that instant, she remembered the car in the garage. Before either Hörður or Sævar could say a word, Elma had spun round and was off. The garage was locked, as it had been earlier that day, but after a brief search she located the key in a small cupboard in the hall. The garage lights came on automatically after flickering for a few moments, to reveal a small grey car.

'Look,' Elma called to Sævar, who had followed her out of the house. She was standing by the front wing on the left-hand side. 'There's a small dent here but it's hard to say what caused it. We'll have to get forensics to take a look.'

'That dent could have been caused by anything,' Sævar said, examining it.

'Yes, it could have been caused by anything,' Elma repeated, but instinct told her he was wrong. They stood there in silence for a while, contemplating the car. The sequence of events was becoming clearer to Elma. The picture she had found in Elísabet's car was like the ones Ása had shown her – same girl, same place. And the girl in the other pictures had been Ása's daughter Sara. There could be no doubt about that.

'Which of them do you think was driving?' Sævar asked. 'Was

it Ása, or did Hendrik know that Elísabet had been here, wanting to tell her story?'

'I don't know. Ása didn't say. All she said was that she hadn't believed Elísabet when she claimed Hendrik had abused her. She didn't believe it until she was sent the photos.'

'Did Elísabet send them to her?'

'I doubt it,' Elma said. 'Or presumably Ása would have acted sooner.'

Sævar sighed and rubbed a hand over his eyes. The lights went out and Elma pressed the switch to turn them on again.

'Perhaps they were afraid Elísabet would repeat her accusations to a wider audience,' Sævar said. 'In any case, they had a motive to want to shut her up.'

'But if Ása was so sure that Elísabet's accusations were lies, why bother? Would she really have gone that far to protect Hendrik's reputation?'

'Not only Hendrik's – Bjarni's too. In a small town like this, people are very protective of their reputations, as you said yourself.' Sævar went over to the garage door and called Hörður, who was standing outside, talking to the technicians.

Shortly afterwards the garage was full of police officers and members of forensics, and Elma retreated outside onto the pavement. Only then did she notice the crowd that had gathered around the house. Cars had stopped nearby and curious eyes were trying to get a glimpse of what was going on. The news would be all over town in a flash.

Later that evening Elma parked outside her building. After switching off the engine, she slumped back in her seat. When her phone started vibrating in her pocket and her parents' number flashed up on the screen, she left it unanswered, unable to face talking to anyone just yet. The moment she closed her eyes, she saw the blood again. The floor of Hendrik and Ása's bathroom had been covered in a dark-red lake. She couldn't get the cloying iron stench out of her nose. But the sick feeling in her stomach wasn't due to the blood. It had started when she spoke to Ása; when Ása had shown her the photos of the girls. She could still hear her sobbing; it seemed to ring louder in her ears now that it was quiet. A symphony of grief and rage. But the grief had weighed more heavily, as Elma was only too aware from her own experience.

As she went inside, the door of the flat opposite opened.

'Hi.' It was her neighbour. He leant against the doorpost, smiling at her. 'I thought I heard you coming home.'

He must have been listening out for her. Elma groaned under her breath.

'I was just wondering if you were up for a beer?' he went on. But his smile vanished when he saw Elma's face. 'No pressure, though.'

'I think it'll have to keep,' Elma said, giving an exaggerated yawn. 'I'm absolutely shattered.'

'No problem,' he said with a wink. 'Just knock on my door if you change your mind.'

Elma gave him a perfunctory smile and shut her door behind her. Alone at last. She flopped onto the sofa and closed her eyes. She had seen Ása again down at the station later in the evening but the woman had been in no state to provide a more detailed account of what had happened. She had stopped crying and just sat there, staring into space without saying a word. It was as if her mind was far away, completely detached from the upheaval around her.

Akranes 1992

She had spent several days converting the pallet into a raft. It had been lying there one day when she went down to the beach. One of the planks was broken but it was an easy matter to mend it. Solla's husband had been happy to give her some nails and pieces of wood, and lend her his hammer, though he had looked at her a bit doubtfully and asked what she wanted them for. She'd had to think quickly. The raft was her secret.

Since the weather was mild and dry, she could stay outside all day without getting cold or people thinking it was strange. She hadn't told anyone what she was planning. She had never told anyone her daddy's story about Helga sailing to Greenland on a raft. She knew it almost certainly wasn't possible and that the story was probably made up, but that didn't really matter. At least she could daydream that she was going away somewhere. Fantasise about sailing over the sea on the raft and drifting ashore in some exciting new place. Far from her mother, far from Sara and Magnea and the man who owned the house. She would be free of all that and this thought alone was enough to raise her spirits. The only hard part was when she thought about Sara. Sara had hurt her more than anyone else. None of the rest would have mattered if Sara had still been her friend.

She was overcome with rage whenever she thought about Sara. The throbbing in her head drowned out the plashing of the waves and she could feel her fingertips tingling. Usually it helped to kick some loose object. Once she had stamped on the little limpets clinging to the rocks. But at other times it was as if nothing in the world could relieve the restlessness and anger inside her.

She didn't hear them arrive because she was standing over the raft, banging in nails with the borrowed hammer.

'What are you doing?' she heard a voice ask behind her. Turning, she saw them both standing on the rocks above her, Magnea a little to the fore, staring at her provocatively. Sara avoided her eye, keeping her head down.

'Nothing,' Elísabet answered, turning back to the raft.

'Why's your mum so ugly?'

The spiteful remark came from Magnea. Elísabet didn't answer, just pretended not to hear and raised the hammer again.

'Elísabet,' Magnea snapped.

When Elísabet didn't react, she tried again. 'Elísabet!' Her voice was loud and hectoring. 'I asked you why your mum's so ugly. Was that why your dad died – because he couldn't stand being with someone so ugly?'

Elísabet could feel herself growing hot all over. She aimed the hammer and brought it down on the nail again and again. She could hardly hear Magnea's voice over the clang of metal on metal. Her arm was beginning to ache from the effort.

Suddenly a shower of sand rained down on her. The grains caught in her hair and slipped down the neck of her T-shirt. She stopped and blinked. The sand had got into her eyes and mouth. She could hear Magnea's jeering laughter behind her.

Her hand lifted before she could stop it. Spinning round, she threw the hammer as hard as she could. But it didn't hit Magnea.

Sara clasped her forehead and collapsed. Her head hit the rocks and a bright red river of blood started pouring down over them.

'What have you done?' Magnea's voice was shaking and she glanced round, terrified.

Elísabet didn't move. She stood there rigid, watching as Magnea pushed at Sara. There was no reaction.

'What have you done?' Magnea said again. She was crying now.

Elísabet didn't answer. She didn't know how long it was before either of them moved again. They just stood there waiting. Waiting for Sara to move or for someone to come, but no one came. And Sara didn't move.

'We'll go to prison,' Magnea whispered. 'You'll go to prison.'

'Shut up, Magnea,' Elísabet hissed. She began to drag the raft over to Sara, then tried to lift her body onto it. 'Help me,' she ordered Magnea, who was just standing there, gaping.

Eventually the two of them managed to heave the inert body onto the raft. Elísabet pulled off her shoes, then began to drag the raft down to the sea. The water was up to her waist before the pallet finally started to float and slowly began drifting away from shore. She waded back to the beach, where Magnea stood watching, her face red and swollen from crying. Elísabet went up to her and looked her in the eye. Magnea had stopped crying apart from the odd sob.

Then they walked away in different directions, without looking back.

Wednesday, 6 December 2017

Ása looked completely different next morning. Elma was disconcerted to find her sitting there with her head held high. Elma could have sworn she was smiling slightly.

Hörður had asked Elma and Sævar to conduct the interview on the grounds that he knew Ása too well, and Elma had been privately relieved. It wasn't that she didn't trust her boss but on this point she agreed with him. When she arrived, Hörður had been on the phone to Bjarni, whose voice could be heard blaring out of the receiver. Elma couldn't help feeling sorry for her boss as he patiently fielded Bjarni's questions.

'I hope you weren't too uncomfortable last night,' Elma began, smiling at Ása, although the circumstances were anything but pleasant.

'Not in the slightest,' Ása said formally. 'I don't think I've ever slept better.' She coughed discreetly, then started talking. 'The day my daughter vanished, the weather was beautiful. It had rained the night before and the trees were beginning to put out their leaves with that lovely scent of spring – it was just glorious. I remember going out in the garden that morning, weeding the spring onions and watering the seeds I'd just planted. Then I had a cup of coffee on the deck and enjoyed the fact I could sit outside.' She paused and looked at them both in turn, her expression suddenly clouded with pain. 'I'd always thought I'd sense it if something bad happened. You know, you hear about this connection – that parents can sense it when something bad happens to their children. Maybe that's why I've always felt so guilty. I've always felt as if I should have known … I should have sensed that something was wrong. But I hadn't the faintest idea. It was a lovely day until that evening. I didn't start wondering where she was until then.'

Ása broke off her account to ask for a glass of water, then resumed: 'We found her shoes on the beach but we never found her. My darling girl was never found. I still see her as she was dressed that morning, in her pink dress and her favourite white tights with the pink hearts on them.' Tears began sliding down Ása's cheeks and she quickly wiped them away with her shawl, then asked for a tissue and blew her nose. 'Just imagine it. She'll stay like that forever. Forever nine. Never grown up.'

'What did Elísabet say when she came round to see you that day?' Sævar asked.

'She murdered Sara.' Ása's face grew hard.

Elma gaped at her. 'What do you mean?'

'Just what I said. That's what she came to tell me. She said she'd lost her temper with Sara. She threw a hammer at her, and Sara fell over and hit her head. Elísabet said she was so scared by what she'd done that she lifted Sara's body onto the raft and watched the waves carrying her further and further out to sea. She watched her disappear and didn't do a thing. Just watched my little girl until she was out of sight, then walked off. And all these years she never said a word. Not until just over a week ago.'

Elma and Sævar exchanged glances. This wasn't what they had been expecting at all.

'Just imagine what it was like,' Ása said, raising her voice. 'No one believed me. I knew it wasn't an accident. I always knew. But that Elísabet – there was something wrong with her. I told you when you came to see me yesterday. There was something evil inside her.'

'Did Hendrik know that Elísabet had come round?' Elma asked. She clearly remembered what Ása had said when she visited her. But it had never occurred to her that this was what she had been talking about.

Ása shook her head. 'No, of course he didn't.'

'What did you do after Elísabet told you?'

'What did I do? The moment she told me I froze. Every single nerve in my body seemed paralysed. Then she started making excuses, claiming she was abused as a child. That some man used to come into her room in the evenings and do things to her. Then she told me that she'd seen the same man at Sara's funeral. To think that she actually dared to show her face there. Anyway, she said she'd seen the man there with me. That he was Sara's father. And then she said that … that Sara had told her things she hadn't understood at the time but did now. That Sara had been forced to do the same things by her father, Hendrik. That's when I threw her out. I didn't know how she dared to come round to my house and accuse me of letting something like that go on under my roof. I'd convinced myself I was the sort of mother who would have noticed if something like that happened. I was so angry. I don't think I've ever been so angry in my life.'

'Did she leave after that?'

Ása nodded. 'Oh yes, she left.'

'How did you know she would be at the lighthouse?'

'I was on my way round to Bjarni's with a meat thermometer. He and Magnea were having a dinner party and he'd asked if he could borrow ours. I spotted her outside their house and watched her get into her car. I thought … I thought she'd gone to talk to Bjarni about it. Then I realised she'd stop at nothing. She was going to spread those lies about me … about our family, all over town. So I followed her. I saw her get out of her car by the lighthouse. It was raining and the sea was rough, so I suppose that was why she didn't hear me until the car hit her. I didn't even think, I just put my foot down and headed straight for her. I didn't brake until after the blow.'

Elma suddenly remembered the woollen thread that they had found in the car. Ása's shawl was made of rough wool. Everything was falling into place.

'I did it for Sara,' Ása continued. 'I did it for my children.' She sighed. 'I'm sorry if Elísabet had a difficult childhood. And I'm devastated that Hendrik should have played a part in that. I'll never forgive him. But he hurt my Sara too and knowing that is more painful than anything else. I can't believe Elísabet never spoke a word about it all those years. Can you imagine how I've suffered? It's eaten me up inside, not knowing what happened to my little girl. And all this time Elísabet knew but didn't say a word. That's another thing I couldn't forgive her for.'

Elma handed her another tissue and Ása blew her nose again.

'Did you deliberately try to conceal the evidence by disposing of her in the sea?' Sævar asked.

Ása folded the tissue neatly and put it down in front of her. 'To be honest, I didn't care. I managed to drag her down to the beach but I'm an old woman and couldn't get very far. I hoped the sea would wash her away. I thought God would make sure that she disappeared forever, just like my Sara. There would have been a kind of justice in that, don't you think?'

'Are you sure she was dead?' Elma asked, ignoring Ása's comment. There was nothing just about this case.

'That was the worst part,' Ása said and for the first time since she had opened her mouth, she seemed reluctant to go on. 'I thought she was dead, but then...'

'And then?' Elma prompted.

'She started moaning,' Ása said, a sudden tremor in her voice. 'But by then it was too late to stop.'

Elma found it hard to picture Ása with her hands round Elísabet's neck. But then she found it equally impossible to imagine this dainty little woman lugging Elísabet's body over the rocks.

'What about her car?' Sævar asked.

'That was quite a good idea of mine, don't you think?' Ása smiled dully but didn't wait for a response. 'Elísabet's car keys were in her bag. I took them, then later threw them in the sea. I still had the keys to our old neighbours' house – as you know we've recently moved; we used to live nearby. Anyway, I knew they were abroad. Of course I realised the car would be discovered eventually but I won myself some time to cover my tracks, didn't I?' Ása stopped to catch her breath and adjusted the shawl round her neck. 'Anyway, I'm tired of talking. You should have all you need by now. You couldn't do me a tiny favour, could you?'

'What's that?'

'I'd really like to have my knitting stuff here. You see, I'm expecting a grandchild and I'm knitting a dress, a pink one. I'm sure it's a girl.' As she said this Ása's face lit up for the first time since they had entered the room.

'Well, the case is more or less solved,' Hörður said. 'If neither Hendrik nor Tómas are prepared to confess, it'll be impossible to establish which of them abused the girls or what exactly happened. The victims are both dead and we have nothing to go on but the photos and Rúnar's claim that Tómas used to go up to Elísabet's room. And since Rúnar was probably drunk at the time, his testimony won't be enough to prove anything.'

Elma knew Hörður was right. The case was solved: Ása had confessed to Elísabet's murder and there was nothing more they could do. In the next few days, forensics would run tests on the woollen thread found in Elísabet's car to see if it came from Ása's shawl. They had her confession and there was nothing to suggest that she'd had an accomplice, yet they were still puzzled as to how Ása had managed to drag Elísabet's body all that way. Still, she flatly denied that anyone else had helped her, and Elma knew that people were capable of performing the most extraordinary feats under pressure. The case was solved, yet she wasn't satisfied that justice had been done.

'Naturally we'll summon them both for questioning. The only possibility would be if one of them were to confess, but I find that highly unlikely.'

Elma nodded glumly. She was sitting by Hörður's desk, immersed in paperwork.

'What about Sara?' she asked.

'What about Sara?' Hörður glanced up. 'It's nearly thirty years since she died in what appears to have been an accident. Even if Elísabet was telling the truth, it comes down to the same thing – they're both dead.'

'But what about—?'

'Elma, Elísabet's husband Eiríkur is on his way here and after that I need to talk to the press. Take the rest of the day off. Go for a swim or a walk or whatever. You deserve it.' He smiled dismissively, as if he couldn't wait to get Elma out of his office. She bit her lip and got up. When she turned back in the doorway to add something, Hörður was already on the phone.

Her mother answered a few seconds after she'd selected her number, as if she'd been sitting waiting by the phone. Elma felt a pang of guilt for not having returned her call the previous evening. She was well aware that her mother was dying of curiosity but she couldn't tell her anything, though she had the feeling her mother wished she was more like Dagný in that respect.

'Hi, Mum,' she said, giving her mother just enough time to return her greeting before carrying on: 'Remember when you said that Hendrik's brother, Tómas, used unscrupulous methods to collect the rent? What did you mean by that?' She had suddenly remembered what her mother had said when they were walking in the cemetery.

'Why are you asking?' her mother asked, her voice alive with curiosity, but when Elma wouldn't reveal her reasons, she gave in and said: 'He used to sleep with the women. There were rumours about him taking advantage of single mothers who couldn't pay the rent. I don't know how much truth there was in it but that's what you used to hear. And that Hendrik knew but turned a blind eye to it. Why do you ask? Does it have anything to do with…?'

'I don't know,' Elma interrupted hurriedly. 'I hope not.'

She rang off with the promise that she would come round to supper that evening. Then she put down the phone and stared thoughtfully at the black computer screen in front of her. It was as she had suspected. It had always struck her as suspicious that Elísabet's mother Halla had been able to afford the rent for such a large house. But now she believed she understood. Her thoughts went to the photos of Elísabet standing in her room, looking so vulnerable. It seemed Halla's contribution had not been sufficient to pay the rent on its own. The very idea brought an acid taste to her mouth.

Sævar was in the kitchen when Elma went in. He was leaning against the counter, nursing a mug in both hands.

'Is it drinkable?' Elma asked, fetching a cup.

'No more than usual,' Sævar said.

Elma stood beside him. It was snowing outside. It had hardly snowed at all so far this winter but now it was coming down heavily.

'Do you think it'll settle?' she asked.

'What? The snow?' Sævar glanced at her. 'I doubt it.'

Elma was silent and they stood there watching the flakes floating down, gradually obliterating the dark concrete outside the window.

'Hendrik's conscious,' Sævar said. 'They reckon he'll make a full recovery.'

'Has anyone spoken to him?'

'No, not yet.'

For a while neither of them spoke.

'The brothers look quite alike, don't they?' she said at last.

Sævar glanced up at her again. 'What are you implying?'

'I was just thinking about what Ása said. She said Elísabet had seen the man who came round to her house at Sara's funeral. Tómas must have been there too, and sat in the front pew, maybe even laid a hand on Ása's shoulder. Couldn't a nine-year-old girl have mistakenly concluded that he was Sara's father?'

'Yes, it's possible,' Sævar said. 'But I don't suppose we'll ever find out what happened.'

'My mother told me there used to be rumours that Tómas had unscrupulous ways of extracting the rent from single mothers in difficult circumstances.'

'What did she mean by that?'

'He slept with them. In other words, they paid in kind,' Elma said. 'Do you think Elísabet's mother was one of them?'

Sævar shrugged. 'It's possible, but neither Tómas nor Hendrik will say anything that gets them into trouble. They always stick up for each other and Ása's refusing to say any more.'

'I find it hard to believe that Hendrik would stand by his brother if he found out that Tómas had taken those photos of his daughter.'

'You're probably right,' Sævar said. 'But I very much doubt Tómas will confess to anything. We have no way of proving that he took the pictures.'

'But someone sent them. Someone dropped them through Ása's letterbox.'

'Yes, true. We'll just have to hope that the person in question comes forward.'

'Won't there be any follow-up in connection with Sara's death? No investigation into what Elísabet told Ása about how she died?'

'What would be the point?' Sævar said. 'Elísabet's dead. There's no one to charge with the crime. Anyway, she was only a child and it was almost certainly an accident.'

Elma thought about all the years Elísabet had kept silent. All the years it must have been gnawing away inside her. There was no way of knowing if Sara had really been dead when Elísabet put her on the raft. And although Elísabet wouldn't have realised that when she was nine, it must have occurred to her later. Perhaps Sara would still have been alive if Elísabet had gone to get help.

'So it's only Ása who'll have to go to prison, then,' Elma said, pulling out a chair and sitting down. She felt a degree of sympathy for the old woman. What she'd been forced to endure wasn't fair. Then again, it was her fault that two young boys had now lost their mother, and there was nothing fair about that either.

'I expect she'll be sentenced to sixteen years. Which means she'll be out after serving ten, maybe less,' Sævar said.

Elma nodded. She knew there was no point dwelling on it anymore. The people who could have answered her questions were either dead or refusing to break their silence. She sighed and gazed out at the snowflakes as she finished her coffee.

'I could do with a bit of company this evening,' she said at last, looking up at Sævar with a smile.

Magnea stroked Bjarni's broad shoulders. He was sitting on the edge of the sofa, hunched forward, his head in his hands. Somehow they had got through the day. The seconds had crawled by, becoming minutes and finally hours in which the world seemed to stand still. But evening had come round at last. Their big house was wrapped in darkness. She looked forward to the time when its rooms would be filled with the sound of a child's laughter; when the afternoon would consist of something other than sitting and waiting, which was all they had done today. And the worst of it was that she hadn't a clue what they were waiting for. Magnea had played the role of the loving, supportive wife, despite feeling so weak that all she really wanted was to crawl into bed. She'd had to sit on her hands at times to hide her trembling.

The phone rang. Bjarni picked up so fast that there was no time for more than a single ring. He stood up and went aside, a habit Magnea couldn't stand. What was it that she wasn't supposed to hear? But she didn't say anything, merely waited patiently for him to come back.

'Dad's awake,' he said. His shoulders slumped and he dropped back onto the sofa.

Magnea sat down beside him and put her arms round him. Bjarni leant against her with his eyes closed.

'She deserved to die,' he whispered. 'Elísabet murdered my sister. It was her fault that Sara died, and she kept quiet about it all these years. Can you imagine anything worse?'

'What do you mean?' Magnea stared at him in horror.

'Hörður told me everything,' he said. 'That's why Mum knocked that woman down. She went crazy when she heard how Sara had died. Apparently she was sent some photos of Sara too, photos that make it look like someone abused her, and somehow Mum got the idea that it was Dad who...' Suddenly all the fight seemed to go out of him, he started silently shaking and clutched her tighter, like a small child seeking comfort from its mother. 'Dad denies everything but I just don't know what to believe anymore. I don't know what the hell's happening.'

'Hush, darling,' Magnea whispered, kissing him on the forehead. She'd never seen him so upset. She often cried herself and let her feelings get the better of her, but Bjarni never did. 'It's all in the past – we don't need to think about it anymore.' She took his hand and laid it on her belly. 'Here's the future, Bjarni. Here with us.'

Bjarni raised his head to look at her. His eyes were red but dry and he smiled faintly. As he stroked her belly, Magnea felt the tension leaving his body. She smiled and kissed him again, on the mouth this time. Her tremors were slowly but surely ebbing away. Soon the whole thing would be over and she'd be able to breathe easy again.

She would have nothing to fear anymore.

She didn't get a room to herself. She wasn't even in a special section. The bed was in a big, general ward on the third floor of the hospital, with only a thin curtain separating her from her neighbour.

Ásdís had left the house early that morning, sneaking out without Tómas noticing. The shame was coursing through her body. She had found the photos. She knew what had happened. Knew what he had done.

But what had happened after she posted the photos through Ása's letterbox was a mystery to her. She couldn't understand why Ása would believe that Hendrik had taken them. She simply hadn't a clue what could have led her to that conclusion. And now Hendrik was in hospital. Although he was recovering, Ásdís was afraid of what would happen when he got out. Tómas had already been summoned to the police station for questioning and had been silent and moody when he got home. He had drunk until the early hours and refused to tell her what it was about. But Ásdís had already heard the details from her grandmother and was sure that the whole town must know what Tómas had done. She tried to make herself invisible, hardly leaving the building, tiptoeing around the flat, hoping to God that he'd never find out that it was her who sent the pictures. Who knew what he'd be capable of if he did?

'Look at the lion. Can you remember what the lion says?' asked a woman's voice behind the curtain. A small child made a loud growling noise and the woman gently shushed it. 'Yes, that's right, darling. And look at the elephant. Can you remember what the elephant does?' They both laughed.

Ásdís lay quite still and for some reason a hot tear trickled down her cheek. She slipped a hand inside the gown the nurse had told her to put on and placed it on her stomach. She was probably imagining it but she thought she could feel something. The warmth flowed up her arm. She closed her eyes, trying to forget where she was. She had to go through with this. She couldn't have his child. Couldn't do it.

Reaching for the small handbag beside her, she felt the bundle of notes for what must be the hundredth time. It was still there – the money she'd stolen from Tómas. He hadn't a clue that she knew where he stashed all the money that mustn't go into his bank account. Of course, it was only a question of time before he noticed that some of it had gone. But by then hopefully she would be far away. She smiled at the thought and double-checked the email on her phone as if to convince herself that it was real. The confirmation was there: a one-way ticket to Germany that evening. She would just have to be brave and take some strong painkillers if necessary.

She didn't know why she'd chosen Germany. Perhaps because she spoke the language well. It was the only connection she had to the country. There was no one waiting for her there and that thought alone was enough to make her smile. She had enough money to stay at a cheap hotel for a while, until she found a job. Later she could rent a flat.

'Ready?' asked the nurse who had booked her in that morning. The nurse had asked her an awful lot of questions, questions she found difficult to answer, and the lump in her throat had grown bigger all the time. Yes, she knew who the father was. No, she had never been pregnant before. She must be two or three months gone.

She nodded and sniffed. The voices behind the curtain had fallen silent. Perhaps the child had gone to asleep, safe in its mother's arms. It was as if the nurse could see her hesitation. She looked at her searchingly. 'Are you absolutely sure?' she asked. Ásdís was going to answer but the words stuck in her throat and she shook her head. Before the nurse could say another word, she was off, pulling on her clothes over her hospital gown and running out of the ward.

She wasn't crying any longer. The relief at getting out was so great that she felt almost as if she were floating on air. The two of them could do it. Of course they could. They would make a life for themselves together in a new country – she and the little creature that was now growing inside her. She would give it a good life, a better life than she herself had ever had.

When she got back to their flat it didn't look as if anyone was home but she knew he was there. His car was in the drive. She cursed herself for having forgotten to take her passport with her to the hospital. She had everything else she needed. Now she would have to go inside and explain where she had been, then sneak out again. With any luck he'd be asleep. It wasn't midday yet, so there was a good chance he wouldn't be up. She entered quietly and to her relief all was quiet inside. He must still be out for the count.

Her passport was in the wardrobe so she had no choice but to go into the bedroom. She opened the door warily, making a face when the squeaking of the hinges pierced the silence in the flat. But to her astonishment, Tómas wasn't in bed. She glanced round nervously as if expecting to see him standing behind her, watching. All she could think was that he must have gone out somewhere.

She hurried over to the wardrobe and rooted around in the sock drawer until she found the passport. Now she just had to get herself to Reykjavík and from there to Keflavík Airport. She would have to take the bus, then the airport bus, but that was part of the adventure. How she looked forward to being free. She couldn't wait to leave this town, this country. She had no good memories from here, though she felt a faint pang of guilt when she thought about her grandmother. The old lady had done her best, there was no doubt of that. She would just have to write her a letter. Maybe even invite her out to visit, though she doubted her grandmother would be strong enough to undertake such a long journey alone. Ásdís glanced round the flat one last time, then closed her eyes. She didn't want to remember this place. It was a chapter of her life she couldn't wait to forget.

She had just locked the front door behind her when she heard footsteps on the gravel. He was there in the garden, watching her.

Ásdís froze, terrified he would be able to tell by looking at her that she was leaving him for good. But he didn't seem to notice anything out of the ordinary.

'Fetch your passport and get in the car,' he ordered. Ásdís snatched a look around her. Could she make a run for it? Would she be able to get away? Of course the idea was hopeless; where was she supposed to run to?

'What are you waiting for?' he asked when she didn't move. 'We're leaving. Now.'

Ásdís shook her head slowly, feeling her eyes growing wet.

'Why do we have to leave?'

Tómas walked towards her and she started to shake. What was he going to do now? Did he know she'd taken the money? To her astonishment, he put his arms round her, hugging her tight, then kissed her on the forehead.

'Isn't this what you've always wanted? To leave this miserable dump of a town and make a new start somewhere else?'

She nodded and sniffed. She didn't want to complicate matters by asking why they had to go so suddenly. Opening the door, she went inside and waited in the hall for a minute or two, just long enough for her to have gone and fetched her passport from the bedroom. He obviously hadn't noticed yet that some of the money had gone. Perhaps she'd get away with it.

Tómas was already in the car when she came back out. She got in beside him and in no time they were roaring off down the road. Ásdís gazed out of the window, thinking to herself that at least she was leaving the country. She was still going away, even if he was coming with her. Perhaps it would be better like that.

Perhaps everything would be better somewhere else.

Akranes 1992

The memorial service was held at Akranes Church. Elísabet hadn't wanted to attend but all her classmates went, and so did their teacher, so she'd had no choice. Everyone was dressed in black. There were lots of people there she'd never seen before, people who hadn't known Sara like she did. It was all so solemn. Some of the mourners wept, others blew their noses.

Elísabet felt uncomfortable in there. She wriggled around on the hard pew and stared towards the door. She was sitting at the back of the church – would anyone notice if she sneaked out? She caught Magnea's eye, and the other girl instantly looked away. Magnea hadn't spoken to her since it happened. Had hardly even looked at her. Elísabet didn't care. She was never going to make another friend as long as she lived. No one would be allowed to come near her. She didn't care about anything anymore.

When she saw the people in the front pew stand up, she stiffened in shock. There he was – the man who owned the house; who came to visit. He was Sara's father – the father who was always at work.

Elísabet resigned herself to having to sit through the entire ceremony. She emptied her mind, trying to think about anything but Sara. Trying to remember her stories; all the nice ones with happy endings. It wasn't until later, at the reception, when she was sitting with an untouched piece of cake in front of her and met the eye of Sara's mother, Ása, that she couldn't take any more. She got up, went to the exit and ran away. Ran as fast as her legs would carry her, not stopping until she was at home in her cupboard and had shut the door. There she sat in a huddle, reciting to herself all the stories she knew. Her daddy's stories and the ones she'd read in books. She was oblivious to the pain as her nails split on the wood and didn't stop her clawing until blood was running down the wall.

But it wasn't until long afterwards that it occurred to her that perhaps she hadn't been the only one with a secret. Perhaps Sara had had a secret just as ugly as hers.

Several Weeks Later

The cemetery was covered in snow which creaked under her shoes as she walked through the dusk towards the grave. There was no other sound apart from the distant roar of traffic.

Although it was the first time she'd visited him, she found the grave at once. She stopped in front of the white cross. There was a black plaque in the middle on which his name had been engraved: *Davíð Sigurðarson. Rest in peace.* Nothing else. Nothing to say who he was or what he had done. It would be forgotten in the end, like everything else.

She knew he had been in a bad way for a long time. Sometimes it had seemed as if he were pursued by a black shadow wherever he went, but she hadn't realised how serious the situation was, ignoring all the telltale signs. The nights she had woken up to find him sitting on the side of the bed, staring into the darkness. The way his eyes were sometimes so far away that it was impossible to reach him. He had hidden it well but even so she should have been able to see through him. She should have recognised the danger he was in. She, who knew him better than anyone else.

First had come the anger. How could he do this to her? How could he go without saying goodbye, without warning her? She couldn't look his family in the eye. When his sister Lára had rung her a few weeks ago, she had hardly been able to speak to her. She couldn't talk about him, not yet.

But there was little of that initial anger left now. Now all she felt was grief.

Bending down, she brushed the snow off the candle that someone had placed on the grave. It took a little while to light it but finally the cold wick caught and a small flame began to flicker in the dusk.

She stood there for a while, thinking about their life together. About all the good times and all the bad. Letting the final shreds of her anger burn up with the candle. She didn't leave until the cold began to penetrate her bones. Then she got back into the car and headed for Akranes and home.

ACKNOWLEDGEMENTS

This book would never have been written were it not for my husband, Gunnar, who has far greater faith in me than I do in myself. Not every husband would order his wife to give up all her 'proper' work to concentrate on writing instead. I'll never understand where he gets his extraordinary equanimity, positivity and optimism. Apparently it's true what they say – opposites attract!

Special thanks are due to my Icelandic publishers, Bjarni Þorsteinsson, Pétur Már Ólafsson and co. at Bjartur & Veröld, for taking on an inexperienced young author and giving her a bit of a polish.

Thanks too to Yrsa Sigurðardóttir and Ragnar Jónasson for giving me the opportunity to realise my dream and for introducing me to the wonderful world of crime fiction.

I really got lucky when I signed a contract with David Headley of the DHH Literary Agency as he is so much more than just an outstanding agent.

Many thanks to Karen Sullivan and Orenda Books. I'm incredibly grateful to be part of Team Orenda and can't wait to get to know you all better in the near future. I would also like to thank Victoria Cribb for her faultless translation. My book has certainly been in good hands.

Last but not least, I would like to thank my children, Óliver Dreki, Benjamín Ægir and Embla Steinunn, for forcing me to put down the computer and focus on what really matters.

—Eva Björg Ægisdóttir